Kia Abdullah is an author and travel writer. She has contributed to the *Guardian*, BBC, and Channel 4 News, and most recently *The New York Times* commenting on a variety of issues affecting the Muslim community. Kia currently travels the world as one half of the travel blog **Atlas & Boots,** which receives over 200,000 views per month. kiaabdullah.com

Take It Back

Kia Abdullah

ONE PLACE. MANY STORIES

This novel is entirely a work of fiction. The names, characters and incidents portrayed in it are the work of the author's imagination. Any resemblance to actual persons, living or dead, events or localities is entirely coincidental.

HQ
An imprint of HarperCollins*Publishers* Ltd
1 London Bridge Street
London SE1 9GF

www.harpercollins.co.uk

HarperCollins*Publishers*
1st Floor, Watermarque Building, Ringsend Road
Dublin 4, Ireland

This edition 2022

1

First published in Great Britain by
HQ, an imprint of HarperCollins*Publishers* Ltd 2020

ISBN: 978-0-00-853550-6

MIX
Paper from
responsible sources
FSC™ C007454

This book is produced from independently certified FSC™ paper
to ensure responsible forest management.

For more information visit: www.harpercollins.co.uk/green

Printed and Bound in the UK using 100% Renewable Electricity at
CPI Group (UK) Ltd, Croydon, CR0 4YY

For Peter

CHAPTER ONE

She watched her reflection in the empty glass bottle as the truth crept in with the wine in her veins. It curled around her stomach and squeezed tight, whispering words that paused before they stung, like a paper cut cutting deep: colourless at first and then vibrant with blood. *You are such a fucking cliché*, it whispered – an accusation, a statement, a fact. The words stung because Zara Kaleel's self-image was built on the singular belief that she was different. She was different to the two tribes of women that haunted her youth. She was not a docile housewife, fingers yellowed by turmeric like the quiet heroines of the second-gen literature she hated so much. Nor was she a rebel, using her sexuality to subvert her culture. And yet here she was, lying in freshly stained sheets, skin gleaming with sweat and regret.

Luka's post-coital pillow talk echoed in her ear: 'it's always the religious ones'. She smiled a mirthless smile. The alcohol, the pills, the unholy foreskin – it was all so fucking predictable. Was it even rebellious anymore? Isn't this what middle-class Muslim kids *did* on weekends?

Luka's footsteps in the hall jarred her thoughts. She shook out her long dark hair, parted her lips and threw aside the sheets, secure in the knowledge that it would drive him wild. Women like Zara were never meant to be virgins. It's little wonder her youth was shrouded in hijab.

He walked in, a climber's body naked from the waist up, his dirty blond hair lightly tracing a line down his chest. Zara blinked languidly, inviting his touch. He leaned forward and kissed the delicate hollow of her neck, his week-old stubble marking tiny white lines in her skin. A sense of happiness, svelte and ribbon-like, pattered against her chest, searching for a way inside. She fought the sensation as she lay in his arms, her legs wrapped with his like twine.

'You are something else,' he said, his light Colorado drawl softer than usual. 'You're going to get me into a lot of trouble.'

He was right. She'd probably break his heart, but what did he expect screwing a Muslim girl? She slipped from his embrace and wordlessly reached for her phone, the latest of small but frequent reminders that they could not be more than what they were. She swiped through her phone and read a new message: 'Can you call when you get a sec?' She re-read the message then deleted it. Her family, like most, was best loved from afar.

Luka's hand was on her shoulder, tracing the outline of a light brown birthmark. 'Shower?' he asked, the word warm and hopeful between his lips and her skin.

She shook her head. 'You go ahead. I'll make coffee.'

He blinked and tried to pinpoint the exact moment he lost her, as if next time he could seize her before she fled too far, distract her perhaps with a stolen kiss or wicked smile. This time, it was already too late. He nodded softly, then stood and walked out.

Zara lay back on her pillow, a trace of victory dancing grimly on her lips. She wrapped her sheets around her, the expensive cream silk suddenly gaudy on her skin. She remembered buying an armful years ago in Selfridges; Black American Express in hand, new money and aspiration thrumming in her heart. Zara Kaleel had been a different person then: hopeful, ambitious, optimistic.

Zara Kaleel had been a planner. In youth, she had mapped her life with the foresight of a shaman. She had known which path to take at every fork in the road, single-mindedly intent on reaching her goals. She finished law school top of her class and secured a place on Bedford Row, the only brown face at her prestigious chambers. She earned six figures and bought a fast car. She dined at Le Gavroche and shopped at Lanvin and bought everything she ever wanted – but was it enough? All her life she was told that if she worked hard and treated people well, she'd get there. No one told her that when she got there, there'd be no *there* there.

When she lost her father six months after their estrangement, something inside her slid apart. She told herself that it happened all the time: people lost the ones they loved, people were lost and lonely but they battled on. They kept on living and breathing and trying but trite sentiments failed to soothe her anger. She let no one see the way she crumbled inside. She woke the next day and the day after that and every day until, a year later, she was on the cusp of a landmark case. And then, she quit. She recalled the memory through a haze: walking out of chambers, manic smile on her face, feeling like Michael Douglas in *Falling Down*. She planned to change her life. She planned to change the world. She planned to be extraordinary.

Now, she didn't plan so much.

*

It was a few degrees too cold inside Brasserie Chavot, forcing the elegant Friday night crowd into silk scarves and cashmere pashminas. Men in tailored suits bought complicated cocktails for women too gracious to refuse. Zara sat in the centre of the dining room, straight-backed and alone between the glittering chandelier and gleaming mosaic floor. She took a sip from her glass of Syrah, swallowing without tasting, then spotted Safran as he walked through the door.

He cut a path through soft laughter and muted music and greeted her with a smile, his light brown eyes crinkling at the corners. 'Zar, is that you? Christ, what are you wearing?'

Zara embraced him warmly. His voice made her think of

old paper and kindling, a comfort she had long forgotten. 'They're just jeans,' she said. 'I had to stop pretending I still live in your world.'

'"Just jeans"?' he echoed. 'Come on. For seven years, we pulled all-nighters and not once did you step out of your three-inch heels.'

She shrugged. 'People change.'

'You of all people know that's not true.' For a moment, he watched her react. 'You still square your shoulders when you're getting defensive. It's always been your tell.' Without pause for protest, he stripped off his Merino coat and swung it across the red leather chair, the hem skimming the floor. Zara loved that about him. He'd buy the most lavish things, visit the most luxurious places and then treat them with irreverence. The first time he crashed his Aston Martin, he shrugged and said it served him right for being so bloody flash.

He settled into his seat and loosened his tie, a note of amusement bright in his eyes. 'So, how is the illustrious and distinguished exponent of justice that is Artemis House?'

A smile played on Zara's lips. 'Don't be such a smart-arse,' she said, only half in jest. She knew what he thought of her work; that Artemis House was noble but also that it clipped her wings. He did not believe that the sexual assault referral centre with its shabby walls and erratic funding was the right place for a barrister, even one who had left the profession.

Safran smiled, his left dimple discernibly deeper than

the right. 'I know I give you a hard time but seriously, Zar, it's not the same without you. Couldn't you have waited 'til mid-life to have your crisis?'

'It's not a crisis.'

'Come on, you were one of our strongest advocates and you left for what? To be an *evening volunteer*?'

Zara frowned. 'Saf, you know it's more than that. In chambers, I was on a hamster wheel, working one case while hustling for the next, barely seeing any tangible good, barely even taking breath. Now, I work with victims and can see an actual difference.' She paused and feigned annoyance. 'And I'm not a *volunteer*. They pay me a nominal wage. Plus, I don't work evenings.'

Safran shook his head. 'You could have done anything. You really were something else.'

She shrugged. 'Now I'm something else somewhere else.'

'But still so sad?'

'I'm not sad.' Her reply was too quick, even to her own ears.

He paused for a moment but challenged her no further. 'Shall we order?'

She picked up the menu, the soft black leather warm and springy on her fingertips. 'Yes, we shall.'

Safran's presence was like a balm. His easy success and keen self-awareness was unique among the lawyers she had known – including herself. Like others in the field, she had succumbed to a collective hubris, a self-righteous belief that they were genuinely changing the world. You could hear it dripping from the tones of overstuffed barristers, making demands on embassy doorsteps, barking rhetoric at political figureheads.

Zara's career at the bar made her feel important, somehow more valid. After a while, the armour and arrogance became part of her personality. The transformation was indiscernible. She woke one day and realised she'd become the person she used to hate – and she had no idea how it had happened. Safran wasn't like that. He used the acronyms and in-jokes and wore his pinstripes and brogues but he knew it was all for show. He did the devil's work but somehow retained his soul. At thirty-five, he was five years older than Zara and had helped her navigate the brutal competitiveness of London chambers. He, more than anyone, was struck by her departure twelve months earlier. It was easy now to pretend that she had caved under pressure. She wouldn't be the first to succumb to the challenges of chambers: the gruelling hours, the relentless pace, the ruthless colleagues and the constant need to cajole, ingratiate, push and persuade. In truth she had thrived under pressure. It was only when it ceased that work lost its colour. Numbed by the loss of her father and their estrangement before it, Zara had simply lost interest. Her wins had lost the glee of victory, her losses fast forgotten. Perhaps, she decided, if she worked more closely with vulnerable women, she would feel like herself again. She couldn't admit this though, not even to Safran who watched her now in the late June twilight, shifting in her seat, hands restless in her lap.

He leaned forward, elbows on the table. 'Jokes aside, how are you getting on there?'

Zara measured her words before speaking. 'It's everything I thought it would be.'

He took a sip of his drink. 'I won't ask if that's good or bad. What are you working on?'

She grimaced. 'I've got this local girl, a teenager, pregnant by her mother's boyfriend. He's a thug through and through. I'm trying to get her out of there.'

Safran swirled his glass on the table, making the ice cubes clink. 'It sounds very noble. Are you happy?'

She scoffed. 'Are *you*?'

He paused momentarily. 'I think I'm getting there, yeah.'

She narrowed her eyes in doubt. 'Smart people are never happy. Their expectations are too high.'

'Then you must be the unhappiest of us all.' Their eyes locked for a moment. Without elaborating, he changed the subject. 'So, I have a new one for you.'

She groaned.

'What do you have if three lawyers are buried up to their necks in cement?'

'I don't know. What do I have?'

'Not enough cement.'

She shook her head, a smile curling at the corner of her lips.

'Ah, they're getting better!' he said.

'No. I just haven't heard one in a while.'

Safran laughed and raised his drink. 'Here's to you,

Zar – boldly going where no high-flying, sane lawyer has ever gone before.'

She raised her glass, threw back her head and drank.

*

Artemis House on Whitechapel Road was cramped but comfortable and the streets outside echoed with charm. There were no anodyne courtyards teeming with suits, no sand-blasted buildings that gleamed on high. The trust-fund kids in the modern block round the corner were long scared off by the social housing quota. East London was, Zara wryly noted, as multicultural and insular as ever.

Her office was on the fourth floor of a boxy grey building with stark pebbledash walls and seven storeys of uniformly grimy windows. Her fibreboard desk with its oak veneer sat in exactly the wrong spot to catch a breeze in the summer and any heat in the winter. She had tried to move it once but found she could no longer open her office door.

She hunched over her weathered keyboard, arranging words, then rearranging them. Part of her role as an independent sexual violence advisor was filtering out the complicated language that had so long served as her arsenal – not only the legalese but the theatrics and rhetoric. There was no need for it here. Her role at the sexual assault referral centre, or SARC, was to support rape victims and to present the facts clearly and comprehensively so they could be knitted together in language that was easy to digest. Her team worked tirelessly to arch the gap between right and wrong, between the spoken truth and that which lay beneath it. The difference they made was visible, tangible and repeatedly affirmed that Zara had made the right decision in leaving Bedford Row.

Despite this assurance, however, she found it hard to focus. She did good work – she knew that – but her efforts seemed insipidly grey next to those around her, a ragtag group of lawyers, doctors, interpreters and volunteers. Their dedication glowed bright in its quest for truth, flowed tirelessly in the battle for justice. Their lunchtime debates were loud and electric, their collective passion formidable in its strength. In comparison her efforts felt listless and weak, and there was no room for apathy here. She had moved three miles from chambers and found herself in the real East End, a place in which sentiment and emotion were unvarnished by decorum. You couldn't coast here. There was no shield of bureaucracy, no room for bluff or bluster. Here, there was nothing behind which to hide.

Zara read over the words on the screen, her fingers immobile above the keys. She edited the final line of the letter and saved it to the network. Just as she closed the file, she heard a knock on her door.

Stuart Cook, the centre's founder, walked in and placed a thin blue folder on her desk. He pulled back a chair and sat down opposite. Despite his unruly blond hair and an eye that looked slightly to the left of where he aimed it,

Stuart was a handsome man. At thirty-nine, he had an old-money pedigree and an unwavering desire to help the weak. Those more cynical than he accused him of having a saviour complex but he paid this no attention. He knew his team made a difference to people's lives and it was only this that mattered. He had met Zara at a conference on diversity and the law, and when she quit he was the first knocking on her door.

He gestured now to the file on her desk. 'Do you think you can take a look at this for the San Telmo case? Just see if there's anything to worry about.'

Zara flicked through the file. 'Of course. When do you need it by?'

He smiled impishly. 'This afternoon.'

Zara whistled, low and soft. 'Okay, but I'm going to need coffee.'

'What am I? The intern?'

She smiled. 'All I'm saying is I'm going to need coffee.'

'Fine.' Stuart stood and tucked the chair beneath the desk. 'You're lucky you're good.'

'I'm good because I'm good.'

Stuart chuckled and left with thanks. A second later, he stuck his head back in. 'I forgot to mention: Lisa from the Paddington SARC called. I know you're not in the pit today but do you think you can take a case? The client is closer to us than them.'

'Yes, that should be fine.'

'Great. She – Jodie Wolfe – is coming in to see you at eleven.'

Zara glanced at her watch. 'Do you know anything about the case?'

Stuart shook his head. 'Abigail's sorted it with security and booked the Lincoln meeting room. That's all I know – sorry.'

'Okay, thanks. I'll go over now if it's free.' She gestured at the newest pile of paper on her desk. 'This has got to the tipping point.'

Carefully, she gathered an armful of folders and balanced her laptop on top. Adding a box of tissues to the pile, she gingerly walked to 'the pit'. This was the central nervous system of Artemis House, the hub in which all clients were received and assigned a caseworker. It was painted a pale yellow – 'summer meadow' it had said on the tin – with soft lighting and pastel furnishings. Pictures of lilies and sacks of brightly coloured Indian spices hung on the wall in a not wholly successful attempt to instil a sense of comfort. The air was warm and had the soporific feel of heating left on too long.

Artemis House held not only the sexual assault referral centre but also the Whitechapel Road Legal Centre, both founded with family money. Seven years in, they were beginning to show their lack of funds. The carpet, once a comforting cream, was now a murky beige and the wallpaper curled at the seams. There was a peaty, damp smell in the winter and an overbearing stuffiness in the summer.

Still, Zara's colleagues worked tirelessly and cheerfully. Some, like she, had traded better pay and conditions for something more meaningful.

Zara manoeuvred her way to the Lincoln meeting room, a tiny square carved into a corner of the pit. She carefully set down her armful and divided the folders into different piles: one for cases that had stalled, one for cases that needed action, and another for cases just starting. There she placed Stuart's latest addition, making a total of twelve ongoing cases. She methodically sorted through each piece of paper, either filing it in a folder or scanning and binning it. She, like most lawyers, hated throwing things away.

She was still sorting through files when half an hour later she heard a gentle knock on the door. She glanced up, taking just a beat too long to respond. 'May I help you?'

The girl nodded. 'Yes, I'm Jodie Wolfe. I have an appointment?'

'Please come in.' Zara gestured to the sofa, its blue fabric torn in one corner, exposing yellow foam underneath.

The girl said something unintelligible, paused, then tried again. 'Can I close the door?'

'Of course.' Zara's tone was consciously casual.

The girl lumbered to the sofa and sat carefully down while Zara tried not to stare.

Jodie's right eye was all but hidden by a sac of excess skin hanging from her forehead. Her nose, unnaturally small in height, sat above a set of puffy lips and her chin slid off her jawline in heavy folds of skin.

'It's okay,' misshapen words from her misshapen mouth. 'I'm used to it.' Dressed in a black hoodie and formless blue jeans, she sat awkwardly on the sofa.

Zara felt a heavy tug of pity, like one might feel for a bird with a broken wing. She took a seat opposite and spoke evenly, not wanting to infantilise her. 'Jodie, let's start with why you're here.'

The girl wiped a corner of her mouth. 'Okay but, please, if you don't understand something I say, please ask me to repeat it.' She pointed at her face. 'Sometimes it's difficult to form the words.'

'Thank you, I will.' Zara reached for her notepad. 'Take your time.'

The girl was quiet for a moment. Then, in a voice that was soft and papery, said, 'Five days ago, I was raped.'

Zara's expression was inscrutable.

Jodie searched for a reaction. 'You don't believe me,' she said, more a statement than a question.

Zara frowned. 'Is there a reason I shouldn't?'

The girl curled her hands into fists. 'No,' she replied.

'Then I believe you.' Zara watched the tension ease. 'Can I ask how old you are?'

'Sixteen.'

'Have you spoken to anyone about this?'

'Just my mum.' She shifted in her seat. 'I haven't told the police.'

Zara nodded. 'You don't have to make that decision now. What we can do is take some evidence and send it to the police later if you decide you want to. We will need to take some details but you don't have to tell me everything.'

Jodie pulled at the cuffs of her sleeves and wrapped them around her fingers. 'I'd like to. I think I might *need* to.'

Zara studied the girl's face. 'I understand,' she said, knowing that nerve was like a violin string: tautest just before it broke. If Jodie didn't speak now, she may never find the courage. She allowed her to start when ready, knowing that victims should set their own pace and use pause and silence to fortify strength.

Jodie began to speak, her voice pulled thin by nerves, 'It was Thursday just gone. I was at a party. My first ever one. My mum thought I was staying at my friend Nina's house. She's basically the daughter Mum wished she had.' There was no bitterness in Jodie's tone, just a quiet sadness.

'Nina made me wear these low-rise jeans and I just felt so stupid. She wanted to put lipstick on me but I said no. I didn't want anyone to see that I was … trying.' Jodie squirmed with embarrassment. 'We arrived just after ten. I remember because Nina said any earlier and we'd look desperate. The music was so loud. Nina's always found it easy to make friends. I've never known why she chose me to be close to. I didn't want to tag along with her all evening – she's told me off about that before – so I tried to talk to a few people.' Jodie met Zara's gaze. 'Do you know how hard that is?'

Zara thought of all the corporate parties she had

attended alone; how keen she had been for a friend – but then she looked at Jodie's startling face and saw that her answer was, 'no'. Actually, she *didn't* know how hard it was.

Jodie continued, 'Nina was dancing with this guy, all close. I couldn't face the party without her, so I went outside to the park round the back.' She paused. 'I heard him before I saw him. His footsteps were unsteady from drinking. Amir Rabbani. He— he's got these light eyes that everyone loves. He's the only boy who hasn't fallen for Nina.'

Zara noted the glazed look in Jodie's eyes, the events of that night rendered vivid in her mind.

Jodie swallowed. 'He came and sat next to me and looked me in the eye, which boys never do unless they're shouting ugly things at me.' She gave a plaintive smile. 'He reached out and traced one of my nails with his finger and I remember thinking at least my hands are normal. Thank you, God, for making my hands normal.' Jodie made a strangled sound: part cry and part scoff, embarrassed by her naivety. 'He said I should wear lace more often because it makes me look pretty and—'. Her gaze dipped low. 'I believed him.'

Jodie reached for a tissue but didn't use it, twisting it in her hands instead. 'He said, "I know you won't believe me but you have beautiful lips and whenever I see you, I wonder what it would be like to kiss you."' Jodie paused to steady her voice. 'He asked if I would go somewhere secret with him so he could find out what it was like. I've never known what it's like to be beautiful but in that moment I got a taste and …' Jodie's eyes brimmed with tears. 'I followed him.' She blinked them back through the sting of shame.

Zara smarted as she watched, dismayed that Jodie had been made to feel that way: to believe that her value as a young woman lay in being desirable, but that to desire was somehow evil.

Jodie kneaded the tissue in her fingers. 'He led me through the estate to an empty building. I was scared because there were cobwebs everywhere but he told me not to worry. He took me upstairs. We were looking out the window when …' Jodie flushed. 'He asked me what my breasts were like. I remember feeling light-headed, like I could hear my own heart beating. Then he said, "I ain't gonna touch 'em if they're ugly like the rest of you."' Jodie's voice cracked just a little – a hairline fracture hiding vast injury.

Zara watched her struggle with the weight of her words and try for a way to carry them, as if switching one for another or rounding a certain vowel may somehow ease her horror.

Jodie's voice grew a semitone higher, the tissue now balled in her fist. 'Before I could react, his friends came out of the room next door. Hassan said, "This is what you bring us?" and Amir said he chose me because I wouldn't tell anyone. Hassan said, "Yeah, neither would a dog."'

Jodie gripped her knee, each finger pressing a little black pool in the fabric of her jeans. Her left foot tap-tapped on the floor as if working to a secret beat. 'Amir said, "She's got a pussy, don't she?" and told me to get on my knees. I didn't understand what was happening. I said no. He tried to persuade me but I kept saying no ...' Jodie exhaled sharply, her mouth forming a small O as if she were blowing on tea. 'He— he told his friends to hold me.'

Zara blinked. 'How many were there?' she asked softly.

Jodie shifted in her seat. 'Four. Amir and Hassan and Mo and Farid.'

Zara frowned. 'Do you know their surnames?'

'Yes. Amir Rabbani, Hassan Tanweer, Mohammed Ahmed and Farid Khan.'

Zara stiffened. A bead of sweat trickled down the small of her back. Four Muslim boys. Four Muslim boys had raped a disabled white girl.

'I—' Jodie faltered. 'I wasn't going to tell anyone because ...' her voice trailed off.

'You can tell me.' Zara reached out and touched the girl's hand. It was an awkward gesture but it seemed to soothe her.

'Because if a month ago, you had told me that any one of those boys wanted me, I would have thought it was a dream come true.' Hot tears of humiliation pooled in her eyes. 'Please don't tell anyone I said that.'

A flush of pity bloomed on Zara's cheeks. 'I won't,' she promised.

Jodie pushed her palms beneath her thighs to stop her hands from shaking. 'Farid said he wasn't going to touch a freak like me so Hassan grabbed me and pushed me against the wall. He's so small, I thought I could fight him but he was like an animal.' Jodie took a short, sharp breath as if it might stifle her tears. 'Amir said he would hurt me if I bit him and then he … he put himself in my mouth.' Jodie's lips curled in livid disgust. 'He grabbed my hair and used it to move my head. I gagged and he pulled out. He said he didn't want me to throw up all over him and …' A sob rose from her chest and she held it in her mouth with a knuckle. 'He finished himself off over me.'

Zara's features were neutral despite the churning she felt inside. 'What were the others doing?' she asked gently.

Jodie shook with the effort of a laboured breath. 'I— I couldn't see. They were behind me.' She clasped her hands together in her lap. 'Hassan pushed me and I fell to the ground. He tore my top and undid my jeans and then … he started.' Jodie's features buckled in anguish. 'He— he came on my face, like Amir.'

Zara closed her eyes for a moment, stemming the weakness knotting in her throat.

Jodie's words came faster now, as if she needed them said before they broke inside. 'Hassan turned to Mo and said, "she's all yours". Mo said he didn't want to but they started calling him names and saying he wasn't man enough, so … he did it too.' Jodie's voice cracked, giving it a strange, abrasive texture. 'Mo has sat next to me in class before. He's helped me, been kind to me. I begged him to stop, but he didn't.' She swallowed a sob, needing to get through this.

Zara listened as the words from Jodie's mouth fell like black spiders, crawling over her skin and making her recoil. The sensation unnerved her. Part of Zara's talent as a caseworker was her ability to remain composed, almost dispassionate, in the face of the painful stories told between these walls. Today, the buffer was breached.

'Jodie.' Zara swallowed hard to loosen the words. 'I am so, *so* sorry for what you went through.' Her words, though earnest, rang hollow, echoing in a chamber of horror. 'We're nearly there. Can you tell me what happened after?'

'They just left me there.' Her words held a note of wonder. 'I wiped everything off me using some old curtains. I tucked my top into my jeans so it wouldn't keep splitting open and then I walked home.'

'Did you see anyone on the way? Any passing cars or revellers from the party?'

Jodie shook her head. 'I stayed off the path. I didn't want to be seen.'

'Were you injured at all? Bleeding?'

'No.' Jodie took a steady breath, appeased by the simplicity of this back and forth questioning.

'What time was it when you got home?'

'I walked for fifteen minutes so around twelve I think.'

'Did you tell your mum?'

'Not that night. She was in bed and I let myself in. I went to my bedroom and then I cleaned myself up.' Jodie pointed at her backpack, a bare and practical navy so she couldn't be teased for signs of personality. 'I've brought the clothes I was wearing.'

'Washed?'

'No. I didn't want to be stupid like you see on TV.'

Zara blinked. 'Jodie, nothing you did or didn't do could be called stupid. Please understand that.'

The girl gathered her perfectly formed hands in her lap but gave no sign of agreement.

'Did you tell Nina or anyone else what happened?'

'How could I?' Jodie's voice was soft but bitter. 'How could I tell her that a boy who doesn't even want *her* wanted me? How would she ever believe that?'

Zara looked up from her notes. 'Hey,' she said, drawing Jodie's gaze from her lap. 'No matter what happens, I want you to know that I believe you.' Zara studied her for a moment, noting the dozen different ways in which she kept control: the tensing of her jowls and the squaring of her jaw, the curl of her fists and feet flattened on the floor. 'I believe you,' she repeated.

Fresh tears welled in Jodie's eyes. 'So you will help me?'

'Yes, I will help you.' Zara watched her wilt with relief. 'Is there anything else I need to know? Anyone else who was involved?'

'No. That's everything.'

Zara drew two lines beneath her notes. She watched Jodie dab at her dripping nose and wondered how a jury would view her. A rape trial usually hinged on power – one person stripping it from another – but in this case, it would be difficult not to consider desire. Zara believed Jodie – had seen too much devious behaviour, met too many appalling men to doubt the young girl's story – but felt a deep unease at the thought of her facing a jury. Could they imagine four young men wanting to have sex with Jodie even in some twisted gameplay?

Zara reached for her box of tissues and handed a fresh piece to Jodie.

She took it with a quivering hand. 'What happens now?'

Zara's lips drew a tight line, a grimace in the guise of a smile. 'We would like to conduct a medical exam. All our doctors here are female. After that, if you're ready, we can help you make a formal statement with the police.'

Jodie blanched. 'Can we go to the police tomorrow? I want to think about it for one more night.'

'Of course,' said Zara gently. 'We can do the exam, store the samples and see how you feel.'

Jodie exhaled. 'Thank you for being on my side,' she said, each few syllables halting before the next.

Zara offered a cursory nod.

'No, I mean it.' Jodie hesitated. 'I told you it was hard to be at that party alone. The truth is it's hard to be anywhere – *everywhere* – alone.'

Zara leaned forward. 'You won't be alone in this – not

for any of it.' She gestured to the door. 'If you want me in the exam room, I can sit with you.'

Jodie considered this but then shook her head. 'I'll be okay.'

Zara led her to the exam room and left her with the forensic medical examiner, a brisk but matronly Scotswoman who ushered Jodie inside. Zara shut the door with a queasy unrest. A small, delinquent part of her hoped that Jodie would change her mind, that she would not subject herself to the disruptive, corrosive justice system that so often left victims bruised. The law stress-tested every piece of evidence and that included the victim – probing, pushing and even bullying until the gaps became apparent.

Beneath her concern, however, she knew that Jodie needed to pursue this. A horrifying thing had happened to her and only the arm of the law could scrub the stain clean and serve justice.

*

Erin Quinto watched the strange little girl walk to the exit with Zara, her metronomic shuffle almost jaunty in its motion. With unheard words, they said goodbye and Zara headed back to the pit.

'What's *her* story?' asked Erin.

Zara sighed. 'You wouldn't believe me if I told you.'

'Oh yeah, I'm just a babe in the woods, me.' Erin laughed, deep and throaty, and followed Zara to her office.

Inside, she reached into her jacket and pulled out a manila file. 'I've got something for you guys.' She placed it on the desk. 'Can you give this to Stuart when he's back? It's the San Telmo financials he was after.'

Zara raised a brow. 'Of course. I don't want to know how you got them but thank you.' She watched Erin, her angular features and lanky limbs clearly poised in thought. With her cropped hair, leather jacket and big dark eyes, she looked like a comic book anti-hero: an anime goth designed to drive a certain type of man wild.

Fittingly, beneath the dark hair and piercings, she was as wily as a snake. It was why Stuart had hired her as an investigator to freelance for Artemis House. It was five years ago and he was in the midst of his first big battle: Lisa Cox against Zifer Pharmaceuticals. The company's sparkling new epilepsy drug, Koriol, had just hit the market. Alas, no one was told that depression was a rare but possible side effect. When Lisa Cox stepped in front of a moving train, she miraculously escaped without injury. The media went wild, Big Pharma went on the defensive and the Medicine Regulatory Authority denied all wrongdoing. When Lisa decided to sue, she was smeared as a money-hungry whore with little regard for herself or the three children she would have left behind. Lisa lost her job and almost lost her home. She was an inch from surrender when Erin – young, laconic, beautiful – strode into the Whitechapel Road Legal Centre and handed Stuart a file. Inside were memos between regulatory officials and Zifer acknowledging the drug's dangerous side effects. Stuart couldn't use the documents legally but a well-timed leak prompted an investigation that not only exonerated Lisa but made her a very wealthy woman.

Stuart immediately offered the mysterious young Erin a job. She refused to take it and instead offered her freelance services pro bono, and now here she was pushing classified documents across a cheap fibreboard desk.

Zara placed the folder in her bottom-right drawer, the place she reserved for sensitive material.

Erin watched her, then asked, 'Seriously, what's the girl's story?'

Zara locked her drawer and set down the key. In a measured tone, she relayed Jodie's story, recalling the horrors of the story she'd told.

When Zara finished, Erin leaned forward, elbows on the desk, and said, 'Tell me what you need me to do.'

Zara handed her a piece of paper. 'Find out everything you can about these boys.'

Erin scanned the handwritten note. 'Wait.' She looked up. 'They're Muslim?'

'Yes.'

'Jesus. You're telling me that four Muslim boys raped a disabled white classmate?' Erin whistled softly. 'The tabloids will have a field day when this gets out – not to mention the Anglican Defence League. Those right-wing nutjobs will besiege anyone that's brown.'

Zara nodded tensely. 'That's a concern, but we can't

be distracted by what could happen or might happen. We need to approach this with a clear head.'

Erin's features knotted in doubt. She smoothed the note on the desk and traced a finger across the four names. 'What if I tried talking to one of them?'

Zara held up a hand. 'No, don't do that. Leave it to the police.'

'Screw the police.' Erin's voice was heavy with scorn. 'You think they're going to get to the heart of this?' She didn't pause for an answer. 'Look, the way I see it, these boys did the crime or they didn't. Either way, the police are going to fuck it up. You think they can get more information out of these bastards?'

Zara thought for a moment. 'Fine,' she ceded. 'Please just wait until the formal statement. We've overstepped the mark before and we can't do it again.'

Erin's eyes glinted in the sun. 'Tell me which one refused to take part.'

'Farid, but it wasn't out of sympathy.'

Erin smiled. 'Yes, but maybe he'll confess to save his skin. When are you going to the police?'

'Wednesday. Tomorrow.'

'Perfect. I'll scope him out on Thursday.' Erin slipped the piece of paper into her leather jacket and readied to leave. 'Four Muslim boys. Well, no one can accuse *you* of upholding the status quo.'

'Yeah,' Zara said dryly. 'Rock 'n' roll.'

*

The bells of St Alfege Church cut across the quiet, sending birds fleeing across the early evening sky. Canary Wharf shone in the distance – Zara's favourite feature of her tidy Greenwich flat. She watched from the balcony and raised a joint to her lips. A blanket of warmth clouded around her, loosening the painful knots in her shoulders. Her head felt light but her limbs were heavy, almost sensual in effect. She leaned forward and laid her head on the wrought-iron railings, welcoming relief.

Just as her mind quietened, the doorbell cut through the breeze. Cursing, she snuffed out the joint and stepped back inside. Her flat on the top floor of a converted warehouse was large and bright with creaky old ceiling beams and exposed brickwork. The giant cream corner-sofa sat next to her desk, a sturdy structure of reclaimed oak. Opposite, stood a large bookcase stuffed with legal textbooks next to floor-to-ceiling windows. At the far end of the enormous room was her rarely used kitchen, a modern mix of chrome and glass offset by her giant wooden dining table. In a sea of minimalism, the only signs of personality were her antique lawyer lamp – a graduation gift from her sisters – and five large posters on the western wall depicting headlines from what Zara considered the greatest legal achievements of all time. She padded past them now and opened the door to find Luka outside with two bags filled with takeout.

He smiled sheepishly. 'You said you missed lunch so I brought you some food.' His gaze fell to the joint cooling in her hand.

She drew it back. 'I've had a bad day.'

'I didn't say anything.' He gestured inside. 'Can I come in?'

She held the door ajar.

Luka set the food on the breakfast bar and started to unpack. 'So why did my beautiful girlfriend have a bad day?'

She baulked. Six months and she still wasn't used to 'girlfriend'. They were meant to be casual. He was meant to be a distraction, a mindless and uncomplicated diversion, and yet here he was buying her comfort food and calling her his girlfriend.

She waved a hand. 'It's just something at work.'

Luka stopped. 'What happened? Are you okay?' His concern only reminded her that she had told him too much, pulled him too close.

'Don't worry,' she said. 'It's fine.'

He met her gaze, his eyes a stormy green, frustrated by her caginess. She wanted to reach out and touch him, to somehow soften her sharp edges, but opted instead to do nothing. She moved to the dining table and he followed, sitting next to her instead of opposite. *We're closer this way*, he had once said. His hand rested on her knee, a subtle non-sexual gesture. She moved her leg so that he fell away. *Don't forget,* it warned. She poured a large glass of wine and offered it to him.

He waved it away. 'I can't. I'm training for the climb.'

She set the glass on the table, noting the irony of a white

man refusing a drink from a Muslim woman. She pushed it towards him. 'You've still got a few weeks before you leave.'

He reached forward and wiped a crumb off her lip. 'Yes, I do.' His fingers rested there a moment too long. 'I'll miss you.' He paused. 'You know what's happening between us, don't you, Zara?'

She looked at him, eyes narrowed ever so slightly. It was her Ralph Lauren stare: part anxious, part vacant, detached but intense. Was she still playing or not? Even she couldn't tell anymore.

His dark blond brows knotted in a frown. 'I know what this is and what this isn't but … ' He watched her stiffen. 'I know you don't feel the same but I need you to know.'

'Luka—'

'You don't have to say anything.' He leaned forward and pulled her into his arms.

Against her instinct, she let him hold her. If she was going to use him as a salve, at least she could let him heal.

'I love you,' he whispered.

She swallowed hard, as if rising emotion could be curbed at the throat. She held him tight, knowing full well that it was time to let go.

CHAPTER TWO

Zara's black blazer was stark against the windowless white walls. The fluorescent light reflected off the blue linoleum floor, casting a pallor beneath her eyes. She greeted Detective Constable Mia Scavo, gripping her hand a touch too firmly. In the back of her mind, she tried to remember the writer who said the sight of women greeting each other reminded him of nothing so much as prize fighters shaking hands.

Zara appraised the young detective: the sober manner and formless clothes, the light blonde hair scraped back in a bun. Did she know it only accentuated her cheekbones and brought out her blue eyes?

With greetings safely exchanged, Zara took her seat by the left-hand wall of the interview room: in Jodie's eyeline but in the background nonetheless. She was here not to interact but to lend support.

Mia began with a short preamble. 'Jodie, my name is Mia Scavo. I'm a detective constable with the Metropolitan Police. I've been a police officer for six years and I work specifically with victims of sexual assault. My job is to support you from today onwards, right to the conclusion of the case.

'We're going to start with some formalities and then we will go over your complaint. I don't know what happened so try to give me as much detail as you can. Our conversation is being recorded on video so it can be used as evidence. It's important to be as accurate as possible. If you can't remember something, just tell me. If you want to clarify or correct something at a later date, you can contact me and tell me, okay?'

Jodie nodded. 'Okay.'

'Good. Then we'll begin.' Mia glanced at the two-way mirror. 'It is Wednesday the third of July 2019. This is DC Scavo interviewing Jodie Wolfe. Also present is Jodie's independent sexual violence advisor.' She paused for Zara to confirm her name and began with some basic questions: Jodie's name, date of birth, address and school. She then eased into the interview, first asking about Jodie's hobbies and favourite shows on TV, a basic technique to build rapport. After five minutes, she broached the assault and asked her to recount what happened.

Jodie shared the tale of her first real party, of drunken teens and raucous laughter. She spoke of the grinding social embarrassment and how she had fled for air. She described Amir's footsteps – so evocative they could hear the crunch of gravel. There, frozen in frame by his side, she stopped.

'What happened next?' asked Mia.

Jodie hesitated. 'Amir asked me what I was doing there alone. I said I needed a break.' She paused. 'He told me that Nina had left the party and that he could take me to her so I followed him.'

Zara looked up in surprise. This wasn't the story she had told before. What had happened to Amir's overtures? *'Whenever I see you, I wonder what it would be like to kiss you.'*

Jodie gazed at a burl in the wooden tabletop, not daring to look up at Zara. 'Amir said that they were having an after-party. He said I wouldn't normally be allowed to go but since I came with Nina, he'd take me there.'

Zara searched her face for a trace of the lie but she noted nothing.

'Can you take me through what happened next?' asked Mia. 'Take your time and be as detailed as you can.'

Jodie was still for a moment. Her eyes grew narrow and her features creased as if in the midst of a major decision. She took a breath, trembling and thin, and said, 'He took me to an empty building.'

Jodie's account segued smoothly to her original. She spoke with a tight discipline but her voice broke in the grooves of the taunts – *I ain't gonna touch 'em if they're ugly like the rest of you* – and she finished in a curtain of tears.

Zara felt a swelling pity. She could see that Jodie was in pain, but also that she was trying so extraordinarily hard to cling onto composure. Perhaps it was no easier for a sixteen-year-old to cry like a child with abandon than it was for someone older.

Mia reached forward and squeezed Jodie's arm. 'You've been very brave.'

Zara watched the simple act and felt an inexplicable frisson of annoyance.

Mia flipped through her notebook. 'Jodie, you said the accused were boys from your school. Would you say that you were friends?'

Jodie clutched the cuff of her sleeve. 'No.'

'Have you ever been romantically involved with any of them?'

She grimaced. 'No. Never.'

Mia flipped a page. 'You said you had one glass of punch with alcohol that night. Had you taken any drugs?'

Jodie shrank into herself, as if she were being blamed. 'No.'

Mia made a note. 'Were there drugs at the party?'

'I think so but I'm not sure.'

'That's fine. It's always right to say you don't know if you're unsure.' Mia continued to flesh out the night in question and then explained what the police would do next: contact witnesses, interview the suspects, visit the scene of the assault, review CCTV footage and examine any DNA. 'If we can gather enough evidence, we will formally charge the suspects,' she finished.

The whites of Jodie's eyes were wide: fear laced perhaps with shock that this was really happening. 'How long will it take?' she asked, the words low and timorous.

'The suspects will be arrested for questioning immediately. After that, we usually work to charge them within three weeks.'

Jodie flinched. 'Three weeks? But what if I see them in the area?'

'They won't be allowed to talk to you,' assured Mia. 'They can't approach you or communicate with you in any way.' She smiled gently. 'I know this process is scary but we will be with you every step of the way.' She nodded at Zara. 'You will hear from me or your caseworker when we have an update.'

'Thank you.' Jodie stood unsteadily and said goodbye after final formalities.

Outside, Zara led Jodie to her car. Then, in a tone that was perfectly neutral, said, 'Jodie, I noticed a small anomaly in the interview. Can we talk about it?'

The girl frowned. 'What do you mean?'

'When you spoke to me initially, you said you went with Amir because he wanted to kiss you. In the interview just now, you said it was because he was going to take you to Nina. Were you confused?' Zara watched her weigh her options, a lightning-quick process of elimination.

Jodie slumped in her seat. 'I couldn't tell them what he said. How would they believe that Amir said that? Or that I believed him?'

Zara blinked in surprise. 'Jodie, you *must* tell the truth, no matter how unsavoury. Your statement will be examined by the prosecution. If they find a single hole, they will grab it and tear it as large as they can. We need to tell Mia the truth before it gets any further.'

Jodie shook her head. 'Please, Zara. I can't stand up and tell the world that I wanted him to kiss me. I can't. How would that *ever* be the reason I went with him?' She pressed the dashboard to emphasise her plea and left small and sweaty fingerprints on the textured grey surface. 'Please don't make me do this.'

Zara held up a hand. 'Look, I can't make you go in and tell her but I strongly advise that you do.'

Jodie's voice was unsteady. 'I'm sorry I lied but it's such a small thing. It doesn't change anything else.'

Zara grimaced. 'That's the thing, Jodie. It *could* change something. You've got to get your story straight in your head. Those who tell the truth don't need to rely on memory.'

'That's the only thing, I swear,' she promised.

'I hope so, Jodie. I really do.' Zara started the car, the soft thrum sounding her surrender.

They wove through roads lined with building works, past shiny promotional boards touting luxury two- and three-bedroom apartments the locals couldn't afford. You could tell which streets were *really* gentrified: they had a flank of Boris bikes standing sentry on the pavement. Of course, there was no such offering on the Wentworth Estate where row after row of four-storey buildings stood a nose width away from each other. Communal balconies ran the length of the dark-brick buildings, peppered with soggy clothes and the rusting sequins of satellite dishes.

Zara felt a pang of guilt as she parked her Audi on the concourse. 'I'd like to talk to your mother,' she told Jodie.

'I—' Jodie hesitated. 'My mother isn't really in a condition to talk about this right now.' Her tone was neutral but Zara caught the tremor beneath.

'That's why it's important for me to talk to her. You're sixteen and your mum needs to understand what's happening so that she can provide the support you need.'

Jodie shook her head. 'I'm just so tired. Please, another day.'

Zara studied her for a moment. 'Okay, fine,' she said slowly, confused by Jodie's reticence. 'But call me if you need anything.' She unlocked the doors and watched Jodie shuffle across the concourse. She appeared on the first-floor balcony and after a brief pause, opened a door and went inside.

Zara switched on the air conditioning and dabbed at her brow, careful not to smudge her makeup. She felt a wiry sense of unease and instinctively reached for her bag, a tan Céline tote preserved from her days in chambers. She glanced up at Jodie's flat, then took out a brown glass bottle. She shook it once to gauge the number of pills inside. Satisfied with the dull clink of a healthy supply, she lay it on her lap for later. Calmed by the soft weight resting against her legs, she put the car in gear and moved smoothly off.

*

Jodie closed the door, lifting the handle as she pushed it back. She hated the long whine of the hinge for the way it announced that she was home; the way it would draw her mother to the corridor, can in hand and scowl fixed on.

Sure enough, Christine Wolfe shuffled from the living room, white-blonde hair in a mane of tangles. She regarded Jodie for a moment. 'Where've you been?' she asked, her tone already angry.

Jodie felt her nerve desert her. She had hoped to do this on her own terms: in the living room by the TV with a fresh can of Scrumpy and a cushion on the table for her mother's feet – the happiest Christine Wolfe would ever be. Instead, Jodie stood between the chipped grey walls, caught like a deer in the headlights.

'Well?' Her mother stepped forward, the low light casting shadows on her face.

Jodie swallowed. 'Police station.' She said it blankly, without emotion as if it were a fact that could not have been changed.

Her mother jolted in shock. 'You went to the police with your story?' The bluish whites of her eyes grew wide.

Jodie felt the sting of her mother's doubt. 'Mum, it's not a story.'

Christine smacked her palm against the wall. 'Like you ain't punished me enough?' Her raspy voice struggled to climb. 'What'd I do to deserve you?'

Jodie flinched. The snarl still hurt after years of wear. She knew what was coming next.

'I was happy,' said Christine. 'And then you came along. Your father took one look at you and fucked off out the door – and I let him go 'cause of you.'

Jodie remained calm, knowing that her features in anguish would anger her mother further. 'Mum, please. It's the truth.'

'I can't fucking believe this. You're telling me the police will be here asking questions?'

Jodie recognised the stirrings of a storm. The best thing to do was retreat but her mother stood between her and her room, simmering now in fury. Tears would provoke her further so Jodie stood still and listened.

'You're telling me I have to talk to the pigs? I ain't tellin' them nothin'.' She threw up a hand in disgust. 'Why does every fuckin' thing always come down to me? This is *your* story, Jodie. This is *your* mess. Jesus Christ. I clothe you and feed you and take you to all your fuckin' appointments. Do you know how much them bus fares cost?' Christine smacked the wall again. 'I do *everything* round here and you're gonna stand there and tell me I have to do this too? I ain't talkin' to no pigs. They can fuck off. You hear me? They can fuck right off.' She scowled. 'Why couldn't you just talk to your teachers like any other normal girl? Why'd you have to go to the pigs like some kind of idiot?'

Christine Wolfe was angry at Jodie, but angrier still at life, using the first to rail against the second. The indignity of it was too much. Unemployment. Alcoholism. Poverty. The stench of failure and being unable to climb out from under it. It was all too much. The only thing you could do was surrender and Jodie's resoluteness made her livid. You couldn't stand up to life. It would always beat you down. She shouted this at Jodie, hopelessly angry at her ugly, stolid face, needing something or someone to blame.

When the wind finally blew from her rage, she jabbed a finger at Jodie. 'I ain't havin' no part in this,' she warned. 'You're on your own, you hear me?' Can in hand, she shuffled to the living room. 'You're on your fuckin' own,' she called back as she sank to her spot by the TV and propped her feet up on the table.

Jodie felt the adrenaline drain, leaving her hot and empty. She was motionless for a moment to make sure the rage had calmed. Then, she leaned against a wall and placed two hands over her head, not quite touching the scalp, the way she used to as a child pretending to wear a knight's mail armour. The tiny rings of metal were extraordinary in deflecting pain. These were, after all, just words. She stood like that for a long while, working through the words, letting them bounce off her. Only a few remained by the time she reached her room: *you're on your own*, they said. *You are on your own.*

*

Zara leaned on the kitchen counter, still drowsy from the Diazepam. Some days, the pills brought her peace, on others, only senseless fog. Often, she craved something stronger but was too wedded to her past and the sensible, overachieving version of herself to screw up her life that badly. The first time she tried cocaine, in an illicit huddle at a Bar Council conference, it was like pulling back the curtain on the Wizard of Oz. All the myth and notoriety, the unfettered hyperbole, crumbled in the face of reality. Instead of the giddy, addictive rush of lore, she just felt alert and happy. It was almost anodyne in effect. And so she tried it again, this time with a peer at a party, and came to appreciate the sense of wellbeing. And so she tried it again – and that's when she understood how addiction took hold. It wasn't a bolt of lightning that fused you to your poison but a mellow descent into its seductive grip. That was the last time she touched it. East London didn't need yet another junkie.

She poured herself a glass of water and drank it without pausing. The doorbell rang and she remembered that Luka said he would visit. She placed the glass down next to the Diazepam and let him in with a smile.

He kissed her lips, noting the lazy curve of her mouth. He raised the bottle in his hands. 'Colorado's finest Syrah,' he said with a grin, knowing that Zara liked it despite what she said about American wine. He walked to the kitchen and placed it on a counter, his gaze catching on the bottle of pills. He exhaled slowly. 'I thought you were going to stop.'

She blinked. 'I am. When I'm ready.'

He turned to her with a sigh. His right index finger

tapped against his leg the way it did when he was lost in thought: two quavers with a rest in between. 'Zara, it's not even seven. You're taking pills in the afternoon now?'

'So? I have a stressful job.' Her voice took on a steely edge. 'You don't need to worry about it.'

'But I *do* worry about it.' He threw up two hands. 'Seriously, this makes me so uncomfortable.'

She scoffed. 'It's not my job to make you *comfortable*, Luka.'

'You could give it a try once in a while.' He picked up the bottle and tossed it in the bin. 'Zara, seriously, you've got to stop.'

She bristled. 'Listen to me, Luka. There's only one man who could tell me what to do and *he's* dead.'

Temper sparked in his eyes. 'Yes, and even *he* couldn't stand you by the end.'

The words struck her like a fist in the gut. In a moment shorn of reason, she reached out and slapped him.

He jolted back in surprise. A muscle in his cheek flexed beneath the rising colour and his hands clenched in fists by his side. He took a few short breaths to calm himself. His shoulders rose and dipped with the effort, then slowly came to rest. He spoke to her in a low voice: 'Zara, look at you. Look at that rage burning inside. Would you really be so angry if you didn't think it were true?' He waited. 'You think you can bury your feelings in a bottle? You think striking me will wipe your past clean?'

Zara held his gaze. 'Leave,' she said. Luka's words

smarted like wounds. *Even he couldn't stand you by the end.*

'No,' said Luka. 'You can't drug yourself free of your father's shadow. It's everywhere you go. You say you quit your job to do some good, as if walking out didn't sabotage everything you worked so hard for. You remind me all the time that we're just having "fun" – but this isn't fun anymore, Zara. Drugging yourself to oblivion isn't "fun"; it's cowardice.'

Zara squared her shoulders. 'Just go,' she said coldly. The sting of his words mixed now with a feverish self-loathing. He was the first person she'd ever struck.

Luka's lips tensed over gritted teeth. 'Zara, don't do this. Don't just shut down.'

She said nothing, as much as to hide her shame as to control her anger.

'Stop acting like a child.' Luka's patience waned in the silence. 'You're impossible, you know that? Fucking impossible.' He waited for a beat. 'Call me when you grow the fuck up.' He stalked out of the flat, slamming the door behind him.

His ugly words rang in her ears. They felt hot and prickly like blisters on skin. *Even he couldn't stand you by the end.* The sheer ease with which he'd said them, the unthinking indifference, hurt more than a physical blow. Luka knew what her father had meant to her. That he would use him now to carve a malicious taunt stung like betrayal.

Even he couldn't stand you by the end.

Denial flooded her veins. *I was the one who stayed away. I was the one who refused to be to be seen.* Deep down, however, she knew the quiet truth. She knew that even though he had tried, towards the end her father couldn't bear to hear her name let alone see her face.

It was the summer of 2016 that she said yes to an arranged marriage. The grass outside was a burnt brown and the windows were open as far as they would go. Her father was on his second hospital stay of the year so while she can't say she was *forced* or *coerced*, the situation was prime for emotional blackmail. 'You're his only burden,' her mother would say with only the lightest touch of accusation. 'He worries about you' – as if marriage had solved all her siblings' problems.

She sat there in the sweltering heat draped in her impossibly heavy silk sari, all blazing orange and gold-embroidered trim. She was told the colour would look amazing against her long dark hair – an irrelevant point of persuasion since it was now gathered in a bun, modestly tucked beneath the head of her sari. Her face was a mask of makeup, her foundation a touch too light, the sort that cast an ashy pallor if shown beneath the wrong light. Her eyes were lined with kohl and mascara in the heavy, dramatic strokes that made brunettes look sexy but blondes look trashy. Her lips were painted nude to downplay their obvious appeal, far too seductive for a demure little housewife. And jewellery everywhere. Her ears, freshly pierced after she let the last holes close, shone with Indian gold. Her neck was wrapped in elaborate jewels that would look at home on an Egyptian queen. There she sat, elegant, poised, perfected and neutered. She saw herself through a prism; not as a university graduate, not an ambitious lawyer, not a smart and successful woman but something else altogether, something shapeless and tasteless, a malleable being that had lost its way. There she sat and waited.

Kasim Ali was the fifteenth suitor presented to her that year. She had worn out her rightful refusals about five suitors back and patience was wearing thin. He was big and broad with thinning hair atop milky white skin. His shiny suit was just a tad too tight and his navy tie made his neck fat crease. He was neither attractive nor ugly, just unremarkable.

To his merit, he was well-spoken and seemed to have a sense of humour – more than she could say of his predecessors. The conversation was brief and shallow: job, hobbies, favourite books; the sort of thing you might ask a fellow dinner guest, not the person you would shortly marry. It was that day, sitting mute in six yards of silk, that she made the biggest mistake of her life. It was that day she caved into pressure and said yes to a marriage she did not want. After all, she was her sick father's *only fucking burden*.

The engagement came and went and the ball of anxiety grew and grew, contracting in her stomach like some sort of pestilence. Friends greeted the news with disbelief. She, Zara the Brave, was succumbing to tradition. She, with her iron will and unyielding ambition, was bowing to pressure? How could this be?

It was clear that Zara was struggling but her mother did not ask about the circles beneath her eyes or the weight that drained from her frame, for she knew they had reached a delicate *détente*. Granted the smallest concession, Zara would surely bolt, and so she was held to her decision with a cold, unremitting expediency. It was five months after the engagement that she took the decision to get out. Of course, by then the wedding had passed and her marital bed had long been soiled.

When Kasim secretly searched through her phone and found her message to Safran expressing her mortal doubts, his family rounded on her like wolves on cattle. Neither time nor history had thread trust into their relationship and so her husband showed her no empathy or discretion. Perhaps she could have stemmed the crisis before it reached their ears. She could have sweetened him with loving words, secured his silence with a warm tongue, but subconsciously she welcomed the fallout. She couldn't be his wife. She couldn't be a woman who wore elaborate saris and expensive rings; who made fifteen cups of tea every day; who was indefatigably sweet and loving and innocent. She couldn't be that woman. And so she let them round on her and take away her phone and grab at her throat and call her a whore. For four hours she sat, waiting for her family to come. When it was clear that they would not, she gathered her belongings and marched out the door. She fled from the house and went back to a home that welcomed her no more.

Despite the trauma, that night was not the worst one. That privilege was reserved for the one that followed. The memory of it was oddly monochrome in her mind, darkly black and blinding white, film-noirish in its detail. She had recounted it all to Luka. One night, surprisingly sober, she lay in his arms and unlocked the floodgates for no reason at all. It all bled out: the bitter-centred anger and gut-wrenching pain.

Luka held her as the tears from her eyes stained kohl on his skin. He didn't say the words but it was the night he fell in love with her. She knew from the pain he tried to hide from his eyes. Until that moment, all he had known was Zara the Brave. That night, he saw her weak and vulnerable. He touched the sorest part of her and he couldn't let go.

She wondered how he could use it now to hurt her. But then, isn't that what people *did* when you laid yourself bare? Luka would be lucky to ever have her in that position again.

*

Najim Rashid scanned the hall and spotted the four boys in a corner, huddled over a foosball table. Hassan Tanweer, the smallest of the four, danced restlessly around one edge, spewing a stream of obscenities. The others seemed amused, laughing as his wiry limbs flew from one handle to another. Amir broke the string of expletives with one or two of his own.

Fuck yes, son! No, no, no, you wank stain!

Across from them, another group of boys had set up a game of cards. In the middle of the table was a large pile of chips. *Nah, sir,* they had cried last week. *We don't play for money. That's haram,* the last word loaded with scorn. Najim had moved on without mentioning the pictures of naked women he had seen them sharing earlier. *I suppose that's halal, is it*? he'd wanted to ask, but the Dali Centre was a place of acceptance. Supported by government funding, the community centre was set up soon after the 7/7 London bombings to engage disadvantaged youths in the borough. It attracted a ragtag group of kids, mainly boys, mainly brown, who came to be free of judgment. Here, there were no prayer rooms to prompt them to be pious, no parents with lofty immigrant dreams. There were no pushy preachers or angry teachers, no masters they had to please. Here, the boys could be themselves and as long as they weren't breaking the law, Najim let them be. Of course, it was hard not to dispense advice or push college brochures into the hands of his charges. Every year, he lay out a stack of 'Informed Choices' from the Russell Group universities. Every year, they remained untouched but it was not his role to push the boys in the right direction, only to pull them from the wrong one. Of course, sometimes, trouble came knocking regardless.

Najim leaned over the table to interrupt the game. Hassan stepped back from the haze of competition, his face flushed red and pools of sweat dampening his T-shirt.

'Sorry to disturb you boys, but you're needed in my office.'

Amir playfully jabbed Najim in the rib. '"Office?" Since when do you have an office? Do we have to call you *sahib* now?'

Najim smiled good-naturedly while the boys laughed at the jibe. 'Come on. You have some visitors.' He gestured to the door, praying it was nothing serious. 'Bring your things.'

He led them through the main hall, across a small pitch with forlorn goalposts at either end, and into the northern edge of the complex. Outside his cramped office stood a slim woman with shiny blonde hair scraped into a bun. Next to her was a much older man, dressed all in grey. He had hair that verged on ginger and a face like crumpled paper, his features focused in the middle as if someone had scrunched up his face then smoothed it out again. Behind the pair stood two uniformed police officers.

The blonde woman spoke first. 'I am DC Mia Scavo and this is DC John Dexter. Can you state your names please?'

Amir offered a bright smile. 'What's the problem, officer?' Then, to Hassan, 'Has your mum been caught working the streets again?'

A snigger rose in the group and Hassan, never one to take insult lightly, bounced a hand off Mo's chest, silencing the taller boy, knowing that he – nervy, docile, amusingly principled – was the easiest target in the group.

Mia stepped forward. 'State your names please,' she repeated.

Farid complied, then Mo and Hassan too. Amir sighed exaggeratedly, his eyes rolling skyward. *Fine,* it said. *Be a joyless cow.* In a tone dripping with deference, he said, 'I'm Amir Rabbani, ma'am. How may I help you please?'

Mia's lips drew a tight line. 'Mr Rabbani, I am arresting you on suspicion of rape.' Her tone was even. 'You do not have to say anything but it may harm your defence if you do not mention when questioned something which you later rely on in court. Anything you do say may be given in evidence.' While she spoke, her colleagues arrested the other three boys.

Amir looked to Najim for help. 'Rape?' he asked dumbly. 'What are they on about?'

Mo grew pale and Farid flushed red as if the blood had drained from one boy to the other.

Najim reached out a hand, not touching Mia but close to it. 'Excuse me, you can't just arrest them. Don't you need a warrant?'

Mia regarded him coolly. 'We have reason to believe that these young men have committed a serious crime. We don't need a warrant to arrest them for questioning.' She turned to Amir. 'Please come quietly. We can discuss this at the station. Your parents will be informed and will join you there.'

Amir flinched. 'My parents are coming?' His voice was tense with worry. 'They're going to *kill* me.'

Hassan next to him was a coil of anger. 'This is bullshit,' he swore. His last syllable climbed a register, creating the wobble he hated in his voice.

Mia watched them with interest, noting the change in mood at the mention of their parents. 'Cōme on.' She tugged Amir away and turned him towards the exit. He wrenched around and looked at his friends. Before he had a chance to speak, Mia pulled him back and gave him a gentle shove. As he began to walk, he heard Najim behind him. 'Don't worry,' he shouted. And then, in Urdu: *don't tell the pigs anything.*

CHAPTER THREE

Hashim Khan hurried up the stairs but failed to catch the door held briefly open. At sixty-one, his legs were far wearier than even two years before. He had increasingly begun to ask himself if it was time to wind down his fruit stall but his state pension was a few years away and could he really support his wife and three children without the extra income? He pushed open the wooden doors to Bow Road Police Station and followed Yasser Rabbani to reception.

Yasser, dressed in a tailored pinstripe suit with a woollen mustard coat slung around his shoulders, looked like he'd stepped out of a Scorsese movie. Despite approaching his sixties, he was powerfully built and strikingly handsome – clearly the source of Amir's good looks. He placed a firm hand on the counter. 'Excuse me, I'm looking for my son.'

The receptionist, a heavyset woman in her late forties, glanced up from her keyboard. 'What's his name, sir?'

Hashim leaned forward, his solemn eyes laced with worry. '*Woh kiya kehraha hai?*' he asked Yasser to translate.

Yasser held up an impatient hand. '*Ap kuch nehi boloh. Me uske saath baat karongi.*' He urged the older man to let him handle the conversation. He spoke with the woman for a few long minutes and then, in a muted tone, explained that their sons were under arrest.

Hashim wiped at his brow. '*Saab, aap kyun nahi uske taraf se boltay? Mujhe kuch samajh nahi aaygi.*'

Yasser shook his head. In Urdu, he said, 'They don't have interpreters here right now. And I can't go with your son. Who's going to look after *mine*?'

The older man grimaced. What could he – an uneducated man – do for his son? Thirty-five years he had been in Britain. Thirty-five years he had functioned with only a pinch of English. Now he was thrust into this fearsome place and he had no words to unpick the threat. He wished that Rana were here. His wife, who assiduously ran her women's group on Wednesday afternoons, could speak it better than he. For a long time, she urged him to learn it too. *Language is the path to progress,* she would say, only half ironically. The guilt rose like smoke around him. Why had he spent so many exhausted hours by the TV? There was time for learning after a day on the stall. Cowed by embarrassment, he let himself be led away, along a corridor, into an austere room.

Farid sat alone under the fluorescent light, fingers knitted together as if in prayer. He looked up, a flame of sorrow sparking in his eyes. He offered a thin smile. 'It's okay, *Aba*,' he said in Urdu. 'Nothing happened. They just want to question us.'

Hashim sat down with his hands splayed on his knees and his joints already stiffening from the air conditioning. He stared at the wiry grey carpet to still the nerves that jangled in his limbs.

Hashim Khan had learnt to fear the white man. After moving to England in the seventies, he had learnt that wariness and deference were necessary in all dealings with the majority race. Now, called upon to protect his son, he knew no amount of deference would help. The door shut behind him with a metallic thud. He closed his eyes and whispered a prayer.

*

'Mr Rabbani, please take a seat. Would you like a drink? We have coffee, tea, water.'

'No,' said Yasser. 'Tell me what this is about or I'm calling a lawyer.'

Mia was unruffled. 'If your son is guilty, he probably needs one. If not, he'll likely be out of here in an hour.'

Yasser scowled. 'Then tell me what this is about.'

Mia pointed at a chair and waited for him to sit. She explained that the interview was being recorded and ran through some formalities.

Amir shifted in his seat, feeling unnaturally small next to his father's frame.

Mia began, 'Amir, can you tell me where you were on the evening of Thursday the twenty-seventh of June?'

'Yes. I was at home until about 7 p.m., then I went to a party with some of my friends.'

'What time did you get there?'

Amir shrugged. 'I don't really remember.'

'Okay, what did you do after the party?'

'I went home.'

'What time did you get home?'

'I'm not sure. About 1 a.m.'

Mia made a note. 'And you went straight home after the party?'

'Yes, I just said that.'

Mia smiled coldly. 'Well, what if I said we have reports of you attending an after-party of sorts at seventy-two Bow Docks, a derelict warehouse approximately seventy metres from the location of the party?'

Amir frowned. 'That wasn't an after-party. We were just fooling around on our way home.'

Mia glanced at the father. He was like a nervous cat, poised to pounce at any moment. Perhaps a soft approach was best here. 'Okay, it wasn't an after-party – my mistake. What did you boys get up to there?'

'We just hung out.'

Mia tapped the table with her index finger. 'And by that you mean?'

'We just talked, played music and …' He swallowed hard. 'We had a smoke.'

Amir's father snapped to attention. 'A smoke? Of what?'

'Dad, I'm sorry, it's not something we do all the time. Just sometimes.'

'A smoke of *what*?'

The boy stammered. 'Ganja.'

Yasser shot back in his chair. *'Tu ganja peera hai? Kahan se aaya hai? Kis haraami ne tujhe yeh diya hai?'*

'Aba, please. It was just once or twice.' Amir tried to push back his chair but it was bolted to the floor.

'I work all hours of the day to give you the life you have and you're going to throw it away on drugs?'

Amir shrank beneath the ire as if physically ducking blows. 'Dad, I swear to God, it was only once or twice. *Kasam.*'

His father's voice grew stony. 'Just wait until your mother hears about this.' Yasser shook his head in disbelief. 'We'll deal with this later.' He exhaled slowly and turned to Mia. 'I'm sorry, officer. Please continue.'

Mia felt a flicker of grudging respect. It was obvious he cared about his son's mistakes. Too often she saw young men trudge through here like ghosts, floating from one place to another with nothing at all to tether them. Yasser Rabbani clearly cared about his son.

'So you were smoking cannabis,' said Mia. 'Was there alcohol?'

Amir vigorously shook his head. 'No.'

Mia made a note to ask again later. 'Who else was there?'

Amir nodded at the door. 'Mo, Hassan and Farid.'

'Did anyone join you throughout the course of the night?'

'No.'

Mia caught the fissure in his voice. 'Amir, you should know that our officers are collecting your computers as we speak and we'll be examining your phones. If you or your friends are hiding something, we'll find out.' She smiled lightly. 'Don't you watch *CSI*?'

Amir blinked. 'Okay, there was one other person there but I really don't want this to get out. I've been trying to protect her forever.'

'Who's that?'

He hesitated. 'Her name is Jodie Wolfe. She's a girl from school. She has something called neurofibromatosis which messes up your face. We had a class about it at school but the kids called her the Elephant Woman anyway.'

'What was she doing at the warehouse?'

Amir shifted in his chair. 'She's a sweet girl but she can be a little bit ... sad. She's had a crush on me since year seven and even now, five years later, she follows me around – pretends she just bumped into me.'

'Is that what she did that night? Pretend to bump into you?'

Amir shook his head. 'No, even she wouldn't be that sad. She said she was looking for her friend Nina. She's always going off with different boys so Jodie must've lost her. She said she saw a bunch of us heading here and figured there was some kind of after-party.'

'Did you invite her to join you?'

Amir scoffed lightly. 'No, she just turned up. We were hanging out – just the boys.'

'So she turned up at the warehouse or joined you before?'

'Yes, she turned up at the warehouse.'

'Then what happened?'

Amir frowned. 'She asked if she could have a smoke. The boys didn't want to share one with her. I didn't say anything. I mean, she's not diseased or anything but she's scary to look at because of her condition so I could understand why they said that. She seemed upset so I tried to comfort her.'

'How?'

He shrugged. 'I put my arm around her and told her to ignore them.'

Mia couldn't place his emotion. Guilt? Shame? Embarrassment?

'Then she ...' his voice trailed off.

'Then she?'

The boy's face flushed red. 'She whispered in my ear and said she would do something for me if we got rid of the boys.'

Amir's father stood abruptly. He turned to the door and then back to his son. He opened his mouth to speak but then closed it again. Finally, he sat back down in silence and trained his gaze away from his son, as if the space between them might swallow the mortification of what was to come.

Mia leaned forward. 'You said that Jodie whispered in your ear. What did she say?'

Amir glanced sideways at his father. 'She— she said she would give me a blowjob and then started describing it. I was stunned. I always had this idea that she was a sweet girl.'

'How did you respond?'

'I took my arm off her and told her to go home. The boys started laughing and making kissing noises. I was really embarrassed so I started on her too.' He paused, shifted in his chair and made a visible effort to focus on Mia. 'I'm not proud of it but I said there's no way we'd share the spliff with her; that we didn't want to swap saliva with a dog. I knew she was hurt because I've always been alright to her but—' Amir pinched the skin between his brows, as if to ease a headache. Then, he spoke with surprising maturity, 'Look, I have an ego – I know that – and egos are fragile. The kids at school look at me and see the cricket captain, the guy that gets all the girls, the guy that has it all – and if it got out that I was cosying up to the school freak, then my reputation would take a hit. I like Jodie but she's not the kind of girl I want to be linked with that way, so I had to put a stop to it. She got upset and started crying. I felt bad but I told her to leave.'

'And then?'

'She left. She was crying and I think she may have had a drink because she was stumbling about a bit, but she left. Despite what the boys say, I think we all felt a bit bad so we wrapped it up, finished the spliff and went home.'

'And have you seen Jodie since then?'

'No. Why? Is she okay?'

'Jodie says she was raped that night.'

The boy's face turned ashen. '*She's* the one who said I raped her?'

Mia's voice was cold. 'Yes, Mr Rabbani. She's the one.'

*

DC Dexter put his elbows on the table. Calmly, he repeated himself, 'Jodie Wolfe said you, Amir and Mohammed raped her that night while Farid stood by and watched. What do you have to say to that?'

'I don't believe it,' said Hassan, his eyes ringed with pale, uncomprehending horror. He looked to his father. '*Aba, Allah Qur'an*, that's a lie.'

Irfan Tanweer was an older version of his son: short and wiry with tight ringlets of black hair atop a thin and hawkish face. His beady eyes danced with suspicion as he leaned forward and, in a thick Bangladeshi accent, said, 'You must be mistaken. My son – he is a religious boy. He would not do this.' He held out a hand to quieten his son. 'We are good people, sir, Mr Dexter. I have worked hard to make a home for my wife and my boy. I have a decent boy. Of that I am very sure.'

Dexter nodded placidly. 'That may be true, sir, but we need to know what happened. We need to hear your son's side of the story.'

'There is no "side" of the story. My son will tell the truth.' He turned to Hassan. *'Hasa kotha khor,'* he urged him to start.

*

Mo ducked in embarrassment when his father gripped the edge of the table. Each fingernail had a dried crust of blood along the cuticle. His father wore butchers' gloves at work and washed his hands thoroughly but that thin crust of blood seemed to always cling on. The two didn't look like father and son. Zubair Ahmed with his burly shoulders and broad chest was a pillar of a man. Mo was tall too, but thin and awkward. Where Zubair's hands were strong and meaty, Mo's were thin and delicate, almost effeminate in their movement as they fiddled now with his glasses.

He sat forward in his chair, shoulders hunched as if he were cold. 'I'm not confused, sir,' he said. 'We didn't hurt Jodie – not the way you say we did.'

The detective watched him with reproach. 'I think you *are* confused, son, or you would see that the wisest thing for you to do now is to tell the truth.'

Mo remembered the sharp pain in Jodie's eyes and the sting of betrayal when he sided with the lads. His obedience to them had cost him too: his pride, his integrity, his belief in his own valour. His complicity felt viscous in his throat and he swallowed hard so that he could speak. 'I shouldn't have let them treat her that way. They shouldn't have called her a dog.' He hesitated. 'But they were just words. We were in a loose and silly mood and,' his voice grew thick, 'we took it out on her because she was there and she was weak.' He blinked rapidly, sensing tears. He hated that they'd targeted Jodie. He, all too familiar with the sting of mockery, hated that he'd let it happen. With a deep breath to steady his voice, he said, 'We hurt Jodie but not in the way she says.' He swallowed. 'We were awful to her, but what she said did not happen and I'm sorry, sir, but I'm not confused about that.'

*

Amir sat in silence, his mouth open in a cartoonish O. His father spoke to him in a burst of Urdu, the long vowels urgent and angry. A lock of his salt and pepper hair fell free of its pomade and he swiped at it in a swift and severe motion that betrayed a slipping composure.

Mia firmly quietened him and urged Amir to speak.

'But it's Jodie …' he said. 'You've seen her. I – *we* – wouldn't do something like that.' He ran a hand across the back of his head. 'This is so bizarre.'

Mia studied him closely. He seemed neither worried nor guilty – just confused. She spoke to him in a low voice. 'Maybe it wasn't you. Maybe it was Hassan and Mohammed that did it and you and Farid just watched. Could that have happened and Jodie just got confused?'

He frowned. 'Look, we were all together the whole

time. There is no way any of the boys could have done anything to Jodie and they'll all tell you the same. Nothing happened.'

Mia's face grew stony. 'Then you won't mind giving us DNA samples.'

Amir shrank back in his chair, his athletic frame suddenly small. His father held up a hand. 'Don't you need a warrant for that?'

Mia leaned in close. 'Mr Rabbani, your son is under arrest for rape. Do you understand how serious that is? We can take DNA samples if we want to.' She paused. 'And we want to.'

Amir grimaced. 'I didn't do it.'

Mia smiled without humour. 'Then we don't have a problem, do we?'

It was an hour later that she watched the group of men file out of the station. She turned to Dexter. 'I can't work it out. Do you think they colluded beforehand?'

Dexter's face creased in thought. 'I didn't get a sense of rehearsed answers.'

'Were either of yours even a little bit tempted to shop their friends?'

'No. They're too clever for that. They know all about divide and conquer.'

Mia frowned. 'I just can't work it out,' she repeated. She stared at the door, still swinging on its hinges in the wind.

*

Sameena Tanweer sat motionless, her tiny frame comically small on the sofa. A network of fine grey cracks spread across the leather and a fist-sized patch stained one of the seats. She had caught Hassan as a child pouring the contents of her Amla hair oil in a concentrated pool on the spot. She had tried to hide it with homemade sofa covers, flowery and powder blue, but her husband had shouted. He was still bitter about spending two months' wages on the three-piece suite all those years ago and damn him if he was going to cover up real leather with cheap fabric like a *fakir*.

She sat there now, compulsively tracing the stain as the phone beside her hummed with the news. Her husband's tone had been rushed and harsh, untempered by words of comfort as he told her of their son's arrest.

In her mind, she searched frantically through a list. She couldn't call Jahanara's mum. That woman would spread the news to five others before she even came round. What about Kulsum? Wasn't she always talking about her lawyer son? Or was he an accountant? Sameena couldn't remember. Did she, after thirty years in Britain, really have no friends that she could call? Her social circle was limited to her neighbours, each of whom visited her several times a week to gossip about the unruly daughters and unkempt houses of their mutual acquaintances. Sameena always listened with patience but never partook in the gossip. She knew that every family had its flaws and she refused to pick apart another woman's life.

After a long minute of inertia, she stood and hurried to Hassan's bedroom, hitching up the hem of her sari on the stairs. Inside, she was hit by the musty aroma of a teenage boy. Last Tuesday she had hovered by the door pleading to clean his room but Hassan had swatted her away like a fly.

'Leave the boy alone,' her husband had said, the tetchiness clear in his tone. 'He's a teenager. He needs his space.' Interestingly, he often took the opposite view.

Sameena stepped into the smell and opened a window. Then, thinking no further, she gathered armfuls of clothes and in three trips took them to the bathroom. She stripped his sheets and checked under the bed and mattress for secret hiding places. She pulled out his socks and underpants and added them to the pile.

'It's fine,' her husband had said. 'Don't get hysterical.' But she had heard the horror stories. She had heard how Muslim boys were shot in raids and evidence planted in computers. She had to protect her son.

When the bath was full of clothes, she took an armload and stuffed it in the washing machine. The rest she hosed down with two cups of detergent. She hurried back and gathered all the electronics strewn across his room: his laptop, his dusty old Xbox, a mobile phone with a shattered screen and several USB sticks. She took them to her room and scanned her furniture for a lockable hiding place or secret cavity. She thought desperately of a place to deposit the loot.

Finally, she rushed to the kitchen and located the large

piece of Tupperware her husband used for leftovers from the restaurant. Inside, she lay the items in layers: first the laptop, then the console, then the phone and USB sticks slotted around the sides. With everything neatly inside, she shut the lid, wrapped the box in several bags of plastic and took it out to the garden. Gathering a fistful of her sari, she bent with a trowel and began to dig. When she had a hole almost two feet deep, she pressed the container inside and covered it with soil. She patted it down and scattered stones and leaves across the top to disguise the fact that it had been disturbed.

She stood over the spot in silence until the evening breeze made her shiver with cold. A vision of a nine-year-old Hassan crept into her mind, up in his room one sunny afternoon, standing over his cousin as quiet as a mouse. Her hands began to shake. She was doing this to protect her son.

Back inside the house, she laid a fresh set of sheets on his bed and then gathered an armful of her husband's clothes. Carefully, she arranged the garments around Hassan's room: a jumper askew on the back of a chair, balled socks at the foot of the bed, a pair of trousers at the bottom of the closet. It was only when the first wash cycle spun to a close that her heartbeat began to slow. What would those *kafir* do to her boy?

She unloaded the machine and was crouched down beside the basket when she heard the first knock. She froze for a moment, flinching when it came again, hard and insistent. She crept down the stairs and peeked through a window, coming face to face with a uniformed policeman. He pointed to the door.

'Open up please, madam.'

Sameena stepped back from the window, her head thumping with dread. A heavy fist hammered on the door, the calls loud and impatient. She couldn't just leave them on the doorstep, rousing Jahanara's mum and Mrs Patel across the road. She gathered up her nerve, stepped forward and turned the latch.

A heavyset man, too fat to be a policeman, held up a black wallet with a badge and ID. He spoke to her with surprising calm and then, without invitation, he stepped inside. Two other men followed. They asked her questions she did not understand, the only familiar word her son's name said over and over. *Hassan, Hassan, Hassan.* What fate had he drawn to this house?

The men marched upstairs, making her stomach lurch with each staccato step. She had checked everything carefully but what if they found something she missed? What if her efforts had all been in vain? In advancing hysteria, she hurried upstairs after them, standing sentry as they rummaged through her home and gathered up its pieces in evidence bags.

Every so often, one or the other would pause, asking her questions she couldn't understand. One mimed the act of tapping on a keyboard but Sameena simply shrugged, pretending not to understand their search for a laptop. She caught the exasperation edging into his tone, the subtle roll of his eyes, the silent implication: *Stupid woman. You stupid old woman.*

They spent an hour meticulously combing her home. The fat policeman handed her a pile of papers, emphasising some lines of small black text. With a final sigh of annoyance, he gathered the last bag and walked out the door, leaving it open behind him.

Sameena shut it with trembling hands. She made herself some tea and sat on the sweaty leather sofa, mindlessly swirling the cup in her hands. In a low voice, she recited prayers of gratitude, thankful that she'd had time to clear his room and hide his sins.

It was when the clock struck nine that she heard the front door whine open. Her husband, Irfan, walked in, his thin frame hunched against the falling darkness. Hassan trailed in behind him. Sameena hurried to the corridor, biting down her anguish. She embraced her son and wrapped a protective arm around his head.

'What is happening?' she asked.

'*Kuthain-okol.*' Irfan swore, a low growl that rippled with anger. 'A girl from his school is accusing them of such *besharam* things. And these police – they just believe anything she says.'

Sameena's nails dug into her palms. 'What things? What's happening?'

'Mum, calm down,' said Hassan. 'It's nothing to worry about.' His voice sounded strangely hollow as if reading from a script. 'Some girl at school said she got pushed around by me and the boys. It's not true, so it's fine. There are four of us and one of her. It's our word against hers. And everyone already knows that she's crazy.'

'But why is she saying these things?'

Hassan shrugged. 'I don't know why but you don't need to worry about it.'

Sameena threw up her hands. She cooked, cleaned and ran the home but every time there were important decisions to be made, she was told 'you don't need to worry'. Well, she *did* worry. And when her son was dragged to the police station in broad daylight with no stronger defence than his kitchen porter father, she most definitely worried.

'Why would she say such a thing? The police don't just barge into someone's home without reason!'

Hassan's voice rose a register. 'They were here?'

Sameena gripped his shoulder. 'Yes, but don't worry. They didn't find anything.'

He jerked out from under her hand. 'What do you mean?'

'Jahanara's mum told me what these police do, so I took all your things and washed all your clothes. If they say they found something, I will know they planted it.'

Hassan sucked in a short breath. 'What did they take?'

'Your TV and some of your father's clothes. Everything else I took from your room.'

Hassan almost laughed – a sound that was strange and strangled. 'Mum, you're crazy. What did you hide?'

She pictured the items in the Tupperware box. 'Your laptop, that old games machine, a broken mobile phone and the small silver sticks from your drawer.'

'Where did you put it?'

Sameena watched him closely, noting his sharp relief. She held his gaze and said, 'I've thrown it all away.'

He flinched. 'You did what?'

'I've thrown it away.' Her voice was calm and firm. 'In the canal. I didn't want the police to find it.'

Hassan reared away from her. 'You didn't.'

'Your phone was broken anyway. You don't play games on that machine anymore and you're always complaining about your laptop. We can buy you a new one now.'

Hassan's eyes grew narrow. 'Mum, there's no *way* you've thrown my stuff away. Where is it?'

She gestured at her sari, the hem muddied brown by soil. 'I walked to the canal and threw it all in.'

Hassan's jaw fell slack. 'But I need my stuff. It's got my pictures, my files, everything.' He turned to appeal to his father. '*Aba*, she's got to be joking. Tell her I need my things.' His voice was whiny to even his own ears.

'Hassan, go up to your room. Let me talk to your mother.'

'But—'

'*Go,*' he repeated.

Hassan's face burned red but he knew better than to defy his father. Saying no more, he turned and walked upstairs.

'Sameena, what did you do?' Irfan's voice was low.

She held up a hand to calm him. 'Don't worry. His things are safe but he's not getting them until this is over.'

Irfan sighed. 'The boy needs his things.'

'Why does he need these things?' she asked. 'His exams are finished.'

'Boys need ways to keep busy. Do you want him out on the streets?'

'Do you want him in jail?' she shot back. She watched a rift of anger crack open across his face. 'I'm just protecting him,' she insisted. 'You look at your son and you see a nice religious boy and Hassan *is* a good boy, but a mother knows the nature of her son and she protects him no matter what.'

Irfan scowled. 'What is that supposed to mean?'

Sameena smiled serenely. 'Please – just trust that I did the right thing.' She patted on the sofa. 'Sit down. I'll make you some tea.'

He began to protest but she had already turned towards the kitchen, using three quick steps to end the conversation.

At the top of the stairs, Hassan strained to hear but caught only murmurs. In silence, he crept to his parents' room and dialled Amir's home from the landline.

'Jesus, what a fucked up day.' Amir's voice was weary.

Hassan took a shallow breath. 'Have the feds been round?'

'Yeah.' Amir paused. 'You?'

'Mate, you won't believe this. The feds at the station

took the phone you lent me, but my mum threw away the one that got broken. She's chucked all my stuff away. My laptop, my games. Even my stash has gone. The feds got none of it.'

Amir whistled. 'Mate, your mum's a gangster.'

'She thinks she's done me a favour.'

Amir laughed. 'Well, she has, hasn't she?'

'How can you be so chilled about it?' said Hassan. 'We got *arrested*. She told them we raped her, for fuck's sake.'

Amir was silent for a moment. 'Mate, I have to be chill. Mum's hit the roof as usual.' He sighed. 'She's been going on about it for hours: all the tutoring she's spent money on, all the school reports, all the parents' evenings and meetings and on and on. I have to be chill or else I'll go mad.'

Hassan tightened his grip on the phone. 'But aren't you worried?'

'No,' said Amir. 'Jodie won't go through with this. It's a fucked up situation for sure, but once she calms down, she'll take it back.'

Hassan slid onto his parents' bed. 'If you say so.'

'I do. Just be cool. I'll catch up with you tomorrow.'

Hassan swallowed his weaving nerves. 'Okay, man.' He hung up the phone and sat motionless, unable or unwilling to return to his room.

*

Farid Khan let the ball fall from his grip and watched it roll away. Shoulders slumped, he sat on the wooden block by the path and felt his sweat cool, sending chills down his spine. Shivering, he sat still, not quite ready to leave.

He spotted the slim woman with cropped hair walking purposefully towards him. Instinctively, he lowered his gaze. It was only when she stopped directly in front of him that he looked up and met her eyes.

'Hi.' Her voice was husky but soft. It made him think of warm sand slipping through his fingers.

'Hi,' he echoed.

'What's your name?' she asked.

He looked at her leather jacket, her skin-tight jeans and knee-high boots. 'Whatever you're selling, I'm not buying.'

'Ha!' She sounded amused.

'What do you want?' he asked less certainly.

'Can I sit?'

Farid looked over her shoulder, then back up at her. He shrugged.

Erin sat and curled her graceful legs beneath her. 'I'm a friend of Amir's. I know that he's in some trouble.'

Farid smiled faintly. 'Amir never gets in trouble.'

'Not yet, but we both know it's coming.'

Farid looked at her quizzically, his thick, dark brows furrowed in confusion. 'Who are you? How do you know Amir?'

'I'm working the Jodie Wolfe case.' She watched him stiffen. 'I know that Amir and some of his friends did something stupid and they're about to get into some serious trouble. I'm trying to help him.' She paused. 'You *do* know Jodie, right?'

Farid's gaze fell to the floor.

'Is she a friend?'

He shrugged. 'I wouldn't say that.'

Erin studied his face. 'Did you see Amir with Jodie at Kuli's party?'

'Amir doesn't talk to any of the ugly girls.' Farid caught Erin's expression. 'I'm sorry, I didn't mean to call her ugly – she just … well, she *is*, right?'

'Farid, I'd like to talk to you about what happened that night.'

'Nothing happened.'

'Were you drinking?'

He scoffed. 'I don't drink.'

'What time did you leave the party?'

He looked at her sideways. 'Are you from the police?'

Erin smiled. 'No, I'm a private investigator. When someone's in trouble, I go out and find the truth about what happened. If it turns out that whatever they're accused of is an exaggeration or misunderstanding, then I help them. I know you didn't do anything wrong that night, but you're going to go down for it unless you tell the truth.'

'Nothing happened,' Farid insisted.

'Then why does Jodie say it did? She doesn't seem like the kind of girl who would accuse you for kicks.'

'She's just trying to get his attention.'

'Is that so?'

Farid sighed. 'She's not right in the head. She's always sending him secret messages, even leaving notes in his locker. Amir is kind enough to ignore it. If she was anyone else, she'd be made a fool.'

Erin watched him carefully. There was no hint of a quiver in his voice, no nuance of doubt, nothing to suggest his guilt. She shifted to face him. 'You've got to listen to me, Farid. What Jodie has said about Amir is serious. Really fucking serious, and you're about to get sucked into it. If you tell me the truth about what happened, I can help you.'

Farid's fingertips traced the grain of his beard. 'Listen, I've known Amir since we were both five. He plays the big man around town because he can, but he's a good bloke. He wouldn't hurt anybody. This is just Jodie messing with him. I told you – she's not right.'

Erin took in his quiet assurance, his polite manner, his steadfast gaze. She could spot a liar at ten paces and this boy wasn't lying.

'Okay. Can you think of any other reason why Jodie would want to get Amir in trouble?'

'There's nothing else I can think of. He's always been polite to her. He has a thing about the underdog and he cares about things in ways other people don't.'

'Is that so?' Erin's tone was sardonic.

Farid picked up a stray twig and spun it slowly in his hands. 'When we were eleven, we went down to Vicky Park late one evening. It was just gone spring and it was still a bit too chilly for all the Hackney hipsters. Me, Amir and these other boys were there. This boy Omar had a pellet gun. We were arsing about with it, trying to hit trees and bins and stuff. And then, one of the boys dared him to shoot a swan on the other side of the lake. Omar was laughing about it and we were goading him, calling him chicken and all that. Finally, after about ten minutes of this, Omar takes aim. We didn't think he was going to do it. We really didn't. But then he pulled the trigger and hit the thing square in the chest. I've never heard a sound like it. It was like a young kid squealing in pain. It was kicking its legs, trying desperately to stay afloat, fighting desperately for its life. We all turned a shade of pale I've never seen before. That sound still loops in my nightmares. Five minutes passed and it still fought, still desperate, still screaming. Finally, Amir grabbed the gun and aimed it at the swan's head. The look on his face was …' Farid paused.

'That's the only time I saw him cry. He did what needed to be done, what none of the rest of us could do because he cared about that animal. It's not just a one-time thing neither. Two years ago, he brought home this mistreated dog. His parents gave him hell for it but he kept her; named her "Rocky" because she's a fighter. That's who he is. He cares about things weaker than him.' Farid shook his head. 'Whatever Jodie's saying about him, it's not true. It's not.'

Erin studied him for a moment. Then, she stood and thanked him. 'I guess I'll be seeing you.'

Farid shrugged, then watched her disappear into the

distance. He picked up his muddy ball and turned wearily towards home.

*

Mo uncapped the seam ripper and slid it beneath the delicate blue thread. He flicked up the blade and broke the stitch. With practised fluency, he moved across the Banarasi brocade material, unpicking his mother's mistake.

Mo had served as her assistant for years, both of them cramped into the draughty storeroom that she had turned into a tailor's studio. In July, with wedding season in full swing, her work was seemingly endless. Still, at least Mo's exams were now finished. In April, he used to stop studying at three and spend the next two hours sewing. Bushra would insist he return to his studies, but he could see the worry creasing her brows as the work stacked up outside. It was slow and intricate and could not be rushed, but she took on too much, for the money. On a shelf above her sewing machine, she kept meticulous records of all activity: clients, jobs, transactions and leads, every single pound colour-coded into bridal wear, casual wear and Western wear.

As a young child, Mo learnt to think in colours and textures: nylon was frustration, brown was honesty, blue was freedom and silk was carefree whimsy. He had been so proud of their bridal creations: the diaphanous golds and glittering reds and thousands of shiny stones. At age seven, he had unwittingly told his friends about one such garment and was ceaselessly teased for weeks. He came home crying one day and Bushra wrapped him in her soft arms.

'I can't tell you to ignore them,' she said. 'You will always care what people think of you – that's just the way of the world – but you *can* decide how you act in return. You can choose to be cruel like them to make yourself feel tall, or you can treat others with kindness to balance out the shortfall.' She sat him on her lap. 'There will be moments in your life when you must decide in an instant. What you do is up to you, but I hope you never choose to be cruel.'

He watched her now and marvelled at her sleight of hand. Where other parents were pushy and dogmatic, she steered him with the lightest touch. She told him what she believed to be right and let him set his own course. With this skill and subtlety, she weaved him with a sense of justice.

Lanced with guilt last night, he had confessed to her his treatment of Jodie and said that his courage had failed. 'But we didn't do what she said,' he'd added, desperate to keep her esteem. Bushra had hugged him tightly. 'I know you didn't. The son I raised wouldn't act like that.' She kissed his hair and released him. 'I don't know how far this will go and right now it's important that we face it together. I know that you're a good person. When this is over, however, I would like to discuss how you treated that girl.'

'I know,' Mo said quietly. His mother, who loved him fiercely like a child deserved, expected the conduct of an adult. He had failed her, but when this mess with Jodie was over, he would vow to be a better person. A single moment of weakness would not define his entire life. The mistake would be righted and they'd all move on – and surely that would be soon. After all, it was four against one.

*

Zara grappled for her phone and cursed when she saw the time. Sure enough, there were several missed calls: two from Stuart at Artemis House and another one from Erin. She texted Stuart an apology and then stumbled to the bathroom. Her throat was parched and her tongue held the whispery texture of cotton. She slipped two fingers under the cold tap and ran them over her eyes, wiping away the sleep. The cool water of the shower calmed her pounding head.

Her mind snaked to Luka and clasped his words like a bitter nut at its centre. *Even he couldn't stand you by the end.* She heard the sound of her palm on his flesh and saw the rising colour in his cheek. She closed her eyes and willed him away, refusing to accept her guilt.

Drying off, she returned to the bedroom and rifled through her closet for a pair of jeans, a T-shirt and a blazer. She pulled on her ballet flats, grabbed her bag and headed out the door to her car. Her phone began to ring just as she drove off. She answered it clumsily and switched to speakerphone.

'I tried to call you.' Erin was impatient. 'Listen, I spoke to Farid, the spectator. I caught him after football practice. Here's the thing: I'm not sure your girl is being a hundred per cent honest.'

Zara felt the car swerve beneath her. 'You what?'

'I don't think she's telling the whole truth. I believe the boy.'

'Why? What did he say?'

Erin recounted the meeting. 'Either he's telling the truth or he's a complete sociopath,' she said matter of factly.

Zara tutted. 'Come on, Erin. You're better than this.' She knew the barb would annoy her and this was partly intended. How could she decide that Jodie was lying without hearing her account first-hand?

Erin sidestepped the bait. 'All I'm saying, Zara, is tread carefully. This girl may not be as innocent as she looks. People rarely are.'

Zara frowned. Could Jodie's pitiful gait and disfigured face be hiding a secret cunning? She didn't believe it for a second, but placated Erin nonetheless. 'I'll tread carefully.' She said goodbye and focused her grinding mind on the road.

Half an hour later, she was at her desk. Stuart sat opposite, speaking in a measured tone that only occasionally exposed his dwindling patience.

'What are you not telling me?' he asked.

Zara shook her head. 'I overslept. Really, that's all.'

'Yes, and the first time it happened, I believed you. We've been through this, Zara. You're one of the best lawyers I've ever met and you're sure as hell the best advisor we've had in this place, but this isn't a shift at Tesco. You're not stacking shelves. If you don't turn up to work, the women we look after don't get the level of care they're owed.'

Zara bit down her shame. 'I'm sorry. I am. It won't happen again.'

He leaned forward, his voice softening a notch. 'That's what you said last time.' He ran a restless hand through his hair. 'Seriously, what's going on?'

'I overslept, that's all.'

Stuart's lips came together in a tight, thin line, holding back words he might later regret. 'Okay, fine.' He pressed a Post-it note onto her desk. 'The detective on Jodie Wolfe's case called. You might want to call her back.' With that, he stood and left.

Zara tried to shrug off the guilt but it clung heavily to her shoulders. Were it anyone else, she would wave away the criticism but Stuart was one of the few truly selfless people in her life. He wasn't concerned with feeding his ego or chasing profits; he simply wanted to help their clients. The knowledge of that made her cheeks burn hot. She threaded her fingers through her hair and grabbed angry fistfuls. What was she *doing*? Her mind posed then denied a series of accusations: *No, I'm not bad at my job. No, I shouldn't just quit. No, I don't have to stop using – it's just harmless release.*

Listlessly, she picked up the note. Four words were written in Stuart's expansive scrawl: 'I have news. Mia.' Zara's heart rate quickened and she picked up the phone and dialled.

Mia answered promptly. 'I take it you received my message?'

'Yes. Sorry, I've had a crazy morning.'

A short laugh. 'Yes, unfortunately I'm all too familiar with those.' Mia waited a beat. 'So, Jodie's clothes are positive for semen. We're trying to expedite the DNA tests.'

Zara felt a flush of relief. 'That's great news.'

'I haven't spoken to Jodie yet. I thought you might like to tell her.'

Zara was oddly touched by the gesture. 'Thank you. Do you know when we'll get the results?'

'Right now, I'm told three weeks.'

'Christ.' Zara flicked through her diary and marked out a date. 'Have you found anything you can use on the boys' electronics?'

'No, nothing yet,' Mia sighed. 'They use these so-called "ephemeral apps" and everything gets deleted after twenty-four hours.'

Zara tapped a pen against the page. 'Listen, check if the boys are on Jabdam. It's a Korean app that allows users to post anonymous rumours about each other, tagged by location. It came up in a past case of mine. The app's not governed by GDPR and we can access all the data that's ever been posted on their platform – even if it was set to expire.'

Mia brightened. 'What would we be looking for?'

'Anything that's tagged Bow or East London and that mentions Amir or Jodie – or any of them. Maybe one of the boys couldn't help bragging, or a friend of a friend knows something.'

'Good call.' Mia scrawled down the details. 'I'll let you know if we find anything.'

'Okay,' Zara paused. 'Hey Mia, one more thing. When you canvas the neighbours, greet them with *Assalamu Alaikum* if they're Muslim. They'll likely be tight-lipped and this might help disarm them.'

'Thanks,' said Mia. 'I'll keep you updated.'

Zara hung up and glanced at the clock. Stuart had reassigned her appointments and her day was unusually empty. She flicked through Jodie's case file, reading and re-reading random passages. Eventually, after an hour of inertia, she decided to take a break. She walked to Port & Port on the western end of Whitechapel Road. She liked the bar for its unique position between East London and the city, and for the blackboard outside that said in bright yellow chalk, 'I'd eat here,' a quote which was then attributed to, 'The owner'. Inside, an ensemble of high beams, sturdy wooden furniture and dusty artefacts gave it a comfortable old-barn feel.

She ordered a drink and settled in a booth in the corner. She shrugged off her blazer and placed some files across the table: her excuse for drinking alone. She checked her phone and noted acidly that Luka hadn't tried calling. She picked up a file and scanned it blindly. She was bored. She was *always* fucking bored. She glanced at her watch, not even sure what she was waiting for. She put down the file and picked up another. As she did so, she heard a purposeful cough at the next table. Her eyes – trained to ignore such puerile plays for attention – remained fixed on the sheet of paper. After a beat, she sensed movement towards her.

He was dressed in a dark suit, crisp white shirt and slim black tie. As he sat down opposite, she noticed the muscles of his arm flex beneath the suit. He wasn't her type – far too built for that – but he had her attention.

'You probably haven't drunk enough for this. *I* certainly haven't drunk enough for this but,' he paused, 'you're stunning. And I knew that if I left this bar without talking to you, I'd regret it. So tell me to get lost and I'll get on my way. I just have to know that I tried.' He barely waited for her to respond. 'But, if you want – and it's what I really want – I can buy us another drink and we can sit and talk about whatever you want: the perversions of the Marquis de Sade or the plight of the Congolese, who should have won Bake Off or the latest shade of lipstick – anything.' His eyes searched hers and grew confident as he gleaned the reaction he intended.

A smile curled at the corner of her lips. She knew exactly what type of man he was: the type that recycled pet names from each of his flings and used women as landmarks ('you know the place, the one with that sexy blonde waitress with an arse like an onion'), but it mattered less than it should.

'I'm going to take that as a yes,' he said with a smile. He strode to the bar, his frame tall and powerful – almost twice her size.

As she watched him, she felt her conscience tug. She was angry at Luka but could she really sit here with a stranger and pretend he didn't exist? She sat stock-still for a moment and then, making a decision, gathered up her files and strode to the bar. She stopped the stranger mid-order.

'Listen, I'm sorry but I have to go.'

His head tilted back in askance. 'No, come on!'

'I can't. I'm sorry.'

He clasped his hands in mock agony. 'Okay, but please, *please* leave me your number.'

'I don't give out my number.'

'Okay, then give me your phone and let me put in mine.'

She shook her head with a smile. She knew not to do that after a friend of a friend used her phone to call his own hence securing her number, and then doggedly pursuing her for a good six months.

The stranger reached over the counter and picked up a ballpoint pen. From his pocket, he retrieved a receipt and scribbled down his number. 'Then please take this and please call me.' He pressed the note into her hands. 'I'll be waiting.'

She accepted.

'And at least tell me your name.'

'It's Zara.' She glanced at the piece of paper. 'And yours?'

He leaned forward and whispered it in her ear, his breath warm on her skin.

She closed her eyes momentarily. 'Goodbye, Michael.' She left the bar without turning back, knowing he was watching her go.

*

Nina Sahari was on her back. Her cut-off T-shirt revealed a smooth, taut belly and her silken hair fell around her head like a fan. She reached up and threw the ball against the ceiling, catching it again with ease. Her green eyes – a much-desired result of her Pathan roots – blinked off tiny bits of plaster that rained down around her. She chewed her gum and blew it into a bubble, then popped it with her tongue and licked the sticky substance off her lips.

'What is up with you anyway?' She glanced at Jodie in the corner. 'You've been totally deranged lately. I know your mum's been ill but FFS.' When Jodie said nothing, Nina sat up in exasperation. 'Come on. It's not like she's got cancer; she's ill coz she likes to drink. Why should *you* have to stay home and suffer for it?'

Jodie grimaced. 'She's going through a rough patch.' In truth, she was no worse than usual but Jodie needed a reason to hide.

Nina sighed ostentatiously. 'Look, I don't mean to be a bitch. It's just that there's nothing to do in this shitty place. I'm bored and I've missed you.'

Jodie stirred in surprise. She felt a sudden warmth for her friend, normally so poised and aloof.

'Christ, don't get all emosh on me.' Nina rolled her eyes but then gestured to the bed. 'Come on, tell me what's up.'

Jodie walked over and sat gingerly. Nina, for all her bluff and bravado, showed a keen sense of awareness whenever things were wrong. At school, she wielded this power for both good and evil, lending succour to the girls she liked and cruelly skewering those she did not. In year eight, she would pick out the girl who'd started her first period, or the one wearing a bra for the very first time and use it to tease them without mercy. Now, eager to learn what was wrong with Jodie, she honeyed her voice so that it was soft and warm, and encouraged her to speak.

Jodie shifted on the bed, wanting to please her friend but sick at the thought of sharing her story.

Nina placed an arm around her. 'Come on. Whatever it is, I'll help you fix it.'

Doubt lanced through Jodie's stomach, mixing with the dead weight of fear. She opened her mouth to speak, then quickly closed it again. She took two rapid breaths, then gathered her strength and said, 'You remember Kuli's party?'

Nina's interest was piqued, her brows arching over jade green eyes. 'Yeah. What about it?'

'At the party, the last time I saw you, you were dancing with that boy from Redbridge.' Jodie's words were soft and stilted. 'After a while I couldn't find you so I went out to the canal. I felt stupid in your clothes and wanted to be alone. After a while, I heard footsteps.' Jodie tensed, fearing Nina's reaction. 'It was Amir.'

Nina's face flushed red. 'Who was he with?'

'No one.'

Her eyes narrowed. 'Okaaay. And then?'

Jodie picked at a thread in her quilt. 'He came up to me and started talking.'

Nina frowned but said nothing.

'I told him that I couldn't find you and he said he knew where you were; that you had gone to a private party.'

Nina stiffened. 'That bastard. What rumours was he spreading about me?'

'It— it wasn't about you,' stuttered Jodie. She searched her friend's face for clues. Nina acted indifferent to Amir but she had once pondered to Jodie that since both she and Amir had green eyes, their children would certainly inherit them.

Jodie was tempted to backtrack, to bury her worry and tell Nina nothing. But wouldn't it all be revealed regardless? And wouldn't Nina be angry that she hadn't been honest? Jodie laced her hands in her lap and cautiously continued. 'He told me he would take me to the party. Instead, he took me to this warehouse a few metres down the canal. I don't know if you know it – the tall one with all the broken windows?'

Nina shrugged impatiently.

'When we got inside, the others turned up.'

Nina threw her ball against the far wall. 'They had a party without me? And *you* were there?'

'Nina, please, that's not what happened,' said Jodie, needing her friend to listen. 'Hassan, Mo and Farid came out of nowhere. They were all drunk and rowdy.' There was a catch in her voice and she willed herself to be calm, for Nina couldn't stand theatrics. 'They started to tease Amir, egging him on, and he … he started touching me.'

Nina's eyes grew impossibly wide. Then after a pause of breathless silence, she burst into peals of laughter. 'Ha, good one!' She pushed Jodie's shoulder in jest. 'You're such a fucking psycho sometimes but you know what? I fucking love you.' When she saw that Jodie was silent, her laughter grew shrill. Then, it came to an abrupt stop. 'Jodie?'

Big glassy tears welled in Jodie's eyes. 'They took turns.'

Nina stiffened. 'Doing what?' Her voice was suddenly hard. 'What did they do?'

Jodie pulled her hoodie tight around her body. 'They raped me.'

Nina's face grew pink. 'Jo, tell me you're kidding.'

Jodie shook her head, blinking quickly so that her tears would spread on lashes and not across her cheeks.

Nina shot up from the bed. 'What the fuck?'

Jodie registered her anger and worried about what she might do. 'Nina, please don't confront them. The police are going to—'

'You've gone to the police?' Nina's mouth goldfished open and closed. 'Jesus Christ, Jodie. Everyone always said you were a freak but I've always defended you. What the fuck are you doing?'

Jodie flinched with surprise. 'That's not—'

'Those boys didn't touch you!' Nina was suddenly furious. 'Our whole school knows you've been mooning after Amir for years. I've seen the way you look at him, the way you sidle up to me when he's in a three-mile radius just in case he should come up to me and notice that you exist!'

The last three words hit Jodie like blows: a strike to her head, then one to the neck and the last a punch in the stomach.

'My God,' spat Nina. 'How did you come up with something so twisted?'

'Nina.' Jodie's voice was pleading. 'I'm not making it up.'

'Look, no one's going to believe you and you'll make a fool of yourself, not to mention *me* who's always defended you.' She flung a hand at the door. 'Does Massi know about this?'

Jodie bridled at Nina's affectionate name for her mother. 'Yes,' she whispered.

'And?'

Jodie felt her heart contract. 'She reacted like you.' She closed her eyes so that hot tears now spilled across her face. She felt her resolve bend beneath the pain almost until it was broken. Desperately, she willed her friend to believe her. She could accept that her mother in a stupor of drink couldn't see right from wrong, but not that Nina – who had only ever seen Jodie do good – would accuse her now of being a liar.

Noting Jodie's distress, Nina firmly gripped her shoulders. 'Look, Jo, I'm not doing this to be a bitch but if your own mother and your own best friend are telling you something, you should listen to them. If you told me that those boys got you in that room and slagged you off or called you names or pushed you around, I would have gone and ripped their fucking heads off. But everyone knows you've been in love with Amir for, like, ever. No one's going to believe you. Plus …' Nina shrugged, 'they're good boys, they pray and they respect their families. No one would believe they'd do what you're saying – even to a normal girl.'

Jodie's stomach lurched with a deep-seated anger for trusting her friend.

Nina tossed a glance at the wall clock. 'Look, it's getting late. I've got to get home. I'll call you as soon as I get there.' She leaned forward and planted a kiss on Jodie's head. 'We'll fix this. I promise.'

Jodie watched Nina saunter from the room and close the door with a flourish. With shaking fingers, she reached for her phone and switched it off with a sob.

CHAPTER FOUR

The train slid to a stop at Greenwich DLR station. Scores of revellers spilled forward in keen pursuit of rare Saturday sun. They moved as one, pale limbs protruding from too-short shorts and sandals criss-crossing week-wearied feet.

Zara weaved her way through them and stepped onto the train moments before the doors slid shut. Immediately, she felt the draw of attention, a dozen pinpricks piercing skin. She took a seat and made involuntary eye contact with the passenger opposite, an athletic man in a dark green bomber jacket and pepper-coloured crewcut. They both looked away. A second later, his gaze flitted back and seemingly undetected took rest on her face. Over the next three stops, he stared at her body, darting from breasts to lips.

It took her back to the day she was waiting for a friend outside Mile End station. A group of Asian men, all in their early twenties, catcalled from a passing car. Zara scowled and averted her gaze. They laughed derisively and one leaned through a window. *Oh, please!* he shouted. *Look at what you're wearing!*

A red dress, yes, and three-inch heels, but there was no hint of cleavage. She hated herself for making that distinction. Would she otherwise be fair game? The compulsion to bargain with her own sense of decency was a relic of her pious childhood. Now, under the glare of the crewcut's gaze, she struggled with it once again.

When the train stopped at Bow Road, she stepped onto the platform and with practised speed gathered up her hair in a bun. She no longer wore the headscarf but the censure linked to free-flowing hair still bubbled beneath her skin, because of course a woman's mane, full of seduction and deceit, was not to be flaunted lest it tempted men to think about fucking her.

Zara thought about this bitterly as she wrapped a pashmina around her shoulders and, modesty resealed, walked briskly down the stairs and across the street to her childhood home. It was a neat two-storey house wedged between a pair just like it. Pure white curtains hung in all the windows and a row of immaculate plants sat in the little garden out front.

Despite clear effort to the contrary, the place gave off an air of poverty. Perhaps it was the dark brown brick so pervasive on East London estates or the drooping gutter the council refused to fix, but the house felt sad and heavy above Zara's silhouette.

She reached forward and rang the bell. She was the only child of four who didn't have a key. She had left that behind with everything else.

'*Assalamu alaikum.*' She gave her mother a kiss on the cheek, something that only now, at thirty, felt halfway natural.

'*Walaikum assalam.*' Her mother beckoned her inside.

Fatima Kaleel was a tall woman once, the formidable matriarch of the family. Now the streaks of grey, the burden of age and the weight of bereavement pressed heavy on her shoulders, reducing her to a frailer version of her former self. Her harsh features had softened, her cut-glass cheekbones swallowed by aging skin. Even her frown lines of anger now looked like wearied wisdom.

Zara was not yet sure if this softer incarnation comforted her or terrified her. Her mother was now 'elderly' and one day soon they would have to talk about the past and they would have to exchange forgiveness. But not today. Today would be another of words unsaid.

Zara slipped off her coat and hung it by the base of the stairs. She paused for a moment and picked it up again. Sure enough, there was the distinctive dark blue coat that belonged to her older brother, Rafiq.

She turned to her mother. 'Is *Bhaisaab* here?'

Fatima nodded, her lips tight with tension.

'Why didn't you tell me?'

'I knew you wouldn't come.'

Zara swallowed her reaction. 'Where is he?'

'Upstairs.'

Zara sighed. Kicking off her shoes, she marched into the living room. First, she greeted her sisters. Salma, the eldest, sat with her legs crossed primly at the ankles. She tilted her face upwards to accept Zara's kiss and checked her watch while doing so. Salma's life was measured in one-hour slots, always racing against an invisible hourglass. It was Saturday, which meant her kids were at Arabic class, to be collected in precisely twenty-five minutes. After that, an hour for lunch, then the drive home to Ilford, so that her husband could have the car for the second of his split shift.

Lena, the youngest, sat with her legs curled beneath her. She caught Zara's eye and rolled hers discreetly, a signal that their brother was being especially tiresome. Lena was naturally quiet, but nursed a spiky wit. When an uncle recently marvelled that her husband was minding her child, she smiled sweetly and said, 'Yes, Jash is very excited to continue being a father'. Of course, where Lena used wit, Zara used force and she now turned breezily to their brother in the corner.

'Hi *Bhaisaab*, how are you?' she asked evenly.

He leaned back on the kingly sofa while his wife, Amina, fussed over tea. A faint smirk settled on his features. 'It's you.'

'Yes, it's me.'

'Sit down.' His words pulsed with an imperiousness found only in cosseted Asian men and their rich white peers.

Zara leaned on a wall instead, not yet too old for these small acts of defiance.

Rafiq took a bite of *bora*, a puff of steam curling visibly upward. He chewed slowly for a full minute. 'So where are you living now?'

'The same place I was living last time you asked.'

His face grew tight. 'You can never answer something simply, can you?'

'Is "yes" simple enough for you?' She watched a vein contract in his temple.

Salma sighed. 'Would you two give it a rest?'

Rafiq ignored her. 'How much is your mortgage?' he asked.

Zara shrugged. 'The same as the last time you asked.'

'Why don't you rent it out and move back in with Mum? You could be making thousands.'

'If we're going to use that logic, why don't we *all* move back in with Mum?'

His eyes grew wide, surprised as ever by her gall. '*Tafa kayteh?*'

Zara almost laughed at the predictability of his catchphrase. *Do you want a slap?* She straightened. 'Rather not, but thanks for the offer.'

He pushed the table away from him in a single forceful blow, making his teacup rattle on its saucer.

Salma held up a hand. 'Rafiq, that's enough.'

He turned his anger to a more amenable target. 'How many times do I have to tell you?' he growled at Amina. 'Don't make my tea so fucking strong! This isn't Bangladesh. We get our milk from Tesco, you understand?

We're not gonna send you to the fields to milk the cows at dawn.'

'Rafiq,' Salma's voice grew stern. 'I said *that's enough*.' She, though benign in nature, was never scared to step in. As the eldest child, she had the advantage of age, which in their culture, superseded gender. She could scold him with impunity, but she used this power sparingly, aware that allowing some transgressions prevented the ones that mattered most.

Like a defiant child, Rafiq pushed the table again, now spilling tea across the shiny mahogany.

'I am sorry,' said Amina, dabbing at the tea with the corner of her sari. The heavy roll of her 'r' grated on him, she knew, but it surfaced at times of stress despite her best efforts. 'I will make you another one.' She gathered the debris and hurried from the room.

Zara closed her eyes to calm herself. With a slow, deep breath, she followed her sister-in-law to the kitchen.

Amina busied herself with the kettle. 'I know what you're going to say.'

Zara frowned. 'I'm not going to tell you what to do. God knows you get enough of that from him, but you're a smart woman, Amina. You taught yourself English in two years and you speak it better than he does. If you want your own life, I can help you.'

Amina shook her head. 'Zar, I don't need the freedoms you do.'

'But don't you *want* them?'

Amina smiled wistfully. 'I have more than I could ever have imagined. It's enough for me.'

Zara blinked. 'And him? He is enough for you?'

Amina placed the small white teacup in the centre of the saucer. 'He is a good person at heart. He just expected more from life.' She lifted the teacup and dabbed it with a kitchen towel, absorbing the extra moisture. 'He thinks a lot of you, you know. When you're not there, he tells people about his sister, the successful lawyer and property owner. He tells them how you used to beat him at chess when you were only six years old, or how you knew every word he picked from a dictionary.'

Amina spun the cup around, lining the handle in a precise horizontal line. 'In your presence, however, he remembers everything he should have been. He knows he was given every chance to excel when you had to fight for it all and I think that makes him feel small. He uses piety as a shield, but he does think highly of you.'

Zara swallowed. 'Maybe he can learn to feel big without stepping on me to do it.' She sighed. 'Look, if you ever change your mind, promise me you'll call me. I have space, money, whatever you need.'

Her sister-in-law kissed her cheek. 'I know, Zar. Thank you.'

Zara wanted to say more, but knew that dogma was tiresome. Amina knew what was best for her and Zara had to respect that. She said goodbye instead, then turned and left the kitchen. She retrieved her coat and pulled it on with grim determination.

'*Deka oyboh*,' she said, a perfunctory parting tossed inside the living room.

Her mother walked into the corridor. 'Why are you going?'

'I can't deal with him.'

'Why don't you just ignore him?'

'Why doesn't he just shut his mouth?' The words sounded churlish to even her own ears but it was too late to rein them in. She blinked beneath her mother's gaze, wishing she had the words to explain why she couldn't *just ignore him*, why she couldn't *just be okay* with another man controlling the women around her. Perhaps her mother would never understand. After a lifetime of outsourcing her choices, could she appreciate the value of making her own?

Zara took a stiff breath. 'I'll come round another day.' She walked out and closed the door with a decisive thud. The wind snapped at her face, making her eyes water. She clasped her hands together and held the tips to her lips, breathing deeply once, twice, thrice. Then, she walked away just like before.

*

The dark brick exterior of the Wentworth Estate held the stench of peaty damp mixed with stale urine. Cracked white trim lined the balconies while a heap of rust-red bicycles lent the place an eerie dystopian feel. Zara side-stepped a bag of rubbish, ripe in the summer sun, and started up the concrete stairwell. She slipped on a slushy piece of greying cardboard and steadied herself on the black iron banister. Carefully, she rounded the corner onto the communal first-floor balcony and knocked lightly on a brown door marked seven. It swung open with a long whine.

In the corridor stood a woman in her late thirties, rail thin, dressed in leggings and a baggy brown jumper. Her thin lips stretched across a tight face and her hair, gathered in a messy bun, was platinum blonde with streaks of black. She tapped her cigarette and the ash floated down to the grey linoleum floor.

'Who the fuck are you?' the woman rasped.

'Ms Wolfe?' Zara's tone was neutral. 'I'm Zara Kaleel from Artemis House. Has Jodie spoken to you about my visit?' The question was met with silence. 'May I come in?' Zara hazarded a step inside.

The woman jabbed a thumb at the living room. She took a deep drag of her cigarette, her cheeks growing concave like Edvard Munch's *The Scream*.

Zara stepped around her through a cloud of nicotine. She pushed open the living-room door and spotted Jodie on a sofa, knees to her chest and arms wrapped around them. 'Everything alright?'

Jodie glanced up. 'Yes.'

Zara closed the door behind her. 'I take it that's your mum?'

'Yes.'

'She seems angry.'

Jodie nodded plaintively. 'She usually is.'

Zara perched on the sofa. 'Has she spoken to you about what happened?'

Before Jodie could answer, her mother entered the room.

'So,' said Christine. 'Are you the one putting these grand ideas into her head?' She tapped her cigarette and sent another wisp of ash floating to the floor. She didn't wait for Zara's answer. 'That girl's been nothin' but trouble since the day she was born. You wanna make sure you watch her. She ain't so fuckin' innocent.'

Zara gestured at the sofa. 'Ms Wolfe, please sit down.'

'Don't you tell me to sit down,' she snapped. 'This is my home. Who said *you* could sit down?' She stubbed her cigarette into a glass ashtray. 'Tellin' me to sit down in my own home. This is *my* home.'

Zara held up a palm. 'Ms Wolfe, it is perfectly normal to feel what you're feeling. Many parents of victims feel disbelief, denial or even rage.'

The woman laughed – a high, amused trill you might hear wafting from a fairground. '"Victims?"' She laughed again. 'Jodie ain't no victim. Jodie wants attention. It's always been "me me me" with her.'

Zara glanced at Jodie with a fierce tug of pity. It was little wonder she had tried to keep her from Christine. She appealed to her now with gentle sincerity, 'Your daughter needs your support, Ms Wolfe. She needs you.'

The woman glowered. 'I love that girl. I gave up her father for her. Love of my life he was but I let him go. Don't you tell me what I need to do. I done everything for her but I ain't to be made no laughing stock.' She turned to Jodie. 'You need to get your head straight 'cause I ain't havin' no part in this.' She shoved the ashtray away from her. 'I told you, didn't I? You're on your own.' With that, she turned and stalked to the balcony.

Colour washed through Jodie's face. 'Sorry about that,' she said, aiming for upbeat but sounding sad and small.

'Don't worry,' said Zara. 'It's not unusual for parents to feel anger and denial. It's a coping mechanism.'

Jodie grimaced. 'Mum's not trying to cope. She thinks I'm a liar.'

Zara blinked. It was the second time that day that Jodie's story had been questioned. Zara moved onto the seat of the sofa and turned to face the girl. 'Listen, Jodie, I'm here to take care of you. If your mother won't do it, I will. If those boys raped you, they *will* face their day in court.'

Jodie pulled away. '*If* they raped me?' She gripped the cuff of her sleeve. 'I thought you believed me.'

Zara exhaled slowly. 'I do believe you and I want to make sure that we can prove you're telling the truth.' She paused. 'Jodie, we are making very serious allegations against four people so we need to be absolutely sure that we are clear on the details of what happened. We have to be certain that your recollection of events is unmarred by alcohol or drugs or hazy memory.'

Jodie caught the undertone in her voice. 'Something's changed,' she said. 'What happened?'

Zara moved aside a cushion that sat in the gap between them. 'When I first took this role, I wasn't sure that it was right for me. I don't tiptoe around sensitive subjects, offering tea and sympathy, but I soon realised that I'm perfect for it. I understand what the law needs to prosecute a case and I can help tease it from my charges. I can give them the best chance at justice – but I need to know everything, not just an edited version.' She paused. 'I believe you. I will always believe you but I also need to assess what others see and think.'

Jodie threaded her fingers in her lap. 'What happened? Did you speak to Nina?'

Zara pulled back in surprise. Did Jodie's best friend doubt her too? 'I'm going to be honest with you,' she said. 'One of our investigators met Farid last week. I don't know exactly what he said, but our investigator asked me to double-check all the details. She said there were some inconsistencies and she wants to make sure we have everything right.'

Jodie shifted in her seat. 'Your investigator – was she that tall girl in reception with the dark hair?'

'Yes.'

Jodie nodded knowingly. 'She's beautiful.'

Zara pictured Erin's porcelain skin, her jet black hair and long, dark lashes. 'Yes, she is.'

'She dresses like she knows it.'

'Yes, she does.'

Jodie considered this. 'Was life always easy? Being pretty?' she asked.

'I wasn't always pretty.'

She scoffed. 'Your investigator doesn't believe me because when she's around, men don't look at other women. She goes through life knowing that she's better than others around her so she lowers them in her mind – maybe without even knowing that she's doing it. Me? I'm the lowest you can get. I'm a piece of fluff on her jacket, I'm a stick of gum on the floor. I'm someone she wouldn't even notice if I wasn't so ugly.' Jodie's voice grew hard. 'Things happened the way I remember them and, *no*, they're not "marred" by alcohol or drugs or hazy memory.' She met Zara's eyes. 'I am *not* a liar.'

Zara felt a wash of relief. She reached out and touched the girl's hand. 'I know. I'm sorry,' she said. 'I believe you.'

*

DC Dexter smoothed down his jacket and desperately wished the next resident wasn't Asian. With his reddish brown hair and generous sweep of freckles, he was so conspicuously white, so conspicuously different that every potential witness had rejected him without thought. Door after door had been shut in his face – quietly and respect-fully but always without pause. One family after another refused to talk to him, refused to even acknowledge what had happened in their midst.

He approached the next house and knocked lightly on its door, recently painted a burgundy brown. He waited as the person inside undid a series of locks and bolts. Finally, a woman in her mid-forties peeked out through the gap. Dexter noted with dismay that she was indeed Asian.

'Yes?' she asked haltingly.

Dexter recalled Zara's instructions. '*Assalamu alaikum,*' he greeted her.

The woman opened the door a few inches wider. '*Walaikum assalam.*' She hesitated, then asked, 'Can I help you?'

'Afternoon, madam. I'm Detective Constable John Dexter from the London Metropolitan Police. I was hoping to ask you some questions about a party that took place in the area on Thursday the twenty-seventh of June.'

The woman frowned. 'What about it?'

Dexter was pleased to hear her clear London accent. 'I'm investigating an incident that happened at the party and would like to know if you saw anything.' He embellished his glottal stops, hoping to show that he was a local too. 'May I come in?'

She guarded the entrance. 'I'd rather you didn't.' She nodded at his badge. 'Sorry, but those things can be bought on the internet for a fiver. My son got one for his end-of-year school play.'

Dexter broke into a smile. 'That's alright, madam.

Here's absolutely fine.' He was just happy to have someone engage. Notebook in hand, he asked: 'Does your son go to Bow Road Secondary School down the road?'

A bolt of fear flashed across her face. 'Akif? Has something happened to him?'

Dexter held out a hand. 'No, no, madam, he's fine. This is about something else. Has Akif ever mentioned a girl in his school – a Jodie Wolfe?'

'I don't think so. Why?'

'She, uh, has a few facial differences?' Dexter prodded.

'Ah, yes.' She nodded in recognition. 'That poor girl. She passes this way sometimes.'

'Do you remember the party? It was Thursday the twenty-seventh of June?'

The woman rolled her eyes. 'Yes, Akif was in a black mood because I didn't let him go.'

'Did you see any of the kids who went to the party?'

'Ha! See them? I saw them, heard them and cursed them! They were shouting and singing and being fools all night. I can't think what the parents of these children must be like.'

Dexter nodded sympathetically. 'Did you see Jodie?'

'The girl with the face? No, I don't think so. I can't think what she'd be doing at a party anyway.'

Dexter persevered. 'Jodie was dressed in blue jeans and a lacy red top. Did you see anyone fitting that description?'

'A lacy top!' The woman threw back her head and laughed. 'No, I certainly did not see that girl in a lacy red top anywhere. I'm sure I would have noticed it.'

Dexter made a note. 'Did you see anything that was unusual or out of place?'

'No. Why?' The woman grew serious. 'What happened?'

'We're investigating an incident that happened that night.'

'What kind of incident?' she asked.

'I'm not at liberty to say.'

She frowned, annoyed. 'Well, I didn't see anything. There were a few kids throwing things around later at night and the noise went on 'til all hours but that's it.'

Dexter probed her further but discovered nothing more. Finally, he handed her his card and thanked her for her time. Wearily, he moved next door. There, he found no answer. In this community the police brought only bad news. No good would come of helping them, so most didn't deign to try.

It was three houses later that he saw the woman from the burgundy door again.

She approached him tentatively. 'Officer, did the girl with the face have her hair tied up?'

Dexter brightened. 'She did, yes.'

The woman's jaw fell open. 'Would you believe that from the back, that girl looks like a model? I *did* see her that night. I just didn't realise it was her, though now that I think about it, she did have that strange limping walk.'

'Where was she? What was she doing?'

The woman gestured at the big warehouse by the canal. 'They were walking towards there.'

'"They?"'

She smiled. 'Your girl was with a boy. They were holding hands and he was leading her towards the canal. I was putting out the rubbish and I saw them. Unbelievable what kids get up to these days. I tell you, I wouldn't expect it of her. Can't think who'd want to ...' She paused. 'Well, *you know*,' she said, sotto voce.

Dexter ignored this. Instead, he asked, 'They were holding hands?'

'Yes.' The woman arched her brows in judgment.

'Are you sure?'

'Yes, completely.'

Dexter made a note, his features knotted in a frown. 'What happened after that?'

The woman shrugged. 'Nothing. I just saw them go off and disappear. That was it.'

'Okay, thank you.' Dexter took the woman's details and warned that he'd be in touch. He turned the corner and called the office.

*

Zara held up a forefinger. 'I just need to finish this section.'

Erin pulled out a chair and took a seat opposite. She stretched out her long legs and propped one ankle on top of the other. The silver buckle of her sturdy boot glinted in the sunlight and though it made her squint, she watched it while she waited.

Zara turned the page. As she skimmed the lines of text, a memory rose in her mind: she and Safran in chambers, him laughing at her because she always preferred to stop reading on a round page number. He thought it superstition, but it was another way to bring order to her mind. Like lines instead of curves, forty was neat and thirty-nine was not. She smiled faintly at the memory and finished reading the page.

Erin shifted in her seat. 'Well?'

Zara gestured outward. 'I believe Jodie,' she said.

Erin arched a brow. 'I think this is the first time it's happened: you and I on opposite sides.'

Zara laughed drily. 'Oh, I'm sure that's not true.' She and Erin disagreed often, usually on a point of strategy or a bending of the rules: Erin, the breaker and Zara, the stickler. What she didn't realise was that they had never fundamentally disagreed on the truth.

'I pre-empted this,' said Erin. She ripped a sheet of paper from her pocketbook and wrote out a name. 'I need to find a way to convince myself, and hence our future jury, that the four boys are lying.' She slid it across the desk. 'I think she can help.'

Zara read the elegant scrawl. 'Who's Barbara Grant?'

'She's a teacher at Bow Road Secondary. I've had a look at the boys' school records and there are scores of complaints against them – mostly from this teacher.'

Zara frowned. 'What kind of complaints? We can't put her in the witness box if it's just poor punctuality and a little bit of backchat.'

Erin shook her head. 'Vandalism. Bullying. Theft.' She leaned her elbows on the desk. 'Maybe you're right about Jodie, maybe you're not. Either way, I think there's more to the boys than meets the eye. Maybe this teacher can show us what it is.'

Zara thought for a moment. 'Okay, but vet her properly, will you? I don't want to find out later that she's a raging racist with a vendetta or something.'

'Of course.' Erin made a note in her pocketbook.

Zara watched the pen glide in high peaks and deep lows, Erin's milky white hand graceful and slow. Above her wrists, she wore buckled leather cuffs and it occurred to Zara that she had never seen her without them. For the first time, she wondered if there were scars underneath, but knew better than to ask. Erin had known pain she was sure – the sort not easily shared – but Zara would not push for intimacy. She had seen first-hand what happened when you told someone too much.

Even he couldn't stand you by the end.

She swallowed the sting of Luka's words and watched as Erin stood. 'Hey,' she said. 'Is this really the first time we've disagreed like this?'

Erin paused by the door. 'Yes,' she said. 'One of us is wrong.' She raised a hand and parted.

Zara pressed at a knot in her shoulders. She picked up the document and turned to page forty-one.

*

Jodie paced the length of her room, head pounding from the relentless stench of nicotine. She felt boxed inside the walls, by the stained brown carpet and the yellow floral print, now faded to a pale and sickly lemon.

Compulsively, she thumbed through the apps on her phone. She scrolled through Snapchat, taking in all the sexy self-portraits; her female classmates in short shorts, backcombed hair and dark red lipstick. All of them doing a pouty pose they saw on a TV screen, exaggerated to the point of caricature. She clicked on her own profile and looked at her only picture – even her silhouette was freakish with its jutting forehead and sagging chin. She touched her face and pinched the folds of excess skin. People often asked if it hurt. It didn't. Not physically.

She reached forward to scroll just as a banner slid across her screen. Her blood surged when she read the words, 'Amir sent you a chat'. Fear bubbled in her stomach, her hand frozen in mid-air. With a wince, she clicked and a chat window appeared on screen.

'Hi Jodie, how are you?'

She froze. She knew she shouldn't talk to him. She knew she should call Mia or Zara and report the contact immediately but part of her needed this conversation, yearned for explanation. Barely daring to breathe, she typed 'hi' and pressed enter.

'Haven't seen you since the party,' he replied, then continued after a beat, 'Jodie, the police took me and MY DAD to the station. What have you said? You KNOW I didn't do ANYTHING.'

Jodie's hands hovered by the screen. Her heart raced in her chest and sweat pooled in the hollows of her body: under her arms and the crease of her knees. With a snap of her wrist, she quit the app entirely. A whorl of emotion rose around her: fear, anger, shame, and beneath it all, a cold and curling dread of what she had set in motion.

She resisted the urge to open the camera app. It was her favourite form of self-flagellation: spending hours examining her ugly face, almost bringing herself to tears over the injustice of it all. If she were beautiful, would Amir have respected her, protected her instead of just discarding her? Did her subhuman face make him think her subhuman? Something to be procured like a slab of meat, then stripped of its value, and thrown out like garbage?

Her experience that night felt like scarring inside, an indelible streak that ran from her throat down her chest to a knot of tissue between her legs, dry but sticky like sealing wax. She felt it sting inside her, hot and yellow like a wound, salted by words of disbelief: first her mother's, then Nina's, and now Zara's too? Their mistrust was crippling. She, like everyone, had finite ties; moorings that held you in place as you struggled your way through life. All she had was her mother and Nina, and now with those moorings severed, she felt worthless and adrift.

Was it her fault for believing that for just one night, for a few short moments, she could experience what it was like to be normal? To be selfish and desired and wanton? She – usually so wary of being targeted, her senses fine-tuned to threat – *chose* to let her defences down, *chose* to follow Amir that night. Was it all her fault?

The questions circled in her mind, conjuring visions of the night it happened. Jodie raised her fingers to her hair to prove to herself it was clean. *I'm right here, everything's okay and my hair is washed and clean.* There was no vomit clumping the strands, only shampoo that smelled of lilies. Ninety-nine pence it cost in Qessar's cornershop, which meant if she had a twenty-pound note she could buy her mother's cigarettes and a bottle of shampoo and have enough left over for a chocolate bar. She pictured the selection in Qessar's shop and combed through everything in it, from the Freddos and Fudges at the front to Fry's Peppermint Creams at the back, which always sat next to the Flakes and Galaxys. She focused hard on the colours and prices, adding and subtracting to maximise her money, only half aware that her brain was talking her gut into not collapsing. Because her gut was saying help me, help me.

*

Zara stripped off her light navy blazer and slung it over the back of her chair. Behind her, Mia coaxed open a window and wedged it up with a box of cheap printer paper. There was not a whisper of wind and the office was hot and airless in the sapping afternoon sun.

Zara glanced at her watch, a slimline Piaget that fit smartly around her wrist. Its rose gold bezel was too gaudy for her liking but it had been useful in her days in chambers; an important part of the *mise en scène*. It felt garish in this room with its Formica tables, five shades of grey and harsh fluorescent lights that were always on whatever the time of day. She suspected that the police officers resented these meetings – saw it as undue meddling – but she had to ensure that Jodie was a priority. She knew all too well how caseload stunted progress.

A cursory knock drew her gaze to the door. DC Dexter bundled in with an apology and slumped heavily into his seat. 'I found something while canvassing in Bow this morning.' He pushed a thin manila file across the table.

Mia opened it and read the first few lines, her lips parting in disbelief. 'Two witnesses?' she said, scanning down for detail. One witness had seen Jodie being led to the warehouse, contrary to Amir's insistence that she had 'just turned up'. Moreover, an elderly lady across from the warehouse had seen Jodie leaving.

Mia read out a part of the statement: 'Thankfully, I know her from the area or I would have had a fright to look at her. She seemed upset, poor love. It can't have been easy going to a party looking the way she does … Yes, I remember what she was wearing. A red top. She kept adjusting it. These young girls wear next to nothing and then spend all day pulling down their skirts and pulling up their tops.'

Zara listened with blooming hope. Secondary witnesses in rape cases were exceedingly rare. This was a lifeline for Jodie.

Dexter tapped the table to catch their attention. 'There *is* one anomaly I'd like to clear up.' He pointed at the file. 'Jodie told us she was looking for her friend and that Amir told her he'd take her to her. The witness here said she saw Jodie and Amir holding hands and being quite cosy, so which is it?'

Zara stiffened in her seat. She had always known that this lie would hurt them.

Mia flipped forward a few pages and then one back to find the portion in question. 'Huh.' She frowned. 'If Jodie followed him to find her friend, why were they holding hands?' She looked up at Zara. 'Do you know anything about this?'

Zara swallowed the truth. 'Jodie's been clear that Amir led her to the warehouse under false pretences.'

Mia held up the file. 'So why were they holding hands?'

'I don't know. I'll ask her.'

Mia shook her head. 'We're going to need to talk to her ourselves.'

Zara reached for her diary. 'Okay. I can bring her in on Monday.' She marked down the date and felt a sense of unease stirring in her stomach. If Jodie came clean now, the lie would undermine her broader credibility.

Dexter leaned forward and caught Zara's eye. 'By the way, thanks for the tip about greeting people with *assalamu alaikum*. I'll be using that from now on.'

Zara nodded, surprised once again by the collegiate nature of this work. In chambers, she was so often lonely, shouldering her victories and failures alone. At Artemis House, she was part of a collective that worked for a greater good. Gratitude, however small and fleeting, took her by surprise more often than it should.

'We have more,' said Mia. She positioned her bulky black laptop next to Zara. 'So we followed your advice about Jabdam. It turns out our suspects *are* on the app.' She tapped the mousepad to wake the screen. 'There was nothing about Jodie in the app, but there *was* a mention of Amir and a girl called Sophie. There were some nasty comments posted about her in 2017 and it seems she left school later that year. Maybe something happened. We're looking into it.'

Zara read a few comments and felt a spark of disgust at the cruelty of children. Who was this Sophie who had drawn such ire?

Mia clicked onto another screen. 'Also, you remember how the suspects conveniently forgot what they were wearing on the night in question?' She clicked open a photo and pointed to the screen. 'We're going to have to pay them another visit.'

Zara examined the image of the four boys at the party. A lanky Mohammed was dressed in a stripy blue shirt and a pair of jeans. Next to him stood a much shorter Hassan dressed in a yellow T-shirt and dark jeans. Amir Rabbani was in a casual white shirt, sleeves rolled up to the elbows, also teamed with a pair of jeans. Finally, Farid Khan stood looking awkward in a brown jumper and khaki coloured trousers. His beard was two weeks thinner and his absent-minded gaze was directed just off camera.

Zara glanced up. 'This was on Jabdam too?'

Mia smiled. 'Indeed. The privacy settings were a gift to us. We could see everything anyone in East London has ever posted – deleted or not.'

Zara clicked onto the next image, one of Amir leaning close to a girl, whispering in her ear, his hand on the small of her back. 'This could work for us,' she said.

'Or against us,' countered Dexter. He reached over and zoomed into the girl's face. It was in profile but you could tell that she was smiling, basking in his gaze. 'It's clear that Amir Rabbani is a handsome lad. If he has little trouble with the ladies, why would he risk assaulting someone like Jodie?'

Zara frowned. 'You sound awfully earnest about that.'

Dexter leaned back in his chair. 'Meaning?'

'Meaning that you know it's not as black and white as sexual desire or availability.' Zara flicked a hand in the air. 'Men rape women not because they are sexy, but because they want to exert power over them.'

Dexter tugged at his tie, too tight around a neck already tinged pink in the heat. 'But it's naive to think that desire plays no part at all.'

Zara scoffed. 'So what are you trying to say? Ugly girls don't get raped?' She pushed the laptop towards him. 'There are plenty of handsome men who rape women; plenty of successful and wealthy men who rape women;

plenty of politicians and celebrities who rape women – it's not about them being unable to find anyone else to screw.'

The colour deepened in Dexter's face and he looked to his partner for help, but Mia was busy reading the file. 'Look, I'm sorry.' Dexter swiped at his brow. 'I'm a man – a normal one – so I don't understand why someone would want to sleep with a woman unless he was attracted to her.'

'And that's what scares me,' said Zara. 'There will be men on that jury – "normal men" as you say – and maybe Jodie doesn't have a hope in hell.' Her voice edged louder and she caught herself with a grimace, fully aware that force in this case was useless. She was annoyed with Dexter – baffled how a police officer could take such a narrow view – but also aware he was just telling the truth. Jodie's case was complex with mounds of delicate nuance. Dexter didn't understand it and neither might a jury, but shouting at them was not the way to fix it. Instead, they needed an expert – and Zara knew just the person.

She held a hand up in surrender. 'Look, I didn't come here to attack you. I'm just worried about the case.'

'I get it,' said Dexter. 'I'm sorry.'

Zara accepted the truce, then tore a page from her diary and scribbled down two names. The first was Dr Tilda Bussman, an expert on sexual behaviour that she had used in previous trials. She was good with juries, said Zara, and could clearly explain the complexities of a case. The second name was Barbara Grant, the teacher from

Bow Road Secondary who could testify to the boys' bad character. Dexter accepted the note with thanks, his tone no longer frosty.

The three of them sat in the room, windows beating with mid-summer sun, and thought of the troubles ahead. They had a collective four decades of experience in the law and could predict when a case would explode. This one here was going to be one of them.

*

Zara stepped from the lift with two bags of groceries and searched her bag for her keys. As her fingers brushed against the cool metal, she stopped mid-stride in the hallway. Luka stood by her door, leaning against the cream corridor wall. His eyes were weary and the dark circles beneath them told her he hadn't been sleeping. She felt a sudden rush of affection. She walked to him and, standing on tiptoe, leaned in and kissed his lips, possibly the first loving kiss of their relationship.

He blinked in surprise.

She nodded at the door. 'Let's go inside.'

He took the bags from her, his climber's arms flexing beneath the weight. Wordlessly, they unpacked her groceries, he more natural in her kitchen than she. When they finished, he turned to her solemnly.

'I'm leaving for Nepal in two weeks and I want to say something to you before I go.' He tensed for a moment, expecting a rebuff. When there was none, he continued, 'When I started training, I was completely focused. I was in the best shape of my life. I was fit and ready and couldn't wait to get out there. And then I met you. I know you joke and call me "sorbet" – your palate cleanser or whatever – but this isn't casual for me anymore.'

Luka grasped one of her hands. 'I don't want to be five thousand miles away wondering what we'll be when I get back. I don't want to wonder if you're with another man. I don't want to worry. I want to know that I'm with you and that you're with me and I want to know that you'll wait.'

Zara's eyes felt hot with emotion. She felt a tug of tenderness and was thrown by his honesty, overwhelmed by this man and his rugged but gentle manner, his soft Colorado drawl and unimpeachable sense of right and wrong. Dormant emotions hummed to life, beseeching her to yield. But darker instincts kicked into play when she recalled the last time they met: *yes, and even he couldn't stand you by the end*. The shock of those words and the painful truth that lay beneath came to her with startling clarity. She took a step back, physically repelled by the sting.

'Luka.' She swallowed hard and met his gaze. 'I'm happy the way things are.' Why was it that men could say those words with impunity but women always sounded so cold?

'You're happy the way things are?' Luka searched her face. 'Zara, what I said to you last week was *fucking* awful. I acted like an asshole and I'm sorry. I— I'm just …'

A low groan of frustration rose from his chest. 'I just wanted a reaction. I don't know how to explain this, but ever since we met, I— I feel like I've been looking at you sideways, like if I get too close and dare to look at you directly, you'll flee. And so I've been here, by you but not with you.' He ran a hand through his dirty blond hair. 'I want that to change.'

She was silent for a moment, the words still ringing in her ears. *Even he couldn't stand you by the end.* She looked at him impassively. 'I understand, Luka. I want you to know that I'm invested in this but I think we should let it take its natural course instead of trying to define it or mould it into something that may not be right.'

He blinked. 'Don't do this, Zara. Don't be an automaton.'

'I'm not,' she said, shoulders squared and jaw set rigid. 'I'm telling you what I think.'

'Yes, and *that's* the problem,' said Luka. 'Stop thinking for a second and tell me how you feel.'

Zara laced her fingers on the kitchen counter. 'I can't tell you how I feel because I don't *know* how I feel.' She searched for words to soothe him but none seemed right or honest.

'I see.' A muscle flexed in Luka's jaw, his injured ego sounding a retreat. Well, I'll leave you alone so you can figure it out.'

She grimaced. 'You don't have to go.'

'I want to.' He stepped back from her reach. 'Call me

when you work out what it is you want.' With that, he turned and left.

Zara stared at the door, gleaming white in the swelling chasm between them. She swallowed hard, dousing emotion with cold practicality. She turned back to the counter and folded the grocery bags neatly into the recycling bin. Then she sat at her desk, turned on her lamp and immersed herself in work.

*

Fozia Khan stood on her chubby legs and waddled towards the front door. Farid grabbed her by the back of her collar and gently pulled her back just as the bell rang again. He put a finger to his lips and turned down the volume on the *Only Fools and Horses* rerun. On screen, Rodney and Del Boy continued to argue in silence.

Farid pointed to the sofa and told his sister to sit. Their father was still at the market stall. Evening trade picked up before Eid so he usually stayed on to make a little extra. Their mother was at her weekly English class at the library down the road, leaving Farid in charge of his siblings.

The doorbell rang again. 'Police! Open up! We can hear you in there!'

Farid turned to his three siblings assembled on the living-room floor. 'Get up and sit on the sofa. Don't say anything.'

He walked down the dimly lit corridor and paused in hesitation. With a deep breath to brace him, he gently opened the door. There stood two police officers, one in uniform and one whom Farid recognised as DC Dexter, the craggy redhead who had questioned him six days earlier.

Dexter held out his badge. 'Miss me?' he asked. He handed over a piece of paper. 'We'd like to collect these items please.'

Farid gingerly read the sheet. The police had come to his home last week and taken his phone, computer and the family camera, and now they wanted more? On the list was the brown jumper Farid's father had handed down to him three years ago and a pair of beige trousers from his cousin Bilal. The trainers listed were his only pair. He grimaced when he saw that they also wanted his socks from that night. All his pairs had gaping holes.

Dexter pushed the door wider. 'Do you mind?' He took a step inside. 'Who else is in the house?'

Farid stood aside. 'My sister and my two brothers.'

'Where are they?'

'In the living room.'

'Tell them to stay there please.'

Farid nodded, nerves needling in his stomach.

Dexter did a walkthrough and saw that the flat was tiny. There were two bedrooms: one that obviously belonged to the parents and another stuffed with two double beds, occupied by the four children. The bathroom was so small you could touch opposite walls by stretching out your arms. Mould sprouted along the edge of the tiles and the wallpaper puckered with damp. The kitchen reeked of stale spices and fried onion. The living room was the only one that had a bit of space. He could imagine that most of the 'living' happened here where there was room enough to breathe.

Dexter turned to Farid, ignoring the children on the sofa. 'Let's have it then, son.'

With only the briefest pause, Farid led them to his bedroom. He hovered by his closet door. 'Do you have to take my trainers? They're the only ones I've got.'

Dexter smiled without kindness. 'You should have been careful what you did in them then.'

Farid said nothing in response. He opened the closet door and leaned down to a small crate stacked atop another just like it. He rifled through and pulled out a few pieces of clothing. He retrieved his trainers and handed them over. 'Do you know when I'll get them back?'

Dexter shook his head. He inspected the items carefully: one jumper, one pair of trousers, a pair of trainers and a pair of brown socks with yellow polka dots. He nodded to the officer who bagged the items and left the room.

Dexter turned to Farid with a weary wisdom. In a low voice, he said, 'Listen, son, I don't know what you boys got up to that day but we know you only watched. If you tell the truth, we can arrange a deal for you.' He leaned forward. 'I've met your father. I know a good man when I see one.' He waved a hand at the room. 'I know he deserves better than this. You do too, but things are going to get worse for him if you don't come clean. Much, much worse.'

Farid swallowed. 'I told you – nothing happened that night. Not the way Jodie said it.'

'Well, how did it happen?'

'Exactly how I told you.'

Dexter sighed. 'It's a damn shame to see you do this to your parents out of some misguided loyalty to your friends. You think Hassan, Mohammed or Amir would do the same for you? Had they been spectators, they would have sold you down the river by now.'

Farid took a step back, distancing himself from Dexter. 'That may be true but I can't sell them down the river because they didn't do anything wrong. That's the truth.'

'I see.' Dexter nodded curtly. 'Well, thank you for your cooperation. Expect us to be in touch.'

When they left, Farid sank to his knees by his bed and reached for a box beneath it. His fingertips brushed against cardboard and he tugged at the bulk with effort. 'Please,' he whispered. 'Please. Please. Please.' He rifled through the heavy box and pulled out piles of clothes and squares of threadbare sheets. He pushed apart a bobbled scarf and its matching woolly hat. At the very bottom of the box, he found a plastic bag wrapped around a pair of trainers. He pulled it out with a heave of relief. The trainers were falling apart and now half a size too small, but at least he didn't have to ask his dad for money to buy a new pair.

Farid had barely looked him in the eye since the police took their computer last week. Hashim had worked two months straight to fund it: a great big hulk of a Dell that helped Farid get As in all his mock exams. He had promised himself that one day he'd pay his father back, but now the computer was gone with no promise of its return. Farid held the muddy trainers and felt a sense of defeat. Amir had said it would soon blow over, but really it was only beginning.

*

One Canada Square twinkled in the early evening light: 3,960 tiny bright windows all spoke of promise and gain. Flanked by broad blocks of steel and glass – home to hedge funds and investment banks – the iconic tower was a call to arms, a gleaming chalice, an artful promise that were you born poor, you could now be rich.

As a child, Zara would watch the tower's gentle green beacon sweep across the sky, steady like a metronome. She would curl up on the windowsill against the thick plate glass and imagine the life to come: a corner office with a view; a natty assistant, loyal, efficient and somehow always male; a life of strife, yes, but also wealth and laughter. She'd had so much hope, so much expectation as she watched that light at night. Strangely, now with a better vantage, she never seemed to see it shine.

She dwelled on that fact until her landline rang, the trill high and heavy. She sat for a moment, wanting to ignore it, but knowing it would ring and ring. She strode over and snatched up the receiver, sure of who was calling.

She cradled the heavy brass with her shoulder and said, 'Hello, *Assalamu alaikum*.' The two-part greeting used to make her cringe as a child if it was a non-Muslim person calling. She feared they would think it gibberish.

'*Walaikum assalam*.' Sure enough, it was her mother on the line. 'I've tried calling you,' she said. 'Why did you storm off last Saturday?'

Zara pulled the cord taut. She was tired of being the prickly one, the fractious one, the one that nursed a temper. 'I left because of Rafiq,' she said evenly. 'Why does he think he can talk to me like that?'

Fatima tutted. 'What does it matter? They're only words.'

Zara sat on the sofa and gazed up at the posters on her wall: legal victories won only when they gained the favour of men. 'They're not just words, Mum. He thinks he can tell me what to do, that I should shut up and listen because I'm a woman. I won't let him treat me like that.'

Fatima sighed. 'How can you be this age and still not have learnt that our power as women lies in words – in using them wisely but also in ignoring them? When you become angry over every little thing, you give over your power. Don't you see that?'

Zara released the cord, letting it twirl and kink. 'Yes, but I don't agree.'

'You don't agree.' Fatima's tone was clipped. 'That is your response to everything.'

Zara shook her head. 'Don't make this about me. Why

don't you address the way *he* acts?' She knew what her mother was thinking: that she was childish, churlish, spoilt by choices already threefold that of the elder generation, but Zara refused to be grateful for these small scraps of progress.

An edge crept into Fatima's voice. 'You are so smart, Zara, but you don't see the simplest things.' She paused. 'You think that women of my generation have never questioned a man's right to lecture us on our lives. You think that we married a suitable boy and let him control us, and never considered the cost of tradition. You think that, to us, saving face is the most noble act of all.' She gave a short laugh. 'We sacrificed our best years not to please our husbands, but to raise our children; for *you*, so you could be educated and build a better life and have the means to change it if you wished.'

'Then why were you so angry when I *did*?' Zara's fingers curled into fists. If her mother had truly considered the cost of tradition – of marrying a suitable boy – then why ask it of her very own daughter? Why expect the same sacrifice?

Fatima faltered. 'You were a barrister,' she said, the last word soft and reverent. 'And you gave it all up with no explanation. I deserved to be angry.'

Zara closed her eyes, certain her mother had wilfully misunderstood. They both knew it wasn't leaving her career but her *marriage* that angered her mother the most.

Fatima cleared her throat. 'Listen, I didn't call to argue with you. You made your decision and that is that. The past is in the past.'

A distant memory rose in Zara's mind. She, perhaps twelve years old, seated on the living-room floor with her homework scattered across their ersatz Persian rug while Fatima on the sofa read a Bengali newspaper. She made a small, amused sound and Zara glanced up inquisitively. 'Listen to this,' said her mother. 'The reporter is talking about last year's election and writes, "The past is never dead. It's not even past."' She beamed. 'Isn't that wonderful?'

Zara smiled too, surprised to see her mother – her unsparing, abstemious mother – take such delight in language. For the first time, she experienced the strange sensation that her mother was not just a parent; that perhaps she too had interests and ambitions beyond the realm of their home. Her mother was right of course: the past is never past, yet here she was quoting the very opposite.

Zara traced a circle on the soft fabric of her sofa. 'And words are only words, right?'

'Precisely.' Fatima sounded relieved as if they had crossed a minefield without injury.

Zara's eye caught the clock on the wall. 'I'm sorry, Mum, but I have to go.' For once, it was true. 'I'm meeting a friend for dinner.' She hung up with a promise to visit and a cursory goodbye.

She was in no mood to be social, but fetched her bag nonetheless, pulled on her boots and headed out the door to dinner. At the restaurant, she was restless on arrival. She shrugged off her jacket and accepted a table, glancing around as she did so. The dark wooden floors, Chesterfield chairs and green bankers' lamps gave the distinct impression of a gentlemen's club. As she waited, she swapped her cutlery so that her fork sat to the right and her knife to the left – a point of poor etiquette she could not overcome. As a child, she'd been taught that Muslims ate with their right hand because the left was impure, used for unsavoury tasks like cleaning oneself in the bathroom.

There were dozens of these rules that came to her at different times. *Don't cut paper – it will bring you debt later in life. Don't step over your sister's legs – she'll stop growing and stay that size. Thunderstorms invite spirits, so shut the window and say a prayer. Don't swap seats while eating or you'll end up marrying twice.* Thinking of them now, in the impatient tone of her mother's voice, Zara felt a viscous unease. What would happen if she heard about Jodie's case? Would she understand, or would this be yet another source of contention? The prospect bristled on Zara's skin, making her tense and edgy. She took a long drink of icy water. The polished glass was cool, and her touch left little patches of shrinking condensation. She watched them disappear and tried to still her jangling mind. She glanced at the door and the tables nearby, then slid a hand in her bag and found the sturdy shape of a bottle. Wrapping her fingers around it, she used her thumb to open the lid. Carefully, she tipped two pills into her hand. Using her ring finger and little finger to hold the pills in place in her palm, she placed the lid back on and pressed it shut with a click. She drew out her hand and with her hair shielding her profile, slipped the pills in her mouth. She swallowed them without water and briefly closed her eyes, waiting for them to work.

Approaching footsteps paused by her side. 'Zar, you look like shit.' Safran stood above her with an amused smile.

'Well, fuck you too,' she replied, accepting his kiss with a tilt of her cheek.

He took a seat and glanced at his watch. 'Am I late?'

'No, but I wish you'd stop booking places like this.' Zara gestured out at the room.

'What places?'

She shrugged. 'These places where people wear shoes that cost more than my monthly income.'

Safran frowned. He found it hard to digest that Zara Kaleel was intimidated by a place like Sorbero. She was made for a place like this, or at least she used to be. He took in her white cotton dress and ankle-length boots – imitation leather he noted with disdain – and realised that so much had changed. Perhaps this girl, this chimera of sorts, was now a different person entirely.

Zara caught his strange expression and raised a brow in askance.

He waved away the question. 'So how are you?' he asked, catching her stifled yawn.

'I'm fine. Just tired. I'm working on a difficult case which is driving me down.'

Safran's eyes glinted curiously. 'Tell me.'

She shook her head. 'It's a sensitive one. Under wraps for now.'

'Don't be a tease, Zar. If you didn't want to tell me, you wouldn't have brought it up.'

She felt a sweet heaviness in her arms, the first sign that the pills were working. She smiled and said, 'I can't.'

'Oh, come on. I tell you everything.'

She relaxed in her chair, feeling warm and pleasantly calm. 'Not this one, Saf.' She blinked languidly, letting her thoughts come to rest. 'I can't.' As the evening wore on, however, and the Diazepam dissolved her resolve, she began to reveal the details of the case. With Safran's gentle persistence, she told him about her pitiful protagonist and the four villains of the tale. She spoke of Amir, the ringleader, so handsome and respectable. She told him about Mia and Dexter and spoke at length of her concerns.

When she finished, Safran leaned forward with his elbows on the table. 'Zar, this could be big. This could be really, really big.'

'I know.'

'Are you sure you can handle it?' He pre-empted her sarcasm: 'Yes, I know you're Zara the Brave but this could get ugly. Four Muslim boys raping a deformed white chav?'

Zara flinched. 'Don't call her that.'

He rolled his eyes. 'Sorry. *Jodie*,' he said portentously.

'Why are you being snarky about her?'

Safran placed his fork on the plate. 'I'm worried about what this is going to do.'

'I'll be fine,' Zara said with a shrug.

'I don't mean just to *you*. I mean to *us*.'

'Us?' she asked stupidly. 'You and me?'

'Christ, Zar, I mean to *Muslims*.'

'Oh.' Zara caught on. 'Right.' She blinked through her chemical fug. 'What am I supposed to do? Step away just because they're Muslim? Jodie deserves her day in court.'

Safran winced. 'But she can do it without you, no? You're going to be right in the crossfire.'

Zara shrugged. 'Look, things have changed. I'm not the fancy barrister spieling soliloquies outside the Old Bailey. I'll be behind the scenes.'

He shook his head. 'You're a Muslim holding the hand of a girl accusing four Muslim boys of rape. You really think you'll stay in the background?'

She frowned, feeling suddenly sober. 'I'm not sure that "staying in the background" should be more important to me than securing justice for Jodie. Am I supposed to put my religion ahead of the fact that I'm a woman? Do I owe more loyalty to *Islam* than a girl who has been victimised?'

Safran sighed. 'Of course not. I'm just concerned that this will become a spectacle.'

Zara leaned forward in her chair, her right fist on the dark wooden table. 'Saf, I believe her. I *believe* that these boys did what she said they did and if I don't help her, then I don't deserve my job and I certainly don't deserve any fucking self-respect. I have to do this.'

Safran said nothing for a moment. 'Okay,' he relented. 'If you need help, I'm here.'

She nodded plaintively. 'Thank you.'

'How are you in general?' he asked. 'You look …'

'Like shit. Yeah, you said.'

He offered no platitude to temper the comment.

'I'm fine. I'm just tired all the fucking time.' She rubbed a hand over her forehead and felt a film of grease on her fingers. She laughed. 'What happened to me, eh?'

Safran smiled, partly in consolation and partly in agreement.

'I had it all worked out and now look at me.'

'You're not doing so badly. Whatever happens, remember that it was your choice. You could have all of this—' he gestured at the expensive decor, 'but you don't want it. You're doing something worthy now.'

They looked at each other for a beat and then started laughing.

'Being a sincere fucker doesn't suit me, huh?' said Safran.

'Not nearly as much as a cynical bastard.' Zara smiled, warm in the glow of effortless friendship. She knew that even if she didn't see Safran for months, it would still be the same when they finally made time. Mainly, it was because there was no expectation, no drama and certainly no sexual history. Safran's taste in women was comically consistent. His exes were all tall and willowy with honey-blonde hair, inimitable tans and an athletic grace that comes from years of swimming in oceans. They were women that demanded a certain lifestyle and acquired it with ease. He and Zara were more like comrades. They shared some bluster and a bit of bravado but more importantly they had a mutual respect that ran deep and strong. She leaned back now and let him refill her drink, genuinely relaxed for the first time in weeks.

*

Jodie watched the cigarette ash drift to the armchair, singeing yet another hole in the orange-brown upholstery. A cough racked through her mother's body.

'You think I can go in *my* state?' spat Christine.

Jodie blinked. 'Mum, please. It's past nine and the delivery man comes first thing tomorrow.' Even as she said the words, she knew they'd be ignored.

'I'm not going to starve to death just because you're too busy fucking about on your phone. I swear to God, I'll trash that thing – I don't care if you got it for free or not.' She doubled over and coughed violently, her lungs rasping with the effort. She looked at Jodie with contempt. 'I'll do it right now.'

With a cold hand, Jodie reached for the twenty-pound note lying on the cracked glass table. She hadn't left the house in days. The thought of it triggered pools of clammy sweat in the crevices of her torso. She folded the note carefully and placed it her pocket. A vision of Nina rose in her mind. *That's called the condom pocket*, Nina had said, hooking an elegant finger into Jodie's jeans. *You'll never need one of course*. A high-pitched laugh – malice disguised as jest. Jodie had shrugged it off, just as she always did.

Her mother's cough cut through her thoughts, the harsh vowels almost physical in force. Sensing an onslaught, Jodie turned quickly and left the flat. She closed the door and tugged it hard to make sure the lock would catch. A few weeks ago she had woken to a freezing house, the front door wide open because her mother hadn't closed it. She ambled down the stairwell, her hands dug deep in her pockets to stave off the evening breeze. Her thoughts wandered to the documentary she had seen on YouTube the night before. It was about women in Pakistan who had been burned with acid by angry men: jealous husbands and would-be lovers. Some were like Jodie – introverted, withdrawn, desperate – but there were others: confident, outgoing women who walked the world as if beautiful and free. Would she ever be like that? Would she ever be free of this feeling?

Hunkering into her jacket, she walked down the lamp-lit street. Balfor Towers loomed on one side, a forty-five-storey concrete giant slicing into the twilight sky. Its concourse was littered with broken furniture. A pram rested on its side, a broken wheel sitting askew. Next to it, a broken TV, its blue and red wires like earthworms breaking free.

And, of course, a soiled mattress. It seemed that as soon as one was cleared away, another would appear in its place, as if an artist had painted a dystopian scene and insisted that a mattress be part of the tableau.

As she passed Higham Street, she listened for whispers from number seventy-two. *Fish face,* they would call in a hushed singsong tone. *Hey, fish face.* She never dared to look, never dared to challenge them. She hurried to the top of the street and pushed open the newsagent door. She nodded at Qessar, the Turkish clerk who always treated her with kindness. With basket in hand, she walked down a narrow aisle to the dairy section. She selected a pint of milk and checked the sell-by date. She glanced at Qessar and, seeing that he was staring at her, popped the pint in her basket instead of swapping it with another. She walked on and added a few items to her basket, mentally subtracting from the twenty pounds in her pocket to ensure there was enough for her mother's cigarettes. She paused at the confectionary section but realised she didn't have enough for a Milky Way. She headed to the counter instead. Qessar nodded hello and Jodie asked for a twenty-pack of Marlboro Gold.

Qessar glanced right and left, then nodded. 'We're out. I have to go round the back.'

'Okay, thank you.' She watched him walk to the stock-room, casting a backward glance in her direction. She drummed her fingers on the counter, waiting for his return. After a few seconds, she caught something in the reflection behind the counter. She spun round and stared in horror. Her hand, unsteady with shock, reached forward and picked up a copy of *The Sunday Sun*. When she heard Qessar's steps, she stuffed the paper beneath her jacket and spun back to the counter. Qessar slipped the cigarettes into the basket.

'Twenty pounds thirty-nine.'

She dug around in her jacket pocket, her fingers closing around a fifty-pence piece. She handed it over with the twenty-pound note, fighting to keep her hands still. Outside, she shifted the paper beneath her jacket then walked home as quickly as her gait would allow.

Jodie handed over the cigarettes and put away the meagre groceries. With everything in its place, she walked to her room and closed the door. She sat on her bed and tried to still her jangling nerves. After a full minute, she unzipped her jacket and retrieved the paper.

'FOUR MUSLIM TEENS RAPE DISABLED ENGLISH GIRL' the headline shouted in bold black lettering. Jodie's eyes stung with tears, hot and glassy on her skin as they rolled down her cheeks, paused on her malformed chin and then kamikazed to her lap. She thought of Nina's reaction: the pity, the anger, the utter miscomprehension. Now the whole world would know. They would all think she was crazy. With trembling hands, she lay the paper across her lap and read the opening paragraph.

Four East London teens have been accused of brutally raping and humiliating a disabled young classmate in an hour-long ordeal. The accused who cannot be named for legal reasons are all Muslim and from Pakistani or Bangladeshi backgrounds of which there are large quantities throughout the boroughs of East London. The teens reportedly indulged in drugs and alcohol before luring their English victim to an abandoned warehouse nearby, subjecting her to brutal rape and assault. Mere weeks after the gang rape by Asian men of a twenty-year-old girl in Bolton, this latest event underlines the fact that parochial views towards women are not restricted to faraway lands; the hate and misogyny have been brought to our very own doorsteps.

One must question the utter savagery of targeting a victim who has suffered physical disability since birth. Psychologist Linda Bauer says assaults of this nature are not motivated by sexual attraction as much as an all-consuming desire to dominate: 'The fact that the victim is already in a vulnerable position could have actually been more arousing for these boys. They were taking a defenceless creature and using her for their gains. It's easy to see someone "weak" as your plaything.'

Creature. The word rang in Jodie's ears. She turned to page five where the story continued. A picture of five men convicted in a sexual abuse case in northern England sat at the top of the page, its contrast darkened to cast shadows beneath their features. Their smiles seemed mocking – almost manic. The caption read: 'Evil: A ring of Muslim sex abusers in Aylesbury was convicted earlier this year in an eerie precursor to the new case in London.'

The article included her classmates' immigrant histories and more explanatory quotes from Dr Linda Bauer before its rousing finale.

Action must be taken against these predatory men who choose young, native British women on whom to feast. Their actions are symbolic of a wider epidemic that signals to Asian men: 'We can have these women; they are here for the taking.' We must stop them taking. We must call for justice.

Jodie closed her eyes. There was only one person who would have done this. She picked up her phone and dialled Nina. She listened to the phone ring five, six, seven times before it clicked onto voicemail. Nina, dripping with breathy sensuality, explained that she was unavailable to take the call. Jodie hung up in time with the beep. She swallowed, then scrolled through her phone and tried Zara. It rang for a full thirty seconds before it too clicked through to voicemail. There was no personalised welcome message, only the network's automated instruction to speak after the tone. Jodie hung up and immediately tried again. The phone rang on, its high, shrill notes stirring panic as she listened. She felt it shift like iron filings converging and diverging in the pit of her stomach. How could this have happened? How could Nina have done it? And where was Zara?

Jodie hung up and scrolled desperately through her contacts. Her gaze hitched on a name: Mia. Surely, she would know what to do. Jodie called the number and felt a surge of relief when she answered immediately.

'Jodie, are you okay?'

'Yes, I'm … I'm sorry to call like this. I just …' Her voice trailed off.

'Don't apologise,' said Mia. 'I take it you've seen the papers?'

'Yes.'

Mia exhaled. 'Have you spoken to Zara?'

'No. I can't get a hold of her.'

'I see.' Mia's tone was even. 'I can find her for you.'

'No, that's okay. I just— I didn't know if I should do anything so I called you.'

'Don't do anything for now. Just sit tight. We're going to find out who leaked this.'

'I think I know who did it,' said Jodie haltingly. 'I think it was Nina, my best friend.' Jodie's voice caught on the last two words.

Mia was silent for a moment. 'There may be reporters … '

Jodie grimaced. 'I shouldn't have started this.'

'You have to be strong, Jodie.'

'I know. I'm just … stunned.'

'I understand.' Mia softened her tone. 'Do you need me to come over?'

Jodie glanced at the dark sky outside her window. 'No. I'll be okay.'

Mia's breath was audible on the line. 'Okay. I'll let you know as soon as we know something more. Please call me again if you need anything.'

'I will. Thank you.' Jodie's voice was flat and featureless. She swept the newspaper to the floor, curled onto her bed and closed her eyes. *I want to take it back*, rang her sole desperate thought. *Please, God. Please. I just want to take it back*.

CHAPTER FIVE

The first knock didn't rouse Jodie. It was the second, clinking against the window like ice cubes in a glass, that drew her forth from slumber. She blinked against the backdrop of faraway voices. At first, she thought they had bled from sleep, but they wafted to her now in short, sharp bursts without the blurry edges of nightmares or dreams.

The third knock made her bolt upright. Without thought, she drew aside the curtain above her bed. She jerked backwards in surprise as flashes of light popped outside. Faces loomed behind an outsized camera and shards of speech burst inside.

'We'll compensate you for your time!'

'Protect your identity!'

'Your side of the story!'

Her first thought was of her mother. If they lured her out, there would be no end to the lurid headlines. Jodie stole out of bed with a quiet urgency and crept across the threadbare floor, head low and shoulders hunched as if they could see her through the sickly lemon walls.

She found her mother sprawled on the sofa, her fleshy grey T-shirt dotted with ash. A pile of crushed cans lay scattered by her feet. Jodie picked up the debris and walked into the kitchen. Pressing the pedal on the bin, she placed the waste quietly inside. Voices wafted through the single-glazed windows but left her mother unroused. There, next to the bin, Jodie slid to the cold kitchen floor and resolutely waited for her mother to wake.

*

Zara set down the phone with a frown. Jodie had called twice last night: first at 9.33 and again a minute later. Zara had been deep in a chemical sleep and only called back this morning – three times to no avail.

Now, with a sense of disquiet, she switched on her computer and focused on its soothing hum. It was just whirring to life when Stuart marched into her office and dropped a thick stack of newspapers on top of her ordered files.

She stiffened. 'What's this?'

'You tell me.' Stuart's face flushed with fury.

Zara read over the headline and felt her stomach lurch. 'The story broke last night in *The Sunday Sun*.'

Zara thought of Jodie and her calls last night. 'How did they find out?' she asked.

'You tell me,' Stuart repeated, his well-bred vowels sparking with anger.

Zara bristled. 'Are you angry because they know about the case, or are you angry *at me* because they know about the case?'

He slapped down a piece of paper. 'Read what this says.'

Zara picked up the sheet, panic prickling in her throat. She saw that it was an email from a *Sunday Sun* reporter to the news editor. She read fragments of the text: 'The rape counsellor talked in detail about the case. I've drafted the attached copy. I haven't named the counsellor lest the *Mail* try and poach her, but I'm happy to add it. Let me know what you think.'

'Where were you on Saturday at seven p.m.?' asked Stuart.

Zara hesitated. 'I was at a restaurant in Kensington. Sorbero.'

'Bingo!' Stuart tore the email from her hands and read, 'I was in Sorbero in Kensington on Saturday (thirteenth July). Around seven-ish, I was seated next to this posh Indian-looking pair who were talking about a rape case.' Stuart paused. 'What was the date on Saturday?'

Zara searched for a way to calm him.

'What was the date?' he repeated.

'It was the thirteenth of July.'

'I should fire you. I should fire you *right now*.'

Zara flushed red but her voice was calm. 'Stuart. I'm sorry, I wasn't thinking.'

He threw up a hand. 'Zara, I *pay* you to think. That's what you're paid to do. We're doing funding rounds next week. What if they had published your name?' He shook the piece of paper, then slapped it back on the desk. 'The only reason they haven't is to keep you from their competitors. What happens when they find that you won't talk to them, that they won't get their exclusive? They'll tell the world the leak came from us.'

'But they—'

Stuart wasn't ready to let her talk. 'What the hell was going through your head that you would divulge sensitive information about a case in public?'

Zara pointed at the email. 'We were seated at a table alone and had reasonable expectation of privacy.'

Stuart shook his head. 'Not legally and you know it.' He snatched up the piece of paper. 'I'm taking you off the case.'

Zara flinched. 'You can't do that. Jodie needs consistency.'

'Jodie needs competency!' he shouted. 'And this isn't just about Jodie. This is about all the other victims who will suffer if our funding gets cut.'

'Stuart, I'll fix it. I promise.'

'How?' He leaned forward, palms on her desk, his stance unusually menacing. 'How do you intend to fix this?'

Zara urgently rifled through her options. 'I'll file for an injunction. Legally, the papers can't reveal Jodie's identity. I can argue that if they name me as the source, they would be essentially revealing Jodie's identity since I'm her caseworker. Any reporter, or even a layman, can trace me to her even if it's as crude as following me to her home.'

Stuart blinked. He hadn't expected an answer.

'But,' said Zara. 'This will only work if I stay on her case. If you take me off, there won't be any official connection between me and Jodie and the papers can argue that naming me won't lead to her.'

Stuart shook his head. 'That's not good enough. As soon as Jodie is named on social media – and let's face it, she *will* be named – there'll be no argument to keep your name from the papers.'

Zara grimaced. 'Okay, then forget the injunction. I'll promise them an exclusive instead. I'll promise that when this is all over, I'll talk to them and only them.' Zara pushed at the stack of newspapers, toppling over the first few copies. 'But I'll need to stay on the case. They won't be interested in the *ex*-caseworker.'

Stuart rubbed the ridge of bone above his eyes. 'Do you have any idea how ethically problematic this is?'

Zara spoke rapidly, 'Stuart, I made a mistake and I'm sorry, but this is the best thing for Jodie. She's already fragile. If we change her caseworker, it could push her over the edge. I know her. I can help her.'

Stuart's jaw was rigid. 'You've put me in an impossible situation.'

Zara clasped her hands together. 'Stuart, listen, this case could be a watershed moment for us. Having a Muslim face on the prosecution team will show that this isn't a witch-hunt; it's a genuine fight for justice. I can help steer the case. I'll be there every step of the way. If it means going to Magistrates, I'll be there. If it means battling the tabloids, I'll fight. Even pros make mistakes but they're still pros. I know what I'm doing and I won't make another mistake – I promise.'

Stuart held out the printed email. 'Tell me this, Zara. If Erin hadn't tracked this down, if I didn't know the source of the leak, would you have told me it was you? Would you have been honest with me?' His voice was low and threatening.

Zara considered this. Then she nodded softly. 'Yes, I would have.' She watched as he teetered in indecision then, gently, she added, 'This case is going to create a fault line in our community. If we're going after four Muslim boys, then having me on the team will help prove it's a legitimate fight.'

Stuart crunched up the printout. 'One more mistake and you're gone, Zara. I don't care about injunctions to protect our name, or exclusives to keep our funding. One more mistake and you'll be fired.'

Zara closed her eyes. 'Thank you.' Her voice cracked with relief.

'Don't thank me, Zara. Do your fucking job.' He threw the ball of paper in the bin and stalked out of the room, his anger thick and cowing long after he had gone.

Zara prickled with guilt as she gathered her belongings and fled past the pit, her broken ego in pieces at her feet. She walked down the stairwell from the fourth floor to the basement, unwilling to face those she might know. She found her car and with barely a glance over her shoulder, skidded from the parking spot. A single thought swam back and forth like a maddening pendulum. *How could I have been so stupid?* The answer – two yellow pills in the palm of her hand, on her careless tongue, in the base of her throat – was unavoidable. She would not have divulged details of the case nor missed Jodie's calls last night had she not taken those pills. The truth of this fact and what it could mean made Zara feel weak and giddy.

She sped down the A11 towards the Wentworth Estate and tried hard to focus her mind. Her thoughts felt warm and shapeless, a gelatinous mess she couldn't put in order. As a barrister, she would have sprung into crisis mode, directing those around her with the speed of a general. Now, her instincts felt blunted. She blinked against the bright July sun and made a sharp left, wincing as a cyclist swerved in her wake.

Ten minutes later, her Audi swung onto the concourse of the Wentworth Estate. She noted the group of boys eyeing her car as she slipped up the stairwell to Jodie's balcony. There, she saw a pair of reporters knocking on Jodie's window. The man was short and thickset with shoulder-length black hair. The woman was slim and blonde with thin lips and haughty eyes. They both turned to look at Zara.

'May we help you?' asked the woman, her tone clipped and territorial.

Zara ignored them and rang the bell.

'Do you know the Wolfe family?' The blonde's voice sparked with excitement. 'We're looking for Jodie.'

Zara rang the bell again. When she received no reply, she bent and spoke through the letterbox. 'Jodie, it's me, Zara. Open up.' She waited. When she heard nothing, she bent again. 'Hand me the key through the letterbox and then go and wait in your room. I'll let myself in.'

The reporters jostled for position as she placed her hand through the letterbox. After a few seconds, she felt cool metal pressed into her palm. She closed her hand around the key and drew back her arm. After a minute's wait, she slid the key into the lock and opened the door. The reporters snapped in after her and she shut the door angrily in their faces. She latched the bolt, then walked to the living room to find Jodie's mother on the armchair, spread across the upholstery like a dozing bear.

Jodie stepped from her bedroom. 'I thought they'd go away.' Her voice was soft and younger somehow.

Zara shook her head. 'They're tabloids. They never give up.'

The doorbell rang and Jodie's mother stirred on the sofa. 'Would it kill you to answer the fucking door?' she growled. She staggered to her feet. 'I have to do every fucking thing myself.'

Zara stepped forward gently. 'Ms Wolfe, please don't open the door. The press have caught wind of your daughter's case. They will wait outside, possibly for days, to try and get into your home. I'd advise that you keep Jodie sheltered. If you need anything, I—'

'Is it the *Morning Mail*?' Christine cut in.

'No.' Zara stopped, confused. 'It's *The Sunday Sun*. They broke the story.'

Christine pulled the hem of her T-shirt down over her thin black leggings. They were so worn you could see her flesh underneath. 'Old Berta from Higham Street said the *Morning Mail* paid her daughter three grand for her story on that half-caste footballer.'

Zara baulked. She hadn't heard *half-caste* used casually since early childhood.

Christine shuffled to the door. 'I bet they'll give me more since they're so desperate.'

Zara placed a hand on her shoulder. 'Think about what you're doing. She's your child.'

Christine snorted. 'She's sixteen so she ain't no child. She's in my house and I can invite anyone I want into it.' She shook off Zara's hand and pulled open the door. 'Are you from the *Morning Mail*? I want to talk to the *Morning Mail*!'

Zara pulled Jodie into her room. 'She's right. You're sixteen. I can't stop her from letting in the reporters but *she* can't stop *me* from getting you out of here.'

'Out? Where?' Jodie's voice quivered perceptibly.

'Just away.' Zara pointed to the closet. 'Do you want to be covered?'

'Covered?' Jodie's face flushed red.

'I don't mean because of …' Zara stalled. 'I mean … it's very normal to cover up clients in cases like this. They can't print your picture but they'll have it on file and if this goes public, they'll use it.'

Jodie considered it for a second, then nodded. She pulled on a hoodie and tightened it around her face, then added a scarf and a pair of shades. Her bulbous forehead remained uncovered.

Zara reached forward and pulled the hoodie as far down as it would go. 'Ready?'

Jodie grabbed her backpack. 'No.'

Zara held her arm. 'Come on, let's go.' She led her down the corridor past Jodie's mother in the living-room doorway. An excited clatter began behind her. The two reporters sprang from the room.

'Jodie, we just want to talk,' said the blonde.

Zara yanked open the front door and pulled Jodie onto the balcony. Quickly, she led her down the stairwell and onto the concourse, closely followed by the reporters.

'If you tell us your story, no one else will chase you for it.'

The three boys on the corner stared curiously. Zara flung open her car door and Jodie leapt inside. It shut behind her with a decisive thud. In under five seconds, Zara was in her seat, revving her engine. Then, with little regard for the reporters who had to jump out of the way, she pressed on the gas and sped off.

She glanced at Jodie. 'Seatbelt.'

Jodie's hands shook as she fastened the clip. She stared at the road in a daze, faintly aware that Zara was on the phone speaking words in short, rapid bursts – *prohibitory injunction, suppression order* – in a calm but urgent tone.

They were five miles further when Zara hung up the phone. She glanced at Jodie sideways. 'Are you okay?'

'Yes.' After a minute, she said, 'They know who I am.'

Zara swallowed. 'Don't worry. They won't be able to publish a thing your mother says. I've taken care of that.'

'They know everything. My name. Where I live. What I said. I can't believe Nina did this.'

Guilt calcified in the pit of Zara's stomach but she said nothing to acknowledge it. There could be no confession if she were to keep Jodie's trust. They drove without aim, moving smoothly through the streets of East London. When they skirted the boundary of Zone One, Zara suggested stopping for breakfast. She caught Jodie's flinch and added, 'We don't have to sit inside. I could just grab us something. I'm guessing you haven't eaten.'

Jodie nodded so they stopped at a cafe in Aldgate and Zara headed in alone. As she stepped into the surgical chill of the conditioned air, she felt her phone vibrate in her pocket.

'Do you have a moment to talk?' Mia's voice was arctic.

Zara turned her back to the café. 'Yes.'

'Did Jodie get a hold of you yesterday?'

Zara hesitated. 'I'm with her now.'

'Good. Are you bringing her to the station today?'

Zara glanced at her watch. 'Yes. We can be there in twenty minutes.'

'Okay.' Mia paused. 'Please tell her to put the newspaper story out of her mind. We need her to be clear so we can get her story straight. You know what prosecutors do to unreliable witnesses.'

'I know. I will. We'll be there soon.'

'Good.' Without a parting, Mia hung up.

Zara picked up her order and returned to the car. She handed Jodie a fruit smoothie and a flaking almond pastry. 'I know you've had a difficult morning but I need to talk to you about something.' She switched on the air conditioning. 'The police found a witness who saw you with Amir. This is good news because we can place him there with you in contradiction to what he said. The bad news is that the witness saw you holding hands so your excuse that you went with him to look for Nina isn't going to wash. You need to tell Mia the truth. We're going to see her now.'

Jodie's skin turned clammy. 'I— I shouldn't have done this.'

'Don't worry,' said Zara. 'We'll fix it.'

'No, I mean I—'

'We'll fix it.' Zara pointed to the pastry. 'Now eat.' She waited for Jodie to take a bite, then started the car and headed to the station. They rode in silence through light morning traffic and arrived at the station early.

Mia wasted no time with pleasantries as she led them to the interview room. She said nothing of the press leak but Zara presumed she knew the source.

'It's true, yes,' said Jodie when asked about the inconsistency. 'We did hold hands at one point. I'm sorry I didn't mention it.' She glanced briefly at Zara. 'I have trouble walking as you can probably tell. The road to the warehouse is gravelly and I tripped. Amir grabbed my hand to keep me up.'

Zara watched, chilled by the skill with which she lied. She studied the girl's face, hoping for a sign that she had struggled with the lie – a whip of a glance to the right, a sheen of sweat on her face – but there was nothing.

Soon, with Mia satisfied, Zara and Jodie said goodbye and walked to the car in single file, Jodie trailing a few steps behind, her feet shuffling softly on the uneven mottled concrete.

Zara paused by the passenger door. 'Why did you lie?' she asked.

Jodie flushed red. 'I can't do it.' Her voice was thin and strained. 'I can't say in public that I wanted him to kiss me. I won't. I'd rather call the whole thing off.'

Zara sighed. 'Jodie, listen, you're a sixteen-year-old girl. Amir Rabbani is the school heartthrob. You don't have to be ashamed for having a crush on him.'

Jodie shrank into herself. 'That's not what I'm ashamed about. I'm ashamed that I believed he wanted me. I'm ashamed that I was so stupid.'

Zara shook her head. 'Do you think that's more shaming than what Amir did to you? Do you think people will be more shocked by your naivety than his monstrousness?' She leaned down to Jodie's level and spoke, 'Jodie, the law is important to me. It is vast and mighty but it's delicate too. It needs to be treated with respect. We can't pick and choose when we tell the truth and when we lie because if we do that, we can't expect or demand the truth from others. I believe in the law. I *trust* the law and I beg you to trust it too.'

Tears pooled in Jodie's eyes. She blinked to ease them away then turned her head when they spilled on her cheek. 'I'll be humiliated. I'm not going to do it. I won't.'

Zara straightened and closed her eyes. She pressed her fingertips against her brow bone to curb a mounting headache. 'You realise that the defence will tear open every inconsistency they find?'

Jodie wiped her tears with a sleeve and only nodded in response.

Zara threw up her hands. 'Okay, fine,' she relented. 'Fine.' She opened the door for Jodie, then shut it with a slam.

*

The low rumble of the DLR travelled in the wind, caught the car alarm echoing in the distance and carried it through the high-rise windows open to the breeze. Rocky, Amir's honey-coloured Labrador, snapped around his heels, eager for attention. Amir kneeled down and petted her.

'What's wrong, girl?' he asked softly. 'What's wrong? Go on, go and play.' He gave her a gentle push. 'Go on.'

Hassan kicked the football over. 'How's your old lady?' he asked. 'Still angry?'

Amir straightened and caught the ball. 'Christ, I don't know. One day she's trying to feed me to death and the next she can't stop moaning.' He shifted the ball to his right foot. 'I think she's scared, but she's Tiger Mum Extraordinaire and so she roars instead.' With a graceful kick, he returned it. 'What about *your* mum? Did she really chuck all your stuff away?'

Hassan scowled. 'Yeah. I didn't believe it at first 'cause I thought my dad would screw. You know he's tighter than a Jew.'

'Have you searched their room?'

Hassan rolled his eyes. 'Yes, Sherlock, I've searched their room, but she's really gone and done it.'

Amir whistled. 'No offence, mate, but your mum's loopy.'

'Tell me about it.' Hassan kicked the ball with force and it shot past Amir into a ditch beyond. Rocky yelped and chased it.

Mo watched from a brown brick wall on the sidelines, scuffing his knock-off Nikes against the gravel. He took a swig of ginger beer, winced and handed it to Farid. The older boy took a sip and placed the bottle between them. They never normally ventured as far west as Shadwell Park but people in their neighbourhood had started whispering stories and spreading gleeful rumours. None believed that *pathetic white girl* of course, but few would publicly support the boys. Trouble in East London was contagious; just breathe near it and you'd find yourself infected.

Mo picked up the bottle and watched his friends, now in the middle of the gravel concourse, mock-wrestling over the football. Their shouts were loud and joyful, almost musical with laughter.

Farid cast his eyes away. 'It's like they don't have a clue what's happening.'

Mo turned and studied his friend, noting the bags beneath his eyes and the sallowness of his skin. 'Are you worried?'

Farid nodded softly. 'Yeah, course I'm worried.'

Mo felt a jab of anxiety. If Farid – smart, prudent, pragmatic Farid – was worried, then shouldn't he be too? 'Why?' he asked his friend.

'Look at us, Mo. Even if we could prove that we didn't touch Jodie, we'd still be four darkies in the dock. You think we'd get a fair chance?'

Mo gripped the neck of the bottle, tethered by its cool thick glass. 'It's not going to go that far. And even if it does, they're not going to send us down just 'cause we're brown. That doesn't happen in real life.'

Farid stared at the horizon. 'I read that, in America, there aren't many rich people on death row. There are many levels of justice, Mo. You get one level if you're rich and white, you get the next if you're rich, you get the next if you're poor and white, and you get the shittiest if you're poor and dark – and you best believe it's the same here in Britain.'

Mo bobbed his heels in the gravel, a nervous flutter

of denial. 'Nah, man. That's not true, not here. Besides,' he cocked his head towards their friends, '*they're* not worried.'

'Yeah but they're different.' Farid gestured outward. 'If things went south, they could move somewhere else, somewhere no one knows their names or their history. Amir's old man is loaded and Hassan's uncle has the restaurant in Birmingham. We'd be stuck here as the boys who raped a disabled white girl. I'd lose my place in college and we can forget university.'

Mo fell silent, doubting for the first time that it would all work out. Was Farid right? Could they be sent down on word alone? He felt a queasy roiling in the base of his gut and imagined his family without him. He, while not naturally clever, was their great white hope, the only son who would pull them from poverty, from bloodstained fingers that were never quite clean, and endless hours at the sewing machine. Secretly, he wanted a shop on Savile Row, but had decided years ago that he would follow Farid's footsteps. Where his friend got As, Mo got Bs, but that didn't stop him from trying. Farid was the sort of boy who would make something of his life and if Mo shadowed him – picked the same courses, had the same friends – then maybe he would be something too. There would be no branching of their destinies where one boy ends up rich and the other, sad and destitute. Mo would choose the same degree, university, job and company, and with Farid's ultimate success, Mo's would be secured too.

The idea that he might follow him to a jail cell seemed so bizarre, so thoroughly outlandish, that he refused to entertain it. Mo turned instead to watch their friends. Amir had Hassan in a headlock and the younger, scrappier boy was writhing to get away. Their laughter rang high in the sky, then melted into the fading light.

*

The Dalston din was loud and lively despite the fact that it was Tuesday evening. Homeless men gathered outside Şükran Turkish deli, waiting for the day's leftovers; Spanish expats stood outside restaurant doors loudly discussing their evening plans; and bearded men in skinny jeans pretended they didn't care for attention.

Zara hated Hackney with its pop-up art galleries and organic food stalls. It all seemed so contrived. Luka, however, loved his Dalston flat with its dusty floors and rotting beams. She paused outside his building and slid the bag full of his favourite takeaway to the crook of her left arm. With her right, she keyed 1967 into the security panel. *The summer of love*, he had joked when he first gave her the code.

She had made two vows this week: the first was to stop taking Diazepam. The little yellow pills now sat in a heap at the bottom of her bedroom bin, only six stashed away in her glove box and half a bottle in her bathroom cabinet in case of emergency. Her second vow was to tell Luka how she felt before he left the country next week. She would set aside her pride and tell him the naked truth: that she was a coward, rearing at the thought of human touch, but that to lose him would signify something irreversible and she didn't want to grieve that hope. She wanted to clasp it in her hands and put it somewhere safe and trust that one day it would help her find herself again.

She felt a giddy hope as she paused inside to check her makeup and then climbed the two flights to his flat. Of course it didn't have a working lift. She slid a key into his door and unlocked it. Luka was in the kitchen with a bottle of wine askew in his hand. He spotted her and froze. His gaze shifted leftward, past Zara and into the living room. She turned to follow it and found a petite blonde curled on the sofa wearing Luka's T-shirt and nothing else. Her hair was tossed over one shoulder, so thick and long that it swished seductively around her hips. Zara froze in motion, churning with embarrassment. She was stunned, first by a razor pain and then a cutting self-contempt for feeling that way, as if heartbreak were somehow beneath her. She dropped the bag of food – humiliated by this attempt at affection – then spun and started to flee.

Luka crossed the room in an instant and caught her at the door. 'Wait,' he said, his tone hard and urgent.

She pushed him away. 'Leave me alone.'

'Zara, don't go.'

She shook her head. 'This,' she gestured at the blonde, 'is so fucking boring. So *fucking* predictable.' She took a step back. 'Stay away from me, Luka. Just stay the fuck away.' She slammed the door behind her and fled back to her car. There, skin hot with fury, she locked the doors and sped away. She took five rapid breaths and then five more, and when she found that she couldn't calm down, she turned into a side street and stopped. There, she leaned back in her seat and closed her eyes to stem her tears. *What a fucking mess.* The past two years – it had *all* been a mess. She thought back to the night that her world spun upside down. She rarely let herself think of it but sitting there in the dark, betrayal spidering in her chest, she allowed the bitterness in.

It began two nights after the dreaded wedding. Her husband, Kasim, had discovered text messages to Safran. Two days in and he was already going through her phone. She had noticed the icy silence in the bedroom straight away.

'Is there a Safran in your life?' he asked flatly.

She felt a bolt of alarm. Standing motionless, she said, 'There is.'

'Why is he texting you?'

'He's a friend.'

'A friend? You've told him intimate details about us, told him you want to get out of this. Who the fuck is he?'

She bit down her indignation. Why did she have to appease this man she barely knew?

'Have you slept with him?'

'No.'

'Bullshit!' he spat.

'I'm telling the truth.'

'Don't you lie to me,' he snapped back.

And so it went until his sister knocked on the door to query the raised voices. He pulled her inside and pointed to Zara, spitting ugly words about her past. In a haze, his one sister called another sister and that sister called a third sister and then a brother-in-law and another until they were crowded around her bed. Snatching her phone, one declared that 'if she's slept with one guy, she's probably slept with two and if she's slept with two, she's probably slept with five!'

And so it went: hours of abuse until one of them took pity and let her place a call. Unable to contain her tears, she pleaded with Salma to bring her home, hopeful that her elder sister would take action where her parents would not.

'How can I do that?' Salma had said in anguish. 'I can't. You're theirs now.' The eldest child had powers, yes, but even she couldn't flout tradition.

Alone in her room, Zara first felt shame, red and incisive, as it conjured all the people she would have to face: the acid-tongued aunts and inquisitive cousins, the neighbours who barely concealed their spite when Zara got her pupillage. She could picture them now in their gleeful cliques: *what a fall from grace*, they'd say with a cluck of judgmental tongue. *What a crying shame*, concealing their rictus grins.

Then, came a sodden self-pity. She had only tried to please her family. Why must she feel ashamed?

And, finally, there was fury, which consumed her shame like fuel. It bloomed and billowed and swallowed her whole, and from the embers of the docile daughter-in-law rose Zara as she was before: calm, resolute, defiant.

She packed a suitcase of essentials, leaving behind her sumptuous trousseau of gold jewellery and fine saris. She stepped from her room and was spotted in the hall. The family immediately followed as she marched out to the street. Her husband's menacing bulk pulled the suitcase from her hands. *That's mine now*, he said with a sneer. She pulled it back. *No, it's mine.*

They urged her back to the house, mindful of what the neighbours might say. When she refused to yield, they finally gave up, knowing they couldn't keep her against her will. However, instead of setting her free, they took her to her parents. *You're our responsibility until we take you back,* they said as if she were a purchase to be returned to its vendor.

Of course, her parents' home offered no reprieve. For that night and the next day, she hid in her room, engulfed in silent turmoil. In the evening, there was a gentle knock on her door.

'Dad wants to see you,' said Lena, her voice soft and fearful.

Zara swallowed her dread and soundlessly followed her sister. She paused outside the living room. 'Is Mum in there?'

Lena grimaced. 'No. Dad wants to talk to you alone.'

She smiled weakly. 'Maybe that's for the best?' They both knew he favoured Zara and therefore may be clement where their mother would only be stern.

Inside, her father sat on a chair in the corner, already a break in tradition. His preferred seat on the sofa sat empty and his eyes focused straight ahead. With age, the rings around his pupils had lightened from a warm brown to steely grey. They gave him a rheumy look, which belied the man he was inside: strong and dependable, firm but kind.

Zara sat down and thought of all the ways she had disappointed him. He had lived a hard life, raising four children on minimum wage, but never had he complained. He would come home after work with bags so heavy they seared marks on his skin, then cheerily unpack and peel an apple, popping a piece into Zara's mouth, telling her the seeds would sprout if swallowed.

Despite his factory wage, he dressed like a gentleman. His suits, bought in Whitechapel for a fraction of the retail price, were pressed to perfection and his shirts always blinding white. His shoes were polished and his dark hair neatly combed. He looked distinguished, like a reasonable man. He laughed often and, in her memory, cried only once: at her graduation when she became the first and only of his children to get a degree. He was proud of her then. And now? Now he could barely look at her.

He was matter-of-fact when he finally spoke: 'You have to go back.'

Zara stiffened in her seat. 'I'm not going back.'

'You have to go back. You have to think of the family name.'

'I can't.'

'Can't or won't?' he asked evenly.

'I can't and I won't.'

He paused for a beat or two. Then, with unprecedented viciousness, he said, 'Tomorrow, your brother is going to come and hack you into pieces.'

Zara almost choked in surprise. She had heard stories of such things – these despicable threats of 'honour' killings – but in other families, not in hers and not from her gentle father. Catching her breath, she asked: 'He's going to come and do what?', giving him a chance to soften and retreat.

'He's going to cut you into pieces.'

'Okay,' she said calmly. 'I understand.' She stood and walked out, the hunch of her shoulders the only outward sign of turmoil. In her room, she locked her door, then crumpled against it, winded by horror and grief. She muffled her sobs with both hands. Even in shock, she tried to keep pain from her father. She had no wish to wound him further. She knew his threat was empty – spoken under the maddening spectre of dishonour – but that he could even speak it was intolerable, unforgivable.

She sat there for hours, mourning the loss of something fragile: trust perhaps, or faith, or forgiveness. When dawn broke, she slipped from the house with her tiny blue suitcase. As she walked away along the cracked pavement, she felt something shift inside her. The girl she was, the girl that lived to please her father, was to be no longer. With every step she took from that house, she lost a piece of who she was and kept on losing until six months later, her father passed away and he too was gone forever.

Sometimes, on warm and starry nights, she felt that younger, more hopeful version shifting beneath the surface but to slip back would be weak so here she was instead, alone once again in the dark. Shaking the memories away, she pulled open her glove box and retrieved the brown glass bottle. She tipped two yellow pills into the palm of her hand and clasped her fingers around them. As they pulsed in her fist, she reached desperately for an alternative. After a minute, she loosened her grip and let the pills slide back with a soft tap-tap. She wiped away her tears and retouched her makeup with a hopeless, mechanical resolve. She retrieved the piece of paper she had tucked into her wallet and read the number scrawled across. She recalled the memory of the stranger at the bar, of his arms flexing beneath his suit, of his scent as he leaned in and whispered his name: *Michael*. She smoothed the paper and dialled the number.

'It's Zara,' she said in greeting.

He took a moment to gather himself. 'I was hoping you would call.'

'Where are you?' she asked.

'I'm on my way home.'

'To?'

'To?' he repeated. 'To no one.'

'Would you like to see me instead?' She heard his unsure laugh, a little less cocky than he'd been at Port & Port.

'Seriously?'

'Seriously.'

'Tell me where and I'll come.'

She screwed up the piece of paper in her fist. 'Meet me at Gordon's on Villiers Street.'

His confidence returned. 'I'll be there in half an hour.'

'Good.' She hung up, put her car in gear and sped off towards central London.

*

The tower blocks of Longcross hulked against the sky: three demons rising above the steamy mulch of Bow. The refurbishment had somehow made things worse. The white cladding dirtied in a way that brick did not and the spare design seemed borrowed from a prison.

Farid made his way down Rainhill Walk towards the leftmost block. As he approached, he noticed figures shifting in the dark. By instinct, he drew up his chin and pushed back his shoulders, imitating things that he was not: tough, angry, confrontational; traits you needed to survive in this block. He heard his name and stopped mid-stride, momentarily caught off guard. The figures emerged from the shadows in a scuffle and surrounded him all at once.

A microphone grazed his cheek. 'Farid, what did you do

to Jodie in that warehouse?' asked a reporter, a grey-haired man with a weak chin. 'Tell us the truth, mate. We can help you.' The circle of reporters grew tighter and he felt a hand grab his elbow.

'Is it true that you all planned the attack?'

Farid pulled back in alarm. 'No. Look, you're not allowed to do this.'

'You're not allowed to rape your classmates either. You know that, don't you?' said another reporter, this one blonde and female.

Farid tried to push through the ring but they held him fast inside.

'Amir said it was your idea.'

Bodies pressed against his back and their questions grew to a din. Farid held his arms defensively around his head, then pushed through the barrier to the base of his building. The reporters followed, crowding around him as he punched in his numbers and blindly rushed inside. They knocked on the glass of the door, shouting entreaties for him to speak. Afraid to wait for the lift, he bounded up the stairs and kept on running to the eleventh floor where finally he stopped to breathe. He slumped on the stairs, head on his knees, heart drumming a thousand beats. Would this be his life now? Angry questions about ugly things? A lifetime of doubt for a single deed?

He heard a door open behind him and flinched as he turned, expecting to see reporters. Instead, he found his younger brother, Farhan.

'Mum's been waiting for you,' he said. 'She saw you coming up the road and sent me to see where you were.' He hesitated. 'What's going on?'

Farid drew himself up and led Farhan back to the flat. Inside, Rana was pacing the corridor, her green sari whispering to the wall. She gathered Farid in her arms, a tight sob catching in her chest.

'They've been ringing the bell for hours,' she said, her voice high and strained. 'Farhan went and asked them to stop, but they peppered him with questions and just carried on.' She released Farid and gestured at the door. 'We tried to take off the bell, but we didn't know how. They haven't stopped all evening.'

Farid saw the anguish on Rana's face and felt his courage cave in. When did a boy become too old to cry? When could he no longer run to his mother for comfort, but comfort her instead? He held her now to his chest. 'Don't worry, *Ammi*. It will be okay.' It frightened him to see her like this – Rana who was usually so sturdy and busy, so resourceful when times were tight, and generous when they weren't, who would smile at you warmly but breathe fire when crossed. Just last month, he had watched her approach a queue jumper with the authority of a judge, tap him on the shoulder and send him brusquely to the back. And now here she was, crying anguished tears for her son.

Farid held her tight. 'Don't cry,' he said. 'We didn't do it, *Ammi*. It isn't true.' He closed his eyes and prayed that his parents would one day forgive him.

CHAPTER SIX

'Rough day?' Mia stood to shake Zara's hand.

'Something like that.' Two weeks had passed since they had seen each other last and now they stood together awkwardly. Neither had spoken about the press leak but it hung there between them, silent and heavy like a family secret.

In the two weeks since publication, the leak had sprung wide open. In three days, the boys' names had been discovered and plastered all over social media. In five, Jodie's name was out. On day six, there were injunctions but by day ten, there were too many messages, notices, threads and posts to stamp out. 'Justice 4 Jodie' was fast becoming a war cry.

Mia pointed to a chair. 'I called you here because we've caught a break – two in fact.' She placed a file on the desk. 'First, our mysterious "Sophie" from Jabdam is Sophie Patel who left Bow Road Secondary School in 2017 after an alleged sexual assault by Amir. She's given us a statement and it's possible she can testify.'

Zara felt a quiet triumph chased by nostalgia for the job she'd left behind. These breakthroughs were both the best and worst thing about working with the law. They signified tangible progress but also took someone else's pain and reduced it to a piece of evidence, a mere cog in the machine of justice. This moment of pride for the team had cost a young girl something irretrievable.

Mia pushed a piece of paper across the desk. 'And here's our second break.' She pointed to a section. 'This is Amir Rabbani's DNA profile and *this* is the semen we collected from Jodie's top.'

Zara swallowed. 'They match.'

For the first time that morning, Mia smiled. 'There's a one in one billion chance that the semen from Jodie's top is from someone unrelated to Amir Rabbani.'

Zara's voice was thready with relief. 'That's fantastic news.'

'What's more, we found a strand of Jodie's hair on Mohammed Ahmed's shirt. It's less damning but it helps. The evidence against Hassan Tanweer and Farid Khan is more tenuous but we can place them all there and we can prove that Amir at the very least was intimate with Jodie.' Mia paused. 'We're waiting on the CPS but I'm betting we can charge those boys.'

Zara exhaled slowly. 'Good news for Jodie.'

Mia nodded. 'I thought maybe you'd want to tell her.' She caught the surprise on Zara's face. After a beat, she leaned forward to speak. 'Look, we're essentially going into battle together and I want to know that people by my side are going to have my back the same way I'm going to have theirs, so do I like what you did? No. Do I think it lacked professionalism? Yes. But that girl trusts you and she's relying on you – on *us*. You and I are never gonna go on a spa day together or braid each other's hair, but we have to work together so I want you to know that I have your back. No matter what.'

To Zara's horror, sudden tears welled in her eyes. 'I appreciate it,' she said, then stood up quickly. 'I have yours too.' She shook Mia's hand and said goodbye.

Back in her car, Zara thought over the events of the last two weeks. Luka had left for Nepal and she hadn't let him say goodbye. A dull sense of anger welled in her chest as she recalled that night in Dalston. *This is so fucking boring,* she had told him and fled instead to Michael Attali, the self-assured stranger from Port & Port. She recalled the two nights she had spent with him since – he so bold and eager and she always coldly casual – and wondered if she'd had an honest reaction to *anything* this year.

When she was seventeen, Zara worked at a market research company in Richmond. Every Saturday and Sunday, she would wake up, travel an hour and a half across London and spend eight hours cold-calling people and convincing them to answer survey questions for large corporations. Among the group of East London kids was a dour-faced girl called Shamima. She was quiet and contemplative and said nothing for stretches of time as if she were pondering a great problem of the universe. One lunchtime, one of the kids remarked that it was a great shame Shamima had changed so drastically after her father's death. They spoke of a fun, gregarious version of the girl, one free with words and easy with laughter, a version Zara herself had never met. Shamima had drawn into a shell; a bland, anodyne shell of her former self. Zara thought of her now as she drove from Aldgate to Limehouse and parked outside her mother's home. She rang the doorbell, wondering if Shamima ever found herself again.

Inside the house, she was surprised to find her family gathered like a council of elders: her mother and brother in the centre with Lena and Salma on one side and Amina on the other.

'*Phoonsayn*,' started her mother, her frown lines etched deep in her face.

Zara stiffened. The appeal for her to 'listen' spoke ill of that to come.

'Your auntie from number twenty-six heard something today.' Her mother's voice was low and strained. 'That case against those poor boys from Bow? She said that you were involved.'

Zara bristled. She was amazed by the speed of Asian aunties in finding and spreading news. Given a chance, they'd make excellent hacks. She tried to quip as much, but her mother was unmoved.

'Is it true?'

Zara blinked, her gaze flitting to her sisters. 'Yes, it's true.' Her lips were tight in defiance. Had she been *summoned* here to deny a crime?

Amina stood and left for the kitchen. They listened to the hollow rush of water fill the kettle and the low thud of the switch turning on. The hiss of heat filled the room and then the clink of china: six cups on saucers filled with sugary tea.

Rafiq received a cup first, but pushed it aside. 'Why are you doing this?' he asked.

Zara took a cup from Amina, grateful for the discreet squeeze on her wrist. Her sister-in-law sat down beside her, opposite the rest of the family. Lena stood and took a pastry from the table. Casually, she too sat next to Zara. Their unspoken solidarity strengthened her resolve.

Rafiq pointed a finger at her. 'What's going through your mind? Why are you so fucking determined to drag our name through the mud?'

Their mother drew up in her seat. '*Thuy mukh bonkhor,*' she ordered, her sharp tone reminiscent of the matriarch of old. The demand for silence was directed at Rafiq, but all four children were chastened. 'We are going to discuss this calmly and fairly,' she said.

Zara was maddened by the sheer presumptuousness of it all. She felt no compulsion to plead or explain, and her mother's magnanimousness in allowing a *fair trial* was almost as enraging as Rafiq's resentment.

'What would you like to discuss?' she asked obsequiously.

Fatima's features hardened with reproach. 'Why are you getting involved in this case?'

Zara sighed. 'I'm just doing my job, Mum.'

'But why you?'

'Because someone has to.'

'She has a point though, Zar,' said Salma. 'It doesn't have to be you.'

Zara flinched, surprised by the break in ranks. Whatever mistakes she had made in the past, her sisters had backed her up. Sometimes, Salma abstained from a sense of decorum, but never had she openly opposed her. Her question now felt disloyal and Zara floundered for footing.

Salma pointed at the TV. 'It's been all over the news and everyone in Bow knows you're involved. It's only a matter of time until your name hits the papers and you know what they do to women of colour.'

Zara cocked her head to one side. 'What is it they do?'

Salma sighed. 'Come on, Zar. Don't be like that – not with me. I'm trying to do what's best for you.'

Zara searched her face, torn between her instincts, to defy and disobey, and feelings that ran deeper: hurt, confusion, betrayal. Could she do this without her sisters' support?

Lena beside her picked up her tea. 'Maybe Zara can decide what's best for herself.' She took a sip. 'I mean, I know she's only thirty …'

Rafiq smirked. 'Who asked the *oondur* to speak?'

Lena stiffened at the use of her childhood nickname.

Oondur, or 'mouse', was not only a reference to her ears, which were outsized in her youth, but her quiet and thoughtful nature which occasionally sank to melancholy like when she failed to gain admission to her chosen university, or broke up with the man she thought she'd marry, or – most deeply and dangerously – when their father passed unexpectedly.

Zara felt a flash of anger. 'Don't,' she said. 'Don't use me to get at her.'

'Oh, you think *this* is bad?' Rafiq flung an arm at Lena. 'Wait 'til she has reporters howling at her door.'

Zara caught the flash of fear on Lena's face. Would it really get that bad? Would she – who spent her schooldays protecting Lena from bullies – bring them right to her door? Would this fight be worth that?

'Let them come,' said Lena solemnly. 'I'm not worried.'

Their mother tutted. 'Don't be so naive, girl. There are many things to fear in this country. You think the police can protect your sister if someone decides she's a traitor?'

'Is that what you think?' Zara's voice was strangely shrill, like a freshly plucked violin string. 'That I'm a traitor?'

Her mother hesitated. 'I'm worried that's what people will say.'

'Of *course* that's what she thinks,' Rafiq interjected. 'She doesn't understand why you're doing this.' He gestured to the window, Zara's car framed perfectly in the glass. 'You don't have enough money already?'

Zara swallowed. 'This isn't about money. This is about doing what's right.'

Rafiq laughed. 'Since when are you interested in doing what's *right*?'

Zara's voice grew hard. 'What does that mean?'

He smirked. 'A broken marriage, a tanked career. Tell me: are you still clinging onto that car because it makes you feel more than what you are?'

Zara regarded him for a moment. 'Tell me: does it make you feel *less* than what you are?'

Silence cracked through the room and Rafiq rose to his feet. A vein in his temple throbbed and his fingers drew into fists. He met Zara's gaze with a sneer. 'You're going to lose,' he said. 'There's no way anyone's going to believe that dogface, so good luck.' With that, he turned and marched out.

In his wake, the tension caved. Conflict segued into strained cordiality as it so often did in their family. Zara wanted to flee, but resolved to remain for the evening lest her departure be taken as guilt. She and Salma studiously avoided being left alone, their earlier exchange too fresh for post-mortem. They sat primly in the living room, Zara distracted as her thoughts climbed and clashed over each other, making her tense and restless. She could do this without her mother's support – had *expected* to even – but what did it mean when her own blood was rooting for her to fail? She cared little for Rafiq's rhetoric, but Salma's words weighed heavy on her mind. Her sister would not have opposed her lightly and her concern was therefore real.

Zara's unease was compounded by Lena who cornered her in the kitchen later, distinctly less cavalier in candour. She begged Zara to be careful, to mind the whims and deeds of men. 'Your name is out there, Zar. People know who you are,' she warned.

Zara, filled with gratitude for her sister's support, kissed the top of her head. 'Don't worry, little sister,' she said, her voice carrying only the slightest of tremors. 'For I am Zara the Brave.'

*

The reputation of William Stark QC ran at odds with his gentle grey eyes and compassionate smile. Aged forty-eight, he was six-foot-two with the kind of salt and pepper hair irresistible to young women who craved authority. A co-head at his Bedford Row chambers, Stark was known as a strategic virtuoso unencumbered by obligation to truth and justice. In person, he was affably direct, unfailingly respectful and, to Mia's chagrin, wholly disarming.

He addressed her now with a self-aware smile, revealing perfect teeth only two shades off his pristine white shirt. 'At the risk of sounding like a *Miami Vice* extra, shall we cut to the chase, Miss Scavo? If you have evidence against my client, let's hear it.'

Mia held his gaze. 'I would prefer to ask the boy some

questions first.' She gestured at Amir who had been re-summoned to the station for questioning.

Stark nodded once genially. 'May I request that you refer to "the boy" by his name?'

Mia reined in a sneer. 'Of course,' she said with icy politeness. She refused to be cowed by his cut-glass charm and Hublot watch, peeking now subtly from the sleeve of his suit. It was rare for a barrister of his stature to take on a case at this level. Mia suspected he had a personal connection with Amir's father whose business activities, though not entirely clear, could fund a lawyer like Stark. Still, he was on *her* territory now and the windowless interview room was no fit stage for theatrics.

She addressed Amir. 'Mr Rabbani, do you know why you're here?'

Amir shifted in his seat. 'Yes,' he replied, short and simple just as advised.

Stark loosened his tie and sat back in his chair, the subtext clear to all in the room: *I don't even have to try.*

Mia trained her gaze on the boy. 'Why do you think you're here?'

Amir cleared his throat. 'Because you want to ask me more about Jodie.'

Mia smiled. 'That's right.' She flipped open a file. 'In your first interview with us, you said you had no physical contact with Jodie Wolfe. Is that correct?'

Amir glanced at Stark. 'I put my arm around her but that was it.'

'Did you have sexual intercourse with her that night?'

'No, I did not.'

'Have you ever engaged in sexual activity with her – consensual or not?'

'No.'

Stark raised a forefinger an inch off the table. 'Get to the point, Miss Scavo.'

Mia looked at him coolly. She flicked through her folder, retrieved two pieces of paper and pushed one towards Amir. 'Mr Rabbani, can you tell me what this is?'

The boy leaned forward and scanned it. 'It says it's a DNA test.'

'Do you know whose DNA that is?'

'No.'

'The profile on the left illustrates your DNA. The one on the right you see there? That's the DNA of the semen we found on the top Jodie was wearing that night.' Mia paused to savour the moment, then went in for the kill. 'Can you tell me what's interesting about the two profiles?'

A film of sweat spread on Amir's skin. Before he could speak, however, Stark slid the sheet back across the table. 'Enough of the theatrics. What do you want?'

'If Amir confesses, we can talk about a plea.'

Stark laughed. 'Next option?'

Mia appealed to his good sense. 'Look, William, you heard him. He denied any physical contact with Jodie. How is he going to explain this away? It's better for him – and you – if he tells us the truth. This is going to become a media circus and when the boys are found guilty, there's going to be so much worse waiting for them behind bars.' She pointed at Amir. 'Is that what you want?'

'Nice story, Miss Scavo. What's your next option?' said Stark.

'Next option: we go to court.'

He scoffed. 'On this flimsy evidence?'

Mia frowned involuntarily. 'We have DNA evidence that directly contradicts what your client claims as the truth. We have witnesses who saw him leading the complainant to the warehouse, proving that he lied to us. How does your client hope to explain this away? He—'

'It wasn't rape.' Amir's voice was low and soft, his gaze fixed on the sheet beneath him.

'I'm sorry?' Mia leaned back in her seat, not wanting to spook him.

He cleared his throat and repeated: 'It wasn't rape.'

Mia resisted the urge to smile. 'Then what was it, Amir?'

Stark interrupted, but the boy was already talking.

'It was just a blowjob and it was completely consensual.' He cut off Stark's objection: 'It's okay. I shouldn't have lied in the first place.' To Mia he said, 'I swear to you that's the truth. Look, when a girl – even one that looks like her – starts whispering in your ear that she's gonna get on her knees and do this and that to you, how am I going to say no to that? But I swear to God, she started it. The boys can tell you that.'

'They watched?' Mia remained neutral, taking care

not to betray her glee. Amir's about-turn could cripple his credibility. Citing a consensual blowjob sounded like mere contrivance, an impulsive attempt to explain away the evidence.

Amir glanced over his shoulder as if his friends might be standing behind him, monitoring his answer. 'Yes,' he said, 'but that's all they did. They just watched.'

'Did any of them have intercourse with her?'

Amir shook his head with vigour. 'No. She was ashamed afterwards. They were laughing at her so she left. I had no idea she was going to make all this up.'

Mia raised a doubtful brow. 'So why did you lie to us, Mr Rabbani? And how do we know you're not still lying?'

'I swear to you that's the truth.'

She scoffed. 'Ah, if only our justice system were based on pinky promises.' She stood. 'Make yourself comfortable, Mr Rabbani. You're going to be here a while.'

Stark held up a hand. 'Are you charging my client? If not, I'd like to leave with him.'

Mia smiled. 'Why, Mr Stark. Of *course* we are.'

*

Zara hurried along Bow Road, past her old school towards Thames Magistrates' Court. As a lawyer, she used to stride down here, adrenaline pumping and nerves dancing. She used to tell herself that she was making a difference with her school visits, in giving speeches and handing out certificates to wide-eyed immigrant offspring. Soon she became too busy to give up the time. Eventually, she just stopped trying. She could encourage these malleable young women to aim high and rise above their stations but eventually and inevitably, they would hit the glass ceiling – race, class, sex – and succumb to prosaic dreams. It was inescapable and so she had given up – not just on them but on herself too. Now, the school was just another building.

She walked past it and approached the rust exterior of the Magistrates' Court. A grey-haired man with thin-rimmed glasses and a weak chin stood against an orange banister. He stepped forward, thrusting his phone inches from her face. 'Ms Kaleel, as a Muslim woman, what do you say to all the people who claim that this is a Muslim problem?'

Other reporters gathered around them. 'Have you seen the Facebook groups, Ms Kaleel?' asked a reedy woman dressed in sports leggings and a winter fleece.

Zara pushed passed them with gritted teeth. As a tenant in chambers, she had completed several levels of media training but had never had call to use it. Now more than ever, she needed a lawyer's poise. She stepped through the glass doors as a final question snaked its way in behind her. 'Is it true that Jodie sent Amir love letters through Snapchat?'

Zara smoothed her scowl and greeted the security guard. With practised speed, she emptied her pockets into a small blue tray and stepped through the metal detector.

With thanks, she headed to courtroom five. Inside, she took a seat in the public gallery. Magistrates' courts were the opposite of everything she had imagined of the law as a child. There were no grand Edwardian designs, no elaborate wooden fixtures, no sense of importance or occasion, just a surgical white and battered brown, more fit for a factory than a sanctum of law.

The first thing she noticed when the boys filed in was the sheer immaculacy of their dress. In the muted tones of expensive suits, the four were clean-shaven with fresh haircuts and manicured nails. Even Farid, the greengrocer's son, looked like a Tom Ford model. Zara glanced at Amir's father who sat rigidly in the gallery and wondered if he had dipped into his pockets to burnish the boys' credibility.

With little delay, district judge Anthony Brewer marched into the courtroom and asked the assembly to take a seat. The judge's clerk addressed Amir first and took his name, address and date of birth.

'You have been charged with rape, contrary to section 1(1) of the Sexual Offences Act 2003. The particulars of the offence are that on the twenty-seventh day of June 2019, you intentionally penetrated Jodie Wolfe, the said Jodie Wolfe not consenting to the penetration and you not reasonably believing that Jodie Wolfe consented. Do you plead guilty or not guilty?'

Amir's green eyes shone clear and bright. 'Not guilty,' he said without pause or tremor. Hassan was next, his reedy voice strong with conviction as he echoed Amir's plea. Mo stood unsteadily, his hands gripped behind him, one fist balled into another. He too pleaded not guilty. Finally, it was Farid's turn. He faced the lesser charge of secondary liability for rape, but was visibly more anxious than his fellow defendants. His voice cracked just a touch when he echoed the plea of innocence.

'Very well,' said Judge Brewer, noting the expected result. 'In that case, I suppose we'd better set a trial date, no?' From a big grey folder, he fished out two sets of papers and ran through the case formalities: issues in the case, witness and exhibit lists, estimated length of the trial and availability of witness and counsel. He was pleased to note that there were no quarrels or contests.

'Perhaps the case will run smoother than expected,' he mused. With praise for the counsel's diligence, Brewer set a trial date for 2 December, just over four months away. He reiterated conditions of the police bail – 8 p.m. curfew, electronic tag, and no contact with the complainant – and then adjourned the hearing. The assembly stood and waited for Brewer to exit.

Zara closed her notebook and watched the boys leave. As they filed out, she caught a low whisper, hissed in her direction. '*Khanki.*' *Whore.*

Her gaze snapped towards the voice. She hadn't met the four defendants but in catching Hassan's amusement, she knew it was he who had tossed her the insult. With no pause for good judgement, she marched to the boy.

'What did you say to me?' She had spent her entire life

listening to men brand women as whores. She'd be damned if she was going to let this sixteen-year-old weasel spit the ugly word at her now.

Hassan looked at her sweetly. 'I didn't say anything, Miss.'

She hovered there for a second, her face next to his. Then, with her lips curled into a cold smile, she said, 'I thought so.' She stepped back and glared at his lawyer. 'If your client has something to say to me, perhaps it's best he does it through you.' With that, she turned and strode away.

Later, out of earshot in a holding room, Amir elbowed Hassan in the rib. 'What the hell did you do that for?'

Hassan shoved away the arm. 'Do what?' he asked, boorishly tugging his tie. The windowless room felt stale with four of them stuffed inside.

Amir threw up his hands. 'Why did you call her a whore? You think that's gonna make us look good?'

Hassan shrugged, the lift of his shoulders jerky and aggressive. 'I called her a whore because she's a white-trash wannabe. Look at the way she dresses: skirts up to her arse, heels high like a whore's. She needs to be told.'

Amir scowled. 'I don't care what she wears. Don't talk like that. It makes us look like idiots.'

'Ah, I forgot.' Hassan sniggered. 'We can't let Amir the angel's halo slip, not for one second.'

Amir flinched in surprise. 'That's enough,' he said, firming his tone as he spoke so that the emphasis lay on the last syllable.

Hassan smiled coldly. 'If only they knew the truth.'

Farid took a step towards them. 'Alright, guys, that's enough.' He, the unelected arbiter of the group, knew to quash conflict before it began. 'Come on, just sit down.' He pushed a chair in their direction but both the boys ignored it.

Amir squared his shoulders. 'What do you mean by that?'

Hassan curled his lips in spite. 'We wouldn't be in this mess if it weren't for you.'

Mo spoke now too, emboldened by Farid. 'Come on, lads. This ain't the time or place.' The lack of conviction was clear in his voice, wary of reprisal. Mo was used to being ridiculed. Hassan's sharp retorts and swipes to his chest had taught him to be quiet and follow. Now ignored, he sank into his seat, handing back the mantle.

Hassan sneered at Amir. 'You and Jodie. You *loved* the attention. You've kept her sniffing around you like a fucking lapdog for years. None of this would have happened if you'd just put her down like the dog she is.'

Mo stiffened. 'Come on, Hassan,' he said quietly. 'She's not an animal.' He teetered on the edge of saying more but was afraid to draw his ire.

Amir clenched his fists. 'You know as well as I do that I've never hurt Jodie.'

'Oh, right! Never!' jeered Hassan. 'Just like you never hurt Sophie Patel or Yasmin Madani or even Kristal Lim. All those sluts just dying to be the one that gets Amir

Rabbani. No, you never used any of them to get you off. You're just a *seeda saada beta,* aren't you?'

Amir rushed at Hassan and grabbed him by the collar. He shoved him against a wall, dislodging flecks of peeling plaster. 'You're a fucking prick,' he spat.

Hassan bucked against the wall in a struggle to free himself. 'Fuck you,' he spat back. He wrestled with Amir's wrists now clamped against his throat, but failed to evade the stronger boy.

Farid marched forward and wrenched them apart, holding each at an arm's length. When they lunged for each other, Mo sprang up to restrain Amir, grabbing a fistful of his expensive shirt. 'Calm down, mate. Come on, calm down,' he urged.

Farid stood between them, one hand on Hassan's shoulder, firmly holding him back. 'What the hell's wrong with you?'

Hassan raised a finger at Amir. 'None of this would have happened if you hadn't entertained that dog.'

Amir lunged forward. 'Shut the fuck up!' He strained against Mo's grip but was tightly held in place.

'Why? She's a dog, isn't she?' taunted Hassan. 'A fucking ugly dog.'

'Hassan, stop it!' Farid's voice was high and strained. 'Seriously, just shut the fuck up for once in your life.'

'Oh, you want to be a leader now?' said Hassan. 'You're nothing but a bystander, Farid. Even in Jodie's twisted little tale, you're still just a bystander. No one gives a shit about you.'

Farid drew a deep breath and stepped back, his palms held up in surrender. 'Fine. Gouge each other's eyes out for all I care. I'll stand by and watch.'

'Yeah, you do that,' spat Hassan. 'It's what you do best.'

A leaden silence settled on the room. Mo released Amir, leaving clammy marks on his crisp white shirt. It was mercerised cotton poplin, he noted, with genuine mother-of-pearl buttons. Italian, he guessed. His mother would know for sure.

Years ago, he had looked up a tailor's glossary and delighted over the words: a bodger, a bushelman, a skiffle and a kipper. He had vowed to use them – and not just tongue in cheek – when he set up his own *cat's face* on London's Savile Row. As the years passed, however, he realised that striking out on one's own was not for men of meagre means, so he surrendered his dream, never realising how poignant this was at the mere age of fourteen. He chose then to follow Farid and now here they stood on opposite sides of the same room, facing the same predicament: an accusation of a terrible crime and two friends who were pulling apart. They couldn't fracture now, or point fingers outward. They had to stick together if they were to survive this. And yet, as he stood there among his friends, he couldn't shake the sense of aloneness. Amir and Hassan lashed out at fear while Farid withdrew to his thoughts. Where did that leave Mo? They were heading to trial and he couldn't survive alone. The prospect made his scalp feel tight and his heart beat hard in his chest. He leaned on a wall for support, grimacing when the sweat on his back seeped into his shirt. He ran a weary palm across his face, from chin to forehead as if shedding old skin.

Farid watched him from across the room and grappled with fears of his own. Their future, once so bright and bountiful, was irreversibly tarnished by the words of one girl. Their deferral requests had been denied and now none of the four had a place in college. They had no jobs, no prospects, no future – and it had all happened so dizzyingly fast.

It was this single thought that would cross his mind again and again over the next four months. *How did it come to this?* It would settle cold and thick over his throat at night. It would snake through his sinuses as he lay in his bath, it would pitch him over on the football field, webbing itself across the balls of his feet. By the time it was December, days before the trial, he had become a virtual shadow. His feet were soundless as he walked home at night, his family silent as they shared a meal. Had that one summer evening ruined his entire life? Soon, he would know. Soon, it would begin.

CHAPTER SEVEN

In theory, autumn was Jodie's favourite season: chocolate browns and bright blue skies, bracing air that misted breath through knitted woollen scarves. In reality, London's autumn was an endless taunt of anaemic rain and blustery nights, curling inwards beneath a damp grey sky – just as it was now.

Jodie let the curtains fall shut and picked up the letter once more. Funny how neat black letters could cause such turmoil. Jodie's mother had refused to pay the council tax, livid at the latest hike. *I don't care about bailiffs!* she had shouted at Jodie last night. *If you're so fucking worried, go and get a fucking job!*

Jodie twisted the sheet in her hands as she recalled the last visit from the bailiffs two years ago. She had opened the door to a heavyset man with reed-thin hair greased rigid on his head. His dark leather jacket was pungent on the doorstep as he reached forward and stuck his black boot in the doorway. He flinched when he spotted Jodie, her face in shadow from the falling sun. It started as a stuttered demand for the late electricity bill. Twenty minutes later, Jodie's mother was kicking at the door, bashing it against the bailiff's foot. In her hands was a kitchen knife which she waved in the air, threatening to stab it through the bailiff's boot. It was another twenty minutes before she realised her threats would do no good. Slowly and in stages, she calmed down. Eventually, she retrieved her chequebook and bitterly wrote out an amount of over two hundred pounds: the initial bill of £62 added to the warning letters – £32 per copy – and bailiff visits that had passed unanswered.

We're just doing a job, insisted the lead bailiff but Jodie saw his relish as he reached for the cheque. It was the first time she felt hatred towards another person. After the incident, she took charge of the bills, diligently filing them away in a red plastic folder stored above the kitchen sink. Most months, Christine paid without complaint; on others, Jodie had to dip into the pot of money she skimmed from her alcohol fund. Some months, there was nothing. Today, three bills were overdue. She had called the council for yet another extension but this time, they refused. It made her throat feel prickly and her stomach feel too small.

She set down the bill and restlessly thumbed her phone, eager for distraction. She opened Snapchat and checked the yellow circle in the corner of the screen. Two hundred and twelve notifications. She stared at the number for a few seconds and then gingerly pressed it with a fingertip. The screen burst into a blur of activity. A few names immediately stood out. She spotted a message from Nina and opened it before the others.

'Jodie, seriously, enough is enough. Amir's family is going to kill him. Tell the truth – it's not too late.'

She clicked through to the next message. This one was a note of support from Han, a sweet Vietnamese girl who had recently moved to England. Jodie had bonded with her until Nina cruelly disposed of her, airily stating that there was *only room for one freak in the crew*. Jodie recalled how Han had said nothing, just walked away with a quiet dignity. In that moment, she had felt a sudden and forceful hatred for Nina. Beautiful, nubile Nina whom all the boys loved.

Jodie opened a browser and watched the cursor blink. One by one, she typed the letters of her name and then clicked search. The top result was 'Justice 4 Jodie', a Facebook group with over sixty-seven thousand members. She clicked on the link. With her skin burning hot, she scrolled down and read the updates. Message after hateful message was directed at the four boys. She paused on one with over a thousand likes. It read, 'If someone raped and murdered one of those Paki scum, I'd buy him a drink before shopping him to the police.' Another message read, 'I would say hang the ragheads but it's far better to put them in prison so all the convicts can take turns fucking them up the arsehole.' Yet another, 'I'd love to shove a broken bottle up Farid Khan and film it. See how he likes being watched. First I'd glass his arse, then I'd glass his throat.'

Jodie closed the browser in disgust. She had seen Farid on Higham Street two weeks ago. She had slipped into a side street and watched him walk by listlessly. He had lost his emerging athleticism and now looked thin and weak. Jodie had felt a stab of guilt as she watched him turn the corner. She wished she could talk to him, to explain that she hadn't wanted him involved. But they were legally bound to stay apart and so she had waited for him to pass, then followed in his wake.

She thought back to the party that summer, to the moment she slipped her hand into Amir's. She wished she could take it back. She wished she could rewind time and just take it all back. She set down her phone and lay on her bed. Wrapping the sheets around her tight, she buried her head beneath them. Amir's face flashed through her mind. She felt a surge of excitement, quickly followed by a flood of shame. She squeezed her eyes to shut him out.

*

Zara stood outside the Old Bailey and cycled through her voice messages. The trial was starting in two days and she wanted to make sure there were no last-minute loose ends that had threaded their way free this freezing Friday afternoon.

The tone clicked through to the first message. When she heard the pleading 'Zara', she immediately pressed delete. Luka had called every week since summer. At first she listened with morbid interest. Then, she deleted the messages mid-way. Now, she could barely stand to listen. She didn't know what bothered her more: the sharp pain of betrayal when she heard his voice, or the sick satisfaction of knowing he still wanted her.

She hurried through the remaining messages. All seven were from journalists keen for a quote before the trial, desperate to spin this into a Muslim vs Muslim tabloid sensation: she, the beautiful crusader of justice in one corner and the boys, malevolent and remorseless, in the other. She wanted no part in it. All she wanted was justice for Jodie.

She smiled wryly at her unintentional use of the epigram. Justice 4 Jodie. *What a fucking circus.* She entered the building, cleared security and strode across the concourse.

The Great Hall lay in the heart of the Old Bailey, directly beneath its dome. The Baroque ceiling of elaborate arches and friezes featured a number of paintings commemorating the Blitz. A series of axioms ran across the length of the hall: 'The welfare of the people is supreme', 'The law of the wise is a fountain of life.' Half-moon frescos fanned out above the entrances to the courts, symbolising four mainstays: God, the Law, the Establishment and London.

Jodie was waiting beneath an arch with Mia by her side for the court familiarisation visit. Together, the trio headed to courtroom eight. Inside, four rows of wooden desks sat atop a spotless green carpet. The desks faced the clerk's bench and, above it, the judge's. Directly opposite the judge was the dock, protected by a large pane of bulletproof glass. The press gallery and jury box sat to the judge's right and the witness box and public gallery to the left.

Jodie stared up at the room, physically stooping beneath its leaden weight. As she paused beneath the judge's bench, a door to the court swung open.

'Ever so sorry. I was waylaid.' CPS barrister Andrew Leeson strode in.

Zara had worked with him briefly before, finding him confident and disarming but with the absent air of a busy person thinking three things at once. His heavy-lidded eyes gave him a dim-witted look while his long face and fine blond lashes were somewhat effeminate. Nevertheless, Leeson was known as a competent lawyer with a decisive manner and likeable style. Zara trusted him to serve Jodie well.

She introduced them tentatively, knowing that their interaction, however brief, was subject to scrutiny. A barrister and complainant could meet only under special measures and could not discuss the particulars of the case. As such, despite his intentions to put Jodie at ease, Leeson maintained a detached, business-like manner and offered no more than simple pleasantries.

Mia stood to one side and made notes about the meeting. Mere minutes after his entrance, Leeson patted his pockets officiously. 'Well, one must be off.' He offered Jodie a perfunctory smile. 'Do take some rest this weekend. I shall see you on Monday.' He turned to Zara and Mia.

'Ladies.' He doffed an imaginary cap and strode out of the door he came through.

Jodie listened to the echo of the door as it slammed shut. She gave Zara a watery smile, then wandered around the courtroom, pausing by a table to touch a whorl in the wood or the soft green leather of a chair. Jodie had a certain stillness. With her hands in her pockets and her head held low, she had the hushed composure of someone who had faced many a challenge beyond their years.

As she watched, Zara felt a nameless yearning, the sort she felt when she saw an elderly person eating alone. She wanted to protect Jodie, to create a space around her that could not be breached, to prove to her that hurt could be quashed by justice, no matter how hard to win.

Zara felt a hand on her arm, lifting her from her thoughts. Mia ushered her to a corner of the room. Quietly, she said, 'We have a problem. Sophie Patel is refusing to testify. She's being pulled off the witness list.'

Zara baulked. 'No. She needs to stay on the list. We still have time to convince her. If we pull her now, we won't be able to add her back in.' Zara's hand was a fist, the thumb raised slightly like a politician's plea. 'It's Judge Braun presiding over the case, no? He hates disruptions, but he's sympathetic to young witnesses. If we have to withdraw Sophie at the eleventh hour, he will understand, but he won't let us add her in last-minute. Make sure she's left on the list.'

Mia nodded once. 'I'll call the CPS solicitor and let you know what happens.'

'Okay and please check the rest of the list. The teacher from Jodie's school, Barbara Grant, should be testifying right after our expert witnesses.'

Mia watched Zara's stance, head up and shoulders back, and took in her commanding tone. She smiled softly. 'I can tell you used to be one of them.'

Zara blinked, jolted from her train of thought. She shrugged a single shoulder. 'Not for a long time.'

Mia noted the tinge of nostalgia but did not comment or probe. 'I'll double-check the witness list and ensure the teacher knows her date in court.' She took a step towards the door and gestured out at Jodie. 'You still okay to take her home?'

Zara nodded and they exchanged goodbyes. In the fresh silence, Zara wandered across the courtroom and took a seat at the barristers' bench. Jodie came over and joined her. Zara noticed the hollow of her cheeks – the sort you don't note when you see someone frequently.

'Hey, have you been eating?' she asked.

Jodie pulled at the cuffs of her sleeves. 'Yes.'

Zara watched her for a moment. 'You're used to taking care of yourself, right?'

Jodie shrugged.

'Shopping for food, shopping for clothes. You do it all yourself, so these last few months indoors have been hard.'

'I guess so.'

'How long has your mum been like that?'

Jodie swallowed. 'I don't know. Ever since I can

remember. I used to wake up at seven when I was at primary school and make myself breakfast and sort out my clothes. It was great when I was old enough to use the washing machine. Before that, I'd sometimes have to wear dirty clothes to school. I'm sure no one noticed – all the kids were just as poor – but it made me self-conscious. In the end I figured if someone was going to look at me, it wasn't my clothes they would notice.'

Zara felt a tug of sympathy. 'How old were you when you realised you were different?'

Jodie laughed, bitterness hard in the centre. 'Mum made me aware of it ever since I was young. She'd always tell me I was ugly but I guess I never understood what that meant until I was about five or six.'

'And your dad left when …'

'When I was two.'

'I'm sorry.'

Jodie smiled wistfully. 'You know what I dream of?' She looked up at the ceiling. 'I dream of being about twenty-six. I'm living in New York in a Bohemian area where no one cares if you're different. I'm in a really bright flat – maybe one of those loft conversions – and I work as an architect.' She smiled. 'I dream of going to Barcelona and seeing that amazing church by Antoni Gaudí, or maybe Germany for its castles. Have you seen Habitat 67 in Canada? I don't know if it's beautiful or ugly, but I love it anyway. And then there's Chicago. I hear it's got some of the most beautiful modern buildings ever. But I want to settle in New York where you can be totally anonymous.

'And my dream? My dream is to make a mark on the skyline. You know, the sort you see in the movies. I don't care about money or fame. I just want to make a mark on the most famous skyline in the world.'

Zara watched Jodie and felt a deep sadness swell in her chest.

'And you?' Jodie cocked her head.

'What about me?'

'What's your dream?'

Zara gestured towards the dock. 'What, this isn't living the dream?'

Jodie smiled. 'Seriously, though. What do you want?'

Zara thought for a moment. 'I— I want forgiveness, for others and for myself. I want to accept that the journey is all there is. That when you get there, there's no *there* there and so you keep going, keep trying, keep looking for ways to fill that hole but it will never be filled because we are just human and life has a hole – it just does. That's what I want.'

A smile crept across Jodie's lips. 'Is that a lawyer's long way of saying you want to be happy?'

Zara laughed softly. 'Yes, I guess it is.'

'Me too.' Jodie sat back and closed her eyes. 'I'm glad it's finally starting. These few months have been …'

'Hard. I know.' Zara reached forward and touched Jodie's hand. Somehow it felt more natural now. 'They're just getting started. You know that, right?'

'The papers?'

'The papers, the circus, the baying crowds.'

Jodie blinked. 'Yes, I know.' She tried to smile but it twisted to a grimace. 'I'm ready.'

*

Christine Wolfe flitted around the kitchen, opening and shutting drawers, swearing beneath her breath. Her floral leggings were faded around the seat and her baggy grey T-shirt was stained in three places. The veins in her hands danced as she opened another cupboard, then shut it again impatiently.

Zara made one last appeal to her conscience. 'It's okay to be scared,' she said softly.

Christine continued her search through the sticky brown drawers.

'Ms Wolfe, I know that it's been hard raising Jodie by yourself. She cares about you so much. I know it's hard to talk things out – real life isn't like TV – but if you wanted, I could help you do it. Jodie cares about you and wants to have a relationship where you can talk to each other.'

Christine stilled for a moment, swaying just a little. For a second, she looked like she might cry. But then she turned with a smirk. 'Don't patronise me, miss big-thing lawyer. Just because you went to a fancy school and got a fancy degree and a fancy job, doesn't make you better than me.' She gestured at the window. 'Some of the people here are smarter than you'll ever be but they didn't have the chances you had.'

Zara blinked. 'I'm not patronising you. I'm sorry that it came across that way. What I'm trying to say is that Jodie needs your support; just a few words of encouragement.'

Christine turned her back to the room. 'Just take her and go. She'll be fine.'

Zara bit down her frustration. 'Okay, I'll drop her off at the end of the day.'

Jodie joined them in the kitchen, her entrance marked by her steady shuffle. She was dressed in a black cardigan with buttoned sleeves and a knitted turquoise skirt. Opaque tights, court shoes and a pea coat completed the ensemble. Zara had picked out the items and taught Jodie how to tie her hair in a loose chignon, adding a touch of elegance. She smiled now approvingly.

'Let's go. Mia's waiting in the car.'

Moments later, they set off for Central Criminal Court, the great Old Bailey in St. Paul's. In the car, Jodie raised three fingers and wiped the condensation from her window. She peered at the city streets outside, thronging with commuters, winter frowns etched deep on their faces. Small puffs of air misted at their mouths as they huffed through the December chill. Jodie watched them in silence, her mind empty of thought. There were no dancing nerves or jangling doubts as they neared the court. It was far too late to turn back now.

The car rounded the final corner onto Old Bailey. As a

barrister, Zara would enter the building via South Block, reserved for lawyers, police, witnesses and bailed defendants. Today, they drove on towards the secure gateway reserved for sensitive witnesses and defendants on remand. Zara glanced up at the golden statue of Lady Justice, standing sentry over the hundred-year-old building. Twelve feet tall and twenty-two tonnes, she held a broadsword in her right hand and a pair of scales in her left. Contrary to the maxim that justice is blind, this statue's eyes weren't covered, a fact not lost on Zara as Jodie tensed beside her. Waiting ahead was a group of reporters, some huddled by the gate, others leaned against the mottled concrete wall. They spotted the car and rushed around it just as it reached the gate. They barked competing questions, each of them desperate for an original quote. These reporters worked in an age with more news outlets than news; where the same story was regurgitated in a hundred different places. A story like Jodie's – pure gold even without names and faces – could find its way onto a million web pages. As the car eased through the gateway, the reporters' questions snaked past the barrier.

'We'll compensate you for your time!' shouted a gruff voice to the right.

'A source tells us it was consensual,' said another.

'We want to tell your side of the story!'

The reporters ramped up their pleas. 'Jodie, is it true you sent Amir sexy snaps?'

'Why doesn't your best friend believe you?'

Zara and Mia ferried Jodie to the building and directly through to a waiting room. Inside, Jodie sat down, her shoulders square and spine rigid as if bracing for a blow. Zara sat too and explained the next steps once again: she would leave now for her place in court and Jodie was to wait for the usher. Once in the witness box, Jodie would give her testimony from behind a screen, visible to the judge, jury and counsel. Zara explained that as there were four defendants, Jodie would be cross-examined by four different barristers. She watched the girl react and felt a dull ache. Few victims emerged from this gauntlet unscathed.

Zara gripped her shoulder. 'Remember: this is it, Jodie. You don't have to come back after giving evidence.'

'I know,' she replied. 'Thank you.' She looked up at the ceiling and took a thready breath.

Inside courtroom eight, the four rows of desks were full with barristers, one for each defendant, and behind them their solicitors. Large folders lined the desks, each spilling with documents and transcripts. There was no bustle or noise, however. Instead, the lawyers sat in silence, tensely waiting for proceedings to begin. Zara sat near the witness box, permitted to do so for Jodie's testimony. She glanced at the press and public galleries, full but also silent, the weight of anticipation pressing heavy on tongues.

There was a rising murmur as Judge Nicholas Braun swept into the courtroom and asked the assembly to take its seats. His crimson gown hung squarely off his shoulders and his dark-rimmed glasses, low on his aquiline nose, made him look quintessentially sombre beneath his horsehair wig.

Zara was aware that the judge personally knew one of the defending barristers, William Stark QC. If she remembered correctly, their sons went to the same school. She wondered who Judge Braun with his Oxbridge pedigree and Conservative charm would believe: poor, uncultured Jodie Wolfe with her Estuary accent and mangled face, or four Asian boys held up as shining examples of the immigrant dream: Eastern ethics adorned with Western wealth.

Judge Braun cleared his throat, a needless prelude in a room already silent. 'Mr Stark, thank you for being in attendance this morning.'

'Always a pleasure, My Lord,' Stark replied dutifully.

The judge turned to the prosecutor. 'Mr Leeson, I don't believe I've had the pleasure.'

Andrew Leeson sprang to his feet. 'No, My Lord. Much obliged.' His horsehair wig and fluttering gown seemed distinctly effete as he sat back down.

Judge Braun requested the jury and waited for them to settle. Zara studied them as they took their seats. There was an even mix of men and women: seven white, three black, two Asian. She watched the two Asians. The first was a middle-aged woman in the front row. She had greying hair and heavy glasses and wore a long white tunic with an aquamarine scarf slung casually around her shoulders and chest. Behind her was a younger man in his late twenties or early thirties. He had a meticulously maintained beard and wore black slacks with a light grey summer jacket that held a slight sheen in the light. Zara tried to discern if they were Muslim. Had they lost two jurors already?

With everyone in their places, Judge Braun began to speak: 'Members of the jury, you have already been briefed on the sensitivities around this case but I would like to reiterate them. Over the past few months, much has been printed about this case. Please refrain from reading this material. You must make your decision based only on what you hear in this courtroom, so please be discerning in what you consume outside it.'

Zara watched the jurors and caught a few shifting in their seats. It was clear they already knew too much. Judge Braun ran through court formalities, then handed the floor to Leeson.

The prosecutor stood with energy and greeted the jury. 'Ladies and gentlemen, my name is Andrew Leeson. I will be representing the Crown.' He studied the faces of the jury, making eye contact with each of them. 'I woke up this morning and threw on a shirt and tie. I picked a random pair of black trousers, grabbed a jacket and was out the door. I have a female colleague, Catherine, who is an exceptional lawyer. Unlike me, she spends an hour in the mornings picking out an outfit and getting ready for work. Why? Because she has to craft a persona inside and out of court. She has to create just the right amount of warmth, credibility and self-deprecation. Is this because she's not warm, credible or humble? No. It's because there are very specific standards placed on working women. They need to be feminine but not sexy, firm but not bossy, compassionate but not emotional. Catherine confessed to me the other day that she grew up frightened of turning thirty. She was taught that it was over the hill, the age where beauty begins to fade. No one told her the truth, which is that your thirties are wonderful. She told me that she's finally figured out who she wants to be. She's stopped worrying about the fact that she doesn't look like Scarlett Johansson. She's stopped feeling like an imposter.'

Zara noted a nod from a female juror. Leeson knew what he was doing.

He continued, 'Catherine said her twenties were full of people making judgments. She couldn't go out with her male colleagues – men with no ulterior motives – because aspersions would be cast on her character *and* theirs.'

A male juror now nodded.

'Catherine had to think twice about what she wore, what she said, what she did in case it would be construed the wrong way. With her confession, she made me realise that it's such a privilege to not be judged skin deep; to not have people decide – just by looking at you – what kind of person you are. She made me realise just how precious that privilege is. And because I know how special it is, I beg that you extend it to our complainant, Jodie Wolfe.

'Jodie knows what it's like to be judged. She knows what

it's like to have every single person that ever looks at her make a judgment about who she is, what she is. Jodie has been called every pejorative in the dictionary but the one that has been whispered most between the column inches is *ugly*.' He paused for the muted draw of breath.

Zara felt relief that Jodie was outside. Despite the girl's continued courage, 'ugly' was the word she feared most. Hearing it in the harsh acoustics of the courtroom would have shaken her confidence before even entering the witness box.

Leeson continued: 'Your first thought about Jodie may be that she is shockingly deformed, she is undesirable, pitiful. You will hear that she threw herself at her classmates, that she was "asking for it".

'My learned friends on the defence team will try to beguile you with words, but you must look past the veneer. On Thursday the twenty-seventh of June 2019, Amir Rabbani and his co-defendants *raped* Jodie Wolfe, a defenceless young woman whom they lured into a deserted warehouse with the sole purpose of harming her. They took it in turns to hold her down and rape her.

'We will show you repeated inconsistencies that contradict the defendants' testimony. First, they said she wasn't even there. Then, they claimed that Jodie came to *them* but we have witness statements that prove otherwise. Then, when we found Amir Rabbani's semen on Jodie Wolfe's clothes, they suddenly changed their story again. Suddenly, they remembered that they *did* have sex, but apparently it was consensual! The defence will downplay what happened as modern child's play, as if giving fellatio to a boy while three others watch is just a thing young girls do these days. Amir Rabbani's story has changed again and again. What's to say he's telling the truth now?

'Today, and over the coming days, the Crown will serve to prove that Jodie Wolfe was raped by the accused. You will hear from doctors and DNA experts but, first, you will hear from Jodie herself, a broken young woman who trusted her classmates. We will show you – without a reasonable doubt – that Amir Rabbani and his band of followers are callous rapists who must be found guilty of their crime. I trust you, members of the jury, to look beyond the papers, to look beyond the hysterical tenor of rhetoric and make the right decision. The *only* decision: to find the defendants guilty. Thank you.' Leeson turned to the judge. 'I call my first witness, Jodie Wolfe.'

Hushed excitement pulsed through the room as the doors drew open with a whine. Jodie, shielded from the dock with a screen, entered the witness box, her lopsided shuffle rustling softly on the carpet. The jury stared at her. There was no need for a hundred furtive glances to piece together the horror of her face. Here, they could look to their hearts' content.

Zara willed Jodie to look up, to see her nearby and find solace in her presence. Instead, her gaze was glassy in that vacant way that focused on nothing. Coupled with her hollowing cheeks, it made her deformities more ghoulish than usual. In fact, as Jodie took the oath, Zara noticed one juror lean to another and whisper something. Together, the two men sniggered.

Jodie shrank beneath the jury's attention. She trained her gaze on a large patch of damp by the TV next to the jury's box and traced the dirtied brown lines outwards. She shifted in her seat and turned to the judge. In her mangled diction, she said, 'My Lord, if they can't understand me, are they allowed to say so?'

Judge Braun blanched with sympathy. 'Yes, of course.' He addressed the jury, 'Please, if you feel that you missed a part of Ms Wolfe's testimony, raise your hand and I will ask her to repeat it.'

Jodie nodded gratefully. 'Thank you. I will try to speak clearly but, sometimes,' she gestured to her face, 'it's difficult.'

Zara swallowed a smile. They had already scored points with the judge.

Leeson nodded at the jury then turned to the witness and started. 'Jodie, can you tell me how you know the four defendants?'

Jodie stilled her hands by her side. 'They went to the same school as me: Bow Road Secondary School. I shared some classes with them.'

'Would you say you were friendly with them?'

She hesitated. 'Not really. Maybe Mo ... Mohammed. He's helped me in class before.'

'Who invited you to the party that took place on Thursday the twenty-seventh of June?'

Jodie shifted in the witness box. 'It was Nina, one of my friends.'

Leeson drew out the details of their schedule: where and when the two girls met, what time they left for the party, when they arrived and what route they took.

'Did you have a drink?' he asked.

Jodie swallowed. 'I had a glass of punch which had alcohol in it.'

'Were you drunk?'

'No. I've never been drunk. I need to be in control in case I'm targeted.'

'Targeted? In what way?'

Jodie gestured softly at her face. 'People tend to shout things at me because of the way I look. I need to be able to get away from them quickly.'

Leeson glanced at the jury with a mournful smile. 'Thank you for elaborating, Jodie. We have confirmed that you weren't drunk. Were you even slightly tipsy?'

'No. I had one drink – that was it.'

Leeson led her through the first hour of the party, asking several times for minor details mainly to prove that her memory was sharp. Soon, they arrived on the gravel outside and Amir's approaching footsteps.

'What happened next?' asked Lesson.

Jodie was perfectly still. 'Amir came and sat next to me. I was nervous because he never really talks to me.'

'What did he say?'

'He said "aren't you joining Nina?" and I said she was

busy inside. He told me that she was actually at a private party nearby. He asked me if I wanted to go. I— I wasn't sure but Amir told me he'd take me so I went.' She paused. 'On the way there, I nearly tripped and he reached out and grabbed my hand to steady me.'

Zara watched Jodie tell the lie with skill. It left her with a sense of unease, rough and brackish in the back of her mouth.

Jodie continued, 'When we got there, Amir said I should wear lace more often because it makes me look pretty.' A splutter from the dock carried across the courtroom. Jodie pretended not to hear. 'I went all red. No one had ever called me pretty before. He said that he had always wondered what my lips felt like.'

'Please go on,' said Leeson.

Jodie gripped the cuffs of her sleeves. 'I was really confused. I didn't know what to say.'

'What happened after this?'

'Then, things changed really quickly. Amir was nice until now but then he said, "what do your breasts look like? I ain't gonna touch 'em if they're ugly like the rest of you."' A gasp from the dock echoed through the room, its source unseen by Jodie. She continued, 'Before I could react, his friends came in from another room. They were laughing and shouting, making fun of Amir for bringing me.'

'And what did Amir say?'

Jodie grimaced. 'He said "she's got a pussy, don't she?"'

Amir's voice cried out in disbelief, high and angry over the lip of the screen.

Judge Braun was quick in his reprimand. 'Mr Stark, I will have no interruptions. Quieten your client immediately.' In the fresh silence, he asked Jodie to continue.

Her voice grew unsteady. 'Amir told me to get on my knees. I said no, but he forced me. I thought I could fight him but he was stronger than me.' Tears welled in her eyes.

Leeson looked at the jury, his face now creased with anguish, knowing that this day would be one of Jodie's hardest. Over the next hour, he drew out the events in excruciating detail: the sequence of the rapes, who was standing where, what they said, where they touched her, where they penetrated her, what they used and where they ejaculated. The required level of detail was unremittingly cruel and Jodie broke down in tears despite her efforts not to.

Zara watched in sick relief. These past weeks, Jodie had stopped crying, succumbing instead to numbness. Her tears now revealed her pain and juries needed to see this. Lawyers knew that more than anyone else.

'Once they finished, did they help you?' asked Leeson, driving Jodie on.

'No,' she said, her voice thick from tears. 'They cleaned up and they left.'

'What do you mean they cleaned up?'

Jodie grimaced. 'They wiped the floor and threw alcohol over it.'

'Before they left, did they say anything else to you?'

Jodie seemed to sway a little. 'Yes. Amir said, "it was just a bit of fun, yeah, Jodie?" and then they left.'

'"It was just a bit of fun,"' repeated Leeson, letting it hang in the air for a while. 'Then what happened? Did you call the police?'

'No, then I went home.' Jodie's voice caught on the word. Her mouth curled inward as she tried not to sob. 'I went home. I had a shower and hid the clothes. I thought I could get on with my life. I thought I could forget it but I couldn't.'

'What did you do after this? Did you tell anyone?'

Jodie nodded. 'I told my mum.'

'Did you report it to the police?'

'Yes, I went to Artemis House first. I found them on the internet and they helped me report it to the police.'

Leeson turned to Judge Braun. 'My Lord, the interview transcripts are on page two hundred and ninety-eight.' He paused for the rustle of paper to settle. 'Jodie, the judge has granted your request to read out a part of your victim statement. If you are ready, you may do that now.'

Jodie smoothed the statement in her hand, sculpted over several days so that she could best put across what she had to say. She took a moment to compose herself, then cleared her throat and began. 'I wish I was better at talking to people. I know I don't have a clear voice and my words get stuck in my mouth. I know I don't have the sort of face that people want to look at. I can't smile and win you over because my smile isn't charming. I know the only reason I'd ever be the centre of attention is because I'm so terrible to look at.

'People see me and wonder what sort of life I've had – if it's been really hard.' Jodie looked up at the jury. 'The answer is yes. It's been hard. I don't have a dad and my mum hasn't always coped. We don't have a lot of money and there's this.' Jodie gestured at her face. 'But even with all this, I had ways to be happy. I did well in school and that made me happy. I had some friends who cared about me and I had dreams about the future.' Jodie wavered. 'I wanted to become an architect one day and to build important things. I know I'll never have a big life but I was happy with my small one – until that night.

'Something was taken from me that night and I tried so hard to tell myself that I was okay, that I was fine, that everything was okay. I looked in the mirror and I smiled and said "look at you, you're still the same person, you look strange but you're smart and you work hard and you can still be an architect and you can still build things."' Jodie's voice cracked. 'But I didn't believe it.' She gripped the piece of paper, creasing its borders.

'I live in a small flat with my mum and we have neighbours on every side. There aren't any big parks near my house and the thing I found most hard is that I couldn't go anywhere to scream.' The piece of paper shook in her hands.

'Instead, I stopped eating and sleeping, and I changed. I was never pretty but I was gentle and steady and strong. I could look after myself and my mum. Now, I'm ashamed of how weak I've become, how scared I feel just walking down a street.' A teardrop fell on the sheet of paper, staining it a bluish grey.

Jodie looked at the screen that stood between her and the dock. 'What they will lose are concrete things: a place in college, maybe a future job. What I have lost can't be seen. I've lost my courage, my confidence, my belief that I can have a good life.' Jodie swallowed, fresh tears now streaming down her cheeks.

'Until that night, at least my body was mine – deformed and disabled but mine. That night, it became something else; someone else's. I was terrified of it. I wanted to take it off and burn it. How could it cause me more pain? On top of everything else, if this is what happens, then something must be wrong. How can I believe there are better things ahead? I don't know what I can say to the defendants to make this better. All I can tell them is that I've lost my hope.'

Jodie wiped at her tears. 'There is a quote I used to like, "The sun, with all those planets revolving around it and dependent on it, can still ripen a bunch of grapes as if it had nothing else in the universe to do."' She took a deep breath. 'It used to mean something to me. No matter how hard things got, I always believed that I could handle more. That I could survive. But I don't think that anymore.' She pointed towards the dock. 'They took that from me and I won't ever get it back.'

Silence settled on the room as Jodie folded the sheet in half and gripped it in her hands. Zara felt a rush of affection mixed with a desperate sadness. She was proud of Jodie's performance and saw that the jury was affected too. As they filed out for recess, several fought back tears; one held a scrunched-up tissue tightly in her fist. Zara felt a stir of hope but swallowed it immediately. Optimism could be deadly in a case like this.

After recess, the atmosphere in court felt starkly different. Hushed sorrow became perverse thirst, for this was the spectacle they'd come to see: the defence examining Jodie.

Stark regarded her like one might approach a sleeping lion: slowly and quietly with an alert wariness. His grey eyes, only subtly wrinkled in the corners, were solemn and sympathetic. 'Ms Wolfe, do you mind if I call you Jodie?'

'No.' Jodie's eyes were red from crying but her tone was firm and her voice now steady.

'Thank you.' He hesitated for a moment, as if his first question pained him. 'Jodie, have you ever felt a romantic attraction towards Amir?'

Jodie shifted on her feet. 'I— all the girls in my school did.' She followed Zara's advice. *Don't crumble under Stark. Take a few seconds after everything he says. Think about your answer and then say it.*

Stark made a conciliatory sound. 'Including you? You too were romantically attracted to Amir?'

'At one time.' Jodie swallowed her shame.

'Is it true that you sent him gifts and notes?'

She blinked. 'No.'

'There is nothing to be embarrassed about and you

should bear in mind that you are under oath, so I'll ask again. Have you ever given Amir a gift or a note of affection?'

Jodie hesitated. 'Once, but it was a joke Valentine's.'

'Is it true that it was a £50 computer game he said he wanted?'

Jodie's gaze dipped low. 'That was a long time ago.'

Andrew Leeson was on his feet. 'My Lord,' he started in an exasperated tone. 'I must ask my learned friend, will we be asking all complainants of rape if they *fancied* their assailant?'

Stark held out his palms, asking for reprieve. 'My Lord, I am merely seeking to establish the nature of their relationship in order to interrogate alternative motivations behind the complainant's report.'

'Fine. You may continue,' said Judge Braun.

Stark turned back to Jodie. 'We have established that you gifted Amir a £50 computer game. It wasn't really just a joke Valentine's, was it?'

Jodie looked pained. 'No, but it was a long time ago.'

'Did you ever talk to Amir about your crush on him?'

'No.'

'Why not?'

'Because he would have laughed at me.'

Stark repeated it, '"Because he would have laughed at me."' He arched his brows. 'So you thought he wouldn't entertain the idea of having any romantic or sexual contact with you?'

Jodie hesitated. 'I don't know.'

Zara felt a bolt of anger. She knew this was a game and Stark was merely playing but she hated what he was doing.

'Okay, you said that every girl in the school fancied Amir.' Stark examined a piece of paper as if reading the words off it. 'So, if he wanted to, he could have had sexual intercourse with *several* girls that night?'

Jodie faltered. 'I know. That's why I didn't want to come forward.'

'But you did, Jodie.' Stark's voice grew cold. 'You "came forward" and accused him of forcing himself on you. You accused his friends of raping you. Why? Is it because it was just sex for him? Is it because he didn't return your phone calls?'

'I'm not making this up.' Jodie's voice trembled.

'Did you get angry when he didn't return your phone calls?'

'I don't even have his number.'

'Is he a friend of yours on Facebook?'

'Yes.'

'And you follow him on Instagram?'

'Yes.'

'And also on Twitter?'

'Yes.'

'And you follow him on Snapchat too?'

Jodie's face grew pale.

Stark gestured to the clerk. 'My Lord, I have here a list of conversations – I call them conversations but really they were one-sided – between Jodie Wolfe and Amir Rabbani from the morning of Friday the twenty-eighth of June to the evening of Monday the first of July, the day before Jodie reported her rape to Artemis House.'

Leeson stood. 'My Lord, we haven't seen this evidence.'

'I apologise to my learned friend,' said Stark. 'Amir forgot his password and was only able to retrieve it this morning.'

'Then we should have had it this morning!' cried Leeson with exaggerated dismay.

Judge Braun, however, was in no mood for theatrics. 'You have it now, Mr Leeson. I would like to see where this goes.'

Stark provided a copy for Jodie and asked, 'Can you please read the top line?'

Zara craned in her seat as a howling warning blared at her instincts.

'Ms Wolfe, if you will, please read the first line for the members of the jury,' urged Stark.

'Monday first July, 19.00.'

'And what does it say beneath that?' Stark waited.

'It says "Amir, please talk to me. I can't stop thinking about what happened on Thursday. Please call me."'

'And then?'

'"I won't tell anyone what happened. I just want to talk."'

'How many times in total did you try to contact Amir – on Snapchat alone – from Friday the twenty-eighth of June to Monday the first of July? It says it right there at the bottom.'

Jodie drew in a breath. 'Forty-nine times.'

'Forty-nine times! Why were you so desperate to talk to a boy who you say raped you?'

Jodie's voice shook. 'I couldn't just move on. I needed to speak to him.'

'But he ignored you.'

'Yes.'

'So you plotted your revenge?'

Jodie flinched. 'No, that's not what happened. I didn't make this up.'

'Oh? Can you turn to page nine and read the last line, including the date and time?'

Jodie's hands trembled as she turned the pages. 'Monday first July, 23.00. "Amir, this is your last chance. I swear to God, if you don't reply to this, you'll regret it. I can't take this anymore."'

A wave of noise rippled across the courtroom. Zara shifted forward in her seat and captured Jodie's gaze. There she found concern and confusion, a reflection of her own emotions. Jodie hadn't told her about these attempts at contact – what else was she yet to reveal?

Stark let the noise bloom for a moment. 'Ms Wolfe, what did you mean by "you'll regret it"?'

Jodie floundered. 'I meant that … I just needed him to acknowledge what happened. I was giving him a chance to say sorry.'

'Are you lying to me, Ms Wolfe?'

'No.'

'Are you lying to the members of this jury?'

'No.'

'So you're claiming that these boys lured you into an abandoned warehouse and raped you, and that you only came forward after threatening one of them that they would regret it?'

'No, I—'

'What, Ms Wolfe?'

Jodie's face flushed in anguish. 'I just wanted him to talk to me.'

'You just wanted his attention. Well, now you have it, Ms Wolfe. Now you have it!' He tossed the transcripts onto his desk in disgust. 'My Lord, I think the situation is clear. I don't need to ask her anything more.'

Murmurs broke out in the courtroom and burgeoned to a din. Zara felt a deep unease. The slightest shadow of a doubt could thwart a conviction and Stark was well on his way to crushing Jodie's credibility. She looked on as Judge Braun silenced the crowd, then handed the floor to Rupert Baker, the barrister representing Mohammed Ahmed.

Baker stood and cleared his throat. 'Ms Wolfe, would you say that you are close to any of the defendants?'

'No,' she replied softly, fighting for composure.

Baker flipped through his notes. 'In your interview with Detective Constable Mia Scavo, you said, "Mo has been kind to me before". What did you mean by that?'

Jodie's right shoulder rose in a shrug. 'He's helped me in class.'

'In what way?'

'We— we did a science project together in year eleven. He helped me keep up.'

'Is it safe to say he corrected your mistakes and explained things to you, ultimately helping you get an A?'

'Yes.'

Baker examined a sheet of paper. 'And was it only in school that he helped you?'

Jodie hesitated. 'No.'

'Will you tell the court about the events of Tuesday the 8th of January this year? You remember this day?'

Jodie nodded. 'Yes.'

Baker gestured outwards, handing her the floor. 'Please.'

She took a shaky breath. 'I was walking home when I was stopped by a group of kids from another school. It was a quiet road and they pushed me against the wall. Mo came along and helped me.'

Baker smiled. 'Ah, that's not the whole story, is it?'

Jodie trained her gaze on a spot above the jury. She clasped her hands together and began to recount the story. 'There were four of them. Two boys and two girls. The girls had me up against the wall, calling me names, calling me a frog, saying I made them want to vomit. One put her arm against my throat and began to press. Mo found us like that and pulled the girls off me. He shouted at them, told them to stop. That's when the boys started on him. They pushed him, knocked off his glasses so he couldn't see. They held him against the railing by the canal and told him to leave me there with them but he refused. They hit him but he refused to leave me.' Heavy tears rolled down her cheek. 'Eventually, a family came down the road and the group ran off. Mo walked me home.'

'Because he wanted to make sure you would be safe?

'Yes.'

'So my client, in your words, was kind to you, helped you and looked after you. He took on extra work at school to help you get an A grade. He rescued you from local thugs and took a beating because he didn't want to leave you alone. Is that accurate?'

'Yes.'

'Is it fair to say his actions were heroic that day?' Baker was laying it on thick, but juries loved a hero.

Jodie swallowed. 'Yes.'

'And you want us to believe that a boy like that – a boy who protects the weak and puts himself in the way of danger to do what's right – *forced* you to have sex with him! Does this sound like the same person to you, Ms Wolfe?' When Jodie failed to answer, he continued: 'Only Amir Rabbani's DNA was found on your clothing, Ms Wolfe. Isn't that because you only had sexual relations with Mr Rabbani on the night in question?'

'No, that's not true.'

'Isn't it true that you were ashamed about what was merely banter between young boys, and set out to exact revenge?'

'No.'

'Isn't it true that Mohammed Ahmed did not even touch you?'

'No!' Her voice rang high and bitter, cracking under its own weight.

Baker stared at her for a moment and shook his head slowly in a show of pity and contempt. 'My Lord, I have no more questions for this witness.'

Jodie sagged in the witness box, her energy spent like smoke. She bent her head low, hiding the tears that streaked down her cheek. It was the stance of a woman branded with a scarlet letter. Zara urged her to look up, urged her to be strong for more was yet to come. Over the next hours, Jodie's resolve wavered then broke as first Hassan's barrister and then Farid's asked question after question, demanding a technicolour rendering of the worst night of her life. By the time that court adjourned, she was irreversibly bruised: a punching bag beaten for hours until it lay on the floor in a pool. She left the witness box in a daze, blinking as if she had stepped into sunshine from a pitch-black room. All these words, all these hundreds and thousands of words she had spoken since June, and none of it assured justice, none of it mattered in the face of a single number: forty-nine. Forty-nine times she had tried to contact Amir. The number dogged her as she returned to the witness room, following the usher through a yellow-brown stupor.

Zara, when she joined her, didn't bring up the number but Jodie felt the need to explain. 'I didn't lie,' she cried. 'I just wanted to talk to him. I just wanted him to apologise.'

Zara searched the young girl's face, knowing that the number would haunt the jury. Had he known, Leeson could have introduced the evidence himself, manoeuvred it to work for them, but instead they were caught exposed. Zara leaned forward and said gently, 'I asked if there was any contact between you after the event.'

Jodie looked inexpressibly sad. 'He didn't reply so I didn't think it mattered.'

Zara sighed. Calmly and without accusation, she asked, 'Jodie, is there anything else you haven't told us? Any text messages, sexy snaps, anything that might imply this is a vendetta against Amir?' She caught the girl's eye. 'If there is, I need to know – now.'

'There's nothing else, I promise.'

Zara studied her for a second. 'Christ,' she said softly. *Forty-nine times.*

'I'm sorry.' Jodie traced a stain on the table, her finger whispering on the hard wood surface. 'How bad is it?'

Zara smiled tightly. 'Don't worry. You held up really well in there and that's what matters.' She wanted to offer more reassurance but the truth was that the jury needed just one thread of a credible alternative story. Just one hint of an untruth and there would be reasonable doubt. It was, after all, 'they said, she said'. Four against one. Zara gestured to the door. 'Come on, let's get you home. We'll have to wait and see how this plays out.'

Later, after dropping Jodie off at the Wentworth Estate, Zara found herself cornered by a burly journalist. He leaned a hand against the stairwell and ducked his head towards her.

'Come on, love. Give us a quote. We'll anonymise it. Just one titbit and we'll leave you alone.'

'Fuck off,' she replied coolly. 'Can you anonymise that?' She stepped around him and saw another two reporters hovering by her car. The papers had started to fixate on Zara. Leeson looked like any other lawyer on a prosecution case: tall, white, rich, male. Zara was far more interesting: an attractive Muslim woman leading a charge against her very own brethren. There was enough there for a hundred headlines. She strode to her car, pushed past the reporters, and headed home to safety.

*

Day two began as a typical December morning. Crackling cold snaked between seams, giving Zara's clothes a starchy, wooden feel as she took a seat in the public gallery and appraised Jodie's mother in the witness box. Christine Wolfe's gaunt face seemed old beneath her makeup, her fragile skin dark below the eyes and her red lipstick bleeding at the seams. Her whitish-blonde hair was held back by a scrunchie but wisps had broken free, making her long face seem longer. Her neat navy jumper and grey slacks hung off her frame, making her look sloppy instead of smart. She scanned the room with a suspicious glare, thoroughly outside her comfort zone.

Leeson smiled at her warmly. 'Ms Wolfe, I'd like to talk to you about the days following Thursday the twenty-seventh of June. I know it was a few months ago now so it's absolutely fine if you can't remember certain details. Please just tell me if that's the case. Otherwise, please share as much detail as you can. Does that sound okay?'

The woman's raspy voice was quiet at first, so she cleared her throat and tried again. 'Yes,' she repeated more loudly.

'At what time did your daughter, Jodie Wolfe, leave for the party?'

Christine shrugged. 'I don't know. Around eight or nine I think.'

'What time did she get back?'

She shrugged again. 'Late. I was asleep.'

'Is that normal? For Jodie to stay out late?'

'No. She barely ever goes out because of … you know.' She gestured casually at her face. The action seemed some-how callous.

'When did Jodie tell you about the events of that night?'

'You mean the *rape*?' She failed to keep the last note of incredulity from her voice. 'She told me about it a few days later. On Monday I think.'

'What did she say?'

Christine shook her head. *Those crazy kids, eh?* it seemed to say.

Zara listened to her testimony. If she had a choice,

she would have kept the woman off the witness list, she with her cynicism and disturbing dismissiveness, but the prosecution was bound to call the first person to whom Jodie had told her tale. Zara noted with approval that Leeson kept his questions short and close-ended, forcing the woman to give succinct answers with little room to display her doubt. Slowly, he established consistency between her version of events and Jodie's. Unfortunately, there were no tears. In fact, Jodie's mother seemed decidedly undisturbed by the alleged atrocities her daughter had suffered. It was a fact not lost on Stark who took the mantle with delicious eagerness.

'Ms Wolfe, are you and Jodie close?' he started.

'As close as anyone in my parts.'

'How do you feel about what happened to her?'

She thought about it then shrugged. 'I feel bad. 'Course I do.'

'Do you believe everything she told you?'

Christine hesitated.

Stark nodded sympathetically. 'Has she lied to you before?'

Leeson shot up from his seat but Stark quickly acquiesced.

'I'm sorry,' said the seasoned barrister. 'That was insensitive. I think we'll leave it at that.' He didn't need the witness to voice her answer. It was written all over her face.

*

Zara tugged at the thick wool of her cream turtleneck. The windows in the court canteen didn't open and the air inside held a strange sea-urchin smell. She unwrapped her forlorn sandwich and took a small bite. As she ate, she spotted a familiar figure in the doorway. Erin's boots were surprisingly silent as she strode towards the table.

'Sophie Patel is a tough nut to crack.' Erin slid into the seat opposite.

Zara frowned. 'She's still refusing to testify? She's scheduled for court in two days.'

'I know,' said Erin. 'I want to talk to her myself. Is that okay?'

Zara swallowed a mouthful of dry bread. 'Legally? Yes. Thanks for checking.'

Erin nodded. 'Listen, that's not why I came.' She reached into her jacket, pulled out an iPad and slid it across the table. 'Have you seen this?'

Zara picked it up and swore beneath her breath. On screen was an article from *Visor*, an online journal that fashioned itself as the irreverent voice of the generation. Their lead story in the UK was a profile on Zara. Alongside a headshot taken from her days in chambers sat a thousand words on Zara's life and history. She scanned the first few paragraphs.

'Femme Fatale,' ran the lazy headline and, beneath, a provocative standfirst.

Lawyer Zara Kaleel proves that Muslim women can be smart, subversive and sexy too. In her understated Lanvin suit and unapologetic Pigalle heels, Zara Kaleel sits serenely in the courtroom. Before her unfolds one of this year's biggest legal dramas widely referred to as 'The Monsters of Bow Road'. The case caught the nation's attention after it came to light that a disabled young girl had accused four Muslim males of raping her. This is especially disturbing after the recent spate of cases in which Muslim men have targeted vulnerable native women.

What's notable in this case is that Ms Kaleel, herself a Muslim, is on the prosecuting side. After several years as a barrister, Ms Kaleel left her prestigious London chambers to join Artemis House as an independent sexual violence adviser and agreed to take on the case of the vulnerable young accuser.

The most interesting aspect is that Ms Kaleel hasn't let her Muslim roots hold her back and already a backlash is forming. One young man we spoke to in Whitechapel said, 'When there is so much against Muslims, you would expect that we stick together. The fact that this woman is out there trying to put four Muslim boys away on just what that one girl has said is crazy. She's a traitor.'

Ms Kaleel of course doesn't care about the criticism. The *Visor* team is especially impressed by her don't-give-a-crap attitude.

Here amid the vapid copy sat a video clip of Zara filmed the day before. 'Fuck off,' she said, her English accent perfectly calm. 'Can you anonymise *that*?' The article continued.

> Ms Kaleel says what she thinks and does what's right, never mind the fact that her actions may expose her to a vast crowd of baying Muslims who clearly see her as a traitor to the cause. It's not the first time Ms Kaleel has taken a stance against the groupthink mentality that afflicts certain communities. In a 2014 interview for *Asiana* magazine's 'most powerful Asian women' special, Ms Kaleel railed against the expectations placed on British-Asian women, explaining that her peers are 'more than subservient cooks and cleaners cajoled into arranged marriage by their patriarchal communities'.

Oh, the irony, thought Zara now. She scanned the rest of the article, which styled her as a Westernised 'badass'. In another time, she may have found it flattering but today, here, she knew it would bring only trouble. She wanted no part in the trope of the 'Good Muslim'. She had no interest in being lionised as a role model, or used to peddle a positive, attractive, bourgeoisie brand of Islam. She just wanted to do her job.

She slid the iPad back across the table. 'Thanks for the heads up.'

Erin tapped the screen with a finger. '*Visor* prints a lot

of guff but it has a hefty readership. This is going to put you in the spotlight.'

Zara laughed cheerlessly. 'My mother always used to say that I chased trouble; that I could never just bite my tongue; could never leave something unsaid. Maybe she had a point.'

'Yeah, well…' Erin tucked the iPad into her jacket. 'Just be careful, okay?'

'I will.'

'And stay off social media.'

Zara nodded. 'I will.'

*

Back inside the courtroom, Leeson called his third witness. Dr Tilda Bussman stood in the witness box with an air of quiet confidence. In her mid-forties, she had long blonde hair now tied in a bun and high cheekbones unadorned with blush. Her pale, ethereal face remained neutral as she reeled off her credentials for the court. As a clinical psychologist, she had written three books in the field of sexual deviance, assisted hundreds of criminal cases and testified in dozens of others.

Dr Bussman followed Leeson through a series of questions, answering each with informative but succinct explanations. She described her interview with Jodie and explained that the girl's frame of mind was consistent with other victims of sexual assault: shame, guilt, embarrassment and anxiety – all reasons why Jodie hadn't reported the rape immediately.

It was twenty minutes into the testimony that Leeson asked the deliberately provocative question that stirred the jurors from their afternoon slump. He paused, finger poised thoughtfully on his lips, and said, 'Tell me, Dr Bussman, in your learned experience, why would four healthy, happy, handsome boys want to rape a girl so extensively deformed like Jodie?' His tone was taunting, just the way Stark might pitch it.

Dr Bussman nodded once in understanding, excusing the jury for asking the same. 'Rape is not an act of sexual gratification; it is an act of violence. The large majority of men rape because of anger, power or sadism. They either want to humiliate their victim or they want to exercise their masculinity because of underlying feelings of inadequacy, or they associate sex with violence so the only way they can get aroused is through sexual violence.'

Leeson waved an inquisitive hand. 'So, it's a myth that only attractive women get raped?'

'Absolutely. And even if a hundred per cent of all rapes happened for pure sexual gratification, this still wouldn't preclude the scenario in question. Many people have a desire for the "other".'

'So from your expert point of view, isn't it perfectly feasible that these four boys would have raped Jodie?'

Stark stood and interrupted. 'My Lord, leading the witness to a conclusion.'

'Let me rephrase,' Leeson countered. 'Dr Bussman, from your expert point of view, *is it* feasible that these four boys would have raped Jodie?'

'Yes,' said the doctor. 'Power rapists desire control, dominance, strength and authority. They rape in order to assert their competency. In a group scenario, this is exacerbated by peer pressure – if you don't partake, then you are not masculine enough. Their language, their behaviour as described by the victim, is consistent with the behaviour of power rapists.' She looked to the jury. 'It may be hard to digest why four "handsome and healthy men" would rape Jodie but it is absolutely, one hundred per cent psychologically sound.'

'Thank you, Dr Bussman.' Leeson turned to the judge. 'We have no further questions, My Lord.'

Zara exhaled in relief. Dr Bussman worked frequently with Artemis House as an expert witness on rape cases. Once again, she had proven to be calm, composed, knowledgeable and believable. She was skilful as a witness and had greatly bolstered the prosecution. Zara prayed that she held up under cross-examination.

Stark stood and asked his first question. 'Ms Bussman, are you familiar with the work of Richard Felson and David Tedeschi?'

'Yes.'

'Can you tell me about it?'

'They work in the field of gender, sexual violence and aggression.'

'Have you read their book of 1994, entitled *Violence, Aggression, and Coercive Actions*?'

'Yes.'

'What was the main premise of the book?'

'That the primary motivation for rape is sexual fulfilment.'

'Not anger or power or sadism?'

'No.'

'So what you said before is just one of several theories.'

'It's the prevailing view in the field,' said Dr Bussman.

'Prevailing *view*? So it's not fact?'

'A view supported by evidence. Also, as I said before, even if all rapes were entirely motivated by sexual gratification, many men have a desire to experience the other.'

'What do you mean by "other"?' Stark frowned as if baffled by the ambiguity.

'I mean something that goes beyond the norms of sexual desire. There are entire subcultures dedicated to "other" and so, for these boys, Jodie could have been a special kind of contest. They may not have seen her as they would a traditionally attractive woman but it is feasible that they felt a desire to own her, to experience the otherness of her.'

Stark feigned confusion. 'Ms Bussman, exactly what proportion of the population would you say are attracted to this "other" you speak of?'

'It is difficult to say. First, we would have to classify what categories we would like to include.'

'Can you elaborate?'

She glanced at the jury. 'Well, we would have to decide where we draw the line. Do we include mild deviations from the norm or only those more extreme? For example, some men prefer larger women and society labels that because it goes against the norm. Do we include these so-called "chubby chasers" and men of their ilk?'

A quiet wave of laughter rippled through the court.

'Well, what would be your best guess?'

Dr Bussman smiled kindly. 'I'm afraid I can't answer that without knowing your parameters.'

Stark sighed. It was barely perceptible but a red hue was rising in his neck. 'Okay, would you say this so-called condition that you can't quantify is—'

'I believe you misunderstood me, sir,' she interrupted. 'It's not that I can't quantify it; it's that you haven't given me the necessary parameters.'

'Okay,' said Stark, stretching the second syllable like a sarcastic teen. 'Would you say this condition is common?'

'What would you classify as "common"?'

Stark exhaled audibly. 'Ms Bussman, what would you say are the chances that all four of these boys would be so attracted to this "other" that they would go to the lengths of raping a girl to satisfy their desire?'

'Firstly, I would say it isn't common but it's not unlikely either. Like-minded individuals tend to band together, be it those who are into goth subculture or sports or movies. This holds true when dealing with something darker. Look at the 2012 Delhi gang rape – six men came together to plan and carry out an unthinkable crime. They beat, raped and tortured a twenty-three-year-old woman on a bus they had commandeered for the sole purpose of the crime. Is it common for men to do things like that? No. Is it possible? Of course. Secondly, I would say that even if it were one defendant that instigated it, there is a chance the others followed because of the instigator's strong personality.'

Stark looked at the jury incredulously. 'Ms Bussman, are you saying they raped her because someone *told them* to do it?'

The doctor remained unfazed. 'There is a substantial body of evidence that suggests a strong ringleader can exert enormous influence. Myriad cases have proven this. I can list them if we have time?'

Stark raised a curt hand, keen to downplay her expertise. 'That won't be necessary.' He paused to find a new tack. 'Ms Bussman, as an experienced psychologist in the field, do you know the prevalence of false accusations of rape?'

'Yes.'

'What is it?'

'There is no definitive figure but evidence from England and Wales suggests that three to four per cent is a reasonable estimate.'

'Is it possible that Ms Wolfe is falsely accusing my client of rape?'

'Unless we have concrete proof, then of course there's a possibility. I—'

'Thank you, Ms Bussman. I have no further questions.'

The doctor hesitated for a beat or two, wanting to say more. Then, she stepped down with a polite smile and exited the courtroom.

Zara relaxed in her seat. Despite Stark's attempt to instil doubt, the prosecution had gained a footing. Dr Bussman had successfully unpacked the belief that Jodie's appearance would have dissuaded her rapists. Coupled with the DNA evidence, there was a real chance at conviction. Judge Braun adjourned for the day and Zara slipped out before the courtroom cleared.

She retrieved her phone to find forty-eight emails from various news outlets and publications, a clear consequence of her profile in *Visor*. Just as she began to delete them, her phone began to ring. She cursed when she saw her mother's number.

Fatima's tone was abrupt. 'Your brother said your name is in the news. Is it true?'

Zara swallowed a scoff. 'If Rafiq said it, then it *must* be.' She took a few steps into a corner of the hall and took refuge next to the cool, grey marble.

'Your cousin Munir knows one of the families.' Fatima sounded weary. 'He said there is no possibility that those boys are guilty.'

'Then they don't have anything to worry about.' Zara aimed for reassurance but her tone came off as breezy; an intentional slight in the face of her mother's concern.

'Your name is in the news. Can't you see that it will cause trouble?'

'Few things change without trouble.'

There was a beat of silence before her mother spoke. 'You have always done things your way but you must stop and think sometimes, Zara. There are many things working against those young men. Why must you be one of them?'

Zara leaned into her phone when a group of lawyers strode by, their banter loud in the bustle of the courthouse, stirring sharp nostalgia in her. She turned away from them and cupped a palm over the phone. 'Are you worried about me or *them*?' Her mother's loyalty lay with Rafiq and maybe Zara could understand that – he was the only son – but why the concern for men she'd never met? Did Amir and his friends win allegiance purely for their faith and gender?

Fatima grew impatient. 'I'm worried about you. People won't understand that you're doing a job. They will only see that you're attacking one of your own.'

'They are not *my own*.' Zara's tone grew sharp and drew the gaze of passers-by. She turned to face the marble wall. 'You can cry about their misfortune if that's what you want to do, but don't tell me I owe them anything because they're "one of my own". We are *not* the same.'

Her mother, fazed, said nothing.

Zara waited, then softened her tone. 'Look, Mum, please don't worry. I know what I'm doing.' She glanced up at a guard by the opposite wall. 'I shouldn't be on the phone in here. I have to go.' With an *assalamu alaikum*, Zara hung up, her fingers rigid from gripping the phone. She shook her wrists to ease the tension, but knew that it was useless.

Her mother's words of doubt always slipped beneath her skin, sprouting and wrapping like roots around limbs. Thrumming with frustration, she tossed her phone in her bag and exited the courthouse.

Within a few steps, a herd of reporters surrounded her, shoulder to shoulder to box her in. Her media training had taught her to keep walking without breaking stride so that reporters would move forward with her. When she tried this, however, they held firm in a ring around her frame.

A man in his late forties, dressed in a suit and thick khaki jacket, stuck a microphone beneath her chin. 'Are you confident you will win this trial?' he asked, less a question than a demand.

She met his gaze coolly. *What are you doing?* she wanted to ask. *Is this your fight for justice? Is this your battle for truth? Do you have nothing better to do?* Instead, she just said, 'Excuse me.'

A second reporter pushed forward. 'Ms Kaleel, is it true that Jodie sent Amir love letters?'

A third tugged at Zara's sleeve. 'Is this all just the fantasy of a lovelorn teenager?'

Zara snatched her arm from the woman's grip. The flash of photography popped off around her and she raised a hand to shield her face. She pushed through the crowd, pulling free of eager hands and dodging a dozen cameras. The barked demands and pleading appeals blended to a din as she fought to keep her composure. She struggled through the outer band of the scrum and emerged onto the street.

Without pause, she fled to her car on Limeburner Lane and locked the doors behind her. Her nerves jangled in the sudden stillness and her heart raced much too fast. Her hands moved restlessly from the rear-view mirror to her lap, to the wheel of the car, to the glove box. She took a deep breath and tried to remember when she last felt peace without the aid of a chemical kick. Her thoughts went to Michael Attali and a thrill of remembrance ran through her body when she recalled the last time they met: the comforting bulk of his body on hers, the purity of unthinking sex, the simplicity of parting still strangers.

Zara rifled through her bag for her phone and sent a message to Michael. His reply was immediate and she read it with an oily satisfaction:

I'm leaving the office now. Meet me at Potters Fields Park in thirty minutes.

She noted with approval that it was minutes from his flat. They had seen each other a dozen times since their first night together in the summer and he'd learnt quickly that she needed no pretence at romance and courtship. This was merely transactional.

Half an hour later, Michael found her in the park, flanked by Tower Bridge to her right and the listing silhouette of City Hall to her left. He pulled her off the long concrete bench, both his hands hooked into hers in a simulacrum of love. He pulled her to him and greeted her with a kiss.

'Come on,' he said, wrapping his fingers around the crook of her elbow and leading her along the Thames to his coveted riverside flat. Inside, he pushed her against the wall and breathed in her perfume; a hint of bergamot seductive on her skin. 'You want me to take off that classy little skirt of yours?' he asked, his breath on her neck but his lips not yet on skin. 'You want me to slip my fingers underneath and stroke your little clit?'

Zara pressed against him, feeling her body respond. She closed her eyes and surrendered control. His touch was aggressive and unthinking, and in his forcefulness she found sweet relief from having to think. He gripped her wrists and pinned them above her. She bucked against his weight as he pulled her skirt to the floor. He unzipped his trousers and guided himself to her. She cried out as he pushed inside. He held her to him, then lifted her up and took her to the bed. She lay beneath him and in a state of numbing rapture let him wrap his fingers around her neck, let him pull her hair, let him push into her mouth. Here, in physical surrender to Michael, she forgot that she was angry, forgot that she was lonely, forgot that all she felt was distance when near the ones she loved. Here, she felt a silken oblivion that almost swelled to peace.

*

Day three started solemnly. The courtroom chill lingered despite the full-blast heating and the jurors sat in silence, mindful of the media attention. Tabloid editors had seen soaring performance around their 'Monsters of Bow Road' coverage and were pushing reporters for more of the same. One article in particular – 'Monsters of Bow Road TURNED ON by schoolgirl's deformities' – had garnered over two million shares online. It was a twisted interpretation of Dr Bussman's testimony and the disgusted public lapped it up like sugarcane. Spectators had started to gather by the courthouse, shouting obscenities at the four accused. Those in courtroom eight could not hear the crowd outside but they knew it was there, angry and swaying, lying in waiting.

Dr Benjamin Chase was the first in the witness box. Zara swallowed a smile as she watched the jury watch him. Dr Chase was forty-two years old with a chiselled face and salt and pepper hair that, as Erin once put it in candour, made you think of autumn bonfires. Trusting him felt completely natural.

'Dr Chase, how long have you worked in forensics?' began Leeson.

'I started straight out of college so that's twenty-one years – far longer than I prefer to admit.'

'Would you say you're an expert in your field?'

The doctor smiled. 'If you'll excuse my American immodesty, yes, I would.'

'Why?'

'Well, my major was in Criminological and Forensic Science. I have worked in the field for two decades, published over one hundred papers in the field as well as two books.'

Zara noticed Stark roll his eyes.

'Dr Chase, your team worked on the forensics for Jodie Wolfe's case. Can you describe to the court what this entails?'

'Of course.' He turned to the jury. 'The complainant's clothes were collected for trace evidence – hair and fibre, tissue, footprints, paint chips, soil and dirt, bodily fluids including blood, and, of course, fingerprints. Everything was sent to the lab for analysis. My team was first involved in July of this year. We received one semen sample from the blouse Jodie Wolfe was wearing on the evening in question and four DNA samples from the four defendants. The samples were forensically tested and the DNA found on Jodie's clothes matched the profile from Amir Rabbani's sample.'

Leeson nodded thoughtfully. 'And can you explain, Dr Chase, in layman's terms how this process works?'

'I can certainly try.' He smiled at the jury. 'Profiling works like this: a DNA sample is taken from the crime stain, which can be any piece of human matter left at the scene of the crime. A second sample is then taken from the suspect. In the lab, we cut the samples at specific locations and drag them through a gel to create a unique pattern. We then create a visual representation of this pattern, which allows us to compare one sample to another.' He paused to make sure the jury was following.

'Matching one part of the pattern doesn't prove that the two samples came from the same source. By matching combinations of parts, however, you can gradually build up a more and more accurate comparison between the two samples. One combination, for example, might be shared by one in four of the population, but if you then match another combination, that might reduce it to one in sixteen of the population, or one in sixty-four and so on. Eventually, if the sample is good enough, you can work your way to the point where the match is so accurate that the chance of someone else having the same DNA profile has a random occurrence of one in one billion.'

Leeson bounced on the balls of his feet, eager to ask his next question. 'In Mr Rabbani's case, what did you find?'

Dr Chase faced the jury. 'If the DNA in the semen sample came from some unknown person unrelated to Mr Rabbani, the probability of a match would be in the order of one in one billion.'

A gust of noise rose across the courtroom. As the jurors absorbed this news, Zara felt a looping tightness in her stomach. She recognised it as the thrill of the law done right.

Leeson's features were arranged in awe. 'One in one billion,' he repeated. 'So, even though Amir denied going anywhere near Jodie that night—'

Stark shot to his feet. 'My Lord!' he cried. 'My client has submitted a statement specifying that he and Ms Wolfe had consensual relations that night. It's wilful obfuscation to imply otherwise!'

The judge nodded once. 'He's right, Mr Leeson. Please reflect the facts in your questioning.'

Leeson accepted the rebuke. 'Dr Chase, in what you saw of the evidence, was there anything to suggest that the intercourse was not consensual?'

'Yes. Jodie was examined four days after the fact. There was some bruising in her vaginal area and also on her neck.'

'And are these types of bruises consistent with forced intercourse?'

'Yes.'

The courtroom hummed with noise. As those in the gallery whispered around her, Zara watched the jury. The young Asian man in the back row had a hand on his neck and rubbed his skin as if soothing a bruise. Physical evidence in rape cases was invaluable. When it was one word against another, any shred of tangible evidence supported the complainant's credibility. Dr Chase, another stalwart of Artemis House, had helped the prosecution immensely.

Leeson spent the rest of his time asking short questions with long answers, taking just enough time to wear down the jury before the defence's cross.

When his turn finally came, Stark began matter-of-factly. 'Dr Chase, my learned friend has sought to illustrate two things with your testimony: first, that Amir Rabbani and Jodie Wolfe had sexual relations on the night in question and, second, that some of Ms Wolfe's physical attributes were consistent with rape. Is that correct?'

'Yes.'

'Does the first contradict any of what Mr Rabbani has already stated?'

'No, but he—'

'Thank you. And the bruises – could they have been the result of some overzealous but consensual play?'

'There was sizable muscle contusion so it would have to have been some pretty overzealous "play".'

'But it's a possibility?' pressed Stark.

'Yes.'

'And did you find anyone else's semen on her blouse?'

'No.'

Stark arched his brows as if surprised by the answer. 'So what we know is that the evidence – the tangible, hard evidence – shows that it could have been nothing more than an enthusiastic session of consensual sex with one defendant instead of the depraved orgy claimed by Ms Wolfe?'

'The evidence doesn't suggest that.'

'But it's a possibility?'

'It's possible.'

Stark looked to the jury. 'So, just to be sure, nothing in the forensic evidence contradicts the testimony of my client. Nothing proves the complainant's accusations.'

'Is there a question in that?' asked the doctor.

Stark turned with a smile. 'Not a question – just pure fact.'

*

Barbara Grant shifted uncomfortably in the witness box. With shoulder-length brown hair, thick-rimmed glasses and a peach-coloured twinset, she was the epitome of a forty-something English teacher.

'If all my students were like Jodie, my job would be the easiest in the world. She is a keen and enthusiastic member of my class. She is patient, diligent and extremely hard-working.'

Zara stiffened in her seat as she watched. They hadn't sourced the witness for a report card recital. Boredom in a jury was almost as deadly as doubt.

Mercifully, Leeson shared Zara's concern. 'Ms Grant, I'd like to keep focus on the defendants if that's okay,' he told her in a kindly tone. 'You say that you were their form tutor for five years. Did you see any examples of difficult behaviour during this time?'

Grant nodded, sending her tight curls bouncing around her chubby face. 'Yes, I did. Multiple times. On one occasion, they were caught on security cameras throwing a chair through a classroom window. It smashed into the school greenhouse and shattered the glass.'

'Smashing up a school building?' Leeson sounded scandalised. 'Was this typical of them?'

Grant cocked her head. 'Well, there have been four or five recorded incidents of similar behaviour. They seem to have a problem with authority.'

'I see.' Leeson spent some minutes drawing out the details of the incidents in question. He painted a picture of a group of boys who feared and respected nothing, who scorned authority and acted on whim. These weren't the respectable offspring of hardworking immigrants but insolent youths who cared for very little. With his message rendered clearly, he released the witness to Stark.

Amir's lawyer stood up and regarded her with suspicion. 'Ms Grant, you have been called here today to comment on the general character of my client, Mr Rabbani, and his co-defendants. As such, I assume you feel you know Mr Rabbani quite well?'

'Yes. As their form tutor, I saw them every weekday morning and even taught some of their classes.'

'"Even taught some of their classes,"' echoed Stark. His patronising undertone was barely discernible. 'So you know them well enough to make a judgement of their character would you say?'

'Yes.'

'And you're a good judge of character?'

'I would say so, yes.'

Stark turned to the lower bench. 'For the court please, Mr Clerk.' He held out a file for the clerk who passed it onto the judge. 'If the court will indulge me, Ms Grant, can I take your mind back to September 2017?'

Grant shifted nervously. 'Okay.'

'Did anything significant happen then?'

She thought for a moment. 'Not that I can recall.'

Zara grew rigid in the gallery. Stark had a poker face but she recognised the signs of triumph: the twitching curl of a lip, the gentle coaxing of a trap. What did he know that they did not?

Stark spoke patiently as if addressing a child. 'Okay, can you now fast forward to December that year. Anything of interest now?'

Grant frowned, the lines thick and deep in her forehead. 'No.'

'Ms Grant, did you hire an Adam Pope in September 2017?'

The teacher's face grew ashen.

'Ms Grant?'

She took a shallow breath. 'Yes, I did.'

'Is it fair to say you lobbied for him because as a NEET – for the court, that stands for 'Not in Education, Employment or Training' – he had neither the qualifications nor the experience to work in a school?'

'I don't know if "lobbied" is the right word.'

'Campaigned? Championed?' offered Stark. 'Did you not tell the school council that you saw something in Mr Pope?'

'Yes.'

'How did you know Mr Pope?'

'I taught him.'

'For how long?'

Grant glanced over at the jury. 'Five years.'

'For how many hours a week?'

'I couldn't say. Maybe about six.'

Stark nodded. 'So is it fair to say you knew Mr Pope as well as you claim to know Mr Rabbani?'

'I—'

Stark cut in: 'Do you now recall what happened in December 2017?'

She swallowed. 'Yes.'

'Please do be so kind to share with the court.'

'He— Mr Pope was removed from the school because he contravened the code of conduct.'

'How so?'

'He was removed because of inappropriate behaviour.'

'Can you please elaborate, Ms Grant? There's no point trying to evade the question.'

Grant's chubby cheeks were now pink. She hesitated. 'He had intercourse with one of our students.'

A gasp sprang forth from the gallery, almost as if Stark had planted it. Zara coiled tight with frustration. It was her team that had suggested Grant as a witness. Leeson would be livid.

'And how old was she?' asked Stark. 'How old was the student that Mr Pope, himself twenty-one, had sex with?'

Grant looked beaten. 'Fifteen.'

Stark spun to the jury. 'Ms Grant with her excellent judge of character invited a sex offender into the school – *campaigned* for him even.' His tone turned cold. 'Ms Grant, if you are such an excellent judge of character, why did you not see that Adam Pope was a predator? If you were so wrong about him, what's to say you're right about Amir? What's to say we can trust you on *anything*?'

Barbara Grant opened her mouth but remained at an utter loss.

Stark turned to the judge in triumph. 'I have no more questions, My Lord.'

Judge Braun excused the witness and soon adjourned for the day. Zara stalked from the courtroom and immediately called Erin.

'Madame,' she answered in greeting.

'Christ, Erin. I've just left the courtroom.'

'What happened?'

'I told you to vet the teacher.' Zara's voice was steely.

'What happened?' Erin was concerned but calm.

'She hired a sex offender.' Zara's words were spoken quickly in short syllables that popped with anger. 'Did you check her performance records? The school's dismissal records?'

'Of course I did. There was no mention of any of that.'

'Well, Stark just fucked us. Come on, Erin. If *he* found out about it, we could have too.' Zara knew that this would rile her.

'Well, we don't have huge pockets to pay every dickhead that might discredit a witness.'

'Which is why we have *you*,' snapped Zara.

Erin stalled, entirely unaccustomed to making mistakes. 'Look, I screwed up,' she said. 'I'm sorry.'

'Don't be sorry. Convince Sophie to talk. She's due in tomorrow.'

Erin exhaled slowly. 'Okay. I will.'

Zara hung up with a sigh. The teacher had unpicked the progress made by Dr Chase. The damage was done not by what she said, but that the prosecution chose her to say it. It signalled sloppiness and a lack of diligence – and if they were wrong about her, what's to say they were right about the defendants? They *needed* Sophie to talk.

Zara slipped her phone in her bag and headed for the exit. Stepping outside, she heard a high-pitched male voice: 'There she is!' Across the street, a group of young teenagers – five boys and three girls – stood to attention. One of the boys snarled at her and then swore in a coarse Bengali, '*Oi, sudowri, tuy kitha buzos beh? Amdar bhai-okol-tehrer jailor harayteh?*' The words were low and menacing. *You fucking bitch, how dare you try to put our brothers in jail?*

One of the girls spat on the floor in her direction. '*Fungir-fungi,*' she shouted. '*Boroh beti oygizos, na-ni?*' *You think you're a big woman now, don't you?*

The words struck Zara in staccato bursts, transporting her back to adolescence when her brother would use the refrain to belittle her. She felt immediately defensive and grappled with a need to explain. Here were people from her own community and she wanted them to understand why she was on Jodie's side. It was easy to sit with Safran in a lavish restaurant and insist she didn't care; it was entirely different to face the critics who mocked her so gleefully.

The teens laughed at her now as she stood in indecision. Before she could speak, two officers of the court crossed the street to clear them off. Zara cringed at her pathetic need for their approval. She swallowed the emotion like a stone, then squared her shoulders and stalked to her car, fully aware that reporters were recording her every move.

She drove to the Wentworth Estate with an update on the day's events. In the stale smoke of Jodie's bedroom, she recounted Barbara Grant's testimony.

Jodie sat and listened, nodding only occasionally. 'What happens if we lose?'

'Don't worry,' said Zara. 'We're a long way off from that.'

Jodie's gaunt features were now lined in a frown. 'Doesn't the fact that Amir changed his story mean anything? He said I was nowhere near there and changed his story later.'

'We'll address that when he's in the witness box. Please don't worry. The fight is far from lost.'

Jodie grimaced. 'Some days I wish I'd just forgotten the whole thing.'

Zara shook her head. 'Jodie, it's always worth the fight. Even when you lose, it's worth it. Even when you know you're going to lose, it's worth it. One of my favourite lawyers said that true courage is when you know you're beaten before you even begin, but you begin anyway and see it through to the end. You don't often win, but sometimes you do.'

A soft smile spread on Jodie's lips. 'Atticus Finch? I didn't expect sentimentality from you.'

Zara smiled too. 'He was one of the good ones. I'm just not sure there are that many left in the world today.'

'Lawyers or men?' asked Jodie.

Zara sighed. 'Both.'

CHAPTER EIGHT

Sophie Patel was a doe-eyed girl with the sort of inky lashes that made young boys falter. Dressed in a long-sleeved white blouse and baggy black trousers, she looked like a child playing dress-up. As she waited, her delicate fingers tucked and re-tucked loose strands of hair behind her ear.

Zara sensed Stark's disdain over the admission of this witness. If her experience taught her anything, it was that he wouldn't play nicely today. Still, she was relieved that they'd kept her on the witness list and that Erin had convinced her to talk. Sophie could prove crucial in revealing Amir's nature.

Andrew Leeson stood and smoothed his gown. He turned to the witness and started: 'Sophie, can you tell me how old you are?'

'Sixteen.' The girl's voice was soft and fearful.

'I believe you finished school at Bishop Patterson College in Acton Town this summer. What school did you go to before that?'

Sophie swallowed. 'Before that, I went to Bow Road Secondary School. I left in 2017.'

'Can you tell me why you left?'

Sophie's gaze fluttered to the dock. 'I got into some trouble at school and my parents didn't want me there anymore.'

'What do you mean by "trouble"?'

She hesitated. 'Trouble with a boy.' She glanced again at the dock. 'He, um, Amir Rabbani, was in my class and kept asking me out. I kept saying no. My parents are very strict and never let me go out to the movies or anything like that, so he kept trying to get me to bunk off school. One day, it was inset day and Amir told me there would be a day-party at a warehouse.' Sophie tucked a hair behind her ear. 'I really wanted to go so I pretended I was going to school as normal. I changed clothes in some lifts down the road from where I live. Then I met Amir.'

'What happened next?'

'We went to a warehouse in Bow. There were a few other people there, smoking, drinking and getting off with each other.' She gestured at the dock. 'Amir and Hassan asked me if I wanted to smoke some weed. I had never had any before. I didn't want to embarrass myself so I said yes. I smoked a little bit and tried to give it back because I was feeling lightheaded but they said I wouldn't get the full effect unless I smoked it all, so I did.' Sophie hesitated, trying to find her next words. 'I felt really woozy. They told me to lie down because it would help and then … I felt his hands on me. Amir was undressing me. He had my jeans around my ankle and he took advantage.'

Leeson's voice was gentle. 'Can you tell me what happened exactly?'

Sophie took a trembling breath. 'He put his hands in my knickers and began to push a finger inside me. I tried to move away from him but he told me to relax. He kept telling me to relax but I started to cry. A few others noticed but they didn't do anything. He tried to stop me crying but I couldn't help it. I felt like such an idiot but I'd never done something like that before. It was too fast.'

'And then what happened?'

'He got angry. He said I was killing his buzz and then he left me there on the floor of the warehouse.'

'So, Amir and Hassan took you into a warehouse, fed you drugs, laid you on the floor and then Amir abused you. He got angry when you resisted and then he left you there. Is that right?'

'Yes.'

'Can you tell me what happened after that day?'

Sophie laced her fingers together, her childlike hands shaking perceptibly. 'I tried to talk to Amir the next day. I don't know what I wanted: a confession or apology, something that showed what he did was wrong.'

'And what happened?'

'He acted completely confused. He said he thought I wanted it and that he stopped as soon as I said no. He said he had no idea that I felt forced.'

'And did you feel forced?'

Sophie grimaced. 'Yes, I did.'

'What was his reaction when you told him that?'

'He brushed it off. He said I was making it into a big deal and it wasn't one. He told me to "chill out".'

'And then what happened?'

Sophie blinked back tears. 'Then I tried to do what he said. I tried to "chill out". I tried to focus on classes but everything was in a jumble. I started to lose weight. I was having mood swings. I didn't know who to talk to. Eventually I told my sister, and then my parents were told. The next thing I know we were moving away to the other side of the city.'

'Why didn't you go to the police?' asked Leeson.

Sophie hesitated. 'In our culture, these things don't happen. We don't talk about them. Me being there in the first place, that was bad enough. What happened to me – that didn't bear thinking about.'

'What are your feelings towards Amir Rabbani now?'

Sophie looked to the dock. 'He ruined the person I used to be.'

'And that's why you're here today?'

'Yes, I couldn't let him ruin someone else.'

Leeson nodded dolefully. 'Thank you, Sophie. You're very brave.' With that, he concluded his questions.

Stark rose with a genial smile as his gown spread around him like a vulture's wings. 'Ms Patel, thank you for being here today. Before we go on, I want to tell you that I was brought up in a household of women. I have a mother but no father, two sisters but no brothers. I was taught to have respect for women so I take things like rape and abuse very, very seriously.'

Sophie nodded and visibly relaxed.

Zara tensed in her seat in contrast. Stark's words were only borrowed platitude, a honeyed gambit designed to disarm. She willed the girl to stay wary but could see she was already yielding to his charm.

Stark frowned sympathetically. 'I am saddened by the low conviction rate of rape. Unfortunately, the problem comes down to a "he-says, she-says" situation and without proof, we must always give the accused the benefit of the doubt.' He paused. 'Now, what's happening here with you and Amir is slightly different in that you say A and B and C happened, and Amir *also* says that A and B and C happened. He doesn't disagree that you went with him to the warehouse, that you chose to smoke marijuana and that he – with the zeal of a then fourteen-year-old boy – initiated physical activity. He *agrees* that you didn't like it and he agrees that he stopped as soon as he realised you wanted to go no further. Now, can you tell me what in his version of events doesn't tally with yours?'

Sophie hesitated. 'I don't know what you mean.'

'Is there anything you say happened that Amir says didn't happen?'

'I— I'm not sure.'

'So, for example, did he force you to smoke marijuana

but is now saying he didn't? Or, did he continue touching you after you said no, but is now claiming that he stopped? What is different between your story and his?'

Sophie considered this. 'He said I wanted it and I didn't.'

'Did you tell him you didn't want to?'

'Yes.'

'Okay, so he starts to unbuckle your belt and you tell him no?'

'Well, not then. I—'

'Okay, so he goes a bit further and your jeans are around your ankles. Did you tell him no then?'

Sophie smoothed a crease in her blouse.

Stark waited a beat. 'When he started to insert his finger into your vagina, did you say no then?'

'I— it was— yes, that's when I said it.'

'Before or after?'

Zara looked on and simmered with anger. It was a common refrain among lawyers that 'the law is a blunt instrument' and nowhere was this more obvious than in cases of sexual assault. It was obvious to any discerning observer that Stark was being hostile but he was allowed to continue because a neat little tick box said he could.

'Ms Patel, before or after?' pushed Stark.

'After.'

'And what was Mr Rabbani's reaction?'

'He told me to relax.'

'And when you didn't?'

'He got angry.'

'So he stopped what he was doing – just as you asked – and then he got angry?'

'Yes.'

Stark nodded thoughtfully. 'So, in essence, you asked him to stop. He asked you to relax and as soon you refused, he stopped?'

Sophie's voice trembled as she answered. 'Yes.'

'So that moment, those few seconds between you saying "stop" and him saying "relax" – was that sexual assault?'

Leeson stood, aware that Stark was within his right but needing to interject. 'My Lord, we all know rape isn't as overt as my learned friend suggests. A woman doesn't have to be repeatedly bleating "no" to deny consent.'

Stark turned on him. 'And we expect a fourteen-year-old boy to be able to tell when a woman's *body language* says no? How can we accuse a fourteen-year-old boy of sexual assault in this situation? A boy who *stopped* when he realised it wasn't what Ms Patel wanted?'

Judge Braun raised a hand. 'Let's all just calm down please.'

Leeson persisted, 'My Lord, Ms Patel's testimony shows that Amir Rabbani has a history of this type of behaviour.'

'What behaviour?' snapped Stark. '*Sexual* behaviour? Like every other man on the face of the Earth?'

'Enough!' The judge's voice rang high across the room. 'Mr Stark, you have made your point. Are you finished with the witness?'

'Yes, My Lord,' he said, suddenly obsequious.

'In that case, Ms Patel, you're free to go.'

Zara watched Sophie leave the courtroom. Stark's spiel about respecting women was pure artifice. Zara – and Stark – had worked enough rape cases to know a woman didn't always say no. She may be scared of getting her head bashed in or a hip caved in. It was unbearably unfair that these crimes were tried by such broad brushes. It was little wonder that Sophie's family chose to move away instead of pursuing justice like Jodie.

A morose silence settled on the courtroom. It was clear that no one had won today. Leeson stood with his head bowed low. 'The prosecution rests, My Lord.'

Judge Braun shifted in his chair. 'Very well. I'm informed that a member of the jury has an unavoidable engagement tomorrow so I think this is a good time to adjourn for the week. We shall reconvene on Monday to hear from the defence.' With that, he dismissed the court.

Zara felt leaden from the day's proceedings. She pulled on her jacket and wearily left the courtroom. Outside, she was surprised to find Erin waiting.

'Come with me.' Erin grabbed her arm and led her into a small room off the main corridor. She pointed to a plastic chair which stood forlornly beneath the sole window. 'Sit down.' Erin reached into her jacket and pulled out her iPad. 'Today's lead story on *Visor*.' She slid it across the table.

Zara read the headline. SEXY MUSLIM LAWYER BRANDED A 'TRAITOR' declared the front page in large block letters. She felt winded when she saw what lay underneath: a video thumbnail picturing Zara and Michael Attali in Potters Fields Park, his lips on hers and hands resting lasciviously on the curve of her arse.

Zara felt a swell of anger. She reached for the tablet but then drew back her hand. 'How did they—'

Erin, as cool and aloof as ever, took a seat opposite. 'I thought you should know before you went outside.' She gave the tablet a gentle shove. 'It's not good but you should watch it.'

'I—' Zara searched for words. 'Why would they do this?' She drew the tablet near and pressed play with fingers that were suddenly clumsy. The video report opened with a montage of newspaper headlines from Jodie's case. The unseen narrator – an English accent with an American twang – spoke over the graphics, 'It has emerged that Zara Kaleel, the lawyer-turned-rape-counsellor on the Monsters of Bow Road case, has a few skeletons of her own. The seductive young Muslim used all her powers of persuasion to win the support of the public.'

The report cut to a picture of Zara, her black hair flowing around a comely scowl. The narrator continued, 'Pictured regularly on the steps of the Old Bailey, Kaleel has been a vocal critic of the culture of *omerta* that keeps secrets festering inside the Muslim community. But now,' the voice grew ominous, 'her motives for speaking out have been called into doubt.'

The footage cut to Zara and Michael in the park, he

pulling her up and giving her a kiss. Zara's stomach rolled with the knowledge that someone had been watching her, filming her, possibly even stalking her.

The narrator's tone grew righteous: 'Ms Kaleel was filmed getting amorous with a white man of Jewish descent, prompting people to ask: is she crusading for justice or taking revenge on a community she hates?' The report cut to a cleric on the steps of East London Mosque, her family's chosen place of worship. The cleric, dressed in a long white robe and a patterned white skullcap, brayed with sanctimony, no doubt handpicked and primed by *Visor*'s production team.

'Zara Kaleel says she represents Muslims but she doesn't,' said the cleric. 'She is a saboteur posing as a Muslim to poison public opinion.' He raised his hand and counted out his fingers. 'One: she had an arranged marriage that lasted only weeks. Two: she has taken up this case against four innocent boys. Three: she is doing things in public with a non-Muslim.' He raised a fourth finger. 'I could go on. My point is, Zara Kaleel is angry with a community in which she's not accepted. She has no business in this case. She has no objectivity. She isn't a Muslim. She's a stain on our people.'

Zara flinched at the word, then felt a spark of fury that they could still make her feel this way, still make her feel that she was deserving of shame. She stopped the video, noting with horror that it had registered over two million views. A red and heavy dread beat against the roof of her skull, making her feel too hot. She pressed the base of her palms against the sockets of her eyes, trying to still the throbbing within.

Erin beckoned her up. 'We should get you out of here ... They're gathering.'

Zara's eyes grew round. 'Who's gathering?'

Erin hesitated. 'Men. Asian mainly. They're angry.'

Zara thought of her family with a churning nausea. She shook her head. 'I can't.' Her voice rasped softly like fingertips on paper.

Erin's tone was stern. 'Look, we just need to get you out of the eye of the storm and then you can work out what to do; if you want to make a statement or what.' She tugged at Zara's arm. 'Come on. I'll get you out of here.'

Through a glaze of shock, Zara followed her out the door and down the stairs to ground level. Outside, the crowd had swelled to around a hundred. Reporters, spectators and protesters stood behind silver-grey barriers that flanked Zara's path. She stood still for a moment, seized by disbelief. In her stationary state, she noticed one group of protestors above all others: ten Asian men gathered at the front of the crowd. They were in their late teens or early twenties, all in stylish Western dress with not a fleck of beard between them. There was nothing to suggest they were particularly traditional. In their hands, however, they held a series of placards. In big bold letters along the top were the words 'Uncle Tom'. The racial slur, crudely borrowed from the black community, accused

Zara of being servile to whites. Beneath the words, she was rendered in a hijab in various subservient poses. In one, she was on her knees with her tongue hanging out like a lapdog; in another, she was prostrate beneath the St. George's Cross; another depicted her obscenely with a pig, her gown hitched up to the waist and her features arranged in ecstasy.

The message was a perfect blend of racism and misogyny. Zara Kaleel is a traitor, it said. Zara Kaleel is a whore. Zara Kaleel is a fawning, mewling servant to the whites but disguised as something pure. She inadvertently made eye contact with one of the men. He lunged towards her and she jerked back in alarm.

'You whore! How dare you call yourself a Muslim?' he shouted. 'What did they offer you? Thirty pieces of silver?' A fine mist of saliva marked the violence of delivery.

Another man dived forward. 'Uncle Tom!' he shouted clumsily. Pleased with the cheering of his companions, he repeated the epithet to the tune of a popular football chant. Soon, his friends joined in.

Zara shrank back from them and felt the brush of a hand on her back. She spun round and was confronted by a group of white teenagers holding a banner with the words 'Justice 4 Jodie' in bright red letters. 'Ditch the bitch!' they cried in unison. One man reached forward and pulled at Zara's skirt. 'I hear you like white man's cock.'

She cried out and jerked her skirt from his grip. His fingers still grappled for her and a police guard stepped forward to smack his hand away. She swayed unsteadily as hands grabbed at her and cameras blazed with flash. The photographers jostled and Zara felt a hand of support. Erin was by her side, trying to shield her from the crowd. As they pushed their way through the jeers and insults, Zara felt something hard and heavy slug against her shoulder. She looked down and saw the yellow-white liquid of a raw egg dripping down her suit. She watched another sail through the air and hit the side of Erin's head, seeping into her cropped black hair. They looked around and spotted the source, a second group of Asian men with bandanas around their faces.

Erin tugged at her arm. 'Come on, let's go.'

The two of them huddled together and rushed down the path. They reached Erin's car and hurried inside. Within seconds, they set off into the unforgiving night. Zara closed her eyes to keep her world from caving in. The December air clung heavy on her skin: damp and close and discomforting. A flurry of images blurred inside her mind: sharp fingernails and grabbing hands, the gruesome banners and angry chants, that obscene image of her straddling a pig, Islam's most impure of animals. Horror at the invasion of privacy spilled into crippling frustration over the timing of the story – right in the middle of trial. Zara was piercingly aware that she had lost the moral high ground. She was no longer a Muslim woman steadfastly pursuing justice, but an imposter posing as such to leaven the blow of Jodie's accusation. She would be thought an interloper, a traitor, a saboteur. Then, there was family and the cold and heavy dread of confronting her brother and mother. Would they understand how she came to be filmed in public, a white man's hands gripping her backside?

When they reached Zara's building, Erin led her inside. It was only upstairs that she spoke. 'What do you know about this Michael Attali?'

Zara sat on her sofa in a daze. Her face was pale and her skin felt clammy.

Erin paced the room. 'It seems too perfect. How was it that someone who knew who you were was in the exact right place at the exact right time? Do you think he stitched you up?'

'What does it matter?' Zara's voice was bitter. 'They've already decided what I am.'

'It matters,' said Erin. 'I can help you but I need to know what we're up against.'

Nausea churned in Zara's stomach. How many times had she said those very words to some hopeless victim or guilty executive?

Erin grew impatient. 'Here's how it is: you're public enemy number one right now. The Muslims hate you because you're a traitor to their cause. Justice for Jodie hate you because you're tainting the case. You need to fight your corner. Things like this don't die easily and it's going to overshadow Jodie's case if we say nothing. We need to think of a strategy.'

Zara wiped the sweat from her brow. 'Okay,' she said. 'We will. I just— I need a second.' She stood and took a long drink of water, then walked unsteadily to her bathroom. She closed the door and stood over the toilet bowl. Visions rose again of sharp fingernails and grabbing hands, the vile image of her straddling a pig. Her clammy skin flushed with heat and bile stung the base of her throat. She jolted forward with a violent retch, then vomited into the bowl. She watched it spatter against the shiny white ceramic and the rivulets of yellow trickle down the bowl. She retched again and vomited. With her stomach spent, she leaned on the bathroom sink and took a deep breath. She rinsed her mouth. Then, not allowing herself to think, she shook open a drawer and slid a hand to the back. She felt around for a moment, then drew out a brown glass bottle. Without hesitating, she twisted it open, shook two pills into her hand and swallowed them with a sob.

*

Hassan ran down the stairs two by two and threw open the door. 'Hey man, come in.'

Amir took off his shoes and placed them neatly in a corner.

Hassan spotted Rocky nipping at Amir's heels. 'Aw, shit, what's he doing here? Mum's gonna screw if she sees it.' As a child, Hassan had been taught that petting dogs was impure. It was only the most modern of Muslims – like Amir's family – that kept the creatures as pets.

Amir kneeled down and stroked the dog's thick honey

coat. '*It* is a she – and she's harmless. C'mon, we'll just hide her in your room.' Amir pulled off his coat, tossed it onto a rack and followed his friend upstairs, Rocky in tow. 'So, have you seen the news?'

Hassan frowned. 'No. Why?'

Amir smiled and handed him his phone. 'Read this.'

After a beat, Hassan's jaw dropped. 'No way.' He clicked on a headline from *Visor*: SEXY MUSLIM LAWYER BRANDED A 'TRAITOR'. 'Oh my God.' His voice was soft and reverent. 'It says here she picked up the guy in a city bar. I *knew* she was a slut.'

'Keep going,' urged Amir. 'There's a video.'

Hassan howled with delight as he watched the clip of Zara in the park. He listened to the cleric and screeched with glee. 'Do the others know?'

Amir nodded. 'Yeah, Mo couldn't believe it. I told Farid too but you know how he gets.'

Hassan rolled his eyes. 'He needs to chill the fuck out. He's got nothing to worry about.' He turned back to the phone and zoomed into a picture of Zara and Michael. 'Jesus, she has an amazing arse.'

Amir laughed. 'Pervert.'

Hassan narrowed his eyes. 'Please, like you wouldn't jizz all over her pictures.' He made a small keening sound. 'Just look at that arse. She's so fucking hot. I'd give anything to have her on her knees.'

Amir grabbed back his phone. 'Well, you can look at porn in your own time.'

Hassan gestured at his empty bedroom. 'On what exactly? My loopy mother chucked my laptop away.'

'Man, I still can't believe she did that. It's so harsh.' Amir sat in a chair and Rocky curled contentedly by his feet. He ran his fingers through her fur as Hassan flopped down on the bed opposite.

With the strange mix of levity and gravity that defines the friendship of teenage boys, they spent the evening trading insults and woes until darkness thickened outside the window and Amir's curfew beckoned.

*

The steady rev of the sewing machine drifted down the hall. Mo closed the bedroom door and the sound dulled to a hum. It was comforting, this soundtrack to his life. It told him that everything was as it should be, in spite of the truth.

He turned to Farid and tossed him a can of Coke. 'Come on, man. Cheer up. This news about the lawyer is good for us.' He took a seat on a stool, clearing it first of his sketchbook.

Farid set aside his can. 'Cheer up?' he asked. 'You saw what they did to Sophie in court. You think she deserved that?'

Mo faltered. 'No, she didn't, but it had to be done.' He watched Farid shrink with doubt. 'Listen, you're the one who told me to worry. You told me that we're just "four darkies in the dock". You were right, so we have to use everything we've got. Amir never lied about what he did with Sophie and that was proven in court.'

'Yeah, but it's not as simple as that, is it?'

Mo flicked a hand in the air. 'But it *is* that simple, man.' He bit down his impatience, not yet mature enough to navigate this challenge. He hadn't the skill to lead his friend through this fog; wanted instead to yank him from its midst. Farid was possibly the only person in the world with whom he could be himself. He didn't have to mask his gawkish manner or the high notes of his voice. He didn't have to worry about the way his wrists lay limp in their natural pose, giving him a foppish, effeminate look. Mo relied on Farid's steadying force, and the fact that his friend was drifting from his reach filled him with the thick red tulle of anxiety.

Farid closed his eyes and listened to the hum next door. His under-eye circles were now dark and deep and his jawline had receded, giving him a sombre, haunted look.

Mo swallowed his stirring angst and searched for a way to help him. 'What are you worried about?' he asked. 'That we'll be found guilty?'

When Farid opened his eyes, Mo saw that they were wet. It made his chest smart with fear and his scalp feel strangely tight. Despite their years of friendship, he'd never seen Farid cry. He was serious and studious, but rarely melancholic. To see him in distress was deeply unsettling.

Mo took off his glasses and twisted them in his hands as if this might somehow churn the words he needed.

Farid gazed up at the ceiling and tried to stave his tears. 'I'm scared that we'll have to live with this regardless of the verdict.'

Mo shook his head. 'It's four of us against one of her. We'll be found innocent and move on with our lives.'

'Is that what you think?' Farid's words were short and bitter. 'You think we'll just carry on and everyone will forget what happened? That's not how it works. Not for men like us.'

Mo instinctively rejected this. 'You can't honestly believe that this one thing that happened to us at the age of sixteen is going to control our lives forever. People get accused of all sorts of things and they get cleared and carry on and enjoy their lives. Mate, some people are even found *guilty* and are given a second chance. You need to stop stressing.'

'You think we'll get that, do you?' asked Farid. 'A second chance?'

Mo considered this. 'Yes, I think we will.' He had to believe it, or else what were they even fighting for? They might as well say that *yes, we did it*. Mo wanted to help Farid, but he would not follow him into this miasma. He was his family's great white hope and he had to believe that things would get better and that all would be forgiven.

Farid stood up. 'I'm going for a walk,' he said. He picked up the can of Coke. 'Thanks for this.' He did not meet Mo's eyes nor ask him for his company. He simply drifted from the room and left the squat brown house that hummed with the sounds of a sewing machine.

*

Zara watched Stuart read over her statement, his clear blue eyes zig-zagging left and right over the seven lines of text: 'On Tuesday third December, a person unknown to me committed a gross invasion of my privacy. This private moment has since been used to drive an agenda of division and hate. It has been claimed that I have a vendetta against the Muslim community but nothing could be less true. I have taken an active role in fostering harmony between my community and the progressive values of the country we live in. Integration does not happen through entrenched views and harmful invective, rather through tolerance and change. I, along with my colleagues, am fighting hard for justice and I plead that you allow me to do this work. I will be making no further comment on this matter.'

Stuart placed the sheet on his desk. 'Zara, when that man called you a "stain", did it hurt?'

She faltered. 'Yes, but I—'

'Then *say* that.' Stuart tapped a finger on the piece of paper. 'This *sounds* like it was written by a lawyer. It's impersonal, passive and vapid. What he said *hurt* you. Be honest about that. You are not a traitor and you are not a stain. You are doing your job and you're doing it with the logic and objectivity of a first-class barrister. To be told otherwise is hurtful and unjust. You should tell the truth about that.'

Zara opened her mouth to speak, then paused. She considered his words, then firmly shook her head. 'I can't do that, Stuart. I'm not letting them in. They can't have that.'

Stuart exhaled slowly then folded the statement in half and pushed it across the desk.

Zara hovered above it. 'Listen, Stuart—'

He held up a hand. 'Look, you don't need to apologise. This case has become a circus but it's not your fault.'

'I know but I need to tell you that I'm sorry.'

'I'm not accepting an apology. Now go.'

Zara lingered for a moment but then turned and left the room. She walked past the pit and took refuge in the Lincoln meeting room. She sat on the sofa and thought over the last twenty-four hours. Michael had called her and spoken words of sympathy, but beneath the sombre tone of his voice, was a note of amused incredulity, as if he really rather liked being known to have fucked her. He had made a polite attempt to keep seeing her, but they both knew it was over. What point was there in a diverting fling if it itself became a problem?

Zara dispatched him with a cool expediency and Michael did not resist. *I'll miss you*, he said, straining for sincerity. At another time, Zara may have laughed lightly and told him he needn't spend those words on her. Instead, she said *good luck* and *goodbye*.

It was strange. This man had meant so little but changed

so much. The image of him – hands pressing into her body – would be linked to her indelibly. *A stain*, they had called her. *A stain on our people.* Would her family secretly think the same? She hadn't heard from them, not even Lena or Salma. Her sisters forgave her indiscretions – first her refusal to marry, then the divorce, then her estrangement from family – but perhaps this latest was one too many. Her fling with a white man was spread across the papers and it wasn't she in her ivory Greenwich tower that had to face the front line of shaming. It was them with their husbands and children and in-laws and neighbours that would shoulder the dishonour. Her sisters couldn't escape judgement with a careless shrug or breezy *bon mot* for they were embedded in the community. The thought of them bearing her tarnish made Zara feel giddy with guilt. She did not welcome their silence but certainly understood it. She only wished it wouldn't last too long. Silence in her family spun conversation into cobwebs; broad and shallow and fragile, easily broken when shaken too harshly, often beyond repair.

How are you feeling? It was the question she always asked her charges. How are you feeling? This is a safe place to talk. This is where you can bare your soul without judgment. Numb? Empty? Angry? Her answer came to her in a single word: lonely. It felt like cold liver slipping down her throat – *lonely*. She had been lonely for years now.

A light knock on the door splintered her thoughts. Zara glanced up and saw Jodie waiting at the threshold. She beckoned her inside. The girl came in and pulled off her gloves. Her dark blue duffel coat was too big on her shrinking frame; not nearly snug enough to keep in the warm. She shrugged it off and hung it on a rack, then placed her hands on a heater.

'I saw you on the news,' she said softly.

Zara nodded plaintively.

'Do you think it will affect the case?'

Zara didn't want to lie to her. 'Possibly. People may think that I'm on your side not because it's the right side, but because I have a vendetta against my own people. My motivations have been called into question and that may affect the narrative of the case.'

Jodie sat down and thought this over. After a while, she glanced up. 'I'm glad you're here,' she said. 'I'm glad you're on my side.'

Zara smiled faintly. 'I am too.' After a beat, she reached for a folder. 'So tell me, Jodie. How are you feeling?'

*

Farid sat at the top of the hill, ripping strands of grass from their roots. He wondered if pulling grass was human instinct. *It figures,* he thought. *We like destroying life.* He watched the small figures below running around the field, shouting obscenities whenever outside the referee's earshot. He should be down there. It was the only place that gave him true peace. He thought about his family and his home, its air heavy with words unsaid. His father had always warned him about Amir. Somehow, he saw through the perfect looks, all the *sasijis* and *sasajis* he employed to beguile the elder generation.

'This son of a gangster is no good for you,' his father would say, speaking in broken English as if that would connect where his Urdu could not. Farid had defended his friend with the vigour of an acolyte. Sure, he made him smoke the odd joint but who *didn't* do that? And, yes, Amir had a thing for the ladies but didn't *all* the boys their age? Their parents were of a different generation. Their fears belonged to a different time.

Farid's eyes welled with tears as he thought of his father coming home at eleven every night after packing up the stall and then doing a shift at the cash and carry. His mother always waited up and made sure there was a warm meal to greet him. They were good people. They worked hard to give him the life he had. They didn't deserve this public shame. He didn't deserve to be sitting here like an outcast instead of down there, playing with his friends.

He lay back on the grass and slung an elbow across his face to block the watery sun. He heard footsteps behind him, crunchy on the cold grass. He sprang up, always alert, and squinted at the approaching figure.

'I know you,' he said.

'Yeah, we met a couple of months ago down there.' Erin nodded at the football field.

'What do you want?'

'To talk.' She sat next to him but said nothing, instead watching the figures below.

'That guy there in the red, his name is Muamar,' said Farid. 'You know, like Gadaffi. We take the piss out of him. There's an Osama too but he calls himself Sam. We used to joke that all we needed was a Saddam and we'd have our very own axis of evil.'

Erin smiled. 'Do you think it will affect them later on in life?'

Farid shrugged. 'Probably.'

Erin pulled at a blade of grass. 'Way back before I was in this job, I worked at this big corporate place. They once asked me to recruit a junior investigator and I remember having a whole bunch of CVs. There were lots of foreign names and I consciously decided to interview a few. There was Susa Garrido and then a Cuban guy whose name I can't remember and another one called Venkatesh Rao. And all three of them couldn't really understand me properly. I mean, they understood me but they couldn't really express themselves or answer the questions properly. The other interviewer said, "I hate to say it but there's a British premium, isn't there?"

'I hated that he said that but I also understood it. From then on, I chose either people with British names or people who went to a British school because then I'd know they had been here for a while. I didn't want to waste my time.' She paused. 'Is that wrong?'

'Nah, it's just the way it is.'

Erin looked at him. 'I'm sorry for the shit you're going through.' She paused for another moment. 'I feel like you've been dragged into this when you didn't do anything wrong – I know the prosecution also feels that way.'

Farid looked out to the horizon. 'I'm not going to turn on my friends.'

'But you didn't do anything wrong, Farid. Why go down with them? If you testify to what actually happened that night, we can get immunity for you. You didn't do anything.'

'I'm glad you came here.' He cracked a humourless smile. 'It proves you think you'll lose.'

'We're just trying to get to the truth.'

'Aren't we all?'

Erin blinked. After a beat, she turned back to the game. Together, they watched the sun set in a dusky purple sky.

*

Luka's voice was gruffer than usual. 'Zara, I'm flying to Chile for the Vinson climb and won't be back 'til January. I wanted to talk to you before I left, but I know that you're not interested. I know I screwed up but so did you. We could have had something and now we have nothing.' He paused. 'What I do know is that I can't have you in my head on this climb, so this is me letting you go – finally. I hope you find some peace, Zara. I really do.' A beat. 'Goodbye.' A click.

Zara listened to the message again. She could have loved

Luka back – a part of her almost did – but she knew it would not be fair. He would have always been the chaser, the soother, the crutch on which she leaned. To let him go was kinder.

She reached out and erased the message. 'Goodbye, Luka.' She ran her fingers through her hair, from crown to nape as if shaking something free, then sat for a moment, feeling strangely untethered beneath a dark melancholy. To stem the unease, she swallowed two Diazepam with an icy glass of water. As they took effect, she glanced at her watch. She was meeting Safran and hated to be late. She pulled on a coat over a chunky white jumper and jeans, then gathered up her suit bag for the twenty-four-hour laundrette. The egg stain had dried into the suit shoulder, marking it a whitish grey. She grabbed her keys and made the five-minute walk to the corner of Baffin Way. When she handed over her bag, she noted the recognition on the young clerk's face. *I guess he reads the tabloids.* She exchanged cash for a ticket and exited the tiny shop. Just as she left, she bumped into Najim Rashid, an old university friend who lived in the area.

She stopped and smiled in surprise, glad for a familiar face. 'Hey, stranger. It's been a long time.'

He paused in confusion, as if trying to place her.

'How are you?' She reached forward to greet him.

He baulked. 'Are you serious?'

She stopped and stepped back. 'Najim?' she asked, unsure what else to say.

'Are you serious?' he repeated slowly and loudly.

'What are you talking about?'

He scoffed. 'I mean *you*.' He plastered on a fake smile and mimicked her, his voice unnaturally high: '"Hey, long time, no see! How are you!"' He shook his head. 'Are you being fucking serious?'

'I don't—'

'You know, at first I thought you were just doing a job that you were assigned, like you had to do it – helping that girl accuse four Muslim boys of such *kachra* things. And then, the truth comes out about your *gora* fuck buddy. So why are you doing this? Some sort of rebellion against our community?'

'Najim, are you fucking with me?' She half expected him to break into laughter.

'No, but apparently everyone else is.'

Her jaw fell slack. She was truly speechless. Najim had been the ultimate playboy at university. Fresh from the constraints of his private single-sex college, he had fucked his way through first-year law class as if approaching Armageddon. He had spent three years trying to convince Zara to drink, back when she was still teetotal. He had accosted her in the library once, begging her to convince his girlfriend to have an abortion. And here he was, snarling at her with a hate that was shockingly genuine.

He took an irate step towards her. 'I know those boys. Have you seen what the papers have been saying about them? Have you seen what's happening to our community because of that white girl? Do you know they set fire to Leyton mosque?'

'I—' Zara faltered briefly. 'Listen, my case is about a young girl who was raped by four boys. What happens outside it has nothing to do with her.'

Najim held up his hands in mock defeat. 'Ah, I see. The media is just this siloed thing that has no effect on the case, on the boys, or on us, right?'

'What the hell happened to you?' snapped Zara. 'When did you become a crusader for the *brotherhood*?'

'This isn't about crusading,' he snapped back. 'This is about our community, about our honour. Can't you see the damage this is doing?'

Zara's voice grew cold. 'Would you suggest we discharge these boys on merit of their religion?'

'I'm saying you don't need to be a part of this.'

'Well, I *am*.'

He shook his head. 'And that's all you have to say about this?'

'Yes. That's all there is to say.'

'Fine. Well, we all know just how *honourable* you are.' Backing away from her, he spat on the ground near her boot. Then, he turned and stalked away.

Zara watched in astonishment, choking back angry words in his wake. Then, she spun and marched to the station. Twenty minutes later, she was in Hirsch's Bar on Old Street, scanning the room for Safran. She spotted him in a booth in a corner. She wished they had chosen a bigger bar, somewhere that offered the comfort of anonymity. She asked for a glass of wine and took a seat opposite him.

'So …' said Safran. 'I'm so miffed.'

'Why?' Zara pulled off her coat.

'I've been in chambers for what? Thirteen years now and not once have I got a headline case. You go and become a rape counsellor and you're in all the papers.'

She scoffed. 'We can trade places if you want. They're calling me a traitor, a bitch, a whore.'

'Yes, but are they saying anything bad?'

She sighed. 'I hope my family will feel the same way.'

'Ah, yes. Have you heard from them?'

'No.' Zara felt a kick of anxiety. 'I think it's best to give them some space. I hope that when the case is over, they'll understand that it doesn't matter what the papers say, I'm doing a job that matters.' She paused. 'At this stage, I don't know what will be worse: a not-guilty verdict that makes me look stupid, or a guilty one that brands me a traitor forever.'

Safran took a long drink of whisky. 'It doesn't matter what you say or do, Zar. They were always going to call you that.'

She grimaced. 'I knew this case would get bad but …' She searched for words to describe her frustration. 'I have to admit I've been blindsided by the sheer tribalism.' She thought of Najim's rage. 'I expected the fury and hyperbole from the ADL and the right-wing media, but I didn't think the Muslim community would so wholly, so *unthinkingly* band together in support of these boys. Do they really think that because they share a skin colour or belief system with them, that they're incapable of evil? Or that I, for the same reasons, should suspend a pursuit for justice?'

Safran shook his head. 'I think a bit of tribalism is to be expected, no? When Muslims are so gleefully targeted, don't you think a de-facto support system is important?'

Zara scowled. 'I don't buy that. That feeds into the idea that Muslims are all one big, featureless mass – and that those who aren't are traitors or Uncle Toms.' She winced. 'God, I fucking hate that phrase.'

Safran offered a doleful smile. 'Do you think you should sit the rest out?'

She baulked. 'Of course not.'

'Why not?'

'Because then it will look like I have something to be ashamed of.' She straightened in defiance. 'I'm not ashamed of what I'm doing.'

Safran studied her for a moment, noting the dark circles beneath her eyes. 'Zar, have you been sleeping?'

She shrugged ruefully. 'No, I'm too busy fucking white guys.'

He laughed a delighted laugh and drained his whisky in praise. 'Seriously though – have you been sleeping?'

'Some nights.'

'What are you worried about? The case?'

Again, she shrugged. 'The case. My family. Jodie.' Her

gaze turned upward, staving sudden tears. 'I'm just so tired.'

Safran leaned forward. 'Zar, listen, why don't you come and stay with me for a while? I know your cooking is awful – I can fatten you up again.'

She shook her head. 'No, I want to be somewhere familiar.'

He nodded. 'Okay, but the offer's always there.'

'I know. Thank you.' She leaned back in her chair and drained her glass, failing to notice the two Asian men behind Safran, watching them both intently.

CHAPTER NINE

Zara stood by the bathroom sink and peeled off her waterfall coat, shaking the rain off the soft cream folds. The damp sleeves of her smart black sweater clung clammily to her wrists as she rifled through her bag and pulled out a paddle brush. She swept it through her hair, swallowing up the tiny wisps of frizz and leaving it sleek once more. She gathered it up in a neat bun, taking care to secure the few stray strands. The reporters outside had already stolen a hundred pictures of her today but she wanted to look immaculate in the courtroom. More than ever, she needed her armour of poise.

Soon after she took her seat in the gallery, she heard a noise to her right. A man – white, balding and in his mid-forties – imitated grabbing her arse and shoving his crotch into it. Zara averted her gaze and fixed it on the judge. In her periphery, a marshal marched out the offending man while the reporters gleefully scribbled in his wake.

Judge Braun met Zara's gaze. Something in his expression dislodged a distant emotion: an unspoken yearning for forgiveness tinged with bitter shame. She choked it down and looked away.

'Good morning, ladies and gentlemen,' he began. 'I trust you have had an eventful weekend.' A brief pause. 'Before we start, I would like to take a moment to repeat what I said at the beginning of this trial. It is your duty as members of the jury to disregard anything related to this case that you see, read or hear outside this courtroom. This applies to everyone including the victim, the defendants, the counsel and even myself. I may look like a boring old codger but I have some interesting habits, I can tell you.'

A shock of laughter rose across the courtroom. Zara flushed with gratitude. The judge's words, deftly delivered, had defused the stifling tension.

Stark stood for his opening speech. 'Members of the jury, thank you for being here today. I'd like to start with a question if I may. Do any of you have teenage daughters?' More than half the jurors raised their hands. 'Then you'll know that there's no obsession stronger than that of a teenage girl's. Mine? She loves a boy called Tyler King. He's an American *YouTube star* of all things. I don't understand it but millions of teenage girls are in love with him. They watch his videos religiously, they send him messages of love on Twitter, tag him in provocative pictures on Instagram, send him marriage proposals and fan mail. They are, to all intents and purposes, genuinely in love: a normal teenager's way of processing the feelings of love before maturing.

'Amir Rabbani is no YouTube star but he's had a taste

of obsessive attention. Jodie Wolfe is obsessed with my client and has been so since they started secondary school five years ago. We will call witnesses that will corroborate this; witnesses that know Ms Wolfe better than any of us.

'Now, what does an obsessed teen do when a boy ignores her advances? She escalates her behaviour. She sends him suggestive images, she corners him at parties and she persists. She may even get him alone and offer him oral sex and relay it in all its descriptive glory. Amir's only mistake was relenting to Jodie. After five years of issuing rejection and rebuffs, he finally gave in to her. They went to the warehouse together and there, she proceeded to fulfil those promises she had so enticingly whispered in his ear. After the fact, when she saw that Amir's friends were watching, she realised that this wasn't the beginning of a blossoming romance, but a fleeting, purely physical encounter. She realised that Amir wasn't going to whisk her off her feet and announce to the whole school that now the cricket captain was committed to her and her only. She knew she would be ridiculed for offering herself up and so she hit back in the only way she could: she threatened to ruin their lives.

'Amir was too scared to admit the *consensual* sex he had with Jodie because he is exceedingly aware of the great expectations placed on him by his family. Amir was trying to protect his parents from pain. Jodie Wolfe lied because she was hurt – *emotionally*, not physically. Nobody forced her to do *anything*.

'Members of the jury, these four young boys are from honest, hardworking families. Farid Khan's father is a greengrocer and his mother runs a women's group that meets every week to learn English. They have worked their whole lives to give that boy the opportunity to pull his family out of poverty. This summer, he was awarded ten A-grades at GCSE. His request to defer his place in college because of this trial has been denied.

'Amir's father is a local businessman and has donated thousands to charities over the years, most recently saving the Brockney Bridge community centre. Amir's mother was a parent governor at his school for five years, heavily involved in policy.

'Mohammed's father is a local butcher who has worked for years in the community. His mother is a tailor and runs a small business of her own. Hassan's father works in a restaurant and his mother supports the family. These are good, hardworking people who have brought up their sons to be diligent and dedicated. To think these boys would throw it all away for a tryst with Jodie Wolfe is an insult to their families. You have a great responsibility. You must choose: do we opt to ruin four boys' lives because of one girl's unproven tale – sad as it may be – or do we listen to what the evidence actually proves? Again: do we listen to what the evidence actually *proves*?'

Stark regarded the jurors gravely. 'You must choose the only tenable verdict in this case. Amir Rabbani and his friends are *not guilty*. That is the *only* verdict that is just and fair and right. You *must* choose a verdict of not guilty. Thank you.'

Zara's heart felt leaden in her chest. Stark was an extraordinarily skilled barrister. Presenting the boys as products of the immigrant dream was deeply affecting. Their parents' struggles in the country and their efforts to raise good children chimed with Zara's own story. As she looked to the jury, she saw that they felt the same. They sat, still and solemn, in a patchwork of empathy and doubt. Could they really convict four promising young boys based on Jodie's word? How could they know for sure? Stark took a moment to allow his words to echo. Then he called his first witness.

Nina Sahari entered the witness box, dressed in a cream smock dress with a pale blue Peter Pan collar. Her silky black hair was tucked chastely behind her ears and her bare skin was radiant despite the sickly fluorescent lights.

She looks like a fucking choirgirl, thought Zara, unnaturally angry at Nina's betrayal.

'Ms Sahari, may I call you Nina?' asked Stark, pausing for permission. 'Nina, you went to the party in question on Thursday the twenty-seventh of June 2019. Is that correct?'

'Yes.'

'Who did you go with?'

'With Jodie, my best friend.' Nina's voice was calm and measured, her Valley Girl exuberance dialled down to zero.

'Did you meet her at the party?'

'No, I picked her up at her house. I was lending her some clothes.'

'Oh?'

'Yes, I was lending her this red lace top I thought she would look really pretty in. She asked me to bring these low-rise jeans I always wear at home. I—' she hesitated. 'I told her that she couldn't wear underwear with them because they were so low but she had a new pair she wanted to try out: a black thong.'

The courtroom stilled. Zara sat rigid as she watched Nina's wide-eyed innocence and false hesitation. She cast the jury a glance and was disheartened to see them entranced.

'And was there anything else unusual about that night?' asked Stark.

Leeson stood up to object. 'My Lord, highly ambiguous.'

The judge agreed. 'Mr Stark, ask something answerable please.'

Stark apologised and turned back to Nina. 'Did Jodie often wear clothes that exposed her underwear?'

'My Lord!' cried Leeson, back on his feet. 'This is appalling! Are we *really* to resort to victim blaming?'

'The Crown has a point, Mr Stark,' said the judge.

Stark bowed his head in contrition. 'I apologise but, My Lord, I'm not calling into question Ms Wolfe's morality. I merely want to establish if she was behaving out of character that night; if perhaps the party spirit had induced her to take actions she would not normally take.'

Judge Braun frowned. 'Okay, Mr Stark, but you're treading a fine line.'

'Thank you, My Lord.'

Zara stewed in her seat. The genteel parlance and joshing overtures of the British courts were charming on the surface but glossed over things so ugly. 'Appalling' is not the word she would use to describe Stark's question. Outrageous, disgraceful or fetid were more fitting.

Stark turned back to the witness box. 'I'll repeat the question: did Jodie often wear clothes that exposed her underwear?'

'No, she didn't,' said Nina. 'She … was embarrassed about the way she looked.'

'Can you tell me about Jodie's relationship with Amir Rabbani?'

Nina hesitated. 'Well, it wasn't really a relationship. Jodie was in love with Amir but it was entirely one-sided.'

'And do you have proof of this?' Stark picked up a piece of paper as if it were written proof.

Nina shrugged. 'Well, she would tell me. She would send him messages online and stare at him in the cafeteria. Everyone knew it. They teased Amir about it but he tried not to respond.'

Stark bowed his head a touch. 'Thank you for being honest, Ms Sahari. I know you're Jodie's best friend so this can't be easy.'

Zara exhaled a long, low breath. Was there anything as cold as the gilded betrayal of a teenage girl?

Stark continued: 'On the night of the twenty-seventh of June, did you see Amir with Jodie?'

'No, I lost her a little while after we arrived. I thought maybe she got bored and went home.'

'Did Jodie tell you what happened the next day?'

'No.'

'The day after that?'

'No.'

'The day after that?'

'No.'

Leeson sighed loudly from the prosecution table. Zara would have done exactly the same.

Stark moved on, a smile tugging at his lips. 'When did she tell you?'

'About a week later.'

'And what was your reaction?'

Nina grimaced. 'Honestly? I laughed. Everyone knew she was in love with Amir so I thought it was a joke.'

'My Lord.' Leeson was on his feet. 'The witness cannot possibly know the thoughts of "everyone" and she certainly cannot present it as testimony in court!'

'I'll accept that,' said Judge Braun. 'Members of the jury, please disregard the witness's last statement.'

Zara glared at Nina in the witness box. The damage had been done. It was clear that Jodie's best friend didn't believe her story. With that fact established, Stark happily handed the floor to the prosecuting team.

Leeson stood without greeting and said: 'Ms Sahari, would you say that you are insecure?'

The girl blinked in surprise. 'I'm sorry?'

'Would you say that you are insecure?'

She frowned. 'I would say all sixteen-year-old girls are.'

Good answer, thought Zara. There was more to this girl than her sweet smile and perfect hair.

Leeson remained stony-faced. 'Can you answer the question?'

'Not especially insecure, no.'

Leeson looked to the judge. 'My Lord, if you will indulge me, I'd like to ask some tangential questions to establish the credibility of the witness.' He paused for permission, then turned back to Nina. 'Ms Sahari, are you asked out on a lot of dates?'

She shrugged. 'Yes, I guess so.'

'Has Amir ever asked you out?'

She stilled, eyes flicking to the dock. 'No ... why?'

'Is it true that you asked Amir out to year ten prom and he said no?'

Nina reddened. 'I didn't ask him out. I— I just suggested that we could go together.'

'And did you go together?'

'No.'

Leeson feigned surprise. 'I see. Would it be fair to say that Amir Rabbani is one of the few boys at your school that you couldn't have?'

Nina faltered. 'I never tried to have him so I wouldn't know.'

'Did it irk you when your best friend told you that Amir

had forced himself upon her? The same Amir who had summarily rejected you?'

'No. Of course not!'

'Nina, isn't it true that you were involved in a physical altercation – a *catfight* – with the girl Amir *did* take to the prom?'

'It wasn't my fault. She started it.'

'There is evidence that during this fight, you shouted the words "back off him, you bitch, or I'll kill you". Who was the "him" you were talking about?'

Nina's eyes narrowed. 'I didn't think she was good for Amir.'

A murmur rose in the courtroom. Zara tried not to smile as she noted the change in Nina's body language: chest puffed out defiantly, chin held high haughtily.

'And you *were* good for Amir?' asked Leeson.

'It wasn't like that.' Nina's sweet tone was now testy.

'Yes, it was, Ms Sahari. You imagined yourself with Amir – together the Queen and King of your school – but he repeatedly rebuffed you and when you heard that he forced himself on your best friend, you were livid, weren't you?'

'No!' The word snapped with disgust.

'You were consumed by jealousy weren't you, Nina? That's why you're here? To discredit Jodie for your own gain?'

'No.' Nina's face flushed with colour.

'Why are you lying, Nina?'

'I'm not.' Her voice grew high.

'You *are* lying. Why?'

'I'm not!'

'You are.'

'I'm not fucking lying!' Nina's voice rang high and clear across the courtroom, cutting through the hushed surprise.

Leeson nodded once. 'I have no more questions, My Lord.'

Zara caught the trace of victory dancing on his lips. With a glance around the courtroom, she too allowed herself a smile.

*

In the court cafeteria, Zara spotted Mia a few tables over. She picked up her tray and headed over. 'Please don't say you're here to see me. I'm not sure I can handle another surprise.'

Mia shook her head and swallowed a mouthful of lasagne. 'No, I'm testifying on another case.' She gestured to the seat opposite and waited as Zara slid in. 'The crowds are quieter today.'

Zara shrugged. 'It's still early.'

'You want me to stick around this evening? I heard things got ugly on Thursday.'

Zara felt a jolt of unease. There was something uniquely alarming about a mob on the edge of control, but she refused to be intimidated. 'Thank you, but I'll be fine.'

Mia studied her for a minute, then set down her fork. 'Listen, one thing I've learnt in this job is that it's okay to take slack when you get it. You don't always have to be clutching the end of a rope and desperately dragging yourself up. If someone offers you a respite, it's okay to accept.'

Zara nodded. 'I know.'

Mia pushed away her tray. 'I don't think you do. I'll spare you the life story but I'll tell you this: when I joined the force, I wouldn't give an inch. I knew I had to be twice as good to get half the praise. I knew I couldn't show weakness. I knew I had to be brave. I knew I had to be amazing every single day of every single week. Or so I thought. I've seen grown men break down after a harrowing interview, throw up at crime scenes, drink on the job, go mad with insomnia. I've seen a six foot four hulk of a cop huddled in a corner, sobbing out his guts. So let me repeat myself: it's okay to take slack when you can get it.'

Zara swallowed. After a long moment, she said, 'You're right.' She cleared her throat. 'You're right and I'd be really bloody grateful if you could wait for me tonight.'

Mia nodded once. 'I'll be there.' She glanced at her watch, then gathered up her trash and left Zara at the table, head hung low and shoulders hunched forward.

*

The anticipation was almost predatory in vigour. The court reporters sat poised like jackals, their bodies angled forward as if readying to pounce. Zara recognised one in the front row: the haughty blonde who had chased her way into Jodie's home. The woman sat there now, chin high and pen poised as if she missing a single word would shake the very foundations of truth and justice. Next to her sat a wizened broadsheet reporter. His markedly aloof stance was betrayed by his eyes which darted left and right, then back and forth, restless in expectation. The twelve jurors waited in silence. The older Asian woman in the front row held her scarf to her chest like a concerned mother watching her son. Amir stood in the witness box with his green eyes lowered, solemn and respectful. Dressed in a grey suit, salmon shirt and thin black tie, he looked handsome and wholesome, an exemplary mix of East and West.

'Amir, I know this has been a difficult time for you,' started Stark. 'It's not easy to stay calm like you have, so for that I commend you. Today, I will ask you some difficult questions and I want you to answer honestly and as accurately as possible. Does that sound okay?'

'Yes, sir.'

Stark nodded his thanks. 'Four days ago, we heard the testimony of a young woman called Sophie Patel with whom you had an encounter two years ago. Do you agree with her opinion that you assaulted her?'

'No, sir.'

'And why is that?'

Amir bit his lip. 'Because I thought she was okay with

it. I'm not the kind of person that would force myself on a woman. I have never done that.'

'Ms Patel admitted that she said no only after the fact. Is that correct?'

'That's right. As soon as I realised she didn't want to go any further, I stopped.'

'Thank you. Now, I want to take you to the evening of Thursday the twenty-seventh of June 2019. When, in the evening, did you come across Jodie Wolfe?'

Amir frowned. 'I saw her sitting on a wall outside the party. The boys and I had had enough of the bad pop music and just wanted to relax. They were heading over to the warehouse and I said I would catch up.'

'Why?'

'I wanted to see if Jodie was okay. She— she's a bit of a loner and everyone teases me about her but I've always felt some responsibility towards her. We went to the same primary school and I know what she went through there. I felt protective of her.'

Zara's lips drew open, then closed as if snuffing words already on her tongue. How easily this young boy lied.

'Did you tell Jodie that Nina was at a private party?'

Amir shook his head. 'No, sir. That is absolutely not true. I told her that some of us were relaxing at the warehouse and she could come if she wanted to. I didn't lie to her or try to persuade her to come.'

'What did she say?'

'She said okay.'

'So you went to the warehouse? Did you hold hands along the way?'

Amir's gaze dipped to the floor. 'She— she reached out and held mine. I was embarrassed but I didn't let go. No one was around so I let her.'

'Did she trip and grab your hand to steady herself, as she claims?'

'No, sir.'

Zara studied him as he spoke. She ran through the three different versions of that one small action: first, that they mutually held hands after Amir told Jodie that he wanted to kiss her; second, that Jodie tripped, fell and righted herself with his help; and third, that Jodie had clasped his hand in a show of devotion. If the first were true as Jodie promised Zara, then both she and Amir had lied in court. Zara shifted in her seat and continued to watch.

'What happened when you reached the warehouse?' asked Stark.

Amir pinched the tip of his tie with an index finger and thumb. 'I couldn't find the boys. She started to get giggly because she thought I had brought her there to be alone. She started to get all touchy with me. She … she went to the window and asked me to come over and look at the stars. She had her back to me. When I was behind her, she pressed into me really hard and – I couldn't help it – I started to react.' The boy's face flushed red.

Zara's skin felt hot. His branding of Jodie as a precocious

temptress was so incongruous, so fantastically creative, that she almost scoffed out loud.

'What did you do?' asked Stark.

'At first, nothing. She just kept rubbing against me. I could see her thong above her jeans and it—' Amir grimaced. 'She told me to close my eyes and she whispered in my ear that she would take me in her mouth. I— I closed my eyes. She slid down, unzipped me and put her mouth around me.'

'What happened after this?'

'Well, after a while, I …' The boy's face twisted in embarrassment.

'You ejaculated?'

'Yes.'

'Where?'

Amir was mortified. 'She pulled away so it was sort of on her top.'

'Did she say anything?'

'We didn't have time to talk. The boys – I didn't know they had come in – started cheering and whistling. They couldn't believe what I was doing. They started to make fun of us – not just her, but both of us. They were calling me names and teasing. I tried to make light of it but I think I upset her.'

'Why do you think you upset her?'

'Well, I said something mean.' Guilt danced across his face. 'I said something like "pussy's pussy" and I laughed. I know that's horrible, but I was on the spot. I was so embarrassed, so I just said the first thing that came to my mind. The boys started teasing her and joking around.'

'How so?'

'Just saying things like "Jodie! We didn't know you had it *in* you!" and "How does Amir taste?" Just really, really stupid things. She began to cry. I told the boys to get lost. They wouldn't, so I got angry and shouted at them. They left. I told Jodie I was sorry and then I left too.'

'You left her there?'

Amir cringed. 'Yes. I'm sorry I did that but I thought she was okay. I didn't know that any of this would happen. I made a mistake – *me* – but my friends didn't do anything wrong.' He turned to the jury. 'I swear to you they didn't do anything.'

Stark nodded sagely. 'When did you next have contact with Jodie?'

'The next time was when she started to Snapchat me.'

'Forty-nine times?'

'Yes. I didn't answer because I didn't want to give her the wrong idea. I know it sounds bad after what happened but it was a moment of weakness. I didn't want to string her along.'

Stark murmured in sympathy. 'Amir, when the police first came to you, you denied everything. You said you had barely seen Jodie that night. Your account changed later on. Why is this?'

'I— I said I didn't see her because I didn't want my family to know.' He looked up at his father. 'Baba, I'm so sorry.' His voice cracked.

Zara winced. That crack of emotion would go right to the heart of any parent on the jury.

Amir continued, 'My parents have raised me to be a good person. They taught me honour and modesty and restraint. I didn't want to disappoint them. I didn't want them to know.' He took a deep breath. 'When I realised they were going to find out anyway, I told them what really happened.'

'And if you could do it all again, would you give the true version of events from the very beginning?'

'Yes, I would. Absolutely. No question at all.'

'Thank you, Amir.' Stark turned to the bench. 'I have no more questions, My Lord.'

Amir shifted in the witness box. His right fist was cradled in his left palm and his legs stood apart as if bracing for impact.

Leeson stood. 'Amir, you say you couldn't "find the boys" when you got to the warehouse. Where did they go?'

'I don't know. It's a big warehouse.'

'So you knew there was a chance that they would come upon you and despite being so concerned about your reputation, you decided to have oral sex with Jodie anyway? Is that correct?'

Amir hesitated. 'I— yes, that's correct.'

'So you didn't care about your friends finding you?' Leeson was combative.

'I wasn't really thinking.'

'You weren't really thinking? And were you thinking

when your friends held her down and raped her one after the other?'

Stark was on his feet. 'My Lord, my learned friend is being wilfully inflammatory!' His vowels were round with exaggerated incredulity.

Leeson conceded before the judge could speak, having known full well that his question would be challenged. He turned back to Amir. 'Mr Rabbani, you mentioned that you felt a responsibility toward Jodie; that you went to primary school with her and saw what she went through. Can you tell me a bit more about this? What did she go through?'

Amir's dark lashes fluttered in thought. 'Kids would bully her, call her names, sometimes push her around.'

'What kind of names?'

The boy hesitated. 'She was known as "fish face". They'd call her ugly, a monster, a dog – all sorts.'

'And this continued in secondary school?'

'A bit, but not as much.'

'How did she handle this?'

He shrugged. 'She was just quiet. She didn't fight back, she just seemed sad.'

'Is it fair to say that Jodie has been through a lot of abuse – verbal and even physical?'

'Yes.'

'And she dealt with this by largely ignoring it?'

'Yes.'

'Okay, so if as you say, all Jodie faced that night was a bit of verbal teasing, why would she suddenly have such a nuclear reaction? If she is accustomed to being bullied, being called ugly as a dog, being pushed around, why would she react so badly to a bit of light teasing by your friends? Can you explain that?'

'I guess she felt ashamed because of what happened between us.' Amir remained calm and measured.

Zara could sense disappointment spidering across the room. For weeks, the prosecution had searched for a Eureka moment, a single sticking point, an ingenious question or a new insight that would throw Amir off and hurt his credibility but they had drawn a blank. The boy was so well rehearsed that Leeson failed to ruffle him. Eventually, after an anti-climactic hour of questioning, Amir was released from the witness box.

Court soon drew to a close and Zara headed to the Great Hall to wait for Mia. She thought over Amir's testimony, trying to find holes where there were none. He was simply too earnest, too likeable, too attractive a witness. He had been sharp, clear and contrite compared with Jodie's stilted, wilting style of speech delivered from her impossibly mangled face. All Stark had to do was instil reasonable doubt – not hard with a witness like Amir.

Zara spotted Mia crossing the hall and greeted her with a handshake.

'How did it go?' asked the detective.

Zara sighed. 'Not well. I'll update you on the way home.'

Mia nodded at the corridor. 'DC Dexter's just collecting

Leeson. We want to make sure we get both of you safely home.'

'I appreciate it.'

'Not at all.'

Zara hesitated. 'No, I mean it. I'm glad you're here.'

Mia nodded once, the way police officers did in the movies. 'Like I said, not at all.'

Soon joined by Leeson and Dexter, they headed out together. Immediately, the crowds burst into action and that familiar tune rang out over the cool December mist.

'Uncle Tom, Uncle Tom, Uncle Tom!' As before, the jeers were accompanied by pictures of Zara in obscene, submissive poses. Leeson was unperturbed. He, the Oxbridge-educated white man, was somehow excused for seeking justice against four Muslim boys. Zara on the other hand was pilloried as a traitor. She felt a bitter, coppery taste in her mouth as they walked a fine line between the two crowds. As she entered the waiting car, she felt a deep pang of sorrow at the fissures cracking open across her beloved hometown – sorrow and also fear because the worst was yet to come.

*

The sound roused Jodie's attention: a pair of grace notes, C followed by A, that told her she had a new message. She pushed herself off the bed and ambled to the tiny desk. There, on her phone, was a message from Nina.

> Jodie, I hope you can forgive me for testifying in court. You know I don't believe you – I told you that from the start – so you can't hate me. Listen, I'm messaging you to make you aware of this forum. You should report them so the hosting company will take it down.

Jodie instinctively clicked on the link. It was filled with pages and pages of pictures: Jodie, mouth open against the groins of different men. Large red captions with garish green drop-shadows accompanied the images. One of her and obese comedian Stevie G read, 'Finally! Someone hungry enough found Stevie's dick.'

Other captions called her a whore, a dog, a liar. On page three, she found an animated gif of her and a pig, obscene sounds accompanying the writhing and rolling. It made her want to gag. She continued to scroll, compelled to do it. When she reached the end, she returned to Nina's message and deleted it. She knew what game was being played here. She closed her eyes and lay her head in her hands. This was not what she had intended. This was never what she had wanted.

Her phone chimed again, this time with a text from Zara to say she was waiting outside. Jodie padded down the hall and quietly opened the door.

Zara held out a paper bag. 'I didn't have a chance to get to anywhere decent today, so it's just a sandwich I'm afraid.'

Jodie flushed with gratitude, unspeakably grateful for

these small concessions; the way Zara did not ring the doorbell lest it disturb Christine from her doze, or how she spoke to her like an adult, or the time she casually gave Jodie a bag from Boots filled to the brim with tampons because she was 'clearing out the medicine cabinet'.

'Thank you.' Jodie took the bag and they retreated to her room. 'How was it today?'

Zara perched on a plastic chair. 'It was okay.' Her lips curled in a plaintive smile. 'Amir's testimony was strong, but we anticipated that.' She waved a hand at the window as if he might be standing outside. 'Amir is the leader of the gang, the school cricket captain and he knows how to work a crowd, so he was always going to do well in the witness box.'

Jodie's fingers dug into her palm.

'But Hassan is up next and he won't perform as well. Even his friends can barely stand him.' Zara waited for a response. 'How are you doing?' she asked.

Jodie shrugged. 'I'm okay.' She slid backwards on her bed and leaned against the wall. 'I just … I don't know what to be.' She gestured at Zara. 'I look at you and you're a certain way and your investigator Erin is a certain way and Mia is a certain way, and I— I don't know what to be.'

Zara studied her. 'What do you mean?'

Jodie sighed as if she too were confused. After a moment of thought, she said, 'What I mean is that you're bold and forceful, Erin is cool and cunning, Mia is calm and unshakable. I'm trying to be those things. I'm trying to be strong and serious and unshakable, but I'm none of those things.' She held a hand to her chest. 'I feel hurt and weak and …' Her voice was hoarse. 'I feel small.'

'Oh, Jodie.' Zara shook her head. 'Do you think I was this way at sixteen? Do you think Mia was like that at your age? Women aren't born warriors; we learn to fight because we have to.'

Tears pooled in Jodie's eyes. 'I'm tired of fighting.'

'I know you are, but it's worth the fight and we're going to get through this.'

Jodie nodded listlessly.

Over the next half an hour, Zara tried hard to cheer her and Jodie duly obliged, but their levity held an ersatz quality. They were both playing roles – each upbeat to please the other – and eventually they succumbed to silence. They were in no mood for gallows humour, only melancholy.

Before long, they heard stirring in the living room and Jodie pointed at the door. 'You should probably go before she wakes up.'

Zara nodded and stood. 'I'll call you after court tomorrow.' She pointed at the paper bag. 'There's a muffin in there too. Lemon – your favourite.'

Jodie watched her go and thought what a privilege it was that someone knew her favourite *anything*.

*

Zara dropped her Céline bag on the floor and slumped on the sofa in exhaustion. She thought over her meeting with Jodie with a throbbing sense of unease. The girl's resolve was breaking, the mortar melting in her wall of will. 'It's worth the fight' Zara had told her, but even she worried that the worst was yet to come.

She thought of all the injustices of Jodie's young life. Did Zara really owe more to her community and its nebulous idea of loyalty than to a beleaguered young girl who so clearly needed help? Wasn't this why she had left chambers – to actually do some good?

The word hitched in her mind, drawing her lips into a thin, bitter line. 'Good.' She felt undeserving of it, bereft of its comfort and warmth. She measured up once, bolstered by good grades and modest dress and deference to the men in her life. But then she began to make her own choices. She chose to leave her marriage and prompt those words from her father that tore her apart. She chose to keep distance from family, she chose to sleep with Michael Attali and she chose to support Jodie. Did those decisions exclude her from 'good'?

She pulled off her coat and grappled for her bag, then drew out a bottle of Diazepam. As the hum of questions grew loud in her mind, she swallowed two pills in quick succession, then lay her head on a soft cream cushion. Just as she edged past consciousness, her phone sounded a sharp reminder. Neat white letters spelled 'Pick up dry cleaning' on the screen. Zara looked groggily at her watch.

It was late but the laundrette was close by and the air would do her good. She changed out of her shirt and skirt into a pair of jeans and a jumper. She pulled her coat back on, grabbed her purse and left the flat. The trees outside were stark against the moon, their beckoning arms spindly and sparse. As she walked, the late autumn wind snaked beneath her coat, making it billow around her. It was bracing but in a vaguely pleasant way, as if whipping away the old and making space for new.

'Cold tonight, yes, miss?' Mr Lee welcomed her into the stuffy warmth of the laundrette.

'Yes, very cold.' She handed over her ticket and reached for something to say. The lull made her think of Luka and his easy ability to converse with strangers, unaffected by British reserve. She remembered standing right there with him in January as he and Mr Lee chatted away about family, business and women. Zara had stood in silence, waiting awkwardly for them to finish. Tonight, calmed by the Diazepam, she smiled gently and wished Mr Lee goodnight. Bundling the suit under one arm, she stepped back out into darkness and walked idly towards home.

When the case was over, perhaps she would take a holiday. She had worked so long and so numbly that she had forgotten what living really was. When Jodie was no longer beneath her wing and all of this was over, perhaps she could find her way back to who she used to be. 'Back to "good",' she said softly, the word hopeful on her tongue.

She was lost in these gently stirring thoughts when she

noticed the footsteps echoing her own. She glanced back at the street which shifted and paused in the inky blue darkness. Cars lined each side of the road, the moonlight splashing in pools on the roofs. There was no sound other than the soft rustle of her suit in plastic wrap. She scanned the street and the bordering buildings. On one side stood a large brick warehouse, repurposed as a co-working space for start-ups. On the other was a patch of green which now stood black and empty. She counted down from five and then started to walk again. Sure enough, there was a subtle pounding of feet echoing her own. She paused again and turned around, scanning the street once more.

'Hello?' she called out. When there was no reply, she laughed out loud to relieve the tension. It came out shrill and strangled. She turned back round. This time, there was the unmistakable thud of boots on concrete. She crossed the road to quash her paranoia. With a thumping heart, she realised that the footsteps were following. She turned then and saw two men wearing caps and bandanas advancing in her wake. She quickened her pace and they did too. Panic rose in her throat, then roared at her to run. Her reflexes, blunt from the Diazepam, held her there for a second too long. Her suit fell to the floor in a whisper and, then, they were on her.

A thick hand clamped around her mouth and an arm grabbed her waist from behind. She shrieked but the sound was swallowed by skin. They dragged her into an alley and slammed her against a wall. Her head ricocheted off the brick, sending giant black flowers blooming in her vision. She held up two hands and shielded her face.

'Fuckin' whore,' said the smaller of the two men. His Mancunian accent held an Asian twang.

The bigger of the two slapped her across the face. Still in a daze, her head snapped to one side and her cheek hit brick with a sickening crunch. Horror rendered her inert, unable even to scream. A heavy fist punched her in the gut, jolting her body upward. She doubled over with a strangled cry, then crumpled to the ground. A kick to her stomach sent a wave of pain strafing through her body.

The smaller man pulled her hair, lifting her head off the ground. He waggled it back and forth and laughed when she closed her eyes. 'You like that, you *harami*? You like it when we play rough?'

The second man reached down and slapped her, making her ear pulse with pain. Then, he pulled out a bottle of clear liquid. 'You love that little *kuffar* of yours so much, we're gonna rearrange your face like hers.' He unscrewed the cap, his eyes manic above a black bandana.

Zara screamed but the sound had no lungs behind it, like the rustling of fallen leaves.

He taunted her with the bottle, watching her features contract in terror. 'You're gonna look just like that little whore of yours and then we'll see how many white men will fuck you.'

Gathering air in her lungs, she let out a howling scream, but it was too late: he emptied the liquid all over her face, laughing as she shrieked in terror. Then, with a final kick to her torso, they ran off into the night. She listened to their retreating footsteps and, without further thought or feeling, slipped into a welcome darkness.

*

The early dawn light filtered through curtains that were not quite closed. A watery sliver fell on the stark white tiles in a single unbroken line. Somewhere close by, machines beeped quietly, their steady rhythm lending Zara comfort. She heard a soft knock on the hospital door and a creaking yawn as it opened. Her mother stood at the threshold, her silhouette bulky in a black hijab and thick winter coat. She stepped inside the room and walked to Zara's side.

'*Kitha beh?*' she asked. The common Bengali phrase literally meant 'what?' but held a sea of jumbled emotion. It was an enquiry, an entreaty, an implication and an accusation. *What* has happened? *What* can I do to help you? *What* did you do to deserve this? *What* have you done wrong?

Zara bit her lower lip to keep it from trembling. Even in her state, with a black eye and bruised rib, she bore witness to the fact that tears in her family went against decorum.

Her mother studied her face and though her voice was tight with anguish, her chin was high and her jaw set firm. 'What did they do to you?'

Zara swallowed. 'It could have been worse.' Her words

were unintentionally glib. What she meant was it really *could* have been worse. The bottle of clear liquid with which she was taunted – *we're gonna rearrange your face* – could have really been acid as feared. It turns out her attackers were sadists, reaping pleasure from her terror as they drenched her in vodka. Zara shrank beneath the memory, rendered now in blues and blacks as if recalling a scene from a movie.

Her mother pulled a chair closer. 'Just look at what they did to you.'

'It's just a black eye,' said Zara. Her voice laboured beneath a breezy tone.

Fatima picked up a corner of the light blue blanket and tucked it beneath the mattress, a habit built from rearing four children. 'Your sisters are outside,' she said. 'The doctors won't let them in.' She threaded her fingers in her lap, looking suddenly old. She was silent for a moment then said, 'It is time to stop now.' The words were matter of fact, casual even, as if relaying prosaic news.

Zara shifted in the bed and tried not to wince from pain. 'Mum, it's not like it'll happen again.'

Fatima leaned forward in her seat, fingertips pressed together as if in plea. 'I know you think you're doing your job but this is bigger now. People are calling you an apostate. Do you know what happens to apostates in Islam?'

Zara sighed. 'We're in London, not Tehran.'

'Do you think it's as simple as that? Do you think the English police can protect you?'

Zara shook her head. 'I have to do this or they've won.'

'Who?' Fatima's voice was hard like flint. 'Who is "they"? Who are you fighting, Zara? *What* are you fighting for?'

Zara pressed two palms on the bed and shifted herself up. 'I'm fighting for Jodie. I have to see this through.' She caught the derision on her mother's face and paused to order her thoughts. 'Can't you see, Mum? Oppression doesn't spread through men with guns, or bombs on trains. Oppression spreads when women like you tell their daughters to marry a certain man, or wear a certain dress, or work a certain job. It happens when women like you tell us – gently and with all the love in the world – not to peek above the parapet, instead to stay at home, to be quiet, to be kind, to be *good*.' The last word curdled in her mouth. 'Don't you see? I *have* to finish this.'

Her mother blinked as the sepia dawn washed the room in light. She reached out and brushed Zara's chin, lifting it just a touch. 'My daughter. Look at what they did to you.' She blinked. 'It's a good thing your father's not here. He couldn't bear to see you like this.'

Zara flinched with surprise. She and her mother never spoke of her father.

'You were always his favourite – you know that, don't you?'

Zara swallowed hard and gripped the sheet in her fists.

'What are you doing, Zara?' Her mother searched her face. 'You think because your father's gone, everything was lost along with him?' She gestured to the door. 'You don't think about your sisters? You don't think about me? You don't think what would happen if we lost you too?' Her voice hitched on the last note. 'Even your brother was stunned when he heard what happened. He finds it hard to show it but he cares about you. Please stop this now.'

Zara blinked back tears but said nothing to break her silence.

'Okay,' said Fatima after a long moment. 'You fight the demons that haunt you at night but when this is over, you come back to us because we're the ones who are still here.' She tapped Zara's hand. 'You understand? We're still here.' With that, she stood and left the room.

As the door whispered shut, Zara saw her sisters outside, hushing their children in the cold December dawn. The sight of them in a funereal huddle made her heart blister and ache. Despite everything, here they were in the lobby outside, hushing their children and waiting for news. Zara closed her eyes and, with that simple action, lost the reins on her emotion. Guilt and fear welled in her throat and found their way out in angry, staccato sobs. She curled her hands in fists and wept with horror and rage and pain.

*

'I'm on!' shouted Paul, a tall, muscular boy who was as clumsy as he was big. Farid slid the ball to Stephen instead, a graceful player who was light on his feet.

'Wanker!' shouted Paul.

Farid smiled. It felt good to spend a Sunday on the field, to get some air into his lungs and forget about the case altogether. Court had been adjourned for the week to ease tensions after Zara's attack. Farid pitied her, but couldn't deny that the break had helped him.

Stephen dribbled forward, evaded three defenders, then calmly slotted the ball into the net. The team erupted in joy. They had been 2-1 down and his goal equalised with five minutes to go.

Paul caught up with Farid, boorishly grabbed him into a headlock and messed up his hair with a knuckle. After some protest, he released Farid and playfully slapped his back. 'I'm glad you stopped being a pussy about playing just coz of your minor issues with the feds.'

Farid grinned. 'It's good to be back.' Here on the field, he wasn't the sensible, studious one who struggled with rowdy friends. He wasn't the eldest child with three siblings to oversee. Here, he was an equal and things still felt like they might be okay.

The ball sailed towards him. As a midfielder, he was quick and agile and frequently provided assists for the strikers. This time, they were all too wide to receive the ball so he ran forward and skipped past two boys. He stumbled, righted himself, and continued. He slipped past another defender and then, taking a breath, aimed and fired a powerful shot past the keeper, just as the whistle sounded high across the pitch. He heard his teammates roar and run towards him like a stampede of bulls. And then he was enveloped in them, bundled to the floor beneath a heap of bodies, jubilantly shouting their victory chant. There, caught in the midst of the scrum, he felt truly happy for the first time in months.

Later, when the banter died down and the players showered and changed, they agreed to continue celebrations at the Nando's in Mile End. Farid glanced down at his watch. He had to get home for curfew, so he offered his partings and went on his way. As he walked back across the field, he looked up to the hill, hoping to see the tall, dark-haired girl with the white, white skin and red, red lips. He felt something stir in him and shook his head with a smile. He hadn't felt sexual desire in months. He thought of Erin in that short black skirt. He pictured his hand running up her leg and stroking her through those sheer patterned tights.

He laughed out loud. *I'm not dead yet!*

CHAPTER TEN

Zara twisted open the cap and gripped the base of the brown glass bottle. Its smooth, round bulk felt comforting in her hand. She reached forward and with a sick lurching in her stomach tipped the bottle over the toilet. Two yellow pills fell out and clinked against the ceramic bowl then dipped beneath the water. The rest clung together inside the bottleneck. She shook it to free the pills and watched them tumble out. With three shallow breaths, she reached out and flushed. Instead of panic, she felt a jittery pride. The battle was far from over but this felt like an important start. It was a statement of intention, a quiet admission that she had a problem, and a vow to get better; to *be* better. She threw the bottle in the bin, washed her hands and returned to the kitchen.

Safran stood next to the cooker and threw her a frown. 'Seriously, Zar? You can't boil a pot of rice?'

She picked up the spatula. 'My sisters like to cook, so I never needed to learn.'

He smiled. 'Ah, so the truth comes out. You play the

tortured Muslim girl so well, when actually you were a princess who never set foot in the kitchen.' He took the saucepan off the hob. 'I, on the other hand, was beaten at every possible opportunity.'

Zara rolled her eyes. 'Is that so? Your parents are amazing and even you know it.'

'They are but they didn't let me get away with anything.' His dimples curved deep in his cheeks. 'Whenever my brother and I did something wrong, we would purposely hide all the hard-soled shoes and place the softest slippers closest to Mum. That way, when she found out and grabbed for the closest thing, she would get the slipper.' He laughed. 'God, we were such monsters.'

Zara's smile was wistful. 'At least her actions were honest. I sometimes wonder if anyone in my family has ever said or done what they actually wanted.'

Safran tapped her hand with the spatula. '*You* don't do too badly.'

'Yeah and that's the trouble.' She wrapped her oversized cardigan around her and watched him for a moment. 'Listen, I haven't said this but I appreciate what you've done for me. Staying here this week has been like a reset button.'

He met her gaze. She had covered her bruise with makeup, but its purple-brown outline could still be seen in the skin beneath her right eye. He reached forward and tucked a strand of her hair behind her ear. 'Come on, Zar. We don't do sentimental.'

She smiled thinly and turned towards the window, hiding the tears clotting in her throat. In the week since the attack, she had found herself faltering at the smallest things: a dog dying in the movie last night, a saccharine advert on TV, or heartfelt ballad on Heart FM that Safran listened to ironically. The attack seemed to have melted her nerve. Being with Safran helped. He did not indulge her, but was brisk, almost brutal, in getting her back on her feet.

He drained the rice. Without turning, he said, 'You know you don't need to be there, right?'

Zara squared her shoulders. Court resumed the next day and she was determined to be present. Stuart had urged her to take more time off, but she had roundly refused. 'I do need to be there, or the thugs will have won,' she told him as she told Safran now. In truth, she was scared that if she stayed home tomorrow, she might never feel safe in leaving again.

Safran handed her a glass of water. 'If you want me to come with you, I will.'

Zara instinctively began to decline, but then stopped. After a beat, she said, 'Do you know what, Saf? That would be amazing.'

He nodded. 'Zara the Brave,' he said quietly as if her latest act were her most courageous of all.

*

Judge Braun greeted the assembly with unusual cheer. He was clearly pleased to be back on track. He glanced to the gallery and noted Zara's presence. Today, she was dressed like the lawyer she used to be: dark Oscar de la Renta suit, leather Gianvito Rossi heels, black hair cascading to her waist, subtle makeup and a bulletproof sense of confidence. What the judge couldn't see from his bench was that her fists were balled so tight, her knuckles were turning white, or that her feet tap-tapped on the floor to a silent and skittish beat.

As he readied to begin, the door from his chambers swung open. A slight woman with short copper hair walked in and handed over a piece of paper. He took the sheet and skimmed it, his features tightening as he read. He spoke to the woman in muted confusion. After a few moments, he turned to the court.

'Mr Albany, the defendant Farid Khan—'

Farid's barrister stood. 'My Lord, I apologise. I believe Mr Khan is on his way. I have yet to make contact with him but I am sure he—'

'Sit down please, Mr Albany.' The judge's hands were on the bench, fingers knitted as if in prayer. 'I have just received some distressing news.' He paused and cleared his throat. The square of his shoulders bowed slightly and his gaze dipped briefly low. 'The defendant Farid Khan was involved in an altercation last night. He was taken to A&E with injuries to his head and torso. The doctors worked to revive him for several hours but he succumbed to his injuries. Farid Khan was pronounced dead at eleven forty-one last night.'

His words billowed across the room, the shock spreading like backdraft. There was momentary silence and, then, a discordant explosion of noise. Zara watched the scene unfold as if in slow motion.

In the dock, Amir crumpled as if his very spine had snapped in two. 'He didn't do anything,' he said numbly. 'Farid didn't do anything. He just—'

Mo sat in deathly stillness. The colour drained from his face but he did not make a sound.

Hassan next to him sprang against the glass and craned towards the gallery. 'Where is Jodie, that fucking bitch?' The rage shook in his voice as he snapped away from a marshal's grip. He spotted Zara and jabbed a finger towards her with the dull clink of skin on glass. 'This is your fault, you fucking cunt! Look what you've done! Look what you've done!' A sob caught in his throat as the marshal pulled him back from the glass, two sturdy hands heavy on his shoulders.

Zara shrank back in her seat as the judge's call for calm boomed across the courtroom. It had a strange, academic quality, as if she were detached from her body and observing the scene from elsewhere or hearing his voice through a pneumatic tube. She couldn't reconcile the words with reality, or follow them to a logical conclusion.

When shock finally ceded to silence, the judge continued to speak. 'Mr Khan's family was informed last night,' he explained. 'Sadly, I have no more information.' He turned to Farid's barrister. 'Mr Albany, clearly the case against your client can go no further. With respect to the remaining defendants, given the time of the year, I propose we continue as planned.'

Stark intervened. 'My Lord, may I respectfully suggest a short adjournment. My client and his fellow defendants are clearly in no state to give evidence.'

Amir was weeping into his knees while Mo sat stunned and silent.

'Does the Crown have any objections to this?' asked the judge.

'No, My Lord,' said Leeson. 'We're happy to reconvene in a day or two should that help maintain clarity in the case.'

'Very well.' Judge Braun apologised to the jury and adjourned court for that day and the next.

Zara was now on her feet, her grip tight on Safran's arm. 'I need to call Mia,' she said. 'We need to get Jodie to a safe place right now.'

Swelling dread sparked memories of her own attack: the thick hand around her mouth, the crunch of bone on brick, that moment of red terror and then distant relief when it was pungent vodka and not acid that splashed across her skin. The memory was harsh and discordant in her mind and gripped her now in its tentacles of panic. Safran steadied her and led her from the courtroom to the exit. When they stepped outside, the waiting crowds surged forward, rattling the barriers which flanked the path.

Groups of Muslim protestors stood to the left. The

'Uncle Tom' banners were now joined by others: 'We are not your model minority', 'No more silence', 'Stand up to Fascists'. There was an undercurrent of anarchy in their message. These protestors were tired of justifying their faith, tired of appeasing nervous neighbours and tiptoeing around Western sensibilities. They were tired of being silent.

To the right of the path stood the Anglican Defence League who delighted in Jodie's case. They too hefted signs high above their heads: 'Keep Britain white', 'Stop Sharia law', 'Hands off our girls'. Men bared their teeth and flung insults back and forth, whipping the crowd to the first stage of frenzy: a mob on the cusp of snapping.

The first strike came when a steel-capped boot sailed through the air and hit a scarfed girl in the eye. The crowd around her erupted with rage. A group of teens kicked at the silver-grey barriers. Opposite them, the ADL roared with anger. In a second that passed in slow motion, the two sides burst the banks of their fences. Six police officers, three on each side, were swallowed in the surge. And then there was chaos.

Men in bandanas tore at each other with a shocking, savage intensity. There was no sign of restraint or mercy, only the ferocious intent to destroy. Wet sounds of flesh on flesh slopped through the air, joined by the crunch of breaking glass and howling cries of agony. One man lifted a heavy boot and brought it down in a stamp.

Zara jolted and shielded her face. She felt a firm hand

on her shoulder. Safran pulled her back into the courthouse just as she caught sight of a girl, her scarf ripped off by two burly men. Zara screamed out just as the doors were bolted shut.

She stumbled back and crumpled against the cold grey surface of a wall. Outside, sirens seared across the midmorning sky and cameras rolled gleefully as hatred spread to engulf and infest everyone caught in the maelstrom.

*

Mo watched the mourners as they kicked off their shoes and snaked inside. His *thawb* billowed around him, the thin white cotton of the long white robe unfit for fighting the wind. Its icy whip was calming and he let it buffet his skin. He had waited all night for tears as if they might offer absolution of guilt, but he felt nothing but a keening pain. He should have tried harder, had more patience, gained more skill in keeping Farid in reach. Mo had known that his friend was struggling. If he'd done more to allay his fears, he wouldn't have sought solace on the football field.

You think we'll just carry on? Farid's words echoed in his mind. *That's not how it works. Not for men like us.* Mo had been dismissive, but now he saw that his friend was right: that's *not* how it worked. Not for men like them.

He felt a tap on his shoulder. A fellow mourner paused by his side and gestured towards the door. Mo held up a finger. *I'll be one minute*, it promised, but he stood there for many more, waiting for tears under the sting of wind.

Inside the mosque, Amir stood rigid, his heartbeat fast in his chest. The long, snaking line shuffled forward and he, on autopilot, did the same. How could it be that one moment someone could die and then twenty-four hours later, they'd be underground? How could this be the right way?

His thoughts drifted to childhood. He was eight years old. An uncle had died and relatives had gathered to pay their respects. The family had such a beautiful oak coffin that Amir remarked to his father: 'I want a coffin like that when I die.'

His father, slimmer then, ran an affectionate hand through his hair and said, '*Beta*, we are Muslims. We are not buried inside coffins.'

'But *sasaji* is in a coffin,' he countered.

His father explained that they would take the corpse out before putting it in the ground; that the only thing separating him from the earth would be several white sheets wrapped around the body. That knowledge had given him nightmares. How could they leave their bodies so exposed to the elements? Utterly open to every slithery thing that came along to feed?

The line shuffled forward and he did too. He could hear the sobs of the siblings gathered by the coffin. He waited in silence, Hassan ahead and Mo now behind. They had always teased Farid for being a bore, the one who preferred the Bunsen burners of the classroom to more nefarious chemical experiments outside of it. He was their compass, the one who reined them in when they got too wild. Now here he was, lifeless and empty and ready for the ground. It made Amir's eyes water as he stepped to the coffin.

He stared down at his friend. Farid's face was covered with bruises: purple ringed with ugly brown. His lips were grotesquely swollen and his skin had a waxy sheen. Funny how books always said 'he just looked like he was sleeping'. Farid didn't look like he was sleeping. He looked like he was dead. Amir had been told not to touch the body so he put a hand to his heart and then placed it on the coffin. Hot, salty tears ran down his face, dripping to his neck and trickling beneath his shirt.

'I'm sorry,' he whispered. 'I'm so sorry. I wish I could take it back, F.' His voice cracked and his face strained with the effort of keeping composure. He said a prayer then walked away and the line shuffled forward behind him.

He made his way to a small red mat, then knelt and closed his eyes. By now, all the details were in the papers. Farid had been at a football match. His mother had begged him not to go. After that lawyer was attacked, she felt it was unsafe and warned that someone would retaliate. What she failed to see was how swift and hard that revenge would be.

Farid's team had won the match and headed off to celebrate. Farid had cited his curfew and headed home instead. At some point between 7.15 p.m. when he left his friends and 7.45 p.m., he was attacked. The sole witness, an old man walking his dog, said he saw several men run off but couldn't say how many – four, maybe five. Police said the men set upon Farid with a 'disturbing and excessive violence'. Those words would haunt Amir forever.

The men hadn't even tried to hide their attack. It was right there, out in the open amid the playing fields where so many victories were won. They had battered him with punches and kicks but the coup de grace was delivered by hammer – not a big one, the papers had said. The sharp end of a rock hammer, buried right in his skull. The attackers were undisturbed but the men had halted, struck perhaps by the gravity of their actions. It was then that the witness had spotted them – a gang of men frozen on the killing field. In an instant, they were running and it was only when the old man saw the yellow shirt of Farid's crumpled body that he realised the lethal situation.

'I rushed forward as fast as I could,' he had told the police. There in the middle of the green, he and his beloved dog Skipper found Farid, bloodied and bruised with a pierced skull. 'I heard nothing,' said the witness. No screams, no shouts, no cries for help. Nothing.

And now, that's all there was. That's all there would be forever. Amir leaned forward on the prayer mat and brought his head to the ground for *sajdah*. There, once again, he began to weep.

*

Jodie stared at the screen, willing Amir to come online. She needed to talk to him about Farid. The police said it may have been arbitrary but everyone knew the truth: Farid was killed because of Jodie. The papers had likened her case to that of Stephen Lawrence. 'A flashpoint in race relations,' said the pundits.

It's not, Jodie wanted to tell them. *It's not about race but rape.* But the case was no longer about her. It wasn't a flashpoint, it was a war and everyone had their own agenda. It started with one girl, four boys and now Farid was dead. *Because of me. He's dead because of me.* That singular thought clashed against all others in a discordant mix of guilt, fear and regret.

She thought back to the haze of yesterday: being rushed out of the house and placed under watch, Zara uncharacteristically tender when she dropped Jodie off. Her gentle assurance that *it's okay to be scared* was almost convincing in sincerity. Jodie knew what she really thought: that you had to face up to difficult times; that a display of strength was necessary even at your very weakest, so Jodie had nodded and put on a brave face. And why not? She was used to living behind a layer of masks. It couldn't hurt to wear one more.

*

Zara drew her blazer around her and wished for another layer. As a participant in the case, she was one of the few still allowed inside the courtroom. In the two days since Farid's funeral, Judge Braun had closed the press and public galleries in an effort to instil calm and issued a perimeter outside the building to keep protesters at a distance. It was a bold decision given the media's interest in the case.

Zara, as with anyone in the justice system, had worked on cases that blurred the lines of right and wrong. In almost a decade of law, however, she had never had a case as divisive as this. That they were dealing with children, barely out of adolescence, only served to fuel the hysteria. An important part of Zara's job was to uphold the belief that justice always prevailed, that the verdict chosen by ordinary men and women was sacred and true, that the system could and should be trusted. As a new day in court commenced, however, justice sat like a thorn in her throat. It stung on contact and left a scar, and there was nothing she could do but let it run its course.

She watched as Hassan Tanweer entered the witness box. Here was the boy who had so brazenly called her a *khanki*, a whore, in Magistrates Court. Did he think he was vindicated after *Visor* ran their so-called exposé? What delight he must have felt at seeing her filmed with Michael.

As she watched him, she wondered if her community's cries of traitor held a kernel of truth. It was true that she would treat the defendants no differently if they were of another religion, but Zara also knew that she wanted better and expected worse from the men in her community. She had told her mother that oppression happened when good women held back their daughters. It was the same women who pushed forward their sons; who treated them like masters of the universe and taught them to act with impunity. Hassan with all his pride and entitlement was a product of his upbringing. How damaging it had been was yet to be revealed.

Hassan took the oath, his closely packed features set deep in a frown. His dark blue suit was slightly too broad in the shoulders and gave him a droopy, melancholy look. Nonetheless, he answered questions with fluency and reinforced Amir's account of events with touches of credible detail. When asked why Jodie would lie, Hassan took on the mantle of truth-teller.

Taking a ragged breath, he looked to the jury and began. 'Why did Jodie lie? I don't know. Why does anyone lie about something like this?' His tone was weary as if he'd pondered this question many times before. 'Maybe she wants attention? Maybe she needs help? Maybe she's angry that Amir used her and she's embarrassed that she let him. I've been asking myself the same question since all of this began.' His expression grew mournful. 'What I do know is that Jodie looks different to other girls. She says that makes her a target but I think most people feel sorry for her.' Hassan gestured at the jury. 'I bet most of us here feel sorry for her. The thing is: inside she's no different to anyone else. She can still feel anger and jealousy and she can still want revenge. She shouldn't be treated as special. She should be treated like any other woman when her story can't be proven.'

Zara watched him speak, his voice sombre and his stance rigid. He was a picture of respectable calm but she saw the glint of triumph in his eyes. Clearly, he was pleased with his well-practised speech.

Leeson stood for cross-examination and appraised the boy for a second. With a muted look of distaste, he said, 'Mr Tanweer, who did Mr Rabbani take to the year ten prom after rejecting Nina Sahari?'

Hassan was surprised by the question. He floundered for a moment, then said, 'I think it was Aaliya Masanthi.'

Leeson nodded. 'And Mohammed Ahmed? Who did he go with?'

Hassan smiled. 'Jamila Wimal.'

'Why is that amusing?' asked Leeson.

'I— well, he was teased by our classmates because when they stood next to each other, they looked like the number ten because he's so skinny and she's so …'

'So what, Mr Tanweer?'

He hesitated. 'So fat …'

'Ah, I see. And who did Farid Khan go with?'

Hassan's eyes clouded. 'A girl called Rachel Brown.'

'And who did you go with?'

He stalled. 'I— I didn't go to prom.'

'Is that because you couldn't find a date?'

'I—' He took a moment's pause and then smiled dolefully. 'That's partly true, yes. I'm a bit of an ugly duckling. Girls prefer other boys.'

Leeson narrowed his eyes. 'So is it fair to say that when you found a sexual outlet, you took it?'

Hassan drew back as if struck. 'No, that wouldn't be fair.'

'When Jodie Wolfe was on the floor of a warehouse, helpless and vulnerable, you who couldn't get a date to the prom forced yourself on her, isn't that right?'

Hassan grimaced. 'That's not true.'

'Even Mo could find a date! And you couldn't. This was your first chance to be with a woman, isn't that correct?'

Hassan shook his head. 'I didn't touch Jodie. I never have. I don't share any classes with her. I don't talk to her. She wouldn't even know my name if I wasn't friends with Amir. I didn't touch her. I never have.'

Leeson was sceptical. 'Okay, so tell me again, according to your story, once Amir is finished and you are busy taunting Jodie, did you say anything to her directly?'

'I don't remember. We were mainly teasing Amir.'

'Did you and Amir discuss what happened?'

Hassan glanced at the dock. 'No. He told us to keep quiet about it.'

'And do you always do what Amir says?'

Hassan now looked to the jury. 'No. I kept quiet because I didn't want to embarrass Jodie any more than we already had.'

'Is Amir the ringleader of your group? Are you just his lackeys?' needled Leeson.

Hassan shrugged. 'It's fair to say he's the leader of our group – the strong ones always are.'

'And you're just dumb followers?'

A shadow passed over Hassan's face. 'No, I wouldn't say that.'

'Do you get angry often, Mr Tanweer?'

'No.'

Leeson picked up a piece of a paper and studied it closely. 'Would you say you have good judgment?'

Hassan smoothed his tie. 'Yes.'

'Would you ever advocate harm to Jodie because of her complaint against you?'

Hassan shook his head vigorously. 'She needs help, not harm.'

'And you really believe that?'

'Yes.'

'So why is it that you joined an online hate group called "Slay the Wolfe", filled with threats on Jodie's life?' Leeson handed the clerk a set of documents.

Hassan grew rigid with panic. 'It wasn't a group, it was a thread and I didn't join it.'

'So you didn't comment on this thread on the evening of Monday the sixteenth of December under the username "h4sn"? Here's a sample: "Jodie Wolfe deserves to be gang-raped again and again. I'll show that bitch what rape really is." You didn't upvote fourteen other comments in the same vein?'

Hassan floundered. 'I deleted that account straight away.'

Zara watched on with a pang of satisfaction. The evidence, uncovered by Erin and Artemis House, had the desired effect. The older Asian juror pressed her scarf against her mouth, her features a picture of horror. The younger man behind shook his head in disbelief. Zara knew the question now playing in their minds: have we been fooled by this young boy who looks so neat and speaks so calmly?

Leeson scoffed. 'But you did *make* those comments, Mr Tanweer?'

Hassan hesitated. 'I was angry. My friend had just died and I was angry at Jodie, but I didn't mean any harm to her.'

'And did you *mean* to rape her, Mr Tanweer?'

'No, I didn't.'

'You didn't mean to?'

'I didn't rape her!'

'Then why did you say she deserves to be gang-raped *again*? Is it not true that you and your friends gang-raped her first?'

'That's not what it meant. I said "again and again" – it's not the same thing.'

'So you were saying you want her to be raped again and again by other people – not that you wanted her to be raped again after *you* raped her?'

'I didn't rape her.' Hassan wavered for control.

'You just want others to?'

'No! I was angry.'

'You're a rapist, aren't you?'

'I'm not.' Hassan's voice grew high under pressure.

'You *are* a rapist.'

'I'm not!' His hands balled into fists.

'You raped Jodie Wolfe and you frequented forums encouraging other men to rape her again – *after* you and your friends raped her. Isn't that right?

'I'm not a rapist.' His features now creased with anger.

'You are.'

'I'm not a rapist! Jodie's lying! She's a lying, fucking cunt!' Hassan's face twisted with hate and fury.

Leeson let the words hang in the air. Then, with a satisfied smile, he said, 'I have no more questions.'

Zara felt the thrill of victory as the jury stared at the boy, one of them slack jawed. The truth dawned on them that they had been duped. Hassan's articulate, philosophical persona had slipped and beneath lay the version he'd tried to hide. He sagged in the witness box, knowing that he'd blown it. Despite all the pointers and practise, he'd failed in hiding the truth.

*

In the days after the funeral, Amir floated through the house like a ghost, eating little and speaking less. His aunts came to visit and tried to coax laughter from their usually sunny nephew. In the evening, they left without a win. No one understood his guilt, not even Mo or Hassan. After all, *he* was responsible. He was the one who took Jodie to the warehouse. He was the one who ignored her pleas for contact. Forty-nine times she had tried to reach him. Forty-nine chances to have put this right.

When Hassan called after speaking in court and asked Amir to go round, he responded with undue venom. Were they to carry on as normal and forget that Farid had died?

Stuttered by embarrassment, Hassan explained that he needed to talk.

Amir tightened his grip on the phone. Then, with a sigh, he said, 'Fine.'

Hassan hesitated. 'Can you bring some of your stash?'

'No. I had to throw it all away.'

'Can you pick some up on the way here? I just need a little something to help me calm down.'

Amir sighed. 'I don't know. Probably not. You don't know who's out there.'

'Can you try at least?' Hassan pleaded. 'Just call the gardener. Take your dog with you and pick up Mo on the way. I need something, man. I'm climbing the walls over here.'

'Okay, fine. Fine.' Amir dressed and went downstairs, grabbing his cap on the way. He collected Rocky and slipped outside, knowing his mother would try to stop him.

He called in on the gardener, shifting from one foot to the other on the crackly lino flooring. He paid for the weed, dug it deep in a pocket and promptly strode away. He didn't want to admit that he was scared of being seen.

How does a hammer feel wedged in your skull? He called Rocky closer and quickened his pace, trying to ignore the sensation of being watched. By the time he picked up Mo, he was weaving and sweaty with nerves. Neither boy said a word; simply fell in step beside the other as they walked to Hassan's home.

'Man, you two look like shit.' Hassan motioned them inside. He raised his chin at the dog. 'Let's take your bitch to the yard.' He led them down the narrow corridor and out into the garden.

The three boys sat on a wall and watched the fading light. The evening sky was billowing and black as if the whole world were mourning Farid's passing.

Hassan took a drag of his joint. 'I am ready for this to be over.'

Mo zipped up his jacket all the way to the chin. He accepted the joint and took a long, deep drag, letting it cloud his head. He wondered if they would stay friends or be torn apart by trauma. Would the stress of trial and this unnameable grief bond them under pressure or crush them altogether?

Hassan next to him shivered in the wind. 'Do you wish you could rewind to that night and avoid that cunt like the plague?'

Amir baulked. 'I thought we vetoed that word.'

'*You* vetoed that word,' said Hassan. 'I call a cunt for what it is.'

Amir frowned. 'Yeah, course I do. I wish I'd never laid eyes on Jodie Wolfe and her twisted fucking face.'

Mo turned and studied his friend. Amir's words were angry, but his eyes were not. Instead, they were weary as if he were tired of playing a role. It was strange that *yellow* was the colour of deceit. That never sat well with Mo. Surely yellow was the colour of joy. He took another drag and closed his eyes. If Amir was deceitful yellow, then Hassan was wrathful red. And Mo? Mo was Vantablack, the darkest colour ever known.

Amir reached for the joint. As the boys smoked, Rocky fixated on a mound of dirt. She nosed it curiously then sifted it with a paw. Unchastened by Amir, she began to dig.

*

Zara sensed impatience as the courtroom assembled for its final witness: Mohammed Ahmed. In many ways, Mo was the ghost of the trial; ever present but always silent. Today, he would get his chance to speak. Today, he would either prove himself just as inconsequential as he had been thus far, or change the winds entirely. This was his hour, his wretched final hour.

Stark stood and addressed the judge. With a shiver of uncertainty, he said, 'My Lord, a new piece of evidence has come to light which I would like to discuss with Your Lordship and my learned friends.'

'What is it, Mr Stark?' asked the judge. The lead-up to Christmas was fraught with tension and delays weren't granted lightly.

Stark hesitated. 'My Lord, in this instance, I believe we would be best served by discretion.'

The judge sighed. 'Well, since this case has gone swimmingly so far, why not take a detour?' He excused the jury and waited for the gallery to clear.

Stark nodded to the clerk who had in his hands a big yellow envelope. Zara stared at it as she was guided from the gallery. Anxiety churned in her stomach. This was never good. During her years as a lawyer, things of this nature rarely took place. Contrary to courtroom dramas, real barristers rarely sprung evidence on each other. There was an implicit understanding that the game would be played to rules that were fair – and last-minute evidence was rarely fair. Clearly, something major had happened.

Zara strode to a corner of the hall and placed a call to Mia.

The detective answered immediately. 'Are you at court?' she asked, skipping pleasantries.

'Yes. Do you know what's going on?'

'I was hoping you might. I've just had a call from the CPS asking me to procure the complainant.' A pause. 'Why do they want to see Jodie again?'

Dread bloomed black in Zara's stomach. 'I don't know. Stark has something. He wanted to talk to the judge in private. He and Leeson are in there now.'

Mia took a nervous breath. 'Okay. I'll pick up Jodie and bring her in.' She paused. 'Try not to worry.'

'Okay, I'll be waiting.'

Thirty minutes later, a marshal let Zara back into the courtroom, soon followed by the jury. Judge Braun was at his station, his expression indecipherable. Within minutes, Jodie was led in through the judge's door and taken to the witness box. She had dark hollows beneath her eyes and seemed jarringly tiny in a knitted blue cardigan two sizes too big.

'Ms Wolfe, I would like to remind you that you are still under oath. Is that understood?' asked the judge.

'Yes,' Jodie replied softly. She looked up to the gallery and met Zara's gaze.

Zara shook her head once in answer to a silent question. *No, I don't know what's happening.*

The judge questioned Jodie directly. 'On the night of Thursday the twenty-seventh of June 2019, during the events of your complaint, do you recall what the now deceased Farid Khan was doing?'

Jodie blinked. 'No. He— he was behind me.'

'Ms Wolfe, the defence has some new evidence it would like to share with the jury. Now before I allow them to do so, I would like to ask you this: is there anything about your testimony that you would like to change?'

'No, sir.' Jodie's voice trembled with fear.

'Everything you have said has been the truth?'

'Yes, sir.' She seemed to sway on her feet.

'Ms Wolfe, I take the truth very seriously.'

'Yes, sir.' Tears now welled in her eyes.

'Very well.' He turned to the defence. 'You may question the witness.'

Zara's heart thumped in her chest. She tried to catch Leeson's eye but he stared only straight ahead. She shifted in her seat and angled her arms away from her torso to cool the pooling sweat.

Stark's silk gown fluttered as he stood. 'Ms Wolfe, in your earlier testimony, you said, "Amir told me to get on my knees. I said no, but he forced me. I thought I could fight him but he was stronger than me."' Stark looked up at Jodie. 'Is there anything about the testimony you would like to change? Let me remind you that you would be perjuring yourself if you knowingly lie to the court.'

Jodie's voice was thin. 'No.'

'Very well,' said Stark. 'Please remain there for just a moment.' He turned to the judge. 'My Lord, I would like to highlight that the defence gave Ms Wolfe ample opportunity to tell the true version of events. I would have preferred to avoid showing this next piece of evidence but clearly it is necessary.'

The two televisions in the room hummed to life. Zara's stomach twisted as she caught the panic on Jodie's face. What fresh horror was to be revealed?

'Mr Clerk, please play the video,' said Stark. 'May the jury be warned that it contains sensitive material.'

The screen was black but two voices could be heard, muffled and giggling.

'I swear to God, it's true. Turn it on,' said a male voice.

'You're such a fucker, I don't believe you,' said another. The camera shook, the footage blurry.

'Ssh, be quiet.' The camera moved forward. It panned round and showed Hassan's face beaming with delight. He drew a finger to his mouth as if to say 'sssh' before the camera panned back and was handed to someone else. It rounded a corner and was at first completely dark. Then, it zoomed into a black mass at one end of a large room. As the camera caught the moonlight, the mass took on the shape of two people. A girl with her hair tied up, her back to the camera, whispered something in the boy's ear.

The camera panned back to Hassan. This time he opened his mouth in a mock scream and subdued laughter. The girl turned and was now on her knees. The moonlight caught Jodie's profile. She reached forward and unzipped the boy's jeans.

'We should stop.' Amir's voice was nervous but clear.

'Keep your eyes closed.' The camera focused on Jodie's head, following the motions as it moved back and forward. Amir's moans were subtle at first but grew audibly louder. After a few minutes, he cried out loud, his body jerking backwards. Spontaneously, the voices by the door broke out in a cheer. The camera spun into the room and then swept to the floor.

'Waaaahey!' shouted one voice, possibly Hassan's. 'Amir, you fucking freak – who knew you were so kinky?' The camera remained pointed at the floor, hidden from Jodie's view.

'Jodie! We didn't know you had it in you … literally!' Laughter erupted.

'How does Amir taste?' The voices continued to jeer.

Amir's voice cut in. 'Pussy's pussy, you know?' The boys descended into fits of laughter. After a minute, one of them – Mo maybe – was heard over the others. 'Aw, shit, Jodie, don't cry about it. Come on, we're only teasing.'

The camera panned to Jodie, now obscured in the shadows, then to Amir who stood above her. 'Oh Christ, Jodie,' he said. 'They're just messing. C'mon.' He glanced back at his friends and spotted the camera in Farid's hands, still hidden from Jodie's view. He raised his hand and sliced a finger across his throat. It could have been a threat – *you're dead* – but most likely a command: switch it off now. Farid stopped recording and the courtroom screens grew black.

Zara in the gallery closed her eyes. A deep calm settled on her, quenching the fury that threatened to rise. For a bleak second, she thought she might walk out but she was bound for better or worse to the pitiful creature below.

Judge Braun, still perfectly neutral, addressed the prosecution. 'Mr Leeson, does the Crown wish to address the court?'

The lawyer stood. 'I request that I be allowed to consult with the complainant.'

Stark interrupted. 'My Lord, the only safe course of action here is a discontinuance.'

Leeson shot him a glare. 'We can't possibly submit to that without speaking to the complainant. We—'

Judge Braun held up a hand. 'That's fine, Mr Leeson. You may consult with Ms Wolfe. Please be brisk. We shall reconvene in an hour.'

Leeson, Mia, DC Dexter and Zara sat in the room with Jodie. Silent tears streamed down the ridged landscape of her face. As they watched her, a sound caught in her throat: a guttural cry of pain – or guilt.

'Jodie,' Zara started gently. 'The prosecution has submitted verification of the clip. We are checking it but I need to ask you, is it real?'

Jodie's tears evolved to sobs. 'I didn't know they were filming me.'

Zara studied her. 'Is it real?'

Jodie shrank into her chair. 'I don't want to do this anymore.'

Zara leaned forward. 'I know this is difficult but the court is waiting for us and we need to clarify what happened. Is that clip fabricated in any way?"

Jodie shook her head. 'No.'

Zara exhaled. 'What really happened on the night of Thursday June the twenty-seventh?'

Jodie's tears fell to the table and flowered across the rough wooden surface. 'I lied.'

There was a growl of frustration in the room.

Zara held up a hand to silence the adults, then knelt by Jodie's side. Her voice was quiet and pleading. 'Jodie, what's going on here? I've worked with over fifty victims of rape and you … you can't have been lying.'

'I lied.' The girl's voice shook. 'I lied about everything.'

Zara blinked. 'Why?'

Jodie swallowed a sob. 'I just wanted him to talk to me.'

'So you did *this*?'

'I wanted him to talk to me, to care what I said, to think I was important. I wanted to … matter.'

Zara thought of the clip, of Jodie coyly whispering in Amir's ear. How could she have got it so wrong? She had believed every word the girl had said. A bolt of anger rose in her chest. 'Jodie, if you withdraw your claim, you could be investigated for making false allegations and for lying in court. This could have very serious consequences. Do you understand?'

'I just wanted to scare him. I didn't mean for it to come to this.'

'You want to withdraw your complaint?'

Jodie nodded. 'I do.'

Leeson rose to his feet. 'I better call the DPP. He's going to be all over us.'

This case was going to embarrass the Director of Public Prosecutions and the entire CPS. The papers would have a field day. As Leeson left the room, Jodie and Zara locked eyes. The first burned with guilt, the other with anger. Both were asking a single question: *how did it come to this?*

*

Courtroom eight was breathless with tension. Amir, Hassan and Mo sat in the dock, thrumming with hope and worry. They looked suddenly young. Amir still wore a Remembrance Day poppy on his lapel. He sat, gaze trained on the judge's bench, waiting for the lawyers to speak.

Leeson stood and addressed the judge. 'My Lord, I have discussed the case with Ms Wolfe and based on her admission, the Crown submits to a discontinuance.'

Murmurs of confusion rose in the dock.

The judge turned to the jury, his sigh loud and weary. 'Members of the jury, given these extraordinary circumstances, the Crown no longer believes it can safely prosecute this case.'

Cries of joy erupted in the dock.

The judge apologised to the jury, thanked them for their time and said, 'You are free to go, as are the defendants.'

Amir was on his feet, giddy with relief. Mo and Hassan hugged him, the three of them lost in a moment of joy. Amir disentangled himself and the jury saw that he was crying. Tears of relief mixed with sorrow as the stress and horror of the past few months hit him all at once. He sat back down in a daze, the sounds of the court too bright and too close. He drew his hands to his face, palms pressed against his eyes, and then he sat and cried. So much had been wasted. So much had been lost. And for what? One lie. One mistake.

*

Zara turned into the Wentworth Estate and parked on the empty concourse. 'I don't know where to start.' Her hands were clenched into fists.

'I'm sorry,' said Jodie.

'You're *sorry*? That's it? That's all you have to say?' Zara struggled for composure. 'You're lucky you're not sleeping in a jail cell tonight. Do you have any idea what you've done?'

Jodie's face twisted in anguish. 'It wasn't meant to go this far.'

Zara grabbed the girl's hand and held it, cold and bony, between her own. 'Jodie, what is going on here? I am struggling to make sense of it so you have to tell me – what just happened?' Her voice took on a note of hysteria. 'A boy got killed over this. What am I missing? Why did you do it?'

Jodie pulled her hand away. In the distance, faint cries rose from a schoolyard and traffic hummed along Mile End Road.

'Say something.' Zara pleaded. 'Farid got killed over this. I nearly did too. My life's been dragged all over the papers for you. Why?' She gripped the steering wheel, fighting her desire to shake Jodie.

'Amir should have defended me. He should have protected me. He needed to know how I felt.' Jodie's voice was small, a shiver of speech against the hum of traffic.

Zara turned and stared at her. 'So you accused him of *rape*?'

Fresh tears pooled in Jodie's eyes, lending Zara a grim satisfaction. 'I couldn't let him get away with it. He just walked away and left me there.' Her face creased in anguish. 'People like him have no idea how much they hurt people. I wanted him to learn that you can't just act how you want and treat people how you want and then just walk away from it like nothing happened.'

'Oh, Jodie. I wish you knew.' Zara drew in a long breath. 'I wish you knew what real rape victims go through. I wish you could see their pain. I wish you knew how hard it is to come forward, how horrifying it is when they're not believed, how "innocent until proven guilty" means you're a liar by default. And *you* – you so brazenly, so coldly, so utterly *convincingly* – walk into my office and you tell me that four innocent boys did that to you? God, I wish you knew.'

Jodie's voice was ragged through the sobs. 'I didn't mean for it to get this far. I just wanted to scare them, but I didn't know how to stop it.'

'By *talking* to me, Jodie. That's what I was here for. You should have talked to me.'

'I tried,' said Jodie feebly. 'You kept telling me not to give up; to stay strong.'

'Because I thought you were telling the truth!' Zara's voice quaked with anger.

Jodie shrank into her seat. 'I'm sorry.'

'You're unbelievable, Jodie. Unbelievable.'

She wiped her tears with a sleeve. 'What's going to happen to me?'

Zara rubbed her brow bone and closed her eyes to calm herself. 'Mia will talk to the CPS and let you know.'

'Will I see you again?'

'No,' said Zara coldly. 'I work with victims of sexual assault.'

Jodie's mangled features twisted in a grimace. 'If I could take it back, I would.'

'Yes, well, you can't.' Zara turned on her engine, a prompt for her to leave. 'Goodbye.'

Jodie hesitated, then opened the door with a trembling hand and soundlessly stepped outside.

Zara sped off without glancing back. Jodie's stillness that she admired so much now stirred a bleak melancholy. She thought of the unique circumstances that had led them to this moment. The vagaries of misfortune ranged from enormous to minuscule. What if Jodie had been born with a normal face? What if she had a father or loving mother? What if she hadn't gone to the party that night? What if Amir had glanced another way, chosen another girl? Would they be here at this juncture with Farid's life lost and Jodie's ruined?

The thought of Farid – set upon by men as convinced of his guilt as Zara was – made her heart constrict. Her role in the case, her part in casting the boys as villains, made her ache with guilt. And yet she knew she would choose it again. It was her duty to protect the victim. Even when branded a traitor, an imposter, a fucking Uncle Tom, she would do it all over again.

*

Hassan pointed his bottle at Mo. 'You know what I reckon?' he asked, words slightly slurred. 'I reckon they'll write a book about us. Maybe even a movie. Hey, maybe *we* should write something. Remember that American bird in Italy? She got four million for her story!'

Mo balanced his bottle on the grass between his legs. The light layer of frost was seeping into his jeans, but coming to this hill above the football pitch seemed like a vital pilgrimage. 'Do you know the meaning of a Pyrrhic victory?'

Hassan's brow scrunched tight. 'What the fuck does that mean?'

'It's a victory where both sides lose.'

Hassan laughed and punched Mo's shoulder, weaving as he did so. 'Well, I feel like a winner right now.' He took a long swig from his bottle. 'That good old bastard, Rocky. Who knew he would save the day?'

'*He* is a she,' said Amir. 'Shit, if we knew your mum buried your stuff like a freshie, we could've ended this mess ages ago.'

Hassan shook his head in wonder. 'I really believed that she chucked it all away. I would've told her what was on there otherwise.'

'You sure about that, mate?' Amir mimed getting a blow job.

Hassan laughed. 'Yeah, maybe not.' He gestured towards home. 'We're just lucky that your mutt dug it up.'

Amir smiled and raised his bottle. 'To Rocky.'

Hassan raised his too. 'To Rocky, the bitch who saved the day.'

Mo followed suit. 'And to Farid ... who didn't deserve it.' He looked at the pitch below: two rusty goalposts bookending a nightmare. He tried to name the texture of his grief. He thought it leaden at first, but it was more like sludge or tar. As soon as you cleaned one pit of it, it oozed into another. 'Do you ever wonder what his last thoughts were?'

Amir wrapped his fingers around a blade of grass and pulled it from the ground. 'All the fucking time.' He swallowed. 'I hope they find the people who did it.'

Hassan scoffed. 'I hope they kill the cunts.' His words echoed in the glass neck of his bottle. 'Hey, what do you think Jodie's feeling right now?'

'Suicidal?' said Amir.

'I should fucking well hope so.'

'Come on, guys.' Mo shook his head.

'Come on what?' Hassan challenged.

Mo searched for the words to confront him, to ask about his humanity, to remind him of his cruelty. Jodie had caused them pain, but to sit here and wish her dead in a twisted show of masculinity was utterly and thoroughly revolting. Mo remembered his mother's words. *There will be moments in your life when you must decide in an instant*. He took a breath and held it, feeling his heartbeat quicken. Then, he exhaled thinly. 'Nothing. I just— I'm worried about her.' Cowardice spread like oil on his skin.

Amir slapped Mo on the back. 'Why are you worried about *her*? We're the ones who lost an innocent man out of it.'

'I just think—'

'You think too much. Drink.' Amir picked up his bottle and pressed it into Mo's hands.

*

The bruises had faded but her left cheekbone was still tender when touched. She could feel it now, throbbing beneath her mother's gaze.

'Drink your tea,' urged Fatima, her personal panacea.

Zara took a sip and placed the cup back down, the liquid too hot and sweet. As a pupil in chambers, she had been the sole person to take sugar in her tea. It was only when a colleague joked about her roots that Zara realised they thought it working class. Soon after, she cut down to half a spoon and then further to none.

'I saw Farid's parents on the news,' her mother cut through her thoughts. 'His father was crying.'

Zara stiffened. 'I saw him too.' She stirred her tea and waited, but her mother said nothing further. That was their way: ignore the issue long enough and perhaps it would go away. They may pick at it once in a while, but would never hold it fully in their grasp. Even now, three weeks after the story broke, her mother said nothing of her clip with Michael. Zara had ended the fling but it lay heavy on her chest like a scarlet A which her mother tried hard to ignore. One day, it would all be used against her – by her mother in a moment of candour or her brother in angry rancour – but until then, it would sit and gather dust, waiting to be shaken.

The clock on the wall ticked on and Zara counted the beats of silence. It was exactly two hundred and seventy seconds later that Rafiq walked in with Amina. He regarded Zara with a look she couldn't place; it wasn't schadenfreude or glee, but something akin to pity.

'It's you,' he said.

'Yes, it's me,' she replied.

Rafiq hesitated. 'The mosque is having a collection for that boy.' He shuffled on his feet. 'I can put in a contribution if you want. It would help to make amends.'

She watched him for a moment and tried to divine his aim. Was this a barb to rouse her guilt, or a genuine attempt at repair? Unlike Zara, he was steadfast in his faith. Was this a bid to help in a way he believed would work?

Zara swallowed her tea. 'Okay, thanks,' she said, taking him at his word.

'Okay.' He hesitated, then patted his pockets. 'I forgot something from the shops.' He walked out without goodbye. She saw him no more that evening but didn't lament that fact. Perhaps the words unsaid were better left that way.

*

The room tinkled with the sound of glass as the swing band readied for their first song. Safran watched Zara as she watched the stage.

'Penny for your thoughts,' he said.

'We're lawyers,' she replied. 'We don't deal in pennies.'

He smiled. 'If I had to take a guess, I'd say you're thinking of Jodie.' He took a sip of his whisky. 'It's been two weeks and you've not mentioned her.'

Zara sighed. 'I don't know what to say. If I'm honest, it frightens me to death that I was so wrong about her. What happened to my famed barrister's instinct?'

'You're not the only one she fooled.'

'I just—' Zara's hands curled into fists. 'I'm angry for not seeing that she needed help of a different kind.'

Safran frowned. 'You're not a psychiatrist. Besides, your job is to *believe* the women you serve, not question them.'

Zara leaned back in her chair. 'You're right. I just hate the way I left things.'

'That's your problem, Zar. You want life in neat and predictable boxes when it's actually a river of shit.'

She smiled sardonically. 'I'll have to have that framed on my wall.'

He laughed softly and took another sip. After a moment, he asked, 'How are things with your family?'

Zara hesitated. 'They're okay under the circumstances.' She fell silent for a moment then shrugged lightly. 'Look, we're never going to have the angry, cathartic conversations you see on TV but maybe we'll dust off some cobwebs and actually start to talk.'

Safran nodded as soft applause rippled across the room, cutting into their conversation. The band launched into a new song. Zara strained to recognise the lyrics, then threw her head back and laughed. Paul Anka's version of 'Smells Like Teen Spirit'.

'Want to dance?' she asked, only half joking.

Safran smiled. 'You know, it's good to hear you laugh again.'

She rolled her eyes. 'Come on, Saf. We don't do sentimental.'

He set down his drink, slow and deliberate. 'No we don't, but I will say that I'm proud of you.'

She averted her eyes, uncomfortable beneath his praise. The year's events flashed through her mind: meeting Luka, fighting for Jodie, the horrific attack by unknown strangers. And here she was on the other side – still intact.

Safran caught her gaze. 'You're a good person, Zar. I know you don't believe that but you are.'

She scoffed. 'There are about three million Muslims in the country who'd disagree with you.' Soft lines dipped in her forehead. 'And maybe they have a point. Those four boys were innocent but the world won't remember that. Their names have been cleared but this wreck of a case will live on in a hundred different ways: the mother who warns her daughter from brown boys, the man who worries about his surname, the polite mistrust between next-door neighbours. The mess we created will live on, so I don't blame those three million Muslims for thinking what they do.'

Safran leaned forward. 'Maybe, but the question is: do you believe them or do you believe me?'

Zara held his gaze. The broad tones of the swing band soared across the room. After a long moment, she said, 'You.' The word caught briefly in her throat. She cleared it and repeated: 'I believe you.'

CHAPTER ELEVEN

Zara rang the bell and stood back as if expecting a blow. It had been three weeks since the end of the trial and she found herself coming back to this spot time and again, her mind tethered there by the string of words she'd left unsaid. She listened to the rasping cough grow louder in the corridor. A twist of a lock and the door swung open.

Jodie's mother shrugged in greeting. 'You know where to find her.' She took a puff on her cigarette and shuffled back to the living room.

Zara knocked on Jodie's door, then pushed it gently open. She was knelt on the floor, smoothing brown tape over a large cardboard box. The bed was stripped bare and desk broken down.

'I heard that you were leaving for a while,' said Zara. She noted that Jodie looked better now. Her skin was brighter and she had gained a few pounds.

Jodie didn't reply. Instead, she ripped three long strips off the roll of brown tape.

'I think that's good,' said Zara. 'It's a new year and a

break will be good for you.' She took a few steps inside and sat gingerly on the bed. 'Hey, will you stop for a second?'

Jodie put down the roll of tape.

Zara appreciated her maturity. If it were she at sixteen, she would have carried right on, or at least ripped off one last strip in a childish act of defiance. 'So, how are you?' she asked.

Jodie blinked. 'Shell-shocked.'

'I bet.' Zara tried to catch her eye.

Jodie pushed the box aside, its heavy bulk whispering along the carpet. 'What are you doing here?' There was no impudence in her tone, only curiosity.

'I wanted to say goodbye.'

Jodie looked up. 'You already said goodbye.'

'No, I didn't – not properly. I was … angry.'

'And you're not anymore?'

'No.' Sat there in the bleak lemon glow, Zara felt a gentle tenderness.

Jodie leaned against a wall. 'Did they tell you I have to see a therapist?'

'Yes.'

She sighed. 'People in books and movies always say they wish they could rewind time to a certain point. They talk about "a good age". I wish I could rewind time too, but I realised that there's never been a good age for me. I don't know if there ever will be.'

Zara felt a swell of sorrow. 'Oh, Jodie. I promise you there are better things ahead.'

Jodie traced a circle around the roll of tape. 'I never meant to hurt him.'

Zara had vowed not to be combative, but she had to ask, 'Where would it have ended, Jodie? If they hadn't found that clip, where would you have let it get to?'

Jodie's gaze dipped low. 'I thought we'd lose, so it wouldn't matter.'

'And if we'd won? Would you have let those boys go to prison?'

Jodie grimaced. 'I would have told the truth.'

'Really?'

'Yes, really.'

Zara blinked. She wanted to say more but just took a deep breath and stood up. 'You're leaving tonight?'

Jodie nodded. 'Yes. I'm staying with my aunt in Portsmouth 'til Mum gets on her feet.'

'And you'll start college in September?'

Jodie stood too. 'I hope so.'

They stood shoulder to shoulder for a silent minute. Zara swallowed hard, then took the girl in her arms. 'You're going to have a great life, Jodie Wolfe. I promise you.'

'Thank you.' Jodie closed her eyes and let herself be held.

*

The paper ball hit Amir's head then fell to the floor by his feet. He picked it up and unfurled it to read the message inside: Cunt Stain. He turned and caught Hassan's wicked grin, then mimicked a blowjob back to him.

'Yeah, but only if I've got a face like a fish, right?' Hassan threw back.

Amir gasped in mock horror. 'Dude, you can't say shit like that!' They both laughed, their voices bright and happy.

Mo shivered in the January chill and watched the exchange from the corner sofa at the Dali Centre. How could it be that after everything they had been through, his friends were still the same: so careless, so thoughtless, so utterly reckless? The arrest, the trial, the undoing of Jodie Wolfe and the murder of their friend. Someone had *murdered* their friend and here they were, laughing and joking and pretending it hadn't happened; that everything was still okay. Mo could barely stand it.

There will be moments in your life when you must decide in an instant, his mother had told him. That was true, but sometimes you needed time and perspective to walk away from something toxic. Mo rose from his chair and left his friends without a word in parting. He walked through the hall, across the small pitch with its forlorn goalposts and onto the street outside. He walked to Bow Road tube station, then passed through the barriers and strode down the steps to wait solemnly on the platform.

*

Zara made a note in her diary, cracking the spine at January. She traced a finger along the centre seam and

365

felt a stir of hope. This year, she vowed, would be a good year. This year, she would get a bit closer to who she used be; she with her plans and goals and unflinching sense that the world was entirely conquerable. That woman seemed like a stranger now but maybe, with time, she would find her way to herself again.

Zara circled a date and set down her pen. She reached for her coffee cup and heard a light knock on the door. She glanced up and her hand froze mid-air.

'May I come in?'

Zara withdrew her hand. 'Uh, yes.'

Mohammed Ahmed walked in and closed the door behind him. 'May I sit?'

Zara watched him for a second, perplexed by his visit. She nodded towards a chair, her interest sufficiently piqued.

'How are you?' he asked.

Zara's eyes narrowed. 'Why are you here, Mr Ahmed?'

'Call me Mo.'

'Why are you here?'

'I heard that Jodie's seeing a therapist.'

'Yes.'

'I'm glad.' He shifted in his chair and regarded Zara sadly. 'I'm just a boy, you know?' He waved a delicate hand in the air. 'I'm not some champion of morality, I'm not a representation of a people, I'm not a product of a generation or a symptom of a culture. I'm just a boy.'

Zara closed her diary.

'I mean, what is faith anyway? Would you say you're

a Muslim? Would I say *I'm* a Muslim? It's one faith but we're not all the same. The only actions I can represent are mine: a sixteen-year-old boy who lives in East London, who likes Formula One, hates daytime TV, is secretly scared of spiders, and who dreams of being a designer. I'm one person.' He thumped a light hand on his chest. 'And I represent *my* actions.' He grimaced. 'I'm sorry for what happened to you, Ms Kaleel. I'm sorry that all of this got so messed up.'

'It wasn't your fault.'

'That's what everyone says. *It wasn't your fault.* Farid dies but *it wasn't your fault.*' He laughed a bitter laugh. 'Farid told me something before he died. He said that no matter what happened in court, we couldn't just move on. He said, "That's not how it works. Not for men like us." I thought he meant it would be hard because we're Muslim, but that's not what he meant at all. He meant men like *us* – like him and me. We're not like Amir and Hassan. I have a conscience and I can't just carry on.'

Zara waited for more.

Mo reached into his faux leather satchel. 'I came to give you something.' He brandished a USB stick. 'This is for you.'

'What is it?'

He stood. 'Vindication.' And then, without saying any more, he left her alone in the room.

Zara studied the silver stick. Vindication? Was it some sort of revenge? She slotted it into a port on her laptop and waited, impatiently drumming her fingers on the desk. Autoplay launched VLC player and an .mp4 video file began to play. The screen was black and two voices could be heard, muffled and giggling.

'I swear to God, it's true. Turn it on,' said a male voice.

'You're such a fucker, I don't believe you,' said another.

The camera shook, the footage blurry. It was the same clip that had been shown in court. Zara sighed. Why would he give her a copy of this? She didn't need to see it again. She pushed away the laptop in disgust and went to make her coffee.

Was it a slap in the face? she pondered. A rebuke for siding with the wrong team? How was she to know that Jodie had crafted her story from silt? She waited for it to brew, then picked up her coffee and returned to her room. The clip was nearing its end.

'Oh, Christ,' Amir's voice on the tape. 'Jodie, they're just messing. C'mon.' Zara set down her cup and reached to take out the stick.

'Would you feel better if we put another dick in your mouth?' Hassan's voice now.

Zara froze. She crept round to her side of the desk and sank slowly into the chair. The video player had autoloaded a second clip. Jodie was on the screen, face to the wall, crying.

'Oh, come on, Jodie, don't cry. We didn't mean to take Amir's dick away from you. I'll give you mine if you want.'

The other boys fell silent.

'Come on, bruv, you've had yours. Tell the little whore that we're all equals here. What's yours is mine and what's mine is Mo's and what's Mo's is Farid's, right boys?'

Nervous laughter on film. The camera panned down to the floor then swooped back up to Amir. 'Keep filming.' Hassan's whisper was gleeful. It was clear now that the camera was with Farid. 'Keep filming but don't let her see.'

Hassan strutted over to Jodie. He reached out and stroked her cheek. She recoiled from his touch. 'Oh, come on, gorgeous. I know I ain't got pretty green eyes like my boy over there but I have a bigger dick.'

Amir laughed. 'You spend a lot of time looking at my dick?'

'Not as much as Jodie!' he shot back.

Laughter in the room.

Hassan had his hand on her head now, his groin in front of her face. She pushed his hand off her but he grabbed her hair. 'Come on, you white trash whore, you were licking your lips all over Amir's dick a second ago. Don't tell me you don't want more.'

Farid cleared his throat. 'Alright, guys, that's enough now.'

Hassan laughed. 'Don't be such a bore, man. It's finally your chance to get a bit of pussy.'

'Oh, come on, leave it.' It was Mo now, his voice high and nervous.

'Shut your mouth, weasel.' Hassan's voice was suddenly sharp. 'Amir, sort them out.'

The camera jerked as Amir reached out and playfully grabbed Farid. 'If you've got me on film, you're getting *him* on film.' His voice was low but deadly serious.

Farid's hands shook as he righted the camera.

Hassan unzipped and held his erect penis in front of Jodie. 'Come on, gorgeous, I'll close my eyes. Just give it a lick.'

Jodie began to shuffle away, backwards on her knees. He grabbed her by the hair and pushed her to the ground. Suddenly manic, he ripped open her top. 'Well, what do you know? The freak has amazing tits!' He pushed his face into her breasts. Then, he tugged at her jeans.

She started to scream but he silenced her with an arm. Farid moved forward but Amir held him back. 'Leave it.'

Hassan wrapped his hand around her neck and, then, he penetrated her, her screams muffled by his second hand. It was several minutes before he pulled out and ejaculated across her face and hair. He stood, sated, and turned to Mo.

'What's mine is yours, brother.'

'Nah, it's alright. I don't want to.' Mo's voice was strained.

Hassan slapped him on the back. 'Come on, Mo. God knows when you'll next get a chance. Go on. I'll put something over her head if it'll help.'

Mo's voice trembled: 'No, really, I don't want to.'

'Ah, don't be a fucking gay boy about it.' Hassan pushed him towards Jodie. 'Tell him, Amir.'

'Be a man, Mo, go on. It's the only chance you're ever gonna get.'

'Seriously, just have a suck on her breast and it'll put you in the mood,' urged Hassan.

Mo took a few hesitant steps forward. He looked at the camera, then back at Jodie. 'Aw, look at her man.'

'No, no, *don't* look at her; that's the key.' Hassan hooted at his own humour.

Mo walked to her and with all the enthusiasm of a man to the gallows, undid his jeans and climbed on top of her. He rocked back and forth until he too ejaculated over her with a cry.

The camera shifted positions. It now swung round towards Farid. Hassan had the controls. 'And now you, Mr Khan.'

Jodie's cries could be heard in the background.

Farid shook his head. 'No, I don't want to.'

'Oh, come on, man. Don't be such a gayer.' Hassan zoomed into Farid's face. 'What? You don't like women? You prefer to suck on balls?'

Farid shook his head, his jaw set tight. 'I'm not doing it.' He swiped at the camera.

Hassan dodged him, his hyena-like laugh reverberating across the room. 'What you gonna do?'

Farid swiped again, this time making contact. The phone fell to the floor and the screen fell black. The video ended.

Zara put her head in her hands. *Oh, Jodie.* She felt a chasm crack open beneath her and started to career inside, first through a mist of horror at what she had seen on screen, then past the twine of a dozen lies and down to a fog of guilt. She floundered for understanding, lost on a grotesque Escher's staircase where lies turned into truth, and truth stretched into lies.

A fragment of conversation ran through her mind: 'Amir should have defended me. He should have protected me ... I couldn't let him get away with it. He just walked away and left me there.'

The retch of realisation made her skin turn clammy. Jodie's desperation to punish Amir had quashed her chance at justice. She had cried wolf about the boy and ruined her credibility in the process.

Could Zara have changed things? If she had listened a little closer, probed a little further, would Jodie have told the truth? Zara imagined her sense of aloneness and felt her heart constrict. All those words. All the thousands of words they had shared and still they hadn't shared the truth.

Zara pushed away her laptop. Ten minutes ago, all of this was over. Jodie was in a new city with the promise of a new life. Did it really make sense to drag her back to this? Zara thought of the fighting and rioting, the violence and vitriol, the headlines, the hate and the maelstrom of utter chaos. Mohammed had offered her vindication but at what cost? How many other lives would be shred in securing it?

Zara pulled out the USB stick and gripped it hard, its metal bulk cool and heavy in her palm. She breathed deeply to slow her pulse. It would be so easy to just throw it away; to leave things as they were and forget this ever happened. She set down the stick, half on her desk and half hovering above her bin.

She could contact Jodie and ask her, but maybe it was kinder to not give her the choice. What would Zara want in the same position: to move on and forget, or to return and fight?

It was twenty minutes before she made a decision. Her left hand traced the shell of the stick, then tipped it over the desk. At the same time, her right hand reached down and pulled her drawer open, the stick falling in with a satisfying thud. She sent Mia a message:

Call off the press conference and meet me at Artemis House.

She kicked her drawer shut and leaned back in her chair. 'Zara the Brave,' she said beneath her breath. And, then, she smiled.

ACKNOWLEDGMENTS

First, I must thank Jessica Faust for taking on this beast of a novel and finding the perfect home for it. You are a dreamweaver and I'm inexpressibly grateful to have you in my corner.

Heartfelt thanks to my editor, Manpreet Grewal, who shaped this novel with a sorcerer's touch. It wouldn't be half what it is without you.

Thank you to James McGowan at BookEnds and to Lisa Milton and the wonderful team at HQ: Janet Aspey, Sophie Calder, Cara Chimirri, Lucy Richardson and Joanna Rose. Thank you also to Georgina Green, Sammy Luton, Fliss Porter and Darren Shoffren and of course the design and production teams who weave magic behind the scenes. A special thank you to HarperCollins Canada. Your enthusiasm for this book has been incredible.

My boundless gratitude to Lee Adams and Matthew Butt, barrister at Three Raymond Buildings. I am truly astonished by the patience, rigour and generosity with which you answered a hundred of my questions. I hope you will forgive me for any creative license I've taken with your meticulous advice. Thank you also to lawyers Gary Broadfield, David Jugnarain, Kate McMahon, Jeremy Rosenberg and Rabinder Sokhi. I am indebted to Annie Rose and Liz Willows. Thank you for sharing your incredibly important work.

Thank you to Ellie Aldridge, Amit Dhand, Shan Khanom, Kelly Lam, Sathnam Sanghera, Sheeffah Shiraz, Anita Ubhi, Steve Watson, Kevin Wong and Neville Young for helping me get the details right.

A special thank you to my very first readers for your precious time and feedback: Sami Rahman, David Wagner, Peter Watson and Serena Wong. It's finally here!

I'm grateful to my teachers Colin Giles (you always said I'd do this!) and Christopher Talbot for never letting me get complacent.

Thank you, Geoff and Val Watson, for giving me a quiet place in which to finish this novel. Thank you to Kashif Ali for all the unpaid tech support and to Hiren Joshi for Opal Home for Strays and for always having my back. Thank you, Pogs, for the constant laughs and to my friends Dina Begum, Priya Patel, Ariane Sherine, Rabika Sultana and Serena Wong. Friends are hard to hold onto in your thirties and I'm so grateful for you all.

Thank you to my sisters Reena, Jay, Shiri, Forida and Shafia for sending love and laughter wherever I am in the world.

Finally, thank you, Peter Watson, for eight years of silliness and adventure. How improbable have been our lives.

Chapter One

It was a strange thing to be jealous of your sister, yet perfectly natural at the very same time. Perhaps it was inevitable. After all, weren't women taught to compete with one another; to observe, assess, rank and critique, which made your sister your earliest rival?

Leila Syed pondered this as she watched her husband lean close to her sister. Yasmin lit his cigarette and he took a drag with audible pleasure. Paired at the foot of the garden, the two seemed remarkably intimate. It coiled Leila's jealousy just a little bit tighter. It was a good jealousy though; a *healthy* jealousy. It reminded her of Will's appeal: his easy, raffish manner, his dark, contrarian humour and that magnetic confidence that only occasionally tipped into pride.

She couldn't blame him, really, for being drawn to her sister. Yasmin had an arresting softness that men could not resist. It was there in the sway of her long, dark hair and the lazy line of her Bambi eyes. Every part of her seemed to curve and curl next to Leila's hard edges: the strong line of her jaw, the thin purse of her lips. She was well aware of their respective roles: Yasmin the centre of gravity and Leila merely caught in the orbit.

She shifted in her seat, unsticking her thighs from the hard green plastic. The air held a tropical damp that felt heavy on her skin. It was unusually sultry for London; the hottest July on record. It gave the city a heady, anarchic feel – all that flesh and temper simmering in crowded places.

Laughter rose in the air and Leila closed her eyes, basking in the sound. What a surprising delight it was to hear her sister laugh. She wished she could pause this moment and gather all its details: the press of heat on her eyelids, the barely-there hint of wisteria, the bleed of a distant party close enough to bring life to the night but not too close for comfort. She sensed movement next to her and opened her eyes. Her brother-in-law, Andrew, watched the pair at the foot of the garden, huddled together like truant teens. He arched his brows at Leila and she returned a knowing smile. He sat down next to her, the lip of his beer bottle balanced between two fingers. They were quiet for a while.

'It's really helped her,' he said. 'Being here.'

'I'm glad,' said Leila with a cheerless smile.

'I appreciate it, you know. Everything you do for her. For us.'

Leila motioned with her hand, wrist still perched on the armrest. 'It's nothing.'

Andrew turned his gaze on her, his eyes dark and wistful. 'It's not nothing.'

She half-shrugged. 'She's my sister.'

'I know but still.' He tipped his bottle towards her, raised in a silent toast.

She clinked her glass against it and took a sip of the earthy red wine. She gazed across the expanse of grass, blue-green in the falling dusk. She watched Will brush something off Yasmin's shoulder: a fly, a spider, some unknown predator. Her bra strap slid off her shoulder and Will's gaze fixed on it briefly. The two red dots of their cigarettes waxed and waned in tandem until one burned out. Yasmin shifted in the dark and headed back to Leila.

'Will is hilarious,' she said with a scandalised shake of her head as if she *could not* believe his temerity.

'Yep. That's why I married him,' said Leila, her voice climbing high midway, signalling sarcasm or irony or some other bitter thing.

Yasmin paused for a fraction of a second before reaching for the wine. She filled her glass, the liquid sloshing generously, a single red droplet escaping the rim to stain the crisp white tablecloth. She didn't offer Leila a top-up. Rather than irk her, however, the casual act of selfishness reassured Leila. It meant that Yasmin felt secure here; unguarded and relaxed. It meant that Leila had succeeded in her task.

When their mother died two decades ago, just a year after their father, Leila, who was nearly eighteen, did everything to shield her sister, then only ten. She gave up her place at St Andrew's for a London polytechnic. She worked evenings at Marks & Spencer and weekends at a greasy spoon, stitching together pounds and pennies to eke out a meagre living. Her greatest success, she thought, was that Yasmin had grown into a happy, secure, well-adjusted adult. Until life came knocking of course.

'It's so nice here,' said Yasmin, stretching her arms

in a languorous yawn. She gestured at the conservatory. 'God, I wish we could get one of those.'

'We *could* if you want,' said Andrew, his face pinched in a frown.

Yasmin swatted the words away. 'You know we can't afford it,' she said a little sharply.

Andrew bristled, but didn't respond. Instead, he stood and headed over to Will. The two husbands had never quite gelled, but they made a valiant effort.

Leila glanced sideways at Yasmin. 'You know, you can always come and work for me. I could use a PA like you.'

Yasmin rolled her eyes. 'I've told you before. I'm not going to come and be your secretary, Leila.'

'You've always been too proud.'

'It's not pride, it's . . .' Her shoulders rose defensively. 'I don't want to be beholden to you.'

'You wouldn't be beholden to me. It's not charity. You'd be paid for the work you do. We have a training scheme too. If you wanted, you could study at the same time and work your way up.'

'I *like* my job,' said Yasmin.

'I know you do, but it's like you fell into being a secretary at eighteen and have stayed there ever since. Don't you want to do more?'

'No,' said Yasmin stiffly. 'I like my boss. I like my colleagues. I like coming home and spending time with Max. I don't need status like you do.'

Leila gestured with her glass. 'You were *just* saying you wish you could afford more.'

'That's your problem, Leila. You take everything literally.

I don't *actually* want your conservatory. I don't want *your* life.'

Leila fell silent. Will and Andrew were laughing, but the sound was forced and formal; the laughter of acquaintances.

Yasmin sighed. 'I'm sorry,' she said with a hint of petulance. When Leila didn't react, she poked her in the arm. When still there was no reaction, she leaned over and threw her arms around her. Then, she began to sing 'Father and Son', her voice laden with mock gravity. She chose the deeper register of the father, who lectures his son on life.

Leila tried to pull away, but a traitorous smile played on her lips. Yasmin always sang this song when Leila was overbearing. 'Okay, I get it.' She pressed a palm against Yasmin's lips, but she shrugged away and carried on singing.

'You're an arsehole,' said Leila, but she was laughing now, unable to resist her sister's cheer.

Yasmin stopped singing. 'No, I'm not,' she said matter-of-factly.

Leila's smile lingered on her lips. She reached over and neatened a strand of her sister's hair. 'No, you're not,' she said tenderly. They settled into companionable silence and Leila made a mental note to get a quote for a conservatory. Last year, she had lent Andrew some money so that he and Yasmin could move to the area. Perhaps she could lend him a little bit more. If Yasmin had more space, perhaps she would do more of the things she used to enjoy: make those silly giant collages with pages ripped from *Vogue* and *Vanity Fair*. She had even managed to sell a couple.

Will stubbed out his cigarette and walked back up the length of the garden. Andrew followed and made a show of checking his watch, prompting Yasmin to stand.

'We better get going,' she said. 'I have an early start tomorrow and Max will get cranky. He grizzled for hours last night.'

They drifted back into the house, the air inside still humid despite the garden doors slung open. Leila watched as Yasmin and Andrew moved in a domestic rush: she scooping up a sleeping Max, her shoulder hung low with the weight of her bag, while Andrew gathered all the books and toys needed to occupy a three-year-old. More than once in the past, Yasmin had lamented that Max didn't have a cousin to play with. Leila always laughed politely and said 'not yet' as if it were a choice she'd made.

'Thanks for dinner,' said Yasmin, scanning the room over Leila's shoulder to make sure that she'd packed everything. They swapped kisses and the two parents marched out, carrying Max to their house around the corner. Leila shut the door and felt the wash of relief that comes with departing guests, even ones you love.

'I'm shattered,' said Will, flopping on the sofa, raising a few motes of dust. He reached for her and pulled her onto his lap. 'You okay?'

She nodded.

He brushed his lips against her slender brown shoulder. 'Can I stay?'

She tensed. Things were complicated enough between them. 'Not tonight.'

'Are you sure?'

'I'm sure.'

'Okay,' he said reluctantly. 'Message received.' He kissed the fine knot of her collarbone and gently tipped her off his lap.

She listened to his footsteps echo down the hall and the

front door open, then close. How quickly their group had dwindled. That was the value, she thought, of building your own family. You were never forced to be alone. She felt an old, familiar ache and hung her head wearily. How many times would she have to do this?

Perhaps if she were more honest with Yasmin, some of the pain would ease. Her sister knew about the first miscarriage but not the three thereafter. She wanted to confide in her, but Yasmin carried her own trauma and Leila refused to add to it. When she and Will separated in February, she had downplayed it to her sister. 'It's temporary,' she told her. 'A chance to assess our priorities and stop taking each other for granted.' The messiness – Will staying over, their attending events together – made the break look superficial; a passing hiccup in a nine-year marriage. In truth, she wasn't sure that they would make it and the thought of growing old alone sometimes left her panicked.

Yasmin had told her once that parents who lost a child didn't have a word to describe themselves – like 'widow', 'widower', or 'orphan'. That was true but at least they could claim 'bereavement'. It was something to attach to. What did you call a parent who had never had a child?

You can't have everything, she told herself for the thousandth time. She had a highly successful business, a hard-won reputation, a comfortable home and lifestyle, a sister she would die for and a husband she still loved. Surely, *surely,* that was enough.

*

A breeze gusted through the open window but barely eased the heat. Leila dabbed her upper lip with a tissue, careful not to smudge her makeup. She was freshly showered, but sweat already lined the wiring of her bra, making her feel unclean. The day was set to break another record and London barely coped in the heat. Sure, there were ice creams in Hyde Park and boat rides on the Serpentine, but commuting on the Underground was like tightening a pressure valve. Leila preferred to drive to work: barely three miles from her house in Mile End to her office in Canary Wharf.

She scooped up her shoes, a finger hooked into each high heel, and dropped them into a plastic bag, its skin worn thin from repeated crumpling. She smoothed her white shirt and grey pencil skirt, then headed downstairs to the kitchen. This was her favourite room in her four-storey Georgian home: large and airy with raw brick and exposed beams dating back to 1730. She moved efficiently through her morning routine: a glass of freshly squeezed orange juice and a quick glance at her email, followed by a mental vow to finally start Headspace, the mindfulness app that languished on her home screen.

Leila ran an architecture firm and though she prided herself on discipline, time often seemed to swallow itself; a whole day gone in one glance at the clock. Today would be one of those days, she knew. Her partner at the firm, Robert Gardner, was pitching for a major project that would propel them into the big leagues. Leila had worked so hard for so long and this was her reward: financial security and lifelong protection from the shame of poverty. The thought of those early years left a hardness in her stomach. Sometimes, a memory would rise unbidden and wind her for a moment: Leila crouched in a campus bathroom stuffing her underwear with wads of tissue so that she could afford tampons for Yasmin, or keeping her bras meticulously clean so Yasmin would never know they were used. Leila had promised herself that she would never go back there again; had worked night and day to get to where she was. This project with Mercers Bank could be her biggest payoff. She had swallowed her pride and agreed to let Robert pitch, knowing that he – an upper-crust white man – had a better shot by default. She had to wait in the wings and see if all her prep paid off.

She drained her glass and filled it with water just as her phone vibrated on the counter. She saw that it was Andrew and felt a twist of anxiety. Yasmin's husband rarely, if ever, called her.

'Leila, are you home?' Andrew sounded breathless.

'Yes. What's wrong?'

'I'm so, so sorry. The office called and our entire bloody network's gone down. Is there any chance at all that you could drop Max off at nursery? It's practically on your way.'

Leila glanced at the clock, but was already saying, 'Of course.'

'You can say no,' he added, but the strain was clear in his voice. His employer, a web hosting company, was already struggling for profit. This latest outage could be catastrophic.

'I'll be over in five minutes,' she told him.

'I'm sorry,' he apologised again. 'I know we've been a pain since we got here.'

'Not at all,' she assured him, though they both knew it was true. Since moving there last year, he and Yasmin had repeatedly called on Leila, as if her *not* having a child meant she was always on hand to tend to theirs.

She was thankful that Will hadn't stayed over last night. Though he adored Max, he would surely launch into a monologue about Yasmin taking advantage of Leila – as if they should refuse on principle alone. Leila gathered her heels, keys, phone and bag, and headed out to her car, feeling her body slick with sweat. Inside her modest Mini, she tossed her bag on the passenger seat, then eased out of Tredegar Square, a leafy street that housed east London's nouveau riche: small-business owners, a couple of footballers, an actress from a comedy show that was successful in the nineties. Leila liked living here. There was none of the snobbery of better postcodes.

She drove round the corner to Andrew's house, a tidy double-fronted building with a mock Tudor facade. He was waiting outside on the path, pacing back and forth.

She parked behind his Toyota. 'Are you okay?' she asked, stepping out of her car.

'Yes.' He pressed a toe into his lawn and flattened a patch of grass. 'I'm sorry to do this to you.'

'It's fine,' she said briskly. She glanced at Max, who was peaceably asleep in his car seat, his brown hair plastered to his sweaty forehead. She picked up the seat, the handle hot and heavy in her palm. Andrew took it from her, the weight shifting easily on his muscular arm. He ducked into the back of her car and clipped in the seat with some difficulty. He leaned in and kissed his son's hair, then brushed his fingers against a soft cheek. 'It's really hot today.'

'I know,' said Leila. 'He'll be okay.'

Andrew stepped back with a grimace.

'He'll be fine, Andrew. Now go to work.'

'Leila—' he started.

'I know. You're sorry.' She tapped him on the arm. 'Go to work.'

'Thank you,' he said.

She nodded bluntly, then got in her car and moved off, sensing no urgency in Andrew's movements as he watched her go. She headed south towards her dockside office in Canary Wharf and switched on the air-con. As she sped down Burdett Road, her in-car phone began to ring. She answered it with a quick flick, careful to watch the road, though she had driven the route a thousand times.

'Leila?' It was Suki, her assistant at Syed&Gardner. 'We have a problem.'

'What is it?'

'It's Robert. He has to leave for the Mercers meeting, but he's misplaced the blueprints.'

'What do you mean he's misplaced them?' Leila asked sharply. 'Did he take them home?'

'No. He swears they were on his desk, but he can't find them.'

'Then they must be in the office somewhere.'

'We've looked everywhere,' said Suki.

Leila glanced at the clock on her dashboard. It was 8.08 a.m. and if Robert didn't leave immediately, there was a good chance he'd be late.

'Okay, well, I have proof versions in my office. They're not perfect but they'll have to do.'

Suki's voice held a note of panic. 'But your office is locked and no one can find the spare key.'

'Have you asked maintenance?' Leila asked calmly.

'We're waiting for them to send someone, but if they don't get here soon, we'll run out of time.'

'Could you run across the road to the printers?'

'They open at nine.'

Leila cursed. She rechecked the time and did a mental calculation. 'Okay, I'll be there in ten minutes, which gives Robert half an hour to get there. Make sure he has a car waiting and that he's ready to leave asap.'

'Okay. Thank you.' Suki was audibly relieved. 'I'll tell him you're coming.'

Leila hovered on the cusp of the speed limit as she raced towards the office, feeling flushed and stressed in the heat. Ten minutes later, she turned into the private car park. She plucked her heels from their plastic wrapping and slipped them on quickly, then grabbed her keys and hurried upstairs.

Robert spotted her and dashed out from his office. 'Leila—' he started.

She held up a finger. 'Not now, Robert. You need to get going.' She unlocked her office and rifled through a pile of prints, pulling out a set of three. She handed them to Robert along with her iPad. 'I know they asked for hard copies, but at least show them the latest version. I want them to know that we got rid of the portico.'

'I could have *sworn* they were on my desk.'

'It's fine,' she said, ushering him to the door. 'Go, go.' She watched him pause by the lift. 'Oh, and good luck!'

He turned and tossed her the Gardner grin – part Frank Sinatra, part elder statesman.

'Go!' she said as the doors pinged open. Back inside her office, she collapsed onto her leather sofa, jittery with adrenaline. *It'll be okay*, she told herself. All her efforts and sacrifices, the back-and-forth and meticulous planning would not be for nothing. She pressed her palms into the cool black leather as if that might steady her: a keel on a rolling boat. She rested there for a moment and listened to the ticking of her giant wall clock, calmed by its faithful pace. After a minute, she rose again, pulling on her poise.

There was a knock on the door. 'Coffee?' Suki raised a porcelain mug with the words 'Syed&Gardner' printed on the side.

'You're a star.' She accepted it gratefully and placed it on her desk. She switched her fan to full blast to stave off the smothering heat, then settled in for a busy day.

Make sure you've read the shocking and jaw-dropping legal thriller from Kia Abdullah

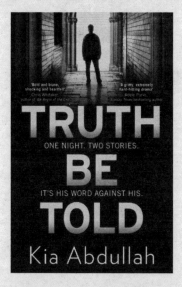

ARE YOU READY TO START THIS CONVERSATION?

Kamran Hadid feels invincible. He attends Hampton school, an elite all-boys boarding school in London, he comes from a wealthy family, and he has a place at Oxford next year. The world is at his feet. And then a night of revelry leads to a drunken encounter and he must ask himself a horrific question.

With the help of assault counsellor, Zara Kaleel, Kamran reports the incident in the hopes that will be the end of it. But it's only the beginning…

ONE PLACE. MANY STORIES

Bold, Innovative and
empowering publishing.

FOLLOW US ON:

@HQStories